Cat's
Magic

BY THE SAME AUTHOR

Stone of Terror

The Dagger and the Bird

A Net to Catch the Wind

HARPER & ROW, PUBLISHERS

NEW YORK

Cambridge
Hagerstown
Philadelphia
San Francisco

London
Mexico City
São Paulo
Sydney

1817

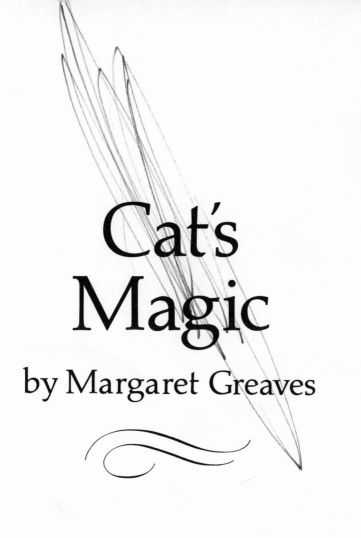

Cat's
Magic

by Margaret Greaves

Library of Congress Cataloging in Publication Data
Greaves, Margaret.
    Cat's magic.

    SUMMARY: Through a cat's magic, Louise meets and
rescues some unfortunate forebears from Victorian
times.
    [1. Space and time—Fiction.   2. Orphans—Fiction.
3. Cats—Fiction]   I. Title.
PZ7.G8Cat 1981   [Fic]   80-8451
ISBN 0-06-022122-4
ISBN 0-06-022123-2 (lib. bdg.)

To Marilyn
who wanted something cheerful

Contents

1
Deep End

As soon as I set eyes on my Aunt Harriet I knew I was doomed to a life of sorrow. Very well, I said to myself, if I am to be an abused heroine I will play my part with courage and dignity. I raised my head proudly, like Joan of Arc in prison. That had been one of the great moments of the film.

"Don't crane your neck like that, child," said Aunt Harriet unkindly. "Like a horse over a hedge."

I am not in the least like a horse. I am small, dark, and curly haired like my mother, who was a French dancer before she married my father. It was from her that I had my names—Louise Genevieve. It's a shame my father's name was Higgs, but there it is. All the same I lowered my chin a little, because I'd nearly tripped over my suitcase. (Joan of Arc would have had devoted soldiers to carry hers.)

"Is this everything? Come along then, there's not

1

much time to catch the bus."

She picked up my zip bag and stalked ahead of me, with long strides like a man's, the pleats of her tweed skirt swinging with each step. Gloomily I followed. Aunt Harriet was clearly the kind of woman who would always travel by bus rather than taxi. My case weighed a ton and it seemed like a long walk to the bus stop. Aunt Harriet, too, seemed glad to set down the other bag.

"Whatever have you got in it?" she asked.

"It's all the knobby things that wouldn't fit into the suitcase. Shoes and pictures and my paint box—things like that."

"Paint box?" She looked at me suspiciously. "You aren't hoping to be an artist like your father, are you? He never managed to make a living at it."

"I don't see how he could," I said reasonably. "Nobody would expect someone called Albert Higgs to be a successful artist."

"That's an odd way to speak of your own father, Louisa."

I didn't think it was odd. My father had died when I was nine months old. In any case I didn't want to be a painter. If anyone had told me the astonishing and improbable things that were soon to happen to me, I don't think I'd have had the courage to get on the bus. But no whisper of that strange excitement, no faintest whiff of magic, came to warn me.

I climbed meekly onto the bus behind my aunt, thankful that it was too noisy for much conversation. I stared out of the window at the April countryside while we groaned up one hill and wheezed down another. Everything looked green and open and I began

2

to feel better. Then I looked sideways at my aunt's thin stern face and felt oppressed again.

I was used to feeling oppressed. I suppose it came of being an orphan. My mother had dumped me in a private school just after my fourth birthday and disappeared. Later someone told me she was dead, but by that time I didn't really remember her. At first I thought it was very interesting to be an orphan, but gradually everyone else forgot about it. The other girls forgot to ask me home, and during vacations Miss Cole, the headmistress, often forgot that I was there. As I grew older I realized that I was an oppressed minority, and I formed a Society for the Freedom of Oppressed Peoples. I called it FOP, but I remained the only member. Miss Cole continued to be remotely kind until all the money ran out. Then she sent for me to explain that I couldn't stay at school any longer, but that she had found my only surviving relative, my father's sister, and I was to go to live with her at once.

So here we were, my Aunt Harriet and I, and neither of us all that pleased about it.

The bus grew emptier. There were only about six people left when we stopped outside a small house with candy and tobacco in one window and a faded board over the door saying MUCH MIDDLING POST OFFICE. Aunt Harriet reached up to the rack for my zip bag.

"This is our village," she explained.

A few minutes later I stood beside her, watching the bus grow smaller in the distance. It was my last link with the only life I remembered. My stomach churned uneasily as I picked up my suitcase again. I shouldn't, I told myself, have drunk that ginger ale on the train.

"Come along," said Aunt Harriet briskly.

She had turned onto a rough track across fields. At the far end sprawled a house that looked tired with age, as if it had sat down there to sleep and sort of grown to the earth in the meantime. I ought to have known from the very sight of it that something queer lay ahead.

"There you are," she said. "That's Deep End."

There were cows in a field on one side of the track, and in the distance I could see a couple of horses.

"Is it a big farm?" I asked.

"It's not a farm at all, not since your grandfather's time. I keep a few poultry and grow some vegetables, but all the land is rented out. I couldn't keep it going single-handed, and your father wasn't interested."

Her voice was reproachful, but I didn't feel responsible for whatever my father hadn't done.

"It's a long way," I said.

"Nonsense. It's only half a mile from the road. Lift your feet properly. Straighten your back. You'll always feel tired if you grumble. They didn't give you enough exercise at that school."

One of the cleaners at Miss Cole's had lent me a book when I had mumps. It was called *The Misfortunes of Millicent.* Millicent's cruel Aunt Mabel must have been very like my Aunt Harriet. I sighed, but not quite loudly enough to be heard.

Just as I changed my suitcase to the other hand for the fourth time, we came to a barred iron gate that squeaked on its hinges. It opened into an untidy yard where hens scratched in the muddy pen along-

4

side a cluster of outbuildings. The house lay to the left of them.

At the sound of the gate an old man came peering out of the dark doorway to a barn. He was yellow and bent and withered, like a shriveled banana. He gave us no greeting but simply stared at me as we approached.

"So this is her, is it? She don't look like a Higgs."

His voice grated as if it wasn't used often enough. I disliked him and I disliked his tone. I put down my suitcase so that I could draw myself up.

"I am Louise Genevieve Higgs."

The old man made a spluttering noise that could have been a cough or a laugh—though I didn't know what he could have been laughing at.

"This is Sid Jennings," said my aunt. "He works for me—when he feels like it," she added tartly, as she looked past him into the barn. "Sid, I thought I told you to clear up those crates while I was gone."

"Ay, you told me right enough. So I will, in time. When I've fed the hens. And set the potatoes. Trouble with you, Miss Harry, is you always wants everything done at once. My name's Sid, not Sampson."

"Those potatoes should have been in a week ago. I can't think why I keep you on."

"Nor I can't think why I stays here, neither," growled the old man.

Aunt Harriet went straight on to the house as if neither of them had spoken at all, and Sid ambled back into the barn. Perhaps bickering was just their normal conversation.

As my aunt laid her hand on the front door there was a scurry of heavy paws on the other side, thuds

5

against the wood, and a deep cavernous barking that made me put down my case and stand well back. I hadn't had much to do with dogs and I didn't like the sound of this one. As the door opened, the creature shot through it, and I gasped. It wasn't a dog at all, it was a small lion!

"Quiet, Bertram!" Aunt Harriet reeled only slightly under the impact. "Sit down. Behave yourself. Come here, Louisa. He won't eat you. This is Bertram."

I was mistaken. It wasn't a lion after all, though it looked like one. He had a huge head and a long plumy tail and was entirely covered with small yellow curls. Sitting down at last, he had an expression of rather fatuous friendliness. I stretched out a cautious hand.

"You've got to be ready for him," Aunt Harriet reproved me a moment later as I picked myself up breathlessly off my toppled suitcase. "I've told you, he's quite harmless."

Time proved her right. No one was ever in danger from Bertram except through accidental encounter with his enthusiasm, uncontrolled energy, and mental muddle. I edged past him into the dim cold hall.

Dimness and coldness seemed the essence of Deep End. Miss Cole's school at least had had central heating. But here there was only a fire in the living room. The rest of the house shivered quietly to itself in the gathering gloom of a misty April evening. I wondered if anyone had slept in my bedroom for a hundred years. I was sure that I myself would never get to sleep there at all. But just as I was thinking it, I discovered that it was already morning.

"Louisa," said Aunt Harriet after breakfast.

"Louise," I told her. "It's French."

"My dear child, it's not your fault that you had a French mother. But your father was English. Louisa is more suitable. Now, it's time that you and I had a talk."

I waited expectantly. When grown-ups say this it means that they want to do the talking and you the listening.

"I knew that my brother had married a French wife and was living in Paris. But, since he never wrote to any of his family from that day forward, I had no idea there was a child. Believe me, I had never heard of you, Louisa, until Miss Cole's lawyer got in touch with me."

Unwillingly I did believe her. It would have been more romantic to be a Neglected and Unwanted Orphan, but my aunt was clearly honest. I'd only been an unknown one.

"I must have been a shock to you," I said with some sympathy.

She looked at me suspiciously.

"What an odd child you are! But yes—the news *was* rather a shock. I have never had anything to do with children. But I wish you to know, Louisa, that I would always do my duty by the family. I shall look after you until you are able to look after yourself. Meanwhile you must do your part by helping me as much as you can. If you are tidy and obedient, and work hard, I'm sure we shall get on very well together."

It sounded like a gloomy prospect but I supposed she had a point. In any case I had a shot at the tidiness and hard work. The tidiness wasn't all that successful. But I learned how to feed hens, and helped with the

7

housework. It was very dull. Sometimes Bertram kept me company, but he wasn't much good at conversation. I thought of enrolling him as another member of FOP since he was clearly Aunt Harriet's slave. Or was he? Can anyone be a slave who willingly makes himself a doormat and so obviously enjoys it?

I was so bored by the fourth day that I could have wept. My aunt was absorbed in *The Poultry Keeper's Weekly*. She was always absorbed in some fascinating reading about egg production or blight on beans or how to make mittens out of your old cat's fur. I sighed with frustration. My aunt lowered her paper to the table.

"What is the matter, Louisa? Don't you feel well?"

"I'm perfectly well, thank you."

"Then what is it? Aren't you happy here?"

"I want to go out," I plunged. "Just to see something different."

"Oh, is that all? Well, I could do with some more slug bait. When you've fed the hens you can go into Much Middling for me and get some."

Big deal! Oh well, the village might not be London, but at least there must be more going on there than at Deep End. I'd met only four people since I arrived, if you counted the cat, Lavinia, Bertram, Aunt Harriet, and Sid. And Lavinia lived in the old stables and was as bored by people as I was by Deep End.

I scurried over the dishes and went out to the hens. I rather liked measuring out the corn, feeling the hard smooth grains run shining through my hands. The hens made their usual greedy flurry for it. All but one. She flew to the wire netting, poking her beak through the holes and beating her wings. As I walked along the run she followed me.

Another oppressed minority! I called an emergency meeting of FOP and the committee decided to enroll her at once. The other hens minded their servitude no more than Bertram did, but this one wanted to get out. I hesitated only a moment. Aunt Harriet had heaps of hens. She could spare one without noticing it. Quietly I opened the door of the run a few inches. The other hens were to busy feeding at the far end to notice it. But the little white rebel could slip out if she wanted to or come back if she didn't like it.

"Chickens never will be slaves," I said to her encouragingly, and walked back to the house.

I washed the hen smell off my hands, dragged a comb through my hair, and called to Aunt Harriet that I was ready. She came out from the kitchen.

"Get it from Slocombe's. Two pounds of the loose stuff—it's cheaper than the packets."

She peered into her purse as she pushed me toward the front door. The warden releasing the prisoner on parole. She gave me a fifty-pence piece, then hesitated and fished for another coin.

"Perhaps you might like—"

My spirits rose hopefully. But at that moment she raised her eyes again to the garden.

"*Louisa! What* is that?"

At the far side of the rough lawn, among the young spring cabbage plants, small triangular white shapes scurried and scuffled. My throat went suddenly dry.

"It looks like hens," I said feebly.

"*Looks* like hens! You naughty, careless child! Don't make it worse by pretending you don't know. You let them out! We'll lose them. And the cabbages—

look what they've done to the cabbages!"

They had certainly done quite a lot to the cabbages. I was surprised that they could do so much in so short a time.

"It was one of the white ones," I explained. "She wanted to get out so much. I didn't think the others would come too. And she seemed so unhappy."

"And how happy do you think she'll be if a fox gets her?" demanded Aunt Harriet. (I must say I hadn't thought of that.) "You will not go anywhere, Louisa, until you have shut every one of them in again. Every one. Twenty-nine white wyandottes and fourteen Rhode Island Reds. You'd better start."

I started. And went on. And on. I'm probably the only person in England who knows how long it takes to drive forty-three hens across a vegetable garden and a yard into a pen on the far side, even with a bait of corn. They were tired of corn, but not of cabbages. It was more than an hour later that I drove in the last few. But before I could shut them in, one dashed out again between my legs before I could stop her. She was probably the original rebel. But by now even the President of FOP had ceased to care whether she had her rights or not. I fastened the hen run securely, then went grimly in pursuit.

I scattered more corn with enticing sounds. She hovered, came nearer, began to feed, moved almost to my feet. I made a swift dive and grabbed at air. Squawking hysterically, she took off over the gate into the unfenced field bordering the track to the road. That gave us about seven acres of open space to play tag in. But I was learning. I made no movement at all until she slowed down. When she stopped, I fol-

10

lowed. I was slowly gaining on her, but by this time we were halfway down the field. Then at last she began to graze along the edge of the track, her nerves apparently restored. I crept closer. Now she had slipped down into the shallow ditch where she could no longer see me. I came as close as I dared, never taking my eyes off her, took a deep breath, and dived.

Triumphantly my hands grabbed feathers. But at the same moment there was a shout and the squeal of metal. Something hit me violently and sent me spinning across the track among a shower of knobbly objects.

"You little idiot!" said a furious voice above me. "Whatever did you do that for?"

2
Charlie

Dazedly I sat up, rubbing a grazed knee. A yard away a boy was picking up a fallen bicycle. A scatter of paper bags, cans, and small packages lay all around us. The boy seemed very tall, and his freckled face was almost as red as his flaming hair.

"Just look at what you've done! The front mudguard's twisted. And if those groceries are spoiled—"

"I'm sorry," I said. "I didn't see you coming."

"Are you blind or something? Or just stupid?"

Injured indignation rose to meet his.

"You must have been coming very fast if I didn't see you and you couldn't dodge."

"Have you ever tried to dodge a charging bull? What on earth did you think you were doing?"

His question reminded me. I looked wildly around for my lost quarry. In the far distance, right in the middle of the open pasture, was a small white speck.

It was too much. My legs and head already ached from my previous exertions, my knee was sore, and I seemed to be covered with white flour from a burst bag that lay beside me. My aunt didn't want me. Sid Jennings hated me. This strange boy was angry with me. I felt suddenly more alone than I ever had in my life. I was oppressed indeed.

"I'll never catch her now!" I shouted furiously to keep back my rising tears, then bit my lip to stop it wobbling. The boy put down his bicycle and stepped over to look at me.

"Here! Are you hurt?"

I shook my head in silence and scrambled up. Suddenly he burst out laughing. My tears dried up in rage.

"I don't see what there is to laugh at. You've—"

"I'm sorry, of course you don't. You can't see yourself. With flour all over your face and hair, and squaring up like a little bantam cock. I know—you must be the kid who's staying up at Deep End."

"I'm Louise Genevieve Higgs," I told him with dignity.

I pushed my hair out of my eyes. A mistake, as my hands too were covered with flour. The boy took a sort of hiccuping breath and bowed with a flourish.

"I'm Charlie. Charlie Parkinson. My dad runs the

12

grocery store in Much Middling." Looking past me, he too saw the small white speck. "Oh, that's what it was? One of Miss Higgs's hens got out? Come on, kid. Help me put this stuff back in the basket and then I'll help you catch her."

No one had ever called me kid before, but I was mollified by his offer. I looked at his bicycle.

"Is it much damaged?"

"Nothing we can't put right. Hold it for me while I shove."

With a wrench of his strong hands he had the twisted mudguard more or less in place again. We propped the machine upright in the ditch, then together picked up the scattered groceries and put them back in the basket. None of them was much damaged except the flour.

"Now," said Charlie, viewing the hen. She had come rather closer without noticing it. "Give me time to get to the far side of her. Then move toward her very slowly—and keep quiet."

He took off his jacket as he went, holding it over his arm. He stopped a few yards beyond her and gently I began to move in. For a minute or two the hen pretended not to notice. Then she clucked nervously and moved away toward Charlie. I waited till she'd forgotten me before I stirred again. So patiently, foot by foot, I urged her toward him. Three yards to go. Two. Only one. And with one swift movement Charlie threw his jacket over her.

"Oh clever!" I said. "Very clever!"

Charlie grinned, scooping up his coat in a neat bundle, but making sure that a ruffled white head could poke through it into the air.

"It's an awful long way back," I said gloomily, as I felt the weight of it in my arms.

"A long way?" He stared. "Don't people ever walk in London?"

He sounded too much like Aunt Harriet.

"Of course they do." I was cross. "But they don't have to chase forty-three hens for hours and hours and then have a mile to walk back home."

"Half a mile," corrected Charlie. He looked at me and grinned. "So that's what you were doing? No wonder you're exhausted. Here, why don't you go up on my bike, and I'll walk with this thing?"

"Thanks, but I've never had a bike. I can't ride."

"Pity," said Charlie. "Oh well, we can walk up together. You push the bike and I'll carry the hen. You'll find it easier."

I was grateful. I was sure the wretched creature would escape again if I carried her myself. I heaved the bicycle out of the ditch and began to push. Charlie looked at me sideways.

"I can't manage all that Louise Genevieve stuff," he told me. "I shall call you Scrap."

"That's a stupid name."

"No, it isn't. You're so little for your age. And you remind me of a little terrier we used to have. His name was Scrap."

I exploded.

"I'm not one bit like a terrier—"

He laughed. "There you go again! You see? Just like him."

I'd never had a nickname before. No one had bothered. Quite suddenly even a silly name seemed friendly.

"All right," I allowed. "Do you always bring our groceries?"

"Only on Saturdays during school—like today. But I help Dad a lot during vacations."

A disturbing thought struck me.

"I will not go back to school," I declared.

"Well, I don't suppose Miss Higgs will bother until next term. You'll get a nice long break."

"I won't go back, ever," I said firmly. "I hate school."

"Oh well," he soothed me. "I suppose there's plenty of time to think about it." But there was to be more time than either of us could guess.

We put the captured hen back with the others before taking the grocery box to the back door.

Aunt Harriet stared at me in horror.

"Good heavens, child! Whatever trouble have you got into now?"

Charlie spoke up quickly.

"It's all right, Miss Higgs. I wobbled into her, but she isn't hurt. There must have been a rut in the path or something. I'm sorry about the flour—I'll bring another bag up this evening."

"That doesn't sound like you, Charlie. Still, there seems no harm done. The flour can wait for a day or two."

"It's a pity she can't ride a bike, Miss Higgs. It would be useful is she could slip down to the village for you sometimes."

"That's not a bad idea," said Aunt Harriet thoughtfully. "It might keep her out of mischief."

I caught the ghost of a wink from Charlie.

"I could borrow a bike from one of my sisters,"

15

he offered, "and give her a lesson next Saturday afternoon if you like."

"Thank you." There was some tartness in my aunt's tone. "But I don't think we need trouble your sisters, Charlie. I believe there's an old bicycle up in the loft over the small barn. Sid can get it down and look it over."

"Then may I come next Saturday?"

"Yes, please," I said quickly. "Thank you, Aunt Harriet. Thank you, Charlie."

"Go upstairs and get clean, Louisa. Then you can peel the potatoes for me. It's too late for you to go out now."

I sighed and went.

I thought quite a lot about Charlie in the next few days. I hadn't met many boys and had never really known one. By casual questions I found out a bit about him from my aunt. He had two sisters much older than himself. He seemed rather the odd man out in his family, but she thought he was a good-enough lad in his way. From Aunt Harriet I suspected that this was praise.

I wondered if she'd forget about the bike. But she and Sid passed the kitchen window while I was washing up the breakfast things on Monday. I stopped clattering to listen.

". . . and check that it's safe. I don't want the child to break her neck."

"Reckon she'll do that one of these days anyway. She's a wild one. What d'you think you're doing with a child that age, and you knowing no more of children than one of them hens?"

"I'm learning," retorted my aunt grimly. "And she's

my brother Albert's child whether I like it or not. So get down that bicycle, you grumbling old man, and . . ."

Their voices faded.

"I'm just a duty," I confided to the breakfast cups. "No wonder she dislikes me."

I began to clatter them again and one of the saucers broke in half. Aunt Harriet appeared in the doorway as I was staring is dismay at the pieces. She strode over to the sink and took them from me with an irritated snort like a rhinoceros with a tickle in its throat. Her restraint was somehow more alarming than any amount of yelling would have been.

"Really, Louisa, don't you know *anything*? You don't want to put all the china in the bowl together. No wonder something gets broken!"

She was always telling me I didn't want to do something. It was the same when she asked me to beat the batter for her.

"The other hand, child. You don't want to do it like that."

She was wrong. I did want to do it. Just like that.

"I'm left-handed," I explained.

"Maybe. But you can't beat batter with your left hand. Use the other."

"It gives left-handed people a stammer if they have to use the wrong hand," I warned her.

"That's only about writing. And don't argue over everything."

So I used my other hand and a lot of batter splashed onto the table. Served her right!

It was bad enough in the kitchen, but worse when she interfered with my own things. She came into

17

my bedroom one day when I was looking through a pile of stories—those thin paper things that look like magazines. The same cleaner who had lent me *The Misfortunes of Millicent* had given me some that she didn't want anymore. My aunt picked some up.

"Good heavens, child, you don't want to read trash like that. Throw them away. Come on downstairs and I'll find you something worth reading. Like Sir Walter Scott. You'll enjoy Scott."

She was wrong again. I did not enjoy Scott. There was a whole shelf of his novels in the dining room, and to satisfy her I tried several. But they all began with long boring descriptions of scenery. And then at the end of the first chapter he'd say something like "But this was all twenty years before my story began. Now I'll start again." I went back to *The Lost Heiress*, which I hadn't thrown away. I'd hidden them all in my winter undershirts.

But life got a bit more interesting that week. Sid Jennings got the bicycle down from the loft—in his own good time—and I brushed off the cobwebs and cleaned the surfaces with an oily rag while he checked the brakes and things. He was muttering as usual.

"As if I hadn't enough to do without jobs that ain't none of my business. Reckon she thinks there's twenty-six hours in the day and I ought to be working every one of them."

"Why do you work for her," I asked with interest, "if you think she's so difficult? Couldn't you get another job?"

The old man pulled himself upright and stood staring at me.

"Another job? Me? I'd have you know, little Miss

Cock Sparrow, Jenningses have worked for Higgses as long as there was either in Much Middling. And that's as long as anyone knows, I reckon. There's a lot you've still to learn, there is."

There certainly was. But I hadn't much time to think about this particular oddity, as I'd something else on my mind just then. Charlie wasn't going to teach me to ride any bike. I was going to teach myself before Saturday.

After I'd fallen off three or four times I had a bright idea. Bertram was quite friendly to me, when he had time to spare from Aunt Harriet, and Bertram was very large and solid. I decided that if I pedaled close by the wall at the far end of the yard, with the dog on the other side of me, I'd have something to grab at whichever way I wobbled.

It worked splendidly at first. Bertram ambled amiably beside me, puzzled but willing. He was so absorbed in trying to fathom what we were doing that he scarcely noticed the times that he took the full weight of me and the bicycle. When at last I managed two trips the length of the wall without actually clutching him, my ambition grew. I wheeled the bike out onto the field track, and Bertram came with me. He had decided that anyone who behaved so oddly needed protection.

The track looked very long and open. There were more stones and ruts in it than I had thought. Centuries of weather and flood had worn a hollow in the land not far from Deep End, so that it sloped slightly downward and then rose again. I took a deep breath and mounted, wobbled for a yard or two, and then suddenly found that I was riding. It was marvelous.

The field flowed past me, the spring wind lifted my hair. I had mastery, speed, power.

"Yippee!" I yelled joyously. "Yippee! Much Middling, here I come!"

Too much speed, too much power! I was going downhill like a bird, but without a bird's wings. And at that moment Bertram solved his problem. Of course! This was my way of taking him for a run, faster than anything Aunt Harriet could do. Barking with enthusiasm he lumbered at my side, thudding along like a runaway traction engine. It was wonderful, it was just what a dog wanted, he adored me. Carried away by gratitude he flung himself at me to tell me so.

It seemed forever before we were disentangled— Bertram, the bike, and me.

"You fool dog!" I stormed at him. "You blundering great idiot! Haven't you got any brains at all?"

Bertram stopped licking my ear and lay down in a big yellow heap with his head on his paws, crestfallen and bewildered. He knew, he said, that he had no brains. People were always telling him so. But he had meant well. It had been a lovely game and now I was cross with him. Why did everything always happen to him?

It didn't, I told him. Most of it seemed to happen to me. Well, there, all right, I was sorry. I hadn't meant to hurt his feelings. We were reconciled and had to get disentangled all over again.

"Do you fall down here every day?" asked an interested voice above us.

Charlie again! Charlie with his red hair flaring in the late afternoon sun, his face crinkled with laughter.

"Do you always come on top of people without any warning?" I retorted.

"No offense, Scrap! I got off school a bit earlier than usual and Dad didn't need me, so I thought I might give you your first lesson."

"Thanks," I said. "I've had it."

"You shouldn't let Bertram teach you," said Charlie. "He's no good at it."

"I've noticed." Suddenly I found myself laughing too. "But I've done it," I told him triumphantly. "I got all the way here by myself until that idiot sabotaged it."

"Good for you! You may not have much sense, Scrap, but you've got guts. I'll say that for you."

Something glowed inside me. Appreciation rarely came my way.

"If you'll keep hold of that dog, I'll show you," I offered recklessly.

It was much harder to mount on an upward slope. For a minute I just plunged giddily from side to side of the track. But I would *not* fall off again in front of Charlie. I was doing it. I was moving in a straight line. I was up the slope and onto the level bit before the gate. My speed increased unexpectedly and the closed gate rushed to meet me as I grabbed for the brakes.

"Great!" called Charlie. "You really can do it."

He was only a few yards behind me, with Bertram trotting after him as meekly as a lapdog. Tactfully he chose not to notice that I was dragging my front wheel out of the gap between the gatepost and the gate.

"Let's go out for a bit of practice."

"All right. Thanks. I'd like to. But I'd better put old Blunderbuss in first. I'm safer without him."

Bertram looked apologetic again as if he understood, so I had to stop to make a fuss of him. Sid came ambling out of the storage shed, caught sight of us, and scowled. He was wearing his cap, his sign that he was knocking off work.

"Just as I warned her. Take in one young one and you'll get half a dozen. Racketing everywhere."

I started to point out that Charlie wasn't half a dozen and that neither of us was racketing. But Sid wasn't listening. He was suddenly intent on watching the far side of the yard. I could see nothing there but Lavinia, slinking along very quietly close to the wall and disappearing with a neat hop into a thick patch of weeds at the end of it.

"So that's where she's taken it! The cunning old devil. I'll find it in the morning, so I will."

"Find what?" I asked.

"The other kitten. I got the first three, but she was away with the other afore I could take it. I've searched them barns a month or more and couldn't see no sign of it."

"What did you want them for?"

"They're awfully clever at hiding them," broke in Charlie very quickly. "Sid, if you see my dad in the Three Feathers you might tell him I'll put up those orders for him. Save him time in the morning."

"Tell him yourself. What d'you think I am? Her Majesty's mails?"

He made a strange creaking noise, amused by his own wit. Then he picked up his battered old bicycle and was off through the gate, the chain making a small clacking sound as he bounced slowly away down the track to Much Middling. Charlie grinned.

"It wasn't a very good message. But he won't give it anyway. And at least it got rid of him."

"Charlie, why did he want the kittens?"

He took my bike from me and leaned it carefully against the wall. He spoke without looking at me.

"You can't find homes for a lot of kittens in a place like this. And you can't keep tribes of them. I'm sorry. He wanted to get rid of them."

Sickness and anger welled inside me.

"You mean—you mean he's *killed* them?"

"Don't take on so, Scrap. Their eyes wouldn't even be open. They wouldn't know a thing."

"And he'll kill this one too?"

"I'm afraid so."

"I won't let him touch it. I'll find it first. I'll hide it and keep it safe."

I marched toward the patch of weeds, but Charlie caught up with me and held me back.

"You'll only frighten her into taking it somewhere else."

The sudden tears stung my eyes.

"What can I do then?"

"She'll have hidden it in the old pigsties at the back there. Go into the field by the far gate and wait. Just watch till she comes out again."

It made sense.

"Are you coming too?"

He shook his head. "She'd notice two of us. You'll be better on your own. See you on Saturday afternoon then?"

"Yes. I'm sorry, Charlie. I feel a bit mean when

you've come up here specially . . ."

"That's all right," said Charlie cheerfully. "Any time with you seems likely to be full of surprises. I'll get used to it. Louise Genevieve to the rescue!" He turned back again just as he was leaving. "What will you do with it, Scrap, if you do rescue it?"

"I'll hide it," I said. "Somewhere in the house. Where Sid can't find it."

I tried to speak confidently, but I didn't feel that way. But someone had to do something. If ever there were an oppressed minority, it was that kitten. For a minute I thought of telling Charlie about FOP. But I wasn't sure he'd understand; boys often think things are silly.

"I'll manage," I assured him—and myself.

He looked at me in silence a moment, and I couldn't read his expression.

"If anything goes wrong—if you need someone— here's our phone number." He scribbled on a bit of paper he took from his pocket. "If anyone else answers you can always say it was a wrong number."

"Thanks," I said.

I watched him as he rode away and felt suddenly happy. I'd never had a friend before.

3
Casca

The yard seemed very deserted when Sid and Charlie had gone. Bertram had ambled indoors in search of Aunt Harriet, but there was no sign or sound from either of them. It might have been an empty house inhabited by ghosts. Perhaps it *was* haunted? I shivered, overcome by chill melancholy. Then I pulled myself together. The Lost Heiress had no one to share her more sensitive moods with either, but she never let it get her down. She would walk through the gypsy encampment like a queen, dreaming of the day when she would meet a kindred spirit with whom she could share her most secret thoughts. I didn't think I could share all my secret thoughts with Charlie. In fact, I don't think it would be very safe for anyone to do that with anyone else. But at least I tried to walk like a queen, until I came to the cow-trampled patch by the gate. It's almost impossible to be queenly while

25

squelching through three or four inches of very slippery mud.

It was too wet to sit down, so I lurked near the hedge, fixing my gaze intently on the row of old pigsties. Time passed slowly. I shifted my weight from foot to foot and began to feel chilly. Just as I thought I'd have to give up, a small head poked through the second door from the right and turned cautiously from side to side. Satisfied, Lavinia slipped out and away into the weeds.

I waited for her to get clear, then went straight to the second sty. The outside pen was empty. There was nothing to do but crawl on hands and knees into the sleeping quarters. I could see nothing. My own body was blocking such dim light as there was. I groped and found nothing but straw. Then, as I paused, there came the faintest rustle from the far corner.

I reached out again, found something yielding and furry, something that tore down the back of my hand like a hot wire, something that made a funny little noise between a hiss and a growl. I grabbed it and backed out.

It was unlike any other kitten I'd ever seen. Coppery brown as a beechnut, with eyes of darkest, clearest honey in a small triangular face with enormous triangular ears. Its legs and tail were long and thin, and it made a protesting wail about three times too loud for its size. I thanked heaven that Lavinia's hunting had taken her out of earshot. No avenging fury came to the rescue.

I set the tiny body in the crook of my arm, cradling it with soothing noises.

"There, there! I'm trying to help you. You don't want to be killed like the others, do you?"

The wail changed suddenly to a tremendous purr like a distant airplane. I stroked the delicate fur and noticed the blood running over my scratched hand.

"Naughty!" I reproached it. "See what a rent the envious Casca made!"

We'd been doing *Julius Caesar* at school. Actually I'd had to read Casca's part and I rather liked him. He was not only a rebel. He seemed to be the only conspirator with a sense of humor.

"That's what I'll call you," I said. "Casca. It suits you."

Casca suddenly bit me and my heart warmed toward him. Here was a member of an oppressed minority quite prepared to fight for his rights.

"You're the new Vice-President of FOP," I told him.

But there wasn't time to explain any more to him, for just then I heard my aunt's voice calling me, and even at that distance I could hear the edge in it. I was already late for tea.

"Coming!" I shouted. "Coming!"

I dashed for the house, stuffing Casca under my Windbreaker as I went. I held my arms wrapped across my chest as if I were cold.

Aunt Harriet grabbed me in the doorway, and I coughed loudly to cover the kitten's indignant protest as my grip involuntarily tightened.

"Louisa! Whatever have you done now? You're *smothered* in mud. Smothered! You look as if you've been crawling in it."

I stifled a rising giggle and the kitten's increasing

objections by another burst of coughing.

"I'm sorry," I gasped. "I fell in it. It's so slippery."

"And given yourself a chill as well. And you fully deserve it. Go up at once and take off those wet things. They smell like a pigsty. At once, do you hear?"

I fled. I was in for another lecture, but it was worth it to escape with Casca so easily. I put him down on the floor while I changed. He began to explore every corner with complete fearlessness. Then suddenly he tired of it and clawed at my leg with loud demanding squeaks.

My first real problem had arrived. The creature was hungry.

I'd meant to hide him in the wardrobe until there was time to think, but this was clearly not to be. We had high tea instead of supper at Deep End, and it was a leisurely meal. By the time we'd finished, his yells would be heard all over the house. Anyway I couldn't bear him to go hungry. I had to take a chance. Carefully picking up my soiled clothes, I rolled them into a bundle around him and carried him downstairs. I ran quickly past the kitchen to the old dairy next to it, which was now used as scullery and larder.

"Where are you going, Louisa?" called my aunt.

"I'll only be a minute, Aunt Harriet. I'm just putting my clothes to soak so that I can wash them more easily after tea."

I turned on both taps in the sink to cover the clinking sounds as I poured out a saucer of milk and set it on the floor. Casca rushed to it, purring, his tail erect and quivering with joy. Thank heaven, he was weaned. I looked around wildly for a hiding place. Two or three old pairs of boots stood in a dark corner near the outside door, my own among them. There was no danger of mine being borrowed—they were smaller than any of the others. As soon as he'd finished I popped him into one of them and dropped my Windbreaker over the top to stifle any sounds. I thought he'd still get enough air for an hour or two. Virtuously I left the muddy side up to get dry. Then I turned off the taps—the sink was getting dangerously full—swished loudly among the wet clothes, and dried my hands.

"A glimmer of sense, at least," conceded my aunt grudgingly as I entered the kitchen. She turned from the stove and put a plate of scrambled eggs in front of me.

"Louisa, when I agreed to take you I thought you would be old enough to be responsible. It seems I was wrong. You are in and out of trouble all the time. I shall be thankful when next term begins."

"Next term?" I faltered. "Oh, Aunt Harriet, do I *have* to go back to school?"

"Of course you have, child. Not to Miss Cole's. I can't afford boarding schools. And how your poor foolish mother ever thought she could pay for one beats me. It'll be Colbury Comprehensive for you. And heaven help them!"

I was dismayed. I'd been clinging to the thin hope that Aunt Harriet wouldn't think of school. But she went on about it. I'd have to behave myself there. Perhaps *they* could get some sense into me. And in any case, was the unspoken addition, she herself would at least be rid of me for a bit.

I let her go on. I was only half listening, for I was anxiously trying to make plans about Casca. Besides,

I was worried about whether he really had got enough air inside that boot. My aunt was still carrying on about discipline when we were interrupted.

Along the stone-floored hallway came the thud of heavy paws and the door was thrust open until Bertram could sidle through it—a trick he had long perfected. He was carrying something in his mouth. He picked a careful way to the rug in front of the wood stove (nothing as labor saving as a gas stove had as yet reached Deep End), and laid it down. Then he stood back with a half wag of his tail, looking from my Aunt Harriet to me with a mixture of hopefulness, surprise, and embarrassment. Shouldn't I have brought it? he was saying. I didn't know what else to do with it.

My aunt made a startled noise, and Bertram stepped nearer to his charge. It was very small, he explained. He didn't know what it was. But he thought it needed kindness and not sudden noises.

Aunt Harriet drew in her breath alarmingly. She reminded me of that bit in the Bible about the horse that saith Ha, ha to the trumpets.

"Louisa!" (It occurred to me how often she said Louisa in just that way, like the horse saying Ha, ha.) "This, I imagine, is something to do with you?"

"It isn't mine," I protested. "It's Lavinia's."

"Lavinia's?" She bent down to examine the small object that was now sniffing its curious way around the rug. "Lavinia never has kittens like that. Hers are always black. She must have—" She stopped and went slightly pink.

"It's all right," I told her kindly. "We did biology at Miss Cole's, you know. There must be a Siamese tom or something in Much Middling."

"It's not even a Siamese." For the moment she was too puzzled even to be cross with me. "Burmese, perhaps. They're dark." Then she remembered the main point. "How does it come to be here?"

I'd made a mistake. If only I'd pretended that Bertram had found it all by himself! But I'd shown I knew something, and there was nothing for it but confession. The words came all in a rush.

"It is Lavinia's. Sid drowned all the others, and he was going to drown this one too if he could find it. But I found it first, and it's too beautiful to be drowned, and Lavinia will probably die of sorrow, and please, oh please, may I keep it?"

Aunt Harriet held out her hand. Interested, the kitten made a sudden pounce and sank all its small sharp teeth into her finger. ("Oh idiot!" I groaned inwardly. "That's ruined it!") But to my astonishment my aunt laughed and lifted Casca to her knee. Bertram reared up with anxious protectiveness, thrusting his lion head forward to lick him. Casca backed, hissing, and slapped him on the nose.

"He's got spirit, anyway," said Aunt Harriet. She rumpled the dog's head. "Poor old boy, he didn't mean it. I don't suppose he's seen anything your size before."

Then she gave me a long considering look.

"You can't keep a kitten for nothing, Louisa. Or without trouble. If you keep him you will be entirely responsible for housetraining him and clearing up the mess if he makes any mistakes. You will earn the money for his keep by helping me or Sid; and out of that you will pay for his extra food, other than

31

the household scraps, his vet's bills, and anything else he needs. On those conditions only."

"Oh, *thank you*, Aunt Harriet! Thank you!"

On impulse I jumped up and kissed her on the cheek. It was the first time I'd ever done it. She went quite pink but I don't think she minded.

"Well, there! Perhaps that will keep you out of any more mischief for a while. Tomorrow you must take him down to Jackson's for his enteritis injections and have him wormed. I'll pay for that. But after that you're entirely responsible. Understood?"

So Casca became mine. Or mostly mine. Bertram insisted that he had found him and that Casca was really his. He doted on him. The kitten's favorite game was to fall off a chair onto the dog's back and cling to his golden curls with outspread claws before diving for the plumy tail. Bertram would turn his head to watch him with fatuous devotion, only giving a small protesting *woof* if his hair was pulled too hard. As for Casca's own opinion, he belonged to none of us, though he was graciously pleased to sleep in my bedroom at night.

The next two days passed very quickly. I walked down to Much Middling, with the kitten wrapped in a laundry bag and shrieking all the way, for the vet's evening office hours. Dr. Jackson liked him.

"Fine little fellow. Belongs to Miss Higgs's stable cat, you say?" He chuckled. "She must have gone a long way to find his dad. He looks almost pure Abyssinian."

"Abyssinian? I've never heard of it."

"Very aristocratic, my dear. And not too common. They're said to be descended from the sacred cats of ancient Egypt."

I was pleased. I knew Casca was something special.

Outside I met Charlie, who walked back with me, pushing his bicycle, and we took turns carrying Casca. Charlie gave me a lot of useful hints on the care of kittens. It was lucky that Casca was recently weaned when I found him, because Lavinia, after a brief search, had suddenly lost interest.

Next day Charlie and I went out for a long practice, and by the time we got back, I could ride without hands—as long as there were no bumps. All together, life was looking up.

I showed Sid his intended victim and he snorted. "Out of her mind she is! First them bicycles and now it's pets! There'll be rabbits next."

I hadn't thought of rabbits.

"You've given me an idea," I said. Sid glared at me.

But good luck doesn't last. I'd learned that in all my years at Miss Cole's, only Charlie's company had made me forget it.

The next day was absolutely pouring. If Noah had had weather like this, I thought miserably, he wouldn't have had time to build an ark. Sid Jennings didn't turn up—Aunt Harriet said he was probably cut off by the rising brook—so we had to do all the outdoor jobs ourselves. Bertram came with us and then left a trail of muddy footprints as if a baby elephant had stampeded through the hall and kitchen. My aunt scolded him and he sulked; and Bertram's gloom was the kind that can fill a house. The fire sulked too, and blew smoke into the room. Casca spent the day thinking up all the things he shouldn't do and then doing them.

I realized more fully than ever before how far Deep

End was from anywhere else. We might be marooned there for days and days of this chilly daytime twilight with the endless slither of rain over the house. For the first time since I'd arrived I really missed Miss Cole's. My spirits sank with every hour and Aunt Harriet grew more irritable. One way and another I was in nearly as much trouble as Casca.

My aunt was one of those women who punish themselves when they get tired or flurried by finding more jobs to do. After tea she suddenly decided to make scones "to save time later in the week." Goodness knows why—there was nothing likely to happen later in the week. Then she went upstairs to tidy something up while they cooked. I heaved a sigh of relief, pulled *Dangerous Desire* from beneath my jersey, scooped Casca onto my lap, and sat down for a good read.

Some time later I was roused by a loud cry and the rush of my aunt's feet across the kitchen. She flung open the oven door. A small cloud of smoke blew out a strong smell of burning. The scones came out looking rather like charcoal biscuits.

"Louisa, why didn't you call me when you first smelled them?"

"I'm sorry," I faltered. "I didn't notice anything. We can still eat the bottom halves."

"You didn't notice anything!" She loomed over me and suddenly twitched *Dangerous Desire* out of my hands. "You just couldn't be bothered, could you? Didn't I tell you to throw all that trash away?" Opening the stove door, she thrust the story into the fire with a vicious prod of the poker. "You're a naughty, disobedient girl, Louisa. You will go to bed this minute. And no reading. I shall come up to see that your

34

light is out. No, leave the kitten here."

I knew she would do what she said. There was nothing for it but to undress and climb into bed and lie there staring bleakly at the blank patch of window. Soon afterward I heard her feet come to my door, pause, and go away again. For a while there was no other sound but rain. Then came a scratching at the door and a small demanding wail. I shot out of bed and opened the door before it could be repeated. Casca pranced straight onto my pillow and sat there purring madly.

"All right," I said. "If I can't read I'll tell you a story. One day we'll run away from here. We'll find a lovely place where no one will tell us what we want to do. We'll just do it. And it will be warm and sunny and there'll be lots of people. . . ."

I was still trying to describe it when I drifted into sleep.

4
Night Happenings

It was Casca who woke me with his strange thin wail close to my ear. He was sitting tautly erect on the pillow, his tail curled around him, its dark tip rising and falling with a rhythmic beat. His fur glowed with a smooth dense sheen as if he were cast in bronze.

It took me a moment to realize how odd it was

that I could see him so clearly in the middle of the night; and another moment—with a cold tingle of the nerves—to understand why. Beyond the end of my bed shimmered a cloudy yellow-green light as if some monstrous unripe lemon had dissolved itself into candle flame. Casca's eyes reflected it in brilliant orbs. He cried again, softly, urgently.

Something was moving in the heart of that queer radiance, forming, growing clearer.

At first I thought it was a giant cat, some six or seven feet tall. It was a nightmare and I must force myself to wake. But Casca, unafraid, had become a single throbbing purr. His eyes were met by other eyes, larger, but round and luminous as his own, with furry pointed ears rising above them. Yet it was not a cat's face, but a woman's. Below the slim neck flowed the pleats of a long straight dress, embroidered in gold. The eyes turned from Casca to me.

"Greetings, child, savior of little cats!"

The voice was deep and beautiful, a throaty purr of a voice that filled the room like a caress. Whatever I said—and I don't remember—came out as a muffled croak, but the cat woman didn't seem to mind. Her voice swelled and I wondered whether Aunt Harriet would hear it and what she would do if she came in.

"I am Bast the beautiful, goddess, sister of the sun, Lady of Bubastis, lover and protector of all the cat kind, who derive their being from mine."

Casca's thrilling admiration filled the pause, which I could find no words to break. But Bast went on.

"Have no fear, child. I come not in power, but in love." (I was thankful to hear it, for now I could see

36

her hand resting on the bed rail, fine and strong, and ending in the curved claws of a cat.) "The grateful prayer of this little one has reached me, for he is directly descended from the royal Egyptian line, the sacred guardians of my temple."

Even in his ecstasy, Casca's eyes slid sideways for a moment to meet mine, conceited, impudent. If he had been difficult before, he would now be quite impossible!

"To her who has rescued such a one," purred Bast, "a gift is due. Ask what thing you wish most in the world, dear child, and it shall be yours."

I was appalled. What a decision to ask anyone to make on the spur of the moment, waked suddenly from sleep, and in the middle of the night! All sorts of ideas flashed through my head. A really super bicycle; no, a horse; no, lots and lots of money so that I could buy the bicycle and the horse and anything else I wanted. But what *did* I really want? It was like choosing a book in the last minute before the library closes. Whatever I picked, I should wish it had been something else. But I sensed that Bast grew impatient.

Outside, beyond the lemon-colored light, I could hear the rain still lashing and sliding against the dark windows. Beyond them were miles of sodden, empty countryside. Inside were the chill, dark, empty rooms of a crumbling house built for a large family and now inhabited only by two people, a dog, and a kitten. I spoke on impulse.

"I wish I weren't here," I said. "I wish I could go far away from here and be somewhere else."

"And where do you wish to be, little one?"

"I don't know." Probably she wouldn't like the answer, but it was true. "I don't know. Just anywhere else. Anywhere away from here."

The goddess smiled, a slow cat smile that was more alarming than reassuring. But her words were kind.

"A dangerous wish, child. You might find somewhere worse. But cats too are restless, wanderers of the dark. Your desire shall be made as safe as I can make it. You shall go wherever and whenever you wish to go, and take with you what companion you will. And you shall return again whenever you wish to return. You have only to utter your request."

"Thank you," I stammered feebly. "Oh thank you. Thank you very much. That will be wonderful."

"Where will you go first, little helper of the sacred cats?"

The million-dollar question. But I knew I had to answer quickly. Somewhere warm. And sunny. And a long way off. Looking at those two green moons of eyes, I suddenly knew the answer, and one that would please her too. I had a vision of white pyramids against a sky of scorching blue, of camels plodding through the sand beside a shining river enormously wide, of luxury hotels, streets full of shiny expensive cars owned by shiny expensive people in Eastern robes, of narrow lanes between small exciting shops full of exotic and beautiful things.

"Egypt!" I said. "Oh please, may I go to Egypt? And take Casca with me?"

The cat smile spread. The round green eyes grew bigger, more compelling. A huge purring filled the room and melted into darkness.

And then there was light. Brilliant light. And heat. And noise.

The noise was too loud for me to recognize the separate sounds that made it. I opened my eyes, half blinded by the sun, and tried to understand what lay before me. It was certainly not the Egypt I'd imagined.

I stood on a terrace, between two massive pillars of stone. Below it ran a broad street of sun-baked earth, and beyond that a river. The river was enormously wide, its surface so solid with light that it gleamed like dull gray satin. But even if the far bank was normally visible, I could hardly glimpse it now. Between me and it floated a long procession of barges, all aswirl with streamers and flowers and lengths of silken cloth, and crowded with people who danced and sang and swayed to the beat of drums and the harsh bray of bronze instruments. The rhythmic din almost drowned the tramp of naked feet in the street below me. But here too people sang and swayed and waved handfuls of flowers that gave out a scent as sweet and heavy as incense. No luxury hotels, no cars, no wealthy businessmen. Most of these people wore nothing but short white kilts and collars of colored beads.

I stepped forward to take a closer look, and the movement caught their attention. The nearest people stopped and pointed and called out something to the others. Heads turned toward me, the stream of bodies eddied and tangled to a halt.

Something slipped out of the dense shadow of one of the pillars, brushed past my ankles, and paused at the top of the great flight of steps that led down from the terrace. It was Casca. The sun was low and the nearly level light turned his brown fur almost to gold.

There was a moment's breathless silence as if the whole vast concourse had been struck suddenly dumb, and through it I heard the wash of water against the barges, the creaking and straining of ropes. Then there broke out a great roar of sound.

"Bast! Bast! Bast!"

Many surged to the foot of the steps. Others dropped to their knees, holding up their flowers. Separate voices reached us, voices raised in greeting, awe, astonished adoration. Even though I could understand nothing but the name of the goddess, their meaning was clear enough, and with a thrill of excitement it dawned on me where I must be. I had asked Bast to bring me to Egypt, and she had set me down in her own temple, apparently on her own feast day and in the ancient times of her worship. Obviously the crowd had taken me for the goddess herself. It was all very embarrassing, though natural enough. Since I had no mother, Miss Cole had always bought my clothes. I was wearing one of the sensible white nightgowns that she always chose and that I hated bitterly; but from a distance it might well be mistaken for a pleated tunic. I was a girl. I was alone. I had appeared suddenly out of nowhere at the very entrance to the temple. No wonder they had taken me for Bast.

I felt acutely nervous. If they found out their mistake their worship might well turn to anger. Besides, I was afraid for Casca. He hated noise and wasn't very keen on strangers. If he took fright and bolted I might never find him again. Certainly at the moment he looked composed enough, sitting in the exact center above the topmost step in the same tall elegant pose in which he had recently sat on my pillow. I wondered desperately how a goddess should behave.

Bast had looked about six foot ten, and I was four foot six. Oh well! Stretching to my full height, I moved gracefully forward, raised my right hand as I'd seen the vicar do in church, and waved the other with a warm but condescending greeting like the Queen's in a state procession. I thought the effect was probably rather good, but I needn't have bothered. No one was looking at me. They had eyes only for Casca. And he knew it.

Without turning his head he slid his eyes around to look at me.

"You poor idiot!" they said as plainly as speech. "It's not you they want. It's me. *I* am the goddess."

He was quite right, of course. Half a dozen men, more richly dressed than most, were now lying prostrate on the steps just below him, kissing the hot stone and chanting some sort of hymn.

Casca preened, smugly approving. This, he said with every burnished hair, this is as it should be. This is the life for me. Just let old Bertram see me now. *And* Sid. Sid would have to bite the dust too, wouldn't he?

"Casca," I said severely, "you are nothing but a small brown kitten, and you know it. You aren't a goddess at all. You couldn't be, anyway. You're a tom."

The kitten looked at me with bland indifference as if we'd never met before. No other creature in the world can make you feel as unnecessary and unimportant as a cat can. I began to worry. We couldn't go on standing there forever. If Casca got bored he might scamper off like a streak and I'd never catch him again. But it was probably sacrilege to scoop up a protesting goddess and the crowd would lynch me. I didn't like either alternative.

It was the worshipers themselves who decided it. They had all joined in the chant, which was now rising to a climax of enthusiasm. As it reached its peak someone threw his flowers toward us. It acted as a signal to the rest. A scented, rainbow-colored storm fell all around us, settling into drifts of blossom at our feet.

It was too much for Casca. With a startled yowl he turned and fled, racing for the shelter of the temple. I raised my arms in a solemn gesture.

"The goddess is weary," I called. "She will take her rest."

But my voice was drowned by the clamor of their dismay. The crowd swayed, swirled, eddied like autumn leaves stirred by a gale. My nerve broke too and I fled in pursuit of Casca.

From the brilliant light of the terrace it seemed I had plunged into total darkness, and the shadow felt almost cool after the heat outside. Then slowly my eyes adjusted to the gloom. The thick walls made a deep twilight of the place so that I could see nothing clearly, and they soared so far away above me that the roof was lost in the dense shade. Dimly I made out huge solemn statues that stood along the walls, and darker oblong patches that might be the entrances to other rooms. The noise of the crowd was now only a confused murmur like traffic heard through closed windows.

"Casca!" I called very softly. "Casca!"

I was afraid to speak too loudly for fear that some-

42

one else might hear. The space felt empty but I didn't trust it. My voice fell dead and small into the silence like a stone slipping into a pond without a splash. Cautiously I moved forward. Step after nervous step— the thing seemed vaster than St. Paul's. But no kitten. Then I stumbled against a stone ledge and fell, bruising my knee. I was lying across three shallow steps, and enormous above me towered the statue of a cat-headed woman. Bast herself. I had reached the center of the sanctuary. She was so impressive that I got up hurriedly and made a kind of curtsey.

"I'm sorry," I said. "I didn't see you. I wish you could tell me where Casca is."

Perhaps she heard me, or perhaps only Casca did. But a small warm body brushed against my leg and sharp little claws dug into it. I picked him up and he snuggled against me, trembling and for once affectionate. He didn't want to be a goddess after all— the temple was too big.

Then, even while I comforted him, he made a great spring over my arm to the very feet of the statue. He had seen something I hadn't noticed. On the topmost step was a row of small bowls, and a steady contented lapping now came from one of them. The sound made me realize that I too was terribly hungry. I stooped and groped in the other bowls. One contained some hard dry things that smelled strongly of dead fish. In the other were some flat cakes, tough in texture and heavily spiced. I couldn't eat either and by now Casca had finished all the cream and was sitting up to lick his whiskers. For a moment I thought almost wistfully of morning at Deep End and a saucepan of oatmeal bubbling on the stove.

43

But soon I had something more than hunger to worry about. I realized it slowly when I had sat for a long while, nervous of what might come through those closed entrances and wondering what to do next. There had been two tall shapes of light in the heavy walls when I first entered—one the door by which I had come and the other apparently another door that faced it far ahead of me. But now the light was changing, from speedwell blue to pale lilac, from lilac to white. And then suddenly a furry darkness pierced by a few great stars. It all happened so quickly I could hardly believe it. Absurdly I remembered Miss Siggs. Miss Siggs had gray hair twisted into a bun and wore dim sweaters and flat shoes and, like Aunt Harriet, was always exhorting me to read *good* books. ("You're too intelligent to waste time on rubbish," she said; but flattery got her nowhere. I bet she read rubbish herself at my age. It's more exciting.) All the same, some of her lessons were the best things at Miss Cole's. I could hear her voice inside my head at that moment, reading from *The Ancient Mariner*.

"The Sun's rim dips; the stars rush out:
At one stride comes the dark."

Wow! It was true then, and I didn't much like it. The crowd seemed to have gone by now, and Casca and I were sealed up in a silence you could almost touch. I held him rather tightly as I made my way cautiously toward the far door. The darkness seemed less heavy as I reached the open air, but only enough to show blacker shapes against it, humps that might be buildings or trees. I could see no lights. I thought I was on a terrace like the one on the other side. I crossed it slowly, feeling with my bare feet for any unseen obstacle.

It was a noise that brought me abruptly to a halt, my heart racing, fear running like water down my spine. From the dark spaces beyond the temple came a roar. Long, crescendo, menacing, it shook itself out across the night until the stars themselves seemed to quiver at it.

Casca gave a little squeak of terror, digging his claws into my chest. I fled back into the temple almost before I knew I had moved.

Not that I felt all that safe there either! The silence was broken by small sounds now and again, faint rustles, raspings of movement. Just drafts across the floor? Mice? Rats? Perhaps snakes? But once and again the cry of the hunting lion shook the night, and I stayed where I was. It was not a comfortable time—especially when Casca slipped off to explore. He came back quite casually just as I feared he was lost. But later I woke from an uneasy doze to find him stiff-legged and growling close to my feet. I never discovered what was worrying him. I had found my way back to Bast's statue, so I just picked him up and curled myself closer to it. After all, since she had brought us here this was probably the safest place to be.

Somewhere, at long last, a cock crowed. As if the sound had torn it open, the darkness shredded, faded, and slowly dissolved.

We were still alone in the temple, but I remembered the offerings in the bowls. Casca's cream had been quite fresh. Probably it was renewed every day. It was time to be moving before any priests discovered us. I tucked the kitten inside my nightgown again and made for the farther entrance. It gave, as I had thought, onto another terrace. I looked out on a landscape that seemed wholly deserted—a broad stretch of green countryside, of fields and silent mud-brown houses. And beyond that, as sharply divided as if two different lands had been laid edge to edge, yellow sand and rock stretched away to distant hills that rose sheer as cliffs beyond the desert.

That was the way to go, to explore in comparative peace before the sun rose too high. And if possible to find food, for by now I was so hungry that nothing else seemed to matter.

At the top of the terrace steps a small blue object caught my eye. Someone had dropped a broken piece of necklet made of little sea-colored stones. It was a pretty thing. I stooped to pick it up, tied the two ends together, and slipped it on like a bracelet. Then I ran quickly and quietly down the wide steps and made for the deep shadow of the nearest wall.

I was in the outskirts of a village or perhaps a town. Yellow-brown houses and trees and walls reached toward and beyond the temple as far as I could see on one side of me. On the other side they ended quite soon at the edge of cultivated fields. Faint busy sounds and an occasional distant voice showed that people were waking up to the new day. I hesitated, clutching the kitten more closely, wondering what welcome I might receive.

I wasn't left long in doubt. Around the corner of an alley came the flap of small bare feet, and a very small boy emerged only a yard or two away. He stopped dead as he caught sight of me, and stood

46

staring, his fingers in his mouth. Then he turned and bolted back like a rabbit into its hole, yelling as he went.

The nearest house came suddenly to life. People called to each other, ran and scurried. A startled group of women, with small children clinging to their skirts, came cautiously out of the alley. They stared and pointed and talked among themselves and tried to push one another forward. At last one bolder than the rest, or perhaps pushed harder from behind, came toward me at a little run and asked some kind of question. I shook my head.

"I'm hungry," I said. "Hungry."

I opened my mouth and pointed to it, but she took no notice. She was staring at my nightdress. She reached out a nervous hand as if I might bite her and touched it with one finger. Since I stood still she felt it more firmly and her exclamation brought one or two of the others hurrying up to stroke it and pat it and wonder and exclaim. Brushed nylon was something new to them.

But the noise and the poking frightened Casca. With a squall of protest he erupted onto my shoulder and I only just caught him in time. At once all the women cried out and fell back from us, bowing and walking backward. My spirits rose. If I was in favor with a goddess they would surely give me something to eat at last.

It was a short-lived hope. From the far end of the lane came a dog—a thin rangy mongrel of a beast, as unlike Bertram as chalk from cheese. He looked hopefully toward us until he suddenly caught sight of Casca on my shoulder. It was clear that whatever anyone else in Egypt thought about cats, dogs just wouldn't believe it. To them a cat was still a cat, and all that divinity stuff was mere spoof. This one said so, loudly and unmistakably. Stiff and bristling, he let out a hideous growl. Casca gave him one appalled look, tore himself out of my clutch, and was off like a streak.

I don't know what happened to the dog. The women surged forward to intercept him, but I fled in pursuit of Casca. Twice I glimpsed him, heading away for the open country like a rocket-propelled bottle brush, but I hadn't a hope of catching him. I was brought to a standstill in the end by a stitch in my side and a pounding in my head. The day was already blazing hot and I couldn't run a step farther. Not far ahead of me the desert danced and quivered in the heat. There was no living soul in sight, not a hair or a whisker of my lost kitten, and I was weary and hungry and by now rather frightened.

"Oh I wish, I wish," I said desperately, "that Casca and I were safely at home together."

It was a quite involuntary thought. But it was no sooner out than one of the great boulders beyond the fields seemed to stir and gather itself, lifting a monstrous maned head to the sun. A great purring rose all around me as if from the very ground, and I found myself slipping into a furry clinging darkness.

The darkness remained even when I opened my eyes. Casca was purring on the pillow beside me. Outside I could still hear the endless brush of the rain.

5
Hooves on the Heath

Despite the chill of the spring night Casca's fur burned hot and springy to the touch. Something bumped against my wrist as I stroked him—the small smooth stones I had found on the temple terrace. It wasn't a dream then! I really had been in ancient Egypt.

The house was very quiet. I was puzzled. I must have left it at least fifteen hours ago. That ought to make it now about midafternoon in Deep End. But even if I'd gotten the time wrong, my absence had surely been long enough to be noticed. There was not any sign of alarm, let alone of search. It seemed that no one was bothering about me at all. I felt aggrieved. Perhaps my aunt was even glad that I was lost.

I was also still very hungry. I slipped out of bed, groped for my dressing gown and slippers, and padded softly out onto the landing. A gentle pulse of sound from my aunt's room showed that she was deeply asleep. I felt my way down to the kitchen, where Bertram heaved himself up with wagging tail. But his greeting was that of most animals disturbed by their owners in the middle of the night—surprised and pleased, but not effusive. Not even Bertram had missed me.

With a good slice of bread and butter in one hand and a mug of milk in the other, I sat down close to the stove and thought. However little my absence had worried anyone, it would still have to be explained, and no one was going to believe the truth—not even with the broken necklace to prove it. I decided to hide the beads in my old paint box, and went back to bed trying to invent a useful story.

As it happened I didn't need one. Aunt Harriet looked around as I came into the kitchen next morning.

"You look tired, child," she said quite kindly. "Didn't you sleep well?"

"Not really, Aunt Harriet. I came down in the night for some bread and butter and milk. I hope you don't mind?"

"Of course not. The best thing to do when you can't sleep. Thank goodness, the rain's stopped at last."

So it had. The sun was shining in a pale, washed sky, its beams still low enough to make every grass blade wink and glitter. I found it rather soothing after the fierce Egyptian morning. At the same time a great sense of relief mingled with bewilderment. Aunt Harriet didn't even know I'd gone! My whole journey had happened in some invisible space between one minute and the next, or time had washed back to close the gap just as dammed water will flow back when released. If I slipped away again no one need ever know. It gave me a marvelous feeling of freedom and excitement.

But I wouldn't try it again just yet. There was plenty of time to find out if Bast's gift still worked, but on the next occasion I would plan it properly and be fully prepared. Meanwhile there were things I wanted to know.

"Aunt Harriet," I said, "do you ever go into Allington?"

"Of course. The village doesn't keep everything. But I did all my shopping there on the day I met you." She looked at me more closely. "Why? Do you want something there?"

"I thought I might go to the public library. If I joined it I could choose something good. As well as Scott," I added hurriedly.

"That's quite a sensible idea, Louisa. A day out would do you good. You probably feel bored here after London. You'll just get the nine-forty bus if you hurry. Oh, and while you're there you might get me some fish from Harrington's. And I need some extra wool."

By the time I was ready she had quite a list of errands for me. But she also gave me my fare and some money for coffee and buns in case I missed the midday bus back.

Allington was quite a small market town, but after the remoteness of Much Middling it seemed almost as bustling as London. I dealt with Aunt Harriet's things first in case I should forget them, though later

I regretted buying the fish so soon. It had a haunting presence that became more apparent as the day went on.

At the public library I went straight to the librarian's counter.

"Have you got any books on Egypt, please?"

The librarian looked slightly anxious.

"Are you doing a project on that at school?" she asked.

"No, I'm just interested."

Her face cleared. "How nice to find a child who really wants to know. Yes, of course, I'm sure I can find you something. Come along." She came from behind her barrier and led me briskly in the right direction.

"Don't you like projects?" I asked curiously. I'd always thought schoolteachers and librarians were in cahoots.

"Of course I do," she said conscientiously. "But it always means twenty children wanting the same book, and a lot of them aren't really interested at all."

Inspired by my keenness, she soon had me seated at a table with half a dozen books and a big encyclopedia. Some of the stuff was dull, and the pictures of modern Egypt seemed flat after my recent experiences. But I found out quite a lot about Bast. I was delighted to be told she was a goddess of pleasure. "Her feast days were occasions of general rejoicing, celebrated with music and dancing." I could have told the author that myself. I was glad she was my patroness and not Horus, whose fierce hawk-headed statues were decidedly alarming.

Just as I was leaving, I remembered about joining the library so that I could pacify Aunt Harriet with the sight of Some Really Good Books. Here again the librarian was helpful. She made out my tickets and helped me to find some books, including one called *The Bright and Morning Star.*

"You'll like that," she said, "since you're so keen on ancient Egypt." (She was right! I read it in two days and it made *Dangerous Desire* look pretty thin by comparison.)

I caught the 2:40 back again and got off just before Much Middling so that I had to walk through the village. I was vaguely hopeful of a meeting. A van, its doors open, stood outside Parkinson's Grocery Store. I dawdled as I approached it, having seen a flash of red hair inside as someone piled up boxes.

"Hullo! Busy?" I said casually as Charlie emerged backward.

"Oh hullo, Scrap!" He glanced after the bus. "Been to Allington?"

I nodded. "It's only a quarter past three. You're home early."

"Oh, term finished today. Didn't I tell you? We always go home early on the day we break up."

I didn't care for the news. One term ending meant another starting in about three weeks time. Still, perhaps it wouldn't be so bad with Charlie there.

"You're looking very pleased with yourself," commented Charlie. "What have you been doing?"

"Shopping for Aunt Harriet," I said virtuously. I waved the fish bag near him. "You can smell it. And I've been to the library too. To find out about ancient Egypt."

He stared. "Ancient Egypt! Whatever do you want to know about that for?"

I put out a feeler.

"Well, I had this queer dream about it. Do you sometimes dream almost as if it's real? I thought I was in a huge temple, and there was a cat-goddess there."

"Here, watch it, kid," Charlie advised me solemnly. "Seems to me you've enough daydreams in your head already, without worrying about night dreams as well."

I gave up, disappointed. Charlie wasn't the kind to believe in peculiar experiences without a lot of persuasion. Whatever had happened, I'd have to keep it to myself for the time being anyway.

If anything *had* happened? I was almost ready to doubt it myself in spite of the blue beads hidden in my paint box. I should have to put it to the test again. But I hesitated, partly through fear of disappointment and partly because this time I wanted to think more carefully about my choice.

For the next few days I went about mostly in a dream, waked now and again by irritated sounds from Aunt Harriet.

"Louisa, look what you're doing! Louisa, I told you half an hour ago to do that. Louisa, didn't you hear me? Louisa . . ."

Charlie came up a couple of times and we went for long cycle rides. I dropped all thought of Bast's gift while I was with him because there were so many other things to do. Charlie knew an awful lot about birds and plants and things. We talked too, and quarreled sometimes, but not for long because he always

made me laugh. But if he knew a lot more than I
did, I could pretty soon ride as well or better. He
was furious the first time I put my feet on the handle-
bars and went whizzing downhill like a rocket.

"You'll kill yourself," he yelled as he caught up
with me. "And serve you right too!"

"No, I won't. You should try it. It's just like flying."

But he wouldn't do it. He said he'd got too much
sense, and I said he was scared, but I couldn't make
him angry that way.

One way and another those were good days. But
in the times between I kept on thinking about other
places. Australia perhaps? But there was a great deal
of Australia and I wasn't sure what part I wanted. I
didn't want to find myself alone in a desert. Peru?
But all I knew about Peru was that it was a very long
way away. In any case, since this would be a kind of
test trip to see if the gift still worked, it would be
sensible to choose somewhere familiar, just to make
sure that I'd arrived in the right place. Well, there
was only one place beside Much Middling that I really
knew. I put down my duster (I was supposed to be
cleaning my bedroom at the time) and spoke aloud.

"I wish I were in Streatham."

I was slipping away into darkness and space and
a vast warm purring. Then daylight pressed on my
eyelids again. The purring note went on but with a
different, colder sound. Indeed it wasn't a purr at
all but the brush of wind over long stretches of grass.
I opened my eyes, and for a moment I nearly panicked.

The gift had half worked. I was certainly Somewhere
Else. But just as certainly I was not in Streatham.
Suppose my return journey should be equally inaccu-

rate! I almost wished myself back home at once, to make sure. Then I pulled myself together. Even a goddess might get fed up with someone who changed her mind every few minutes. I would stay where I was and find out more about it.

I was in a stretch of open country, hummocky coarse grassland, broken by patches of scrub and tangled trees. A few yards away a road led gently uphill to where, perhaps half a mile away, a big house loomed against the sky. There was a flicker of light in some of its windows, for this was not the bright spring morning that I had just left.

There was something scary about the place. I was standing at the edge of a small clump of trees, and instinctively I moved farther back, keeping the trunk of a big oak tree between me and the road. Although I seemed to be quite alone I had the uneasy feeling that there might be other, unseen eyes not far away. Perhaps it was just the dull quietness of the evening that seemed to wait and watch.

I was bracing myself to walk boldly out into the open when I heard a rumbling sound in the distance. Something big and dark was approaching along the road. Out of the rumbling came the beat of hooves and then the jingle and creak of harness. A big coach was swaying and bumping behind four trotting horses, and now I could hear the driver's voice urging them to go faster.

It was very near now. Still I hesitated, uncertain whether or not to attract attention. And at that moment there was a loud report and a spurt of flame.

The leading horses reared and plunged. The coach rocked, lurched sideways with the near wheels caught

56

in a deep rut, then dragged to a halt as a mounted man rose suddenly alongside it and grabbed at the trailing reins. Inside the coach someone screamed.

At that distance details were blurred by the twilight. But there was a dark space where the rider's face should be, and I realized that he was wearing some kind of mask. He leaned over and caught the coachman's arm, pulling him down. I could hear his voice, rough and brutal.

"Cut the nags loose."

The man seemed to protest and the rider raised his arm.

"Cut 'em loose if you don't want a bullet in your gullet."

The man stumbled to obey, fumbling among the harness, while the rider spoke to the passengers inside.

"Shut that noise or I'll shut it for you. Out, all of you."

He dragged open the door and pulled at someone, still keeping his pistol raised. Two women, in long dresses and cloaks, stepped down onto the road, followed by a small thin man who moved stiffly as if he were very old.

The driver stepped back as the harness fell away from the horses, and the highwayman raised his arm and fired. With a whinny of fright the beasts kicked free and bolted away up the road. The rider kept his weapon trained on his victims.

"Give," he ordered them.

He held something out with his other hand and I heard the chink of metal.

"You've a watch there too, I believe."

The old man groped in his coat and slowly held something out. The highwayman snatched it, then bent down and roughly tore something from the neck of one of the women. She cried out and broke into frightened sobbing.

"Stop your sniveling, wench. I'll have the earrings too. Or must I drag those off as well?"

Her hands went to her ears, and something glimmered as they moved.

It was all over in a couple of minutes. The robber laughed, an ugly jeering sound.

"Good night to you all. It won't hurt you none to walk the rest of the way."

He swung his horse off the road.

I pressed myself, shaking, closer to the protecting trunk of my oak tree. Highwaymen in stories and films had always seemed romantic. But this was as cold-blooded and brutal as any mugging in a modern city street. And the man who had done it was riding straight toward me. As he came he pulled away the scarf that had masked him, whistling softly between his teeth. He was near enough for me to see him clearly. He had a middle-aged, blotchy face, coarse and rather stupid.

I stayed absolutely still, holding my breath. He might have gone by, but the horse either sensed or saw me. It shied violently away and the man turned his head and looked at me. I was wearing jeans, and in the dusk he must have taken me for a boy.

"A spy, eh? A sneaking, crawling little spy!"

"Oh no," I faltered. "I'm not. Truly. I just happened to be here. Please don't shoot."

"Shut your trap. There's none to hear you. Not a

58

soul in miles but them poor fools back there. You'll not turn evidence against me, my lad."

He raised his arm, I don't know whether to strike or shoot. I threw myself sideways, around the other side of the tree, and ran. I wouldn't have had a chance, but fate (or perhaps it was Bast?) stepped in. I heard a crack and something hit the ground ahead of me, spurting up leaves and grass. Then there was silence and I glanced back as I ran. He was reloading. It gave me a few seconds' lead, and then I heard the thud of following hooves. Then there was a sudden crash and a cry. The horse must have caught its foot in a rabbit hole or something. It was scrambling to its feet—I was half glad the poor beast wasn't hurt—but its rider was gasping for breath. I never stopped to look back again. I just ran and ran, dodging from one tree to another, making for the big house on the hill. I wondered that no one there had heard the shots and come out, but perhaps they too were afraid.

I was almost there when I heard the hooves again in the distance, and I flung myself at the front door. But no one heard my desperate shout. I groped for the bell, and faintly in some far corner of my mind was surprised not to find it. There was a creaking sound over my head as the wind blew a big wooden sign to and fro. The place was an inn.

There would be stables at the back, and I could hear sounds of movement there. I raced around to it. There was a big stone water trough at the corner of the house, and even in the growing dark I dodged around it without thinking. A young woman with a pail in her hand was just going through the back door.

"Stop!" I called. "Stop! Help! Let me in!"

She swung around, staring at me.

"Lord bless us! It's a child! Whatever's to do?"

I ran to her.

"The highwayman!" I gasped. "He's after me. He robbed a coach on the road back there. Oh please help!"

"Come inside," said the girl.

She pulled me in after her, shut the door, and then looked at me.

"A wench's face and voice and a lad's clothes! And mighty queer clothes too! You'll be one of them rascally players from the town and up to no good."

"I'm not. I'm not. I'll explain later." (Just what I'd be able to explain later I couldn't imagine.) "But there isn't time now. Those people need help. And the highwayman's still out there with a pistol."

"Is he now?" She was watching me with an oddly wary expression. "Robert!"

A man appeared suddenly in the stone hallway where we stood.

"Ay?"

"She says there's a highwayman out there. And folks on the road. See to it. Sharp now."

The man stared at me. He too was puzzled by my clothes, but he was also in some queer way hostile.

"Highwayman, is it? Keep her safe, Rosie. I'll be gone."

He went out and I heard him shout to someone else. The young woman seemed to be thinking, and her face changed.

"I'll believe you," she said, and put her hand quite kindly on my shoulder. "Come along, little miss. You're frightened and tired, that I can tell. I'll take you where you can sit and warm yourself."

She took me along the passage, through a door, and into a spacious hall. A wide, curving staircase led up to the floor above, and I had the oddest feeling that I'd seen it before.

The girl almost pushed me through the first door we came to, and I found myself in a small room where a fire burned low on the hearth. She took a candle from the mantelpiece and lit it.

"You wait here now. I'll bring you some hot milk."

I heard a faint click after she closed the door, and then her footsteps going away. I waited a moment before I tried the door. It was locked.

Slowly and carefully I looked all around the room, and my anxiety was almost forgotten in a sudden wave of excitement. I saw the shape of the two tall windows and, as I raised the candle, the moving shadows of the molded plaster ceiling. I carried the light to the fireplace. There was molding above this too, and I ran my fingers along it. Leaves, fruit—there should be a sort of cherub's head at either end. Yes, there they were. Now I knew why I had groped for the bell, why I hadn't fallen over the stone trough at the corner. I had certainly been here before. The furniture was different and there had been electric light instead of candles. But from the corner where her desk always stood I heard in my head Miss Cole's voice, angry but carefully restrained as it usually was in our encounters.

"Louise, I try to make allowances for your lack of a normal home life. But there is no excuse for sheer naughtiness."

The goddess had kept her word. I was in the headmistress's study of my own old school in Streatham. The water trough at the corner of the building was the one that held all the crocuses in spring. And beyond those darkened windows, in summers far ahead, Miss Cole's sensible figure in its sensible Dacron suit would often be bending over her sensible flowerbeds of geraniums and lobelia. But a shadowy Miss Cole was small comfort to me now. With a sinking of the heart I realized that Bast's gift was a dangerous one indeed. To a goddess thousands of years old, a century or two was obviously neither here nor there. But her vagueness about time had landed me in a fine old mess now.

I'd read about eighteenth-century inns, where the stable hands and chambermaids were in league with the highwaymen and told them when rich travelers were expected. And this was almost certainly one of them. If so, I hadn't escaped at all. I'd walked straight into a trap.

There were heavy footsteps outside, the click of the key in the lock.

I'd always been sure that some of my mother's ancestors had perished nobly on the guillotine. Now was the time to behave like an aristocrat. I swung around to face the door.

It was the highwayman himself who entered. Behind him I caught a whisper from the girl called Rosie.

"She's naught but a child, Jim!"

"What of that? She saw me, didn't she?"

He shut the door behind him and moved so quickly that I hadn't time to make a sound. He had grabbed hold of me, with one great hand over my mouth. In the other was the scarf he had worn, now twisted and knotted into a kind of rope.

My fear-frozen mind clicked into action just in time. I bit hard on his dirty fingers and wrenched my head free.

"Bast!" I shrieked. "I wish I were at home!"

Was there a quiet chuckle beneath the purring that rose all around me? I thought of that slow cat smile and wondered. But the momentary darkness cleared, the April sunshine flooded in, and I was standing in my bedroom with the duster on the chair beside me, and bits of twig and a withered leaf in my hair.

6
Unintended Journey

"Charlie," I said, "what do you think about time?"

"Ten past one," mumbled Charlie, with his mouth full. "Have another sandwich?"

I took one.

"I didn't ask what *is* the time. I said, 'What do you think *about* time?'"

Charlie turned to look at me.

"I wish I could see inside your head, Scrap," he said, not unkindly. "Your brains must look like spaghetti—all tangled up with weird thoughts."

"All brains look disgusting. Haven't you seen pictures of them? But like cold gray oatmeal, not like spaghetti at all. But I really do wish I understood more about time."

"I don't want to understand it. I just want to enjoy it. I mean, it's just there, isn't it? Going on and on."

"But does it?" I persisted. "Does it go on and past like a train, or does it stay put and sort of spread out all around us like a pond getting bigger?" I waved my hand toward the miles and miles of country that lay like a colored map below us. "Look, suppose it spreads out like that? And if you lived long enough— hundreds and hundreds of years—you could look across it like this and it would all look the same from where you were. You could drop someone down in it anywhere and it wouldn't matter. But it would matter to the person—like finding yourself in Glasgow when you wanted to be in Bristol."

Charlie's forehead wrinkled.

"I think I see what you mean. It would go on being there. Louise Genevieve Higgs, you think too much. What does it matter?"

I'd reached the stage where I had to share my secret with someone. After all, Casca wasn't much as a confidant. I took a deep breath and felt in my pocket for the broken sea-colored necklet and dropped it into his hand.

"It matters to me," I said. "What do you think that is?"

"Beads," said Charlie, turning them over. "I like the color. Where did you get them?"

"In the temple of Bast in ancient Egypt," I told him.

I gave him the whole story as plainly as I could give anything that wasn't plain at all, even to me. He didn't laugh. One of the best things about Charlie is that he laughs a lot but never at the wrong things.

But all the same he didn't believe me. In fact, he was clearly worried about my state of mind.

"You must have been having some terribly vivid dreams, Scrap. It couldn't really have happened, you know."

"I know it couldn't. But it did. And if it didn't, how did I get the blue beads? And the oak twigs in my hair?"

"Perhaps they were straws," suggested Charlie unkindly. "No, don't fly off the handle again, Scrap! I can see that *you* believe in it, and perhaps something strange really did happen. But I don't know what."

"Look," I said, "she said I could take anyone I liked with me. Will you come next time? Just to prove it?"

"I don't know." He was puzzled and uneasy. Charlie likes life to be simple. "Well, all right. We can try it and see what happens. Only don't choose the North Pole or anywhere too awful—just in case it works. Shall we try now?"

"No," I said. In one way I wanted to do it there and then, to make him believe in me. If I put it off he'd be all the more doubtful. But my last experience had shaken me. Bast had been right when she called it a dangerous gift. I was going to think all around it in every detail this time. There had to be some harmless place in the world that would be the same at any time in history.

"No," I said again. "I'll wait and think about it, and let you know when I'm ready."

We didn't talk much on the way back, and then only about other things. We both felt a bit embarrassed and awkward. I began to feel miserably that

I'd rather not have met Bast at all if it was going to spoil my friendship with Charlie. But it was a marvelous spring day, with the sky as blue as a thrush's egg and white clouds blowing across it. No one could be depressed for long.

"A sky like that always makes me think of the sea," said Charlie longingly. "It's the sort of light you get at the seaside."

"I wouldn't know," I said. "Have you often been to the sea?"

"Nearly every year. Dorset or Devon mostly."

"I've only been once. One of the girls at school invited me when her parents took her to Brighton for the day. I wish I could see one of the places you've been to."

O fool! Idiot! Mindless half-wit! As the warm purring rose all around me I could have bitten out my tongue with rage at my own stupidity. I supposed, I thought grimly, I should be thankful for a limited blessing. If the goddess had chosen to fulfil my *every* wish, no minute of the day could have been safe from any idle thought. Like this one.

"In modern times," I yelled desperately into the closing dark.

The purr vibrated with a faint irritated rumble, and for a second my stomach lurched as if I were in a car on a fast U-turn. Then as the daylight flowed in again I braced myself for whatever might meet my eyes.

The first sensation was one of pure relief. I stood on a pleasant sunny promenade, with the sea to my right and a row of houses to my left. One carried a large sign saying ROYAL HOTEL.

I was certainly in England, at the seaside, and in modern times. Or were they so modern? The promenade was quite uncluttered—not an ice cream stand, a bus shelter, not even a trash can in sight. The houses were familiar in any long-established part of any town, tall, elegantly bow fronted, or heavily Victorian. But horse-drawn carriages paraded the road that separated them from the promenade. And on the beach below me wooden huts on wheels faced the sea in a neat line.

The goddess had done her best, but what is a hundred years more or less to a lady who has seen thousands? I should be thankful it wasn't Henry VIII's England. I suppose even that would seem pretty modern to her. Oh well, I thought bitterly, full marks for trying.

No one seemed to have noticed my sudden appearance except a plump little girl of about five. She had probably strayed from the woman talking earnestly to a soldier in a red uniform a few yards away from us.

"You weren't there just now," the little girl accused me.

"No," I said, "I've only just come."

She considered me with mild curiosity.

"Why are you wearing those funny clothes?"

"Because I'm a funny person," I said.

I pulled the most horrible face I could think of and wiggled my ears. The child doubled up with laughter and the woman heard. She began to turn, but still keeping her eyes on the soldier as she said good-bye. Luck was with me. There was a flight of steps just beside us from the promenade to the beach.

I put my finger over my mouth before I whispered to the child.

"Hush! It's a game."

I was down those steps in seconds and crouched in the cold dark shadow between the sea wall and one of the huts. Above my head I could hear the woman's voice.

"Miss Marianne, I've told you not to slip away on your own like that. Now, take my hand."

They moved away, the little girl still giggling, and I let out my breath. But the child had shown me a problem. My clothes would give me away at once. There were footsteps coming and going above me. At any moment someone might look down. There wasn't room to crawl under the huts, but I was pretty sure they were empty. The day was bright and cool and fresh like the one I'd just left, and there were few people on the beach itself. I guessed it was still too early in the year for bathing. There was a narrow door at the back of each hut, reached by wooden steps. I stood up quickly, tugged at the nearest door, and found that it opened. A moment later I was inside and shut safely away from any curious eyes.

At first I thought I was in complete darkness. But actually daylight seeped through the cracks around an ill-fitting door at the seaward end, and by groping and peering I could find out what the thing was like. A curtain of some coarse material divided it into two narrow cubicles, a shelf ran along either side about two feet above the slatted floorboards, and each cubicle had its own cork mat. I supposed this was for the bather to stand on when dressing.

I sat down on one of the shelves to think. Bast's

idea of modern times was just about a hundred years out. And girls a century ago would not be wearing slacks and an Orlon sweater. I wouldn't go unnoticed for a minute. But how to get any others? If I tried shoplifting I'd no doubt be caught, and anyway I'd never get as far as the shops unnoticed and I didn't really want to steal even if I could.

I shifted impatiently and my foot tangled with the dividing curtain. Of course! The very thing I needed! I'd only borrow it for a few hours.

I unhooked it from the curtain rings and folded it in half with the hooks inside. They dug in a bit when I moved, but by hitching it up as high as possible I could make a sort of ankle-length skirt. But I couldn't make it stay in place until I had the bright idea of using my tights as a sort of cord underneath the fold. I left my shoes off lest they give me away. I'd have to pass as some sort of beggar girl anyway. Luckily my hair was long, but the Orlon sweater still showed. I peered out of the cracks of the seaward door, wondering what to do next.

The few people on the beach were a long distance away, almost at the edge of the tide. There was not much else to be seen except two or three boats drawn up on the beach a few yards below the huts. They were draped with old nets and pieces of sacking. Sacking! The answer to my problem. The huts hid me from the promenade. I opened the door cautiously and nearly fell down the steps in my heavy skirt, but a quick scurry brought me to the nearest boat. I grabbed the biggest piece of sacking I could see and clutched it around my shoulders. It smelled powerfully of stale fish but it was too late to worry about that. I set off along the beach, practicing walking in the curtain stuff. I soon got the hang of it and was able to walk with my head up instead of watching my skirt and the ground in front of me. I headed toward the promenade. There wasn't much point in staying in whatever place this was unless I found out more about it. I must go toward the town.

There were voices above me as I reached the next flight of steps.

"Come and get it then!"

"Naughty! Don't snatch!"

"Here, Rob. Catch it."

Boys' voices. Mocking, jeering, teasing. Then a girl's, tremulous with unshed tears, but trying to be determined.

"Give it back at once. Don't be so silly! I'll tell the police about you."

I snatched up my skirt and was up the steps while the boys were still laughing. Five of them were capering around a girl of about my own age, throwing a heavy bag from hand to hand, always just out of her reach. She was taller than me but thin and fair and slightly built. She faced her tormentors defiantly, but her eyes had the terror of an animal at bay and at any minute now she might cry. Another oppressed minority.

I let out a battle cry.

"FOP! FOP to the rescue!"

Then I dived at the knees of the nearest boy, who had his back to me. The next two minutes were confused, but the bullies had already been tiring of their game.

"Why, it's only another little nipper!"

"Oh, let 'em alone, Tom. We've wasted enough time. Let the kids go."

There were laughs and the scurry of feet and a final jeering call or two. I picked myself up breathlessly and found myself alone with the fair-haired girl, a heavy shopping basket, and a large bag of apples that had scattered all over the place. The late victim was on her knees, picking them up, and now the tears were out.

"Those horrible boys! Look what they've done! Aunt Gladys will be furious! And they've made me late too."

"Perhaps she'll call the police," I said hopefully.

"No, she won't. She'll say it's all my fault."

"That's not fair."

"She's never fair. Everything's always my fault."

This sounded much worse than my Aunt Harriet. I dived under a seat for two more apples and rubbed them on my sacking shawl before I put them in her bag.

"They aren't much bruised. Tell her they were all the greengrocer had."

"She wouldn't believe it." She stopped sniffing and turned to face me. "I'm sorry, I haven't even said thank you. They'd never have gone if you hadn't helped me."

"Don't mention it," I said grandly. "Anytime."

She smiled at that, but she was staring at me more closely, taking in my odd appearance.

"I've nothing I can even give you," she said uncertainly. "And I expect you're awfully hungry. Here, have one of the apples."

She held out one of the biggest and best, and I

knew it for a pretty generous gesture, considering her obvious fear of her Aunt Gladys.

"Thanks," I said, "but I'm not hungry. I don't want anything, truly."

Her look grew more puzzled.

"How queer you are! You look like a beggar. But you don't talk like one at all. And you're so clean!"

Oh dear! Another unexpected pitfall. Life seemed full of them lately.

"My shawl's filthy," I said. "You can smell the fish."

But I could see that it wasn't going to work. I thought fast.

"Well, I'm not really a beggar, though I haven't got anything and I don't even know where I am. I ran away from home, you see."

"Oh, you poor thing! Whatever happened to your clothes?"

"Some gypsies stole them, because they were so pretty." I began to enjoy my story. Those wide blue eyes seemed likely to believe anything. "I'm really quite rich, you see. But my parents were both killed and my uncle and aunt came to look after me. My aunt's cruel to me and my uncle wishes I'd die so that the manor and the park and all the money would belong to him instead of me. I couldn't bear it anymore and I ran away. I've been walking for days and days and days."

I was so moved by my own invention that there were almost real tears in my voice.

"How dreadful! Look, I'll find some way to help you. I know I can. Walk back with me and wait near the house till I can get out again to talk to you. But hurry, please. She'll be so angry that I'm late."

72

"It's funny that you've got a horrible aunt too," I said.

We contemplated the awfulness of aunts in silence for a moment. But I needed to know more.

"What's your name?" I asked. "And where is this?"

"I'm Flora. And this is Weymouth. Didn't you know? I thought everyone knew Weymouth. Aunt Gladys keeps the Bellevue Boarding House."

"I'm Louise Genevieve," I said.

"What a pretty name! I've never met anyone called Louise."

My heart warmed to her. A nice girl, this. We set off briskly, side by side, each carrying one of the heavy bags. Flora suddenly giggled.

"Didn't that boy look silly when you knocked him over! What was it you were shouting?"

I looked at her sideways, and hesitated. But here surely was one of my own kind who would understand.

"FOP," I said. "FOP to the rescue! It's a Society for the Freedom of Oppressed Peoples."

She was interested and I began to tell her about it. But at the steps near the far end of the promenade she stopped me.

"Look," she said, "that's where I live. We'd better not let Aunt Gladys see us together. Wait for me on the beach and I'll come as soon as I can with something to eat. She usually sleeps after dinner."

"All right. You go on then."

"Promise you'll wait."

"Promise."

She gave me a quick flashing smile that brought her pale face vividly alive. I went far enough down the steps to watch without being noticed and saw her cross the road to one of the big tall houses farther on. For all its size it had a mean look even at a distance. The fading brown paint sneered dingily at the white and pastel blue of its neighbors, and curtains, more faded than the paint, were stuffily half drawn across the windows as if they resented the sun.

I watched Flora hurry past the front door and around the side to a small square porch. But before she reached it a fat woman pounced out of it, grabbed her by the shoulders, and shook her. I thought Flora was trying to say something, but the woman cuffed her and pushed her in, and I could hear the distant slam of a door even from where I stood.

Poor Flora, I brooded. Some aunts were obviously much, much worse than others! I found a sunny patch protected from the wind by the high wall, and sat down to wait. I longed to go closer to that glittering, whispering mass of water, but previous experience had made me cautious. I wouldn't risk some unforeseen encounter that might force me back into my own time before I'd seen more of my new friend. So I huddled in my makeshift skirt and tossed small stones from one hand to the other. Everyone seemed to have gone indoors for dinner and I felt a bit hungry myself. But the sun and the distant sound of the sea made me drowsy, and I was half asleep when Flora's urgent whisper roused me.

"Louise! Louise! I've brought you something."

She sat down beside me, unwrapping a small bundle. From the middle of it came a paper bag containing bread and cheese. They were both rather dry, but out in the crisp air and the sun they tasted good to my sharpened appetite. The other things she unfolded carefully. There was a ragged cotton blouse, a brown shawl, and a very old serge skirt.

"It's lucky I'm taller than you. You can just turn up the sleeves a bit. I'm afraid they're all I could find. She'd notice if I gave you my other skirt."

"My other skirt"—so she had only three in all. And now I noticed that she couldn't help looking at the cheese I was putting into my mouth.

"Flora," I said, "you're hungry too! Hungrier than I am. Was that your dinner?"

Her pale cheeks flushed.

"Only a part of it. I've had enough, really."

I pushed the rest toward her.

"So have I. I'd had a meal not long before I saw you. You finish it."

She argued, and in the end we shared it, bite for bite. But Flora was anxious.

"I'll have to go," she said. "She might wake up anytime, and I haven't finished the dishes yet. But listen, I've had an idea. Bessie—she's the maid—had to go home last week because her mother was ill, and it's difficult to run the house without her. If you come and ask for work she might take you in."

I looked at Flora's hands. They were chapped and red and stained with vegetable juices. If Bessie was the maid what, I wondered, was Flora? But her idea offered a chance worth taking.

"But she won't take me if she thinks I'm a beggar, will she?"

"You don't talk like a beggar," she reminded me. "And you'll look a lot better in ordinary clothes." Her worried frown grew deeper. "But you'd better not tell her the whole truth, in case she tries to send you back home again."

She had taken my story so completely on trust

herself that I felt mean. But this was no time for explanations.

"Perhaps I could say I lost my memory," I suggested.

"That might work. You could try. Louise—if she does take you—you'll find it awfully hard after your kind of life."

"Well, *you* survive it," I said. "And it would be fun to be together."

She flushed again, shy and happy.

"Oh, it would! And at least you'd have shelter and food. Wait about half an hour before you try. She's sure to have finished her nap by then. Good luck, Louise!"

She was gone, scurrying back like a frightened rabbit. I walked back to the bathing huts, making sure the coast was clear, and slipped into the one I'd used before. I changed quickly and risked putting on my shoes again. They wouldn't show under Flora's long skirt.

I waited for what seemed a long time. Then, with my heart beating rather unevenly, I marched across the road to the Bellevue. I stood for a moment, staring up at the name engraved in big curly letters on the grimy fanlight above the front door. The curtains of a downstairs room twitched and someone moved behind them.

I took a deep breath, went around to the side porch, and knocked firmly but politely on the door.

7
Aunt Gladys

There was a long pause. I was just raising my hand to knock a second time when stolid heavy footsteps approached the door from the other side. It opened very suddenly and a woman's head popped out above me as if released by a spring.

"Who is it?"

A thick rasping voice that matched the thick stout body. Flora's aunt filled her shiny black dress as if she'd been poured into it and then left to set. Above it her face rose like a red winter's moon. It was a round, bumpy sort of face, the shape that seems meant to look good-humored, but contradicted by the small sharp eyes.

"Please—"

But her hand was already on the doorknob again.

"No beggars here!"

I took a quick step toward her so that my shoulder

was half inside the doorway.

"Please! I'm not a beggar. There was an accident and all my things were stolen and I'm lost."

"Lost? Then you should go to the police, child."

"I can't do that." I let my voice tremble. "They'd want to know who I am. And you see—you see—I can't remember."

"Can't remember!" Her tone was outraged by such carelessness. It was my business to remember! "Then you should—"

But I broke in before she could suggest anything else.

"I saw the 'Apartments' card in your window. And I thought you could perhaps use extra help—any kind of work—until—until—"

I trailed off pathetically and my eyes filled with real tears of pity for my imaginary self. Some other part of my mind was delighted by this discovery. Perhaps I'd be an actress when I left school.

Flora's Aunt Gladys was much less touched than I was. But there was a thoughtful glint in her eye.

"Work, eh? Well, I don't know, I'm sure. —What's your name?" she barked suddenly.

A trap. I dodged it.

"Louise—Louise—I can't remember. Just Louise."

"Hmmm." She looked me up and down and came to a decision. "You'd better come in." She shut the door behind me. I found myself in a narrow hall, with dark wallpaper and chocolate-brown paint. On a small table wilted a sad aspidistra, without the heart to live or the spirit to die, and above it hung a framed brown print of a large stag. "Wait here. And don't touch anything."

78

There was nothing to touch but the aspidistra, so I obediently waited. She went through one of the doors in the hall, closing it behind her. But she hadn't quite turned the handle and it opened a narrow crack, through which I could hear voices. I moved toward it, then stopped at the sound of a footstep. At the far end of the hallway a face appeared around the corner of the stairs. It was a pale, worried face, surrounded by hair like a haystack after a storm.

"Oh," said the face. "I was looking for—oh, I'm sorry—I was only looking for—"

It disappeared again like a rabbit popping back into its burrow. The sound of voices went on and I moved as close as I could to the door. There was a muffling curtain on the other side, but I could catch phrases here and there. Aunt Gladys seemed to be talking to a man and a woman.

". . . so difficult for you, dear Mrs. Wittering, with Bessie away . . ."

". . . very inconsiderate of her mother to be ill now . . ."

"She speaks well, you say?"

"Quite the air of a little lady." (That was Aunt Gladys, grudgingly but calculating.)

". . . good family . . . perhaps a reward . . ."

". . . dear lady, always so kind . . ." The man's voice was unctuous. It made me think of those big wet snails without any shells, and I almost bolted there and then. But I thought of Flora and hung on. They must have moved closer to the door, for the other woman's voice, thin as a March wind, was suddenly very clear.

"If they don't find her, she can always go on helping

79

Flora. She ought to be very grateful for such protection, I'm sure."

I stepped hurriedly back to where I'd been standing and was clutching my hands with nervous apprehension—not entirely acting this time—as Aunt Gladys bore down on me. Behind her stalked a man and woman who looked at me with no feeling except blatant curiosity.

"These," said Aunt Gladys, with an ingratiating smile toward them, "are my most important boarders—Mr. and Mrs. Merry. *Permanent* boarders. They agree with me that I should give you a few days' trial."

Never had I seen so unmerry a couple. The man loomed over me like a great black crow, with hooded eyes and gaunt stooping shoulders. His wife was more like a starling, busy and aggressive, her sharp nose thrusting forward with a quick stabbing movement as she nodded her head.

"Our dear Mrs. Wittering has a very kind heart," boomed Mr. Merry. "I trust, little girl, that you will not take advantage of it, and will always remember it."

"And be properly grateful," echoed his wife. "Grateful indeed."

"If your story is true," said Aunt Gladys, "we shall try to find your family. Meanwhile you can pay for your keep by helping Flora in the house." She let out a sudden bellow that made me jump. "Flora!"

"Oh thank you," I said, feeling that something was expected of me. "Thank you very much!"

"Thank you—what?" corrected Mrs. Merry sharply.

I hesitated, then caught her meaning.

"Thank you, Mrs. Wittering—ma'am," I dithered.

"Ma'am will be best for the present," said Mrs. Wittering briskly. "Flora! *Flora!* Wherever is that girl?"

"But you will be watched till we know more about you. Watched!" warned Mrs. Merry.

I was sure I should be. That sharp nose would peck out every crumb of misbehavior or scandal.

Feet hurried up the stairs opposite those from which the face had come, and a breathless Flora shot into the hall. She was wiping her hands on her apron.

"Are you deaf, child?" demanded Mrs. Wittering. "And how often must I tell you not to wipe your hands like that? This, Louise, is my niece Flora. She helps me in the house. Flora, you will do Bessie's work as far as possible until she returns, and Louise will do your little tasks for you. Take her downstairs with you now."

"Yes, Aunt Gladys," said Flora meekly. "Shall I give her something to eat?"

"When it is teatime, of course. Louise, can you sew?"

I was about to deny it when I caught Flora's appealing gaze. I had to make a good impression.

"Yes, but not very well," I said cautiously.

Mrs. Merry tut-tutted.

"Well enough, I daresay," said Mrs. Wittering. "I'll find you a dress and apron of Bessie's. You can turn them up yourself tonight. Now go with Flora."

I followed my friend down the steep narrow stairs into a basement kitchen. Its position made it dim enough; and it seemed as well to be haunted by long-dead cabbages, their steam still a ghostly presence in the unmoving air.

"It's awfully dark," I said. "Shall I switch the light on?"

"Switch? Oh, you mean light the gas? What a funny

way of saying it! No, Aunt Gladys always does that herself when she thinks it's time."

Gas, of course. I bit my lip. I really must be more careful.

Flora led me through the kitchen into a stone-floored scullery. Real steam was rising here, from a huge sink still partly filled with plates and cutlery. She was apologetic.

"I'm afraid I haven't finished the dishes yet. I got a bit late through going out. I'm ever so sorry. I know it's not what you're used to."

I felt another pang of conscience at deceiving her, but I couldn't risk losing everything if the truth scared her before she knew me better. I might never find the right spot in time again. Her hands were already in the sink so I took the nearest cloth and began to dry.

"It's all right. I've been in a kitchen before. But what an awful lot of things!"

"Oh, it's not so bad at this time of the year. We're only half full so far. The summer's more difficult."

There was no tone of complaint in her voice; but as I slowly took in my surroundings I began to realize just how difficult it was. I helped her to peel a mound of potatoes for supper, to fill the heavy iron kettles at the scullery sink and carry them to the stove in the kitchen, and to bring in scuttles of coal from the yard. Flora prepared a tea tray with thin bread and butter and little cakes, piled it with plates and cups and saucers, and staggered upstairs with it. I followed with a smaller tray, heavy enough, with a huge teapot and a metal hot-water jug. But only Flora went into the living room. I waited by the aspidistra again until she came back to relieve me of my load.

Soon afterward Mrs. Wittering joined us in the kitchen. She cut us each two thick slices of bread, gave them a passing touch with the butter knife, and allowed us ten minutes to eat them. Then she began to cook the evening meal and had us running everywhere, fetching her this and stirring that, while she complained sharply of our slowness in completing our tasks. Brass jugs of hot water had to be carried up to each bedroom, where slop pails waited to be carried down and emptied later. In each room was a washstand carrying a huge china jug and basin, a carafe of water and a soap dish. The cold washing and drinking water had to be filled up too. I don't think it was ever really changed—a greenish mist clung to the glasses and the insides of the jugs. While the visitors were having supper we carried up buckets of coal to refill the scuttles in the living room. But clearly the fire had not long been lit and the place felt damply chilly in the spring evening. I looked around me at the dingy cretonne of the chairs and the faded streaks in the curtains.

"Whyever does anyone come to stay here?" I asked in amazement.

"Hush," whispered Flora. "It isn't as expensive as some of the other boarding houses. But not many people come twice."

"What about the Merrys? They actually live here?"

"They're sort of friends of Aunt Gladys's. And all their things are better than the others."

Before long I realized that the Merrys did indeed have privileges—the best cuts of the meat, the seats closest to the fire (when there was one), the room with the best view. But Mrs. Wittering kept her other boarders well under her thumb. I caught glimpses of them now and then—elderly ladies and gentlemen, obviously not particularly well off. They'd probably saved and scraped for a vacation. But woe betide anyone bold enough to ask for an extra piece of toast at breakfast or a clean glass in the bedroom or to come in five minutes later than ten o'clock. They never did it again.

It was nearly nine o'clock by the time we had washed the last plate, made up the stove, piled the trays ready with breakfast dishes, and carried in buckets of coal for the next morning. I was almost too tired to drag myself up the third flight of stairs leading to the bleak attic room I was to share with Flora. When halfway up it, I heard Mrs. Wittering's voice from the landing below.

"Here, child! Take this dress and apron. And here are needle and scissors and thread. I shall expect you to be properly dressed by tomorrow morning."

"Oh *no!*" I said despairingly to Flora, as I rejoined her and closed the door behind me. "She expects me to do it *tonight!* And anyway a grown-up's dress will be far too big for me."

But actually the things were only too long. The wretched Bessie was obviously thin with all that stair climbing. I sat as close as I could to the single fizzing gaslight and clumsily began on my task.

Flora watched me for a few moments and then quietly took it from me.

"Let me. I'm more used to it than you are. I'll be much quicker." She gave a happy, conspiratorial giggle. "Isn't this fun? I'd never have dreamed of anything like this when I woke up this morning."

Astonishing girl! She'd worked harder than me and been at it all day. Her face was almost colorless and her eyes shadowed with exhaustion, yet here she was bubbling with the sense of a new adventure. She reminded me suddenly of a snowdrop, so fair and fragile it seems a mere breath of wind will snap it, yet surviving a whole night's frost.

"Now," she demanded, "tell me more about yourself."

"No," I said. "You first. You already know about me. How do you come to be here with your aunt instead of living at home?"

A shadow passed over her happiness.

"I'm an orphan too, you see. My parents died when I was quite little, and at first Aunt Daisy looked after me. She was very kind to me. You'd have loved Aunt Daisy." Her voice shook slightly. "But she couldn't really afford it. And one day Aunt Gladys came and said she'd keep me if I'd help a bit in the house, and so of course I had to say I would."

"What happened to your Aunt Daisy?"

"Nothing. She's still living in Birmingham. She works for a milliner there." She sniffed and rubbed a hand across her eyes. "Oh, I do wish I could see her again."

"Don't cry," I begged her. "Perhaps you will see her again, soon. Oh, please don't cry."

She shook herself like a spaniel coming out of the rain, and smiled at me bravely.

"I'm just being stupid. Here, try this on before I do any more, to make sure it's the right length. Take those things off. You'll have to put it on properly."

I stood up, too tired to think, pulled off my blouse and let the skirt slip to the floor. It was Flora's sudden gasp that brought me to my senses. She looked at my stretch nylon undershirt and tights, touched them very cautiously, then pulled her hand away as if they'd burned her.

"What is it? It's not wool or cotton or anything. And what—what *are* they?"

And I'd meant to choose my time so carefully! I took a deep breath.

"It's nylon. You haven't heard of it because it hasn't been invented yet—not in your time. Don't be frightened. You see, I'm just a sort of visitor in your world. I don't belong to your time at all."

She let out a long sort of sigh and sat down on the edge of her bed again.

"I knew it. There's been something odd about you all along."

Her pale face had gone even paler and her eyes were wide. But her hands rested quietly on her sewing as she watched me. I needn't have worried. My meek, indomitable Flora was not going to be panicked by any ghost, past or future.

"Tell me," she demanded.

So I began to tell her, as well as I could. And after a while she took up the dress again and began to stitch quietly away at it, only looking up now and then to ask a question. She had none of Charlie's doubts about my gift, but she thought I was teasing her when I tried to explain some of the words I used. Horseless carriages that moved very fast, machines that flew in the sky like birds, a box with pictures of things that were happening hundreds of miles away!

Some of these things were quite impossible to her.

"But the lights," she reminded me. "They must be different too. You didn't know how to light the gas."

So she *had* noticed, more than I thought.

She had finished the dress and apron. She stood up, trying them against me, and her hands trembled as they touched my shoulders. Then she pressed them lightly against me.

"You *are* real. Quite real. Just like me."

"I've been telling you."

"You'll go back," she said, in a small flat voice. "You won't want to stay here. You'll go back."

"Not yet," I promised her. "I want to be with you. And I want to know more about your world too. But Flora, when I go—when I do go, perhaps I can take you with me. I can bring someone from my own world with me, so perhaps it works the other way around. Would you come?"

There was longing and doubt and hope in her face, all at once.

"Perhaps," she said. "Perhaps."

But we were both too tired to talk much more, and my eyes were already closing as I huddled down at last into bed. But the memory of a face drifted in front of them, a nervous face surrounded by haystack hair.

"Who was he?" I murmured sleepily.

"Who?"

"The face."

But I was asleep before I could hear any answer.

8
Injustice

Next morning I saw the face again. It belonged to a smallish middle-aged gentleman, shabbily neat, who was crossing the third-floor landing just as I came upstairs with a mop and duster. He stopped as he caught sight of me, and smiled very kindly.

"You must be the child who came yesterday. How are you, my dear?"

"Oh, I haven't been ill. It's only that—"

"That you can't remember. Yes, Mrs. Wittering told me." He came closer and put a light hand on my arm. "Try not to worry about it too much. If you don't think too hard I'm sure it will all come back in time. Perhaps there's something you needed to forget for a little. Some memories are best buried for a while."

The kind smile warmed his face again, but his eyes were sad. I wondered if there were things he himself wanted to forget.

"Thank you, sir," I said with genuine feeling. His was the first adult kindness that had been shown me in that cold unwelcoming house.

He would have spoken again, but just then Mrs. Wittering's voice shrilled from the landing below us.

"Mr. Banting! Mr. Banting! I am waiting."

"I must go," he apologized. He scurried nervously toward the stairs, and I noticed he moved unevenly, almost as if one shoulder were slightly hunched.

I was puzzled at seeing him, for all the other boarders were out at that time of day. Mrs. Wittering made it quite clear that whatever the weather, they were expected not to be in the house except at mealtimes. When I reached the kitchen I asked Flora about him.

"Mr. Banting? Oh, he isn't a proper boarder. Not anymore. He lives here."

"Like Mr. and Mrs. Merry?"

"Oh no. They, as I told you, are friends of Aunt Gladys. I think they've got some sort of share in the business, and it's cheaper for them to live here. Mr. Merry is a lawyer. He's got an office in the town."

"Why does Mr. Banting stay?"

"I think he can't avoid it. I'm dreadfully sorry for him. He's a bookkeeping clerk from Bristol. He came just after I did, for a little vacation after an illness. But the day before he was leaving he lost his wallet with all his money in it. He was greatly distressed, because he couldn't pay his bill and there wasn't even enough for his fare home. There was a dreadful scene when he told Aunt Gladys."

I shuddered. I could well imagine it.

"She fetched the Merrys and I could hear them all bullying and shouting at him, and he sounded frightened."

"He looks frightened even now," I said.

She nodded. "He's good at bookkeeping. But in other ways, you know, I think he is a little less clever than most people. And I could hear Mr. Merry saying things like 'criminal carelessness' and 'debtors' prison' and 'taking proceedings.' So he stayed on to work out what he owed for his board by helping Aunt Gladys with accounts and letters and things, and all sorts of business errands."

"But he must have paid the debt off ages ago."

"Yes, but he'd taken all the vacation he was allowed. He wrote to his employer to explain, but somehow the letter got lost. I found him terribly upset a week or two later, when he showed me a letter from the shop that said he was dismissed without a reference for being absent so long without leave and without any explanation. So he stayed on."

"Can't he get another job?"

"Not without a reference. And they kept on telling him how fortunate he was not to have been prosecuted and to have his board as long as he worked here. Mr. Merry told him he ought to be grateful for such consideration. He told me he wrote to an old uncle for help—twice—but he never got any answer."

"It's weird," I said. "The money and the letters— *all* being lost."

She looked at me sharply. "You're wondering . . . So did I. But I don't know."

"Poor Mr. Banting."

"All the same," said Flora frankly, "it's selfish of me, but I'm glad he's here. We sort of look after each other. Sometimes I can smuggle him a hot drink when he gets one of his bad colds. And once or twice,

90

when she's been in a good mood and given him a little pocket money, he's bought me a meat pie from the town. He's ever so kind."

He was indeed the nicest person in the house, next to Flora herself. He treated us both with the same respect as for grown-ups, and toward me he was specially gentle because of my supposed affliction. I felt almost worse about deceiving him than I had about Flora, but she agreed that he might be terribly worried if he were told the truth. I thought we might risk it later on when he knew me better.

Sometimes the boarders were quite kind too, and even gave us a tip when they left. But that would be the last we saw of it. Mrs. Wittering could have been trained like one of those metal-detecting dogs that the police use.

"What was the coin that Mr. Evans gave you just now, Louise?"

Bother! I'd have sworn she wasn't even in the hall when he'd slipped it into my hand. And it was a more generous one than usual. Reluctantly I pulled it out of my apron pocket. I started to say "ten p.," but just in time I remembered that money was different then. She took it from me.

"A florin. A whole florin! What a lucky girl you are! You'll want it for some special thing one of these days, so I'll keep it safe for you until then. You'll be glad of it one day."

I'd have been glad of it there and then. My dream of meat pies for me and Flora died as suddenly as a fly swatted by my employer's large pink hand. But my protesting tummy rumbles were drowned by Mr. Merry's oily boom as he crossed the hall.

"So thoughtful always, dear Mrs. Wittering! You take such care of these young people. I'm sure they should be properly grateful for it."

Anyone might think Mr. Merry had invented gratitude, he and his wife felt it so often on behalf of other people! I pulled a hideous face at their retreating backs and then tried very hard not to think about meat pies. I'd never thought of food so much in my life as in my time at the Bellevue. I told Flora about it later. She was sympathetic.

"She always does that. She'll lock it away in that carved wooden box on the table in her bedroom. She puts mine there too. And the necklace that my mother left me and the half sovereign Aunt Daisy gave me when she said good-bye." Her eyes filled with tears. "It was much more than she could afford."

"Flora," I said, "as President and Secretary of FOP, we must do something about this."

But though I spoke so grandly, nothing occurred to me for several days.

I hated the Bellevue and its smells and its horrible kitchen, and every night my arms and legs and back ached until I could have cried. Sometimes I got really homesick. Then I would try to make myself laugh by thinking of Charlie still pedaling back to Deep End and not even knowing that I'd disappeared into a slit between two moments of time. I was fond of Flora; but she and I didn't really know each other's thoughts without the need of words as so often happened with me and Charlie. But I stayed stubbornly on in Weymouth. For one thing I was still immensely curious about many things in Flora's world, and for another— in rare brief spells of freedom—I'd discovered the sea and fallen in love with it. But above all I wanted to take Flora back with me, and I knew she was still torn between doubt and decision. I did all I could to prepare her for modern England in case she came, but it had to be her own choice.

But the decision, in the end, was hardly a matter of choice.

Flora and I had just taken up the evening hot-water cans to the third floor. These rooms were occupied by guests poorer in money or spirit and their turn came last. Crossing the first-floor landing on our way back, we heard shrill excited tones from Mrs. Merry's room.

"Listen! The starling's laid an egg!" I whispered, and Flora giggled. She knew my private names for Mrs. Whittering's favorite boarders.

But she hadn't laid an egg. She'd lost one.

Supper was laid; Mrs. Wittering had already been down to the kitchen to carve a dish of very thin slices of cold beef and had then rustled upstairs again to preside at table. Flora was ready to strain and mash the potatoes when one of the bells jangled. They hung in a numbered row along the wall.

"It's Mrs. Wittering's living room," I said. "She ought to be in the dining room by now."

"Bother," said Flora. "I'd better leave these till I've found out what she wants. They'll only get cold."

It was Flora's job to answer all bells, never mine. I suppose they assumed a girl who'd lost her memory was probably an idiot. A minute later she came running down the stairs again, breathless and startled.

"They want you as well. Something's up. Hurry!"

I ran up after her, with a flicker of alarm for which

I had no reason. Mrs. Wittering's small private living room was really her office, and it seemed very overcrowded. Aunt Gladys was sternly enthroned behind her desk, her stout form jutting above it like the prow of a ship. Mr. Merry loomed cavernously beside her, while his wife sat bolt upright on a chair, beating its arms with her angry little claws, a hard spot of color on each cheek. Mr. Banting hovered unhappily in the background, fiddling with a sheaf of papers and looking as if he longed to be anywhere else. By the time Flora and I had edged in behind the door there was hardly room enough left for a cat. Aunt Gladys fixed us both with an eye of steel.

"Which of you took up the hot water to Mrs. Merry's room this evening?"

"I did," said Flora.

"It was her then," burst out Mrs. Merry. "I never did trust her. Too quiet by half. That sort run deep."

"My dear!" Her husband broke in, sleek as a rain-wet snail. "Control yourself, I beg you. Let us hear what the child has to say."

"Did you go in alone?"

"Of course." Flora was puzzled and scared. Her aunt's tone was that of a judge addressing a convicted prisoner.

"And did you at that time see Mrs. Merry's jet pin? You know the pin I mean?"

Certainly we knew Mrs. Merry's pin. Every evening she bore it aggressively aloft on her bony chest, a great black ugly monster of a thing, like the boss of a shield. For the first time I noticed that her plum-colored satin dress was free of its burden.

"I wouldn't have noticed," said Flora. "But it certainly wasn't on the washstand."

"Think carefully, girl," admonished Mr. Merry. "My wife's pin is not in the box where she keeps it. It appears to be lost."

"Stolen," snapped Mrs. Merry.

"Are you sure you didn't touch it?" demanded Aunt Gladys.

Mr. Banting gave a distressed cough, but they all ignored him. Flora looked from one to the other, and her face went white.

"Aunt Gladys," she protested. "You aren't—you can't—you *can't* be thinking that I took it?"

"If it cannot be found," said Mrs. Wittering grimly, "it is clear that *someone* has taken it. That is what we are here to find out."

"Of course she hasn't taken it," I said furiously to Mrs. Merry. "You've probably dropped it or put it in another drawer or something."

The beaky nose jabbed toward me threateningly.

"And who asked *you* to speak, miss? Hold your tongue."

"I won't. How dare you accuse people? Who'd want your beastly ugly pin anyway?"

"Louise!" Mrs. Whittering surged from her chair like a rhinoceros heaving from its mud bath. "You wicked and ungrateful girl! Is this how you repay all my kindness?"

"Perhaps she's the one who took it!" squawked the starling. "Who knows what *you* are or where you came from? A jailhouse brat, for all we know. Oh, I warned Mrs. Wittering of you at the time."

"Please, ladies! Please!" Mr. Banting's tremulous interruption was so unexpected that all three turned to look at him, like a company of astonished stoats challenged by a rabbit. "I am sure that neither of them would take anything that was not theirs. Can we not make a longer and more careful search after supper?"

"I do not think your opinion was ever invited, Mr. Banting." Mrs. Whittering's voice would have made a polar bear feel chilly. "I asked you to be present merely as a witness."

Mr. Merry gave him a long stare out of his hooded crow's eyes and moved closer to the desk as if no one else had spoken. He took up a long slim ruler and stepped toward us, balancing it lightly in his fingers. I think he was enjoying himself.

"I am deeply grieved. Have I not reminded you many times of the gratitude you owe to your protectors?" (Indeed he had!) "And you repay it with dishonesty, deceit, and defiance. So young and so hardened! Well, if the kindness of Mrs. Wittering's inquiry will not move you, we must find other means to make you speak the truth. Hold out your right hand."

I heard Mr. Banting's grasp of protest, and at the same moment the heavy boom of the hall clock announcing half past seven. There had been a moment's eagerness in Mrs. Wittering's face, but luckily for us her business sense was always uppermost. She had a boarding house to run.

"Later, Mr. Merry. We will make further inquiry after supper, but the meal should have been served by now. Flora, you will go straight to your room this minute. Louise will join you as soon as she has brought up the potatoes. You will neither of you have

96

any supper, and neither of you will leave your room until I come to you. Is that clearly understood?"

"Yes, Aunt," whispered Flora.

Mrs. Merry rose with a venomous parting shot. "We shall call the police if necessary. The police."

We were thrust aside as the three inquisitors stalked out. Aunt Gladys never watched to see if she was obeyed. After years of bullying she simply took it for granted. Mr. Banting, summoned by a quick jerk of the head, made his crablike scuttle behind them, but paused to whisper as he passed us.

"It will be found. Don't be afraid. I'll try to—"

"Mr. Banting!" called Aunt Gladys sharply, and he hurried after them.

"Go on," I said to Flora. "I'll be with you in five minutes. I'll think of something."

Conversation stopped as I carried the bowl of mashed potatoes to the long table in the dining room, and there was an embarrassed silence. One or two of the boarders looked shocked or reproachful, but from some I felt unspoken sympathy. I set down my burden and retreated.

Safe at the far end of the passage I paused for thought. Now, if ever, was the moment to return to Deep End and to take Flora with me. Of course I'd always realized that that too might cause some pretty desperate problems, but none could be worse than this. But before leaving I could see to it that at least one bit of justice was done. I slipped silently into Mrs. Wittering's bedroom as I passed it on my way upstairs.

On the small table near her bed lay the carved wooden box which held Flora's necklace and half sovereign and all such small tips as we had received. Maybe it included things of Mrs. Wittering's as well, but as she kept the key in her own pocket I couldn't take them out. I hoped darkly that it did indeed contain something that she valued. After all, if she was determined that we were thieves it would be a pity to disappoint her. I picked up the box and carried it with me.

I found Flora sitting on the edge of her bed, her eyes huge in her pale face.

"Louise," she said despairingly, "whatever shall we do? They just don't *want* to believe us."

"We aren't going to do anything," I told her firmly. "We won't be here."

I took her hand. It was cold as a little fish.

"You mean go? Now? To *your* world? Oh Louise, I don't know—"

But I had no more time for shilly-shallying.

"Listen, Flora. We haven't any choice. After supper Mr. Merry will certainly beat us. And they may really fetch the police as well. Suppose they don't believe us either? You've told me yourself that thieves can be transported in convict ships or left in prison for life."

"We could run away," said Flora uncertainly. "We could try to get to Aunt Daisy."

"Do you really think we'd get there? And even if we did, it would be the first place they'd look for us, and it might get your Aunt Daisy into trouble as well."

There was a heavy creaking on the stairs. Perhaps it had occurred even to Mrs. Wittering that her victims might try to escape. I clutched Flora's hand more tightly.

"She's coming. Quick! Make up your mind."

She looked around that hideous bare little room almost with love, and I felt that she was saying good-bye to all that she knew. Then she squared her shoulders bravely and her fingers tightened on mine.

"All right. I'll come."

"I wish," I said very clearly, "that Flora and I were back home together at Deep End."

At least, I reflected briefly, Bast never seemed to muddle time on the homeward journey. As a heavy step sounded just outside the door, the room faded and we fell away together into the purring dark.

9
A Ghost in the Attic

". . . not that I really don't believe you," Charlie was explaining. "It's just that—"

"Hello, Charlie," I said, as I steadied my bike with one foot on the ground.

"What do you mean, 'Hello'?" said Charlie crossly. "If you just want to be silly about it—"

Then he turned his head and saw us. He stopped so suddenly that he nearly fell off and his hair seemed redder than ever against the sudden pallor of his face.

"What—? What—? And who on earth is *she*?"

"It's all right," I assured him. "She is on earth. Not a ghost. I've just brought her back with me from Weymouth. From a long time ago."

"1862," Flora helped me.

"You mean it really is true? Then you've gone away again and without me! Oh you little beast, Scrap! You said you'd take me with you."

"I know. I'm sorry. But I didn't mean to go at all. It was an awful mistake. Well, not really awful, because I met Flora. This is Flora. Here, I think we'd better all sit down while we straighten things out."

If they didn't sit down I was afraid they might fall down. Both were still trembling. We were at the beginning of the track leading to Deep End. I made them sit close beneath the hedge that separated the first field from the road. The ground of the bank beneath it was fairly dry, and we were screened from any possible passersby.

"Oh Charlie," I said, "you don't know how glad I am to see you again!"

"But you've been with me all morning," he protested.

"Yes, I know. But I've been away for ages as well. Just listen while I tell you what's happened."

He listened, asking questions from time to time, but hardly taking his eyes off Flora. Once or twice he answered absently and I began to feel unreasonably irritated.

"Oh, do *listen*, Charlie," I said crossly. "Don't be so useless! The question is, what are we going to do now?"

"You can't meet your Aunt Harriet in those clothes, for a start," said Charlie.

"I suppose you couldn't smuggle us some of your sisters', could you?"

"Not a hope. Neither of them are anything like your size."

"And none of mine would be long enough for Flora. Look, Charlie, you'll have to distract attention somehow while we slip in around the back. Flora can hide in one of the attics—no one ever goes up there— until I can find a chance to explain things to Aunt Harriet. Keep her at the front door as long as you can to give me time to change."

"How do I do it? I suppose I could let the hens out. But it takes so long to get them back."

"Not the hens," I said firmly. "Anyway I'd be blamed for it."

"You could start a fire," suggested Flora.

"Flora!" I was shocked. "What an awful idea!"

"Just a little one, of course." Fair and delicate, she gazed at us with blue eyes as calm as an angel's. She would never cease to surprise me. "In one of the barns. You did say there were old barns at Deep End."

It was an awful idea, as I've said. It was also a very good one.

"But suppose Sid Jennings caught sight of me?" wondered Charlie.

"Is it Wednesday?" I made a tremendous effort to remember. Surely it had been Wednesday when I was last here, three weeks or half an hour ago. I felt muddled. Perhaps it was jet lag. Three thousand miles in a few hours couldn't be any worse than well over a century in a few seconds. Yes, surely it had been Wednesday.

"Sid won't be there," I said. "It's his afternoon off. And Aunt Harriet will be in the kitchen at the back. She said she was going to do the ironing this afternoon."

"There's one thing, though," said Flora. "Won't she be expecting you to arrive together?"

101

"We can say Louise was just going around the back because she'd got so much mud on her shoes and probably she didn't hear me yell when I saw the smoke."

I nodded. "She expects me to be muddy anyway. You could start it in that little barn near the pigsties. There's nothing much there. There are some muddy old sacks near the door too. They'd stop it from spreading before you could put it out."

"All right," said Charlie. He stood up and looked carefully along the road. "There's nobody about. Come on."

Looking at Deep End as we approached, I felt almost an affection for the place. It might look like an old tree that had sprung up and decayed, but it wasn't just drab and mean like the Bellevue. We were lucky that there was indeed no one about except a few incurious cows. Flora eyed them uneasily and moved closer to me.

"They're quite harmless," I said. "They won't hurt you."

"Perhaps. But they're so big," she complained.

Odd girl! After her Aunt Gladys a herd of wild buffalo would have seemed like mice to me.

"What about matches?" asked Charlie suddenly. "Anyone got any?"

I gaped at him. This seemed the end of our bright idea. But Flora groped in her apron pocket.

"I always carry a few in the evenings," she said, "in case someone asks me to light the gas."

"Oh thanks. Marvelous. Where's the box?"

"Aunt Gladys always keeps that. So I don't waste them. Just use your shoe or the wall."

"But—after all this time—"

I sympathized with his confusion. This time business was muddling us all. "We—I mean they—didn't use safety matches then."

He took them cautiously, and this time I noticed he avoided touching her hand. But his practical mind had recovered from the shock of the first encounter and now he took over.

"I'll go ahead and start the fire. It may take a few minutes. As soon as you see smoke, run as fast as you can for the side of the house, but don't go around the back till you hear me shouting."

He raced ahead. I suppose it was only minutes, but it seemed ages while we loitered in the hollow, praying that nothing would bring Aunt Harriet to the front too soon. Then a thin wisp of smoke slid softly out of one of the barn doors, swirled lightly on the wind, and was gone. I hesitated. Then came a real puff.

"He's done it! Run."

We picked up our skirts and raced for the side of the house. Behind us we heard pounding feet and Charlie's echoing yell.

"Fire! Fire! Miss Higgs, where are you? There's fire in one of the barns!"

The thick house walls swallowed up him and his noise, but by now my aunt must have heard. We crept around the corner and I peered past the edge of the back door.

"It's all right. I can hear them at the front. Follow me quick."

We raced up the two flights of stairs to the attic that stretched the whole length and width of the house. A great beamed wall divided it into two, with a doorway about three feet square leading from one part to the other.

"Stay here until I can get back to you. Nobody ever comes up here. I'll be as quick as I can."

I'd whipped off my blouse and skirt and apron and pushed them under my bed, dragged on jeans and a sweater, and run downstairs again while the others were still out. I felt a brief spurt of panic in case the fire was bigger than we intended, but I tried to keep my voice normal.

"Aunt Harriet! We're back. Where are you?"

I ran to the hall door and looked out. A thread of smoke still trickled through the barn doorway, but much less than at first. I could see my aunt and Charlie moving about and ran over to join them.

"What is it? What's the matter?"

"It's all right," called Charlie quickly. "Everything's under control."

I got the message, with a sigh of relief. Aunt Harriet, with a dark smudge across her forehead, was swinging an empty bucket and trampling purposefully to and fro around the edges of a small blackened heap just inside the opening. Charlie was dragging a damp piece of moldy sacking across it.

"What on earth are you doing?"

"There was a fire," said my aunt. "It's lucky that Charlie spotted the smoke before it really got going. I still can't think what began it."

Something was glinting in the sunshine quite close to me. As she turned to continue her trampling, I rolled it neatly with one foot to the edge of the doorway.

"Do you think this could have done it?" I asked innocently. "You know how you can burn paper by catching the sun with a piece of glass."

They both bent down to examine it.

"One of Sid's empty beer bottles," exclaimed Aunt Harriet. "Must have fallen out of his lunch bag. You know, Louisa, I think you may be right. The sun's quite hot enough to do it with these bits of loose straw lying about. Careless old man!"

But she blamed him out of habit, with none of the real anger that Aunt Gladys would show at the slightest misdoing. I remembered that red, bumpy, falsely genial face, with its hard, sharp eyes and tight mouth. And I looked at my own aunt's features, with her high cheekbones and carelessly brushed hair. If only she took the trouble, I thought suddenly, she'd have quite decent looks.

"Oh, I am glad to see you again," I said impulsively.

The remark astonished both of us.

"Good gracious, child! I thought you'd only been to Broom Hill, not the Antarctic."

I laughed, but reminded myself to be more careful. I wasn't yet ready to explain that I'd been much farther away—in one sense—than the Antarctic. It was obvious that the sooner I told her about everything the better, but it wasn't easy. I felt I needed a quiet moment in which to break things to her gently; but Aunt Harriet never had a quiet moment except when she was sitting down with the daily paper or *The Poultry Keeper's Weekly*. You just can't say, "Oh, talking of North Sea gas (or the price of pullets, or whatever), I've got a girl upstairs from a hundred years ago." And meanwhile, Flora had nothing but an old trunk to sit on, nothing to eat, and nothing to do.

However, luck was still on our side. While I was still wondering how to get back to Flora, the vicar dropped in. He was a nice man, who spoke to me always as one human being to another. This had surprised me at first. The only other clergyman I had known was the minister at Miss Cole's church in Streatham, who spoke to all children as if they were idiots at their present age and miserable sinners in the making. But the vicar of Much Middling had yet another virtue. He too kept hens, at the far end of the vicarage garden, and he and Aunt Harriet could be trusted to spend at least half an hour together in the passionate discussion of fowl pest and the current price of eggs. I murmured vaguely that I must tidy up my room, and left them to it. Closing the door on them, I tiptoed to the larder and foraged for a few things whose loss might not be noticed too quickly—cookies, some cheese, a can or two, and the spare can opener. Then I fled upstairs, going quietly through the empty bedrooms, collecting a cushion here and a blanket there, trying to leave things looking undisturbed. There were old dark family portraits on some of the walls. I'd never taken much notice of them, but now they gave me the strangest feeling that they were watching me. They had sufficient reason to disapprove. I grinned to myself as I realized that our gentle and obedient Flora had already involved us in arson, deceit, and theft.

She had sensibly kept herself well out of sight in the farthest corner of the attic, but came bending double through the little doorway as I softly called her name.

106

"Did it work?" she asked urgently. "Is it all right? You didn't get into trouble, did you?"

"Not yet. Stop worrying. I've brought food and some things to keep you warm." I groped in my pocket and produced *The Lost Heiress.* "And here's something to read to pass the time."

"Oh, thanks. I like reading. I suppose," she asked hopefully, "you haven't got anything longer as well?"

"Not of my own. There are all Scott's novels downstairs. I suppose I could swipe one of those."

I had made the suggestion doubtfully, but she jumped at it.

"Sir Walter Scott! Have you really got them all? Oh yes, please!" she said eagerly. "I would love that."

Extraordinary girl! Then I remembered that there wasn't much of anything to read in Weymouth, so I supposed anything would be welcome.

"I suppose your aunt doesn't take *Household Words?*" she said.

"I've never heard of it."

"Never heard of it? With those wonderful stories by Mr. Dickens? One of the visitors lent me hers last year. There was a serial in it called *Dombey and Son.* I've always wanted to find out whether Florence really did marry Walter."

I had my jet lag sensation again. Dickens had been dead and buried before my grandfather was born, and here I was talking to someone who was still waiting for the next installment of *Dombey and Son.*

"I expect I can get you a copy," I said. "I'll look for it next time I'm in the library."

But she wasn't listening anymore. She was looking at something behind me.

"Oh, the darling!" she breathed. "The little darling!"

I must have left the door ajar at the bottom of the attic stairs. With his little wail of greeting Casca brushed past my ankles, tail erect and quivering, and trotted straight to Flora.

"Oh Louise! Is he yours?"

"Sort of. He's his own really. But he obviously likes you. Tell you what, why don't you keep him up here to keep you company?"

"Can I really? I'll be quite all right if he's here too."

Casca smirked at me from her arms. At last he was properly appreciated. But her welcome of him made me realize even more clearly how nervous poor Flora must be feeling.

"It may be some time before I can bring you down. And there aren't any lights in the attic. Will you mind very much when it gets dark?"

"No," lied Flora valiantly. "Especially if he'll stay."

"I know, I'll get you a flashlight. With any luck they're still talking downstairs."

They were indeed, and I hurried past into the old dairy. There were always two or three flashlights on the shelf above the boots.

"Whatever is it?" asked Flora when I returned.

Of course, she could never have seen a flashlight before. I explained and demonstrated. She was enchanted.

"But don't keep switching it on and off," I advised her. "You'll run the battery down and it won't work anymore. Keep it till you really need it."

She was going to need it all right. The vicar stayed

to tea, then went. Aunt Harriet saw him to the front door, and Bertram, who had been dozing all afternoon in a sheltered patch of sunlight, came ambling in. He got no farther than the doormat, where he stretched himself out again in his best imitation of a heavily doped guard dog, and my aunt tripped over him with irritated noises.

"Aunt," I began. But she didn't even hear me. She was in a hurry to give the hens their last feed before the light faded.

I tried again when she returned, but she was already rummaging through some papers on her desk.

"Not now, Louisa. Whatever it is, tell me later. I simply must finish these tax papers before supper."

She was looking pretty harassed, and it was clearly not the moment to break it to her that there was a Victorian visitor in the attic. Her frown grew deeper. She had never mentioned money since my arrival and I had never thought about it. But I wondered now.

"Am I a burden to you?" I asked suddenly.

"A burden? Of course not. Why do you ask?"

"Well, I just wondered. I mean, there wasn't any money left for me, was there? And I eat an awful lot."

She laughed. "I think we can afford what you eat, Louisa. I know I can't keep this place going properly. The taxes are enormous. I will just hang on here as long as I can. But your coming hasn't made any difference to that. You just get on and finish your schooling, and then we can think about money. Now do let me get on."

We lapsed into silence except for the rustling of her pen over the paper, while I thought of ten different ways of telling her about Flora. Each one seemed more hopeless than the last. I heard Bertram heave himself up off the mat and come padding across the hall. Then he stopped and whined uneasily. My aunt looked up and called him.

"Bertram. Here, boy."

But the dog only whined again. I got up quickly, but she was nearer the door and reached it first. Bertram had moved to the foot of the stairs, and was snuffing around them. The hair along his spine had risen suspiciously. Hearing his mistress's voice he turned his head, gave something between a whine and a growl, and suddenly lumbered off up the stairs, following some disturbing clue.

"Whatever's the matter with the dog?"

"It's probably Casca," I said hurriedly. "Perhaps he's got shut in the attic or something. I'll go and see."

"No," said Aunt Harriet firmly. "Stay where you are, Louisa. I'll go myself."

She reached for a heavy walking stick from the hall stand, then followed close behind Bertram. This was it, then. She'd meet an intruder all right, but hardly the one she suspected. Of course the dog led her straight to the door of the attic stairs and she opened it very quietly. At once Casca shot past her with an angry wail—it was long past his mealtime. But the revelation I expected never came. For about two seconds my aunt stood absolutely still. Then I heard her close the door again and there was a longish pause before she reappeared. Bertram was still worried, and she had a reassuring hand on his neck. But I think she was partly supporting herself as well, and her other hand held tightly to the banister.

"Quite right," she said in rather an odd voice. "It was Casca."

I ran up to join her.

"What is it? Aren't you feeling well?"

She answered indirectly by another question.

"Louisa, have you ever seen anything—unusual—in this part of the house?"

Now that I was close to her I could see that she was shaken, yet in some strange way happy.

"No. I don't think so."

"Come with me. There's something I want to show you." She led the way into one of the empty bedrooms. There were more pictures here than in the others. "This was your father's room, Louisa, before he left home. He liked having the family portraits here. Perhaps that's what made him want to be a painter. Have you ever noticed this one?"

She led me to an alcove, always in shadow in the daytime. I'd had no reason to enter there after dark, but now the electric light from a naked bulb showed up the portrait that hung there among the cobwebs. It was discolored by age and perhaps had never been very good, but to me it was perfectly recognizable. Fair-haired, pale, and rather solemn, in a dress old-fashioned even for her, Flora gazed down at me from the canvas. I caught my breath.

"You *do* know her then?" said my aunt quickly.

"I've seen—someone like her."

She nodded. "I'm glad you weren't frightened either. I've always thought that this house might have a ghost—a nice, friendly ghost because the house itself always feels friendly. It's odd that you've already seen

111

her, and yet I never have until now!"

"Seen her?" I faltered.

"Yes, my dear. That is a portrait of my great-great-great-aunt, Harriet Higgs. And I've just seen her ghost standing at the top of the attic stairs."

10
A Greatness of Aunts

"She isn't a ghost, not really," I said. I'd brought my aunt down to sit near the kitchen stove while I made some coffee for both of us. "It's just that there's something strange going on about time. Though I don't know why on earth Flora should look like your great-great-great-aunt."

"Flora?"

I struggled. "I don't know how to tell you about it. You'll never believe it. Though I've got some beads and things to prove it. And Flora."

"There must be a beginning to all this," said Aunt Harriet. "Why not start there?"

So I started. To my immense surprise she was much easier to talk to about it than Charlie had been. She nodded and asked questions, and wanted to see my blue beads. There was a light in her face as she turned them over in her hands.

"Wonderful!" she murmured. "To think that someone wore them all those centuries ago. And yet you picked them up just after they had broken."

"You do believe me then?" *I* could hardly believe *her* when she said so.

"Oh yes, my dear. Time is very odd, you know. Very odd indeed. I'm not quite sure about Bast, though I'm sure you must be. But time, yes. Go on. Go on about this Flora."

I went on, until she interrupted me.

"Whatever are we thinking of? If that's a real child up there she must be alone in the dark and frightened to death and probably hungry as well."

"She's not hungry. I took some food for her. And she's got a flashlight."

"Well, don't just stand there arguing," said Aunt Harriet rather unreasonably. "Go and fetch her."

Flora was much too sensible to be frightened of the dark (and in any case she'd been having fun with her flashlight), but she was extremely nervous of meeting my aunt.

"The shock was worse for her," I pointed out. "You're prepared for it, but she just thought you were a ghost."

She laughed at that and came down. But she made a funny little curtsey in the kitchen doorway and I could see that her hands were trembling. Aunt Harriet clasped them in both of hers.

"My dear child! Louisa has told me a great deal about you. This must all seem very strange to you. Come to the fire and get warm. Louisa, give her some coffee."

When Flora burst into tears at the kindness of this greeting, I realized how great a strain she must have been under. Hurriedly I sustained her with hot sweet coffee, and a bit of color came back into her face. Bertram scrambled from the hearth and came toward her uneasily inquiring, then decided that this was an approved guest and laid his huge head heavily across her knees.

"You'll feel better when you've had a solid meal," promised Aunt Harriet. "Do you like boiled eggs?"

I had an egg too. All this excitement had made me terribly hungry. My aunt listened to what we chose to tell her while we ate, but waited patiently until we'd finished to ask a question that was urgent to her. She tried to put it casually.

"I don't think you've told us your surname, Flora."

"Wittering, of course," I said.

"No, it isn't," said Flora. "It's Benton."

"But your aunt—"

"She isn't a proper aunt. I thought you knew. She married my Uncle John, and then after he died she married Mr. Wittering."

Aunt Harriet leaned forward.

"But her first husband? Your Uncle John? What was his surname?"

"Higgs," said Flora.

My aunt gave a great sigh and the color flooded into her face.

"I knew it! I knew you must be a Higgs. It's the family face."

"Do you mean that your name is Higgs too?" Flora was equally excited. So was I. Oddly enough the matter of surnames had never arisen between us. I'd assumed I knew hers, and she'd never asked for mine.

"What was your mother's name?"

"Jane Higgs. I don't know much about my family.

114

But I think Aunt Daisy said we came from a big farm somewhere in the Midlands."

"Do you know what your grandfather was called?"

"I think he was James."

"That's it!" said Aunt Harriet triumphantly. "Wait a minute." She went into the living room and returned carrying one of those huge old family Bibles. She laid it on the table and turned over the first pages, where there were columns for births, marriages, and deaths, and space for other notes.

"Here it is. Simon, born 1820, married Frances Smith, died 1850. He was an eldest son and inherited Deep End. My father was in direct line from him. But this must be your grandfather, Flora—James, born 1823. There's a note by his name—'left home in 1840'—nothing more. He was only seventeen then and perhaps they just heard no more about him."

"Do I really look like the family?"

"We'll show you in a minute. The portrait of Simon's eldest daughter, Harriet. It might just as well be you."

I began to feel rather dizzy. I'd been counting back on my fingers.

"If that portrait is of your great-great-great-aunt," I said, "that means that Flora is the same to me, and your great-great-aunt as well."

My aunt and I and our youthful forebear stared at each other in fascinated bewilderment, and then suddenly we began to laugh.

"But what an extraordinary coincidence! That of all the people you might have met, it happened to be Flora."

But was it really a coincidence, I wondered? Bast

might be vague about time, but she was after all a goddess. Perhaps she knew quite well what she was doing.

The next few days must have been far more bewildering to Flora than mine had been to me at the Bellevue. I had at least heard of most of the unfamiliar things I encountered, but everything to her was totally unexpected. Electric light, radio, cars—she had to brace herself for each new startling experience. I was quite thankful for once that we had no television and that the wood stove at least must have seemed homely. But she took it all with that inner quietness of hers although she was sometimes afraid. She was shy, too, the first time she put on the jeans and sweater that Aunt Harriet triumphantly brought back from Allington, but she soon got used to them.

Charlie was a great help. He came up whenever he could and was kindly received by my aunt, although she did once suggest that he might join the Fire Brigade later on. She made no further reference to the mysterious fire in the barn, but I think she had her suspicions. But Flora's arrival had given her a new kind of happiness. It wasn't only its oddity and the sense of adventure that it brought to all of us. Flora too was relaxing, opening out like a sun-warmed flower after a frost. Long ago she had been loved haphazardly by her Aunt Daisy (the more I heard of Aunt Daisy the more I realized that she was a natural muddler), and she had been bullied and exploited by Aunt Gladys. But she had never been cared for, scolded, and organized for her own good, and she loved it. It dawned on me after a while that Aunt Harriet had always needed to organize someone who

116

wanted to be organized. I must have been a disappointment to her, but she and Flora were made for each other.

The first problem, of course, had been how to break her presence to Sid Jennings. The old man had weekends off as well as Wednesday afternoons, so we kept her indoors and out of sight until Saturday. When Sid returned to work on Monday morning, Aunt Harriet took her out to meet him.

"This is Flora Benton, Sid. She's come rather unexpectedly to pay us a visit."

"Benton?" He moved closer, staring at her. Then he turned to my aunt with a grin that showed all the gaps in his teeth. "Benton? You been seeing that lawyer again, Miss Harry? That's a Higgs, that is. Can't you see it?"

"She does look a bit like the family," my aunt admitted. "Indeed she may be distantly related."

"She ain't that distant." He made the creaking noise that was his nearest thing to a laugh. "She be the very spit and image of your own father. Proper Higgs, she is. Not like the other little one there."

"That's enough, Sid," said Aunt Harriet repressively. She'd gone rather pink, but Flora plunged bravely.

"Did you know Miss Higgs's father then, Mr. Jennings?" she asked politely. "You must have worked here a very long time."

"That I have, miss. I've worked at Deep End, man and boy, ever since I weren't no more than knee high to a buttercup."

Fascinated, I tried to fit this vision of an infant Sid to the wizened little lizard of a man in front of me,

117

but the mind boggled. Flora had successfully diverted him, however, from any further talk of lawyers. She was now listening with flattering attention to stories of how, as a barefoot five-year-old, he had scared the pigeons from the corn, and at twelve had been plowing with a team of two horses. At least a quarter of his anecdotes may have been more or less true. Seeing them absorbed in each other, Aunt Harriet drifted back to the house with Bertram at her heels.

I wandered off too and leaned over the gate leading to the cart track. I felt depressed. Flora belonged to Deep End so much more naturally than I did. Aunt Harriet never had to tell *her* not to argue so much; she never did. Sometimes I would hear their voices in another room, chatting away as if they'd known each other all their lives. Even Bertram had taken to following her about, breathing devotion. And now here was Sid, so keen to greet her as "family" that he didn't ask too many questions. I had Higgs blood too. I even had the name. But small and dark and half foreign as I was, no one seemed to notice it. I would be lonely with dignity, I told myself, like Mary Queen of Scots. But I felt too dispirited just then to play the part properly. I was only Louise Genevieve Higgs who didn't really seem to belong anywhere.

I was roused by sharp little needles of pain in the calf of my right leg. Casca was clawing at me crossly, demanding attention. I picked him up, burying my face against his fur.

"Oh Casca! You still love me, don't you? And you know what it's like. You're a half-foreign orphan too."

He wriggled and purred in one of his more expansive moods, permitting my affection. Then the swish

118

of bicycle tires interrupted our conversation, and Charlie dismounted on the far side of the gate.

"Hello, Scrap! I've got the whole morning free. I say, you're looking a bit down. Is it Sid? Have things gone wrong?"

I gave what I hoped was a hollow laugh. I was feeling hollow anyway.

"Not at all. He didn't believe the visitor story, but he's guessed that she's family. He's too pleased about that to worry about how she comes to be here."

"Oh good!" He pushed through the gate and leaned his bike against the wall, lifting a cardboard box out of the basket. "Perhaps she won't need this then. I've brought one of my old jigsaw puzzles for her to pass the time in case she had to stay hidden."

Even Charlie, I thought bitterly. Running after her like Bertram. But as he straightened up he had something else in his hand.

"Here, I've got something for you too. Well, for you and Casca really. I'd meant to give it to you later, but as you're together . . ."

I drew it out of its paper bag. It was a narrow scarlet leather cat collar, with a small metal plate already engraved. "Casca, c/o L. G. Higgs, Deep End, Much Middling."

"Just in case he ever gets lost," explained Charlie, watching me.

"Oh, Charlie, it's lovely! But it must have cost an awful lot. Put it on while I hold him."

It looked splendid against the brown sheen of his fur and he seemed to approve. Charlie laughed at me and was pleased.

"I'll get one for you next," he promised me. "You look more like a terrier than ever."

I punched him and he dodged and I chased him around the yard. The morning was suddenly fine again.

After all, it was quite natural that Aunt Harriet and the old man should feel as they did. I was surprised to find that I'd grown quite fond of Deep End myself; but my aunt Flora loved it with a kind of passion, like a marvelous dream come true. She was always wanting to know more about it. When Charlie and I went into the house she had already returned to it, and she and Aunt Harriet were happily absorbed in going through the drawers of the writing desk in the living room.

"Look what we've found," said Flora. "There's lots of old photographs and letters and things. Here's one of Aunt Harriet."

A tall thin child with pigtails stared at me out of the print, her eyes screwed up against the sun. It was difficult to think of her at that age.

"And here's one of Deep End in 1910." My aunt's voice was wistful.

Despite the faded sepia, the house in the picture seemed somehow more awake than it was now. It had a neat bright look as if freshly painted, barn doors stood straight on their hinges, and there were cows in the field that nowadays held the hen run.

"It looks different," I said.

"It *was* different," said Aunt Harriet. "It was a real farm then and it was kept as it should be. If only your father hadn't wanted to be an artist . . ."

I was hurt by what seemed reproach.

120

"Why shouldn't he paint if he wanted to?" I demanded rebelliously. "Why should he have to be a farmer just because he was born here?"

She laughed. "Bless the child. You sound just like him sometimes."

"Here's another one of you," said Flora, who was still burrowing. "With someone else."

I took it from her. The girl with the pigtails was laughing up at a boy who stood over her, waving a mug. They seemed to be having a picnic in the hayfield.

"Who's he?" I asked.

"Why, that's your father. I remember that day. It was a lovely summer that year."

I was surprised by her tone of affection.

"I thought you didn't like him much."

"Of course I liked him. He was always fun. I hated it when he left home."

I tried to digest this new idea.

"Didn't he ever come back?"

"Once or twice. But he and Father never really got on very well, though they never quarreled. Then he traveled abroad. He sent a postcard sometimes in the first year or so."

There was a shadow on her face, but she turned away and rummaged quickly in the desk again as if to shake off an old sadness. Then she picked up a big sheet of paper and laughed.

"Look at this. He sent it to me soon after he'd gone. Someone had paid for one of his paintings with it. There was a funny little note with it that said he was sorry he couldn't be a farmer, but at least he was sending me a bit of land that no one else wanted."

121

"What is it then?" I asked. I could make nothing of the paper, which was a foreign language.

"It's a conveyance of land," explained my aunt. "A completely barren bit of the Spanish coast that had bankrupted the man who tried to farm it. It's quite worthless, but I've kept it as Albert's last present to me."

She put it away in the drawer and we went on looking at photographs. Among the very early ones was a faded wedding group that greatly entertained us. All the gentlemen were in frock coats and top hats, and stood sternly with folded arms. In front of them the ladies sat stiff and self-conscious in their swirls of muslin, the bridesmaids clutching tight little posies as if they were pigeons that might try to fly away. At each end of the row some very small children were firmly gripped upon female laps and had clearly been commanded to face the camera.

"My grandfather's wedding," said Aunt Harriet.

"Their faces look more like a funeral," said Charlie. "As if they're afraid to smile in case something splits."

"It was such a fuss taking a photograph in those days, I expect everyone got nervous while they were waiting."

"Do you know who any of them are?"

"My grandfather, of course. And I think the little boy in the sailor suit is— Why, my dear child, whatever's the matter?"

Flora lifted a grief-stricken face.

"It's that one, the lady at the end. She reminds me so much of Aunt Daisy. It doesn't seem right, my being so happy here, while she loves the country

122

and has to work so hard for that horrible shop in Birmingham. Oh, I do wish she could be here too!"

"In that case," said Aunt Harriet briskly, "Louisa had better fetch her."

11
Rescue

They were all looking at me. They might have been asking me merely to pick up a package at Allington Station, I thought irritably. But then they'd never had to face those Egyptian crowds, nor the highwayman of Streatham.

"Of course, I'd like to—if I can."

"Then what is the problem?" Aunt Harriet was slightly displeased by my hesitation.

"It's this time thing, isn't it?" Charlie came in quickly on my side. "This goddess of hers does seem vague about it."

"You could name the year," suggested Flora. "It's still 1862, isn't it? I mean, it was—is—"

"Birmingham's a big place," I objected. I didn't want to seem unwilling or to disappoint my friend, but really no one else seemed to realize the difficulties.

"Flora will give you the address," said Aunt Harriet briskly.

"I'd have to say it very quickly before I'm whisked off," I said. "Anyway I can try. But suppose she doesn't want to come? Or doesn't believe me?"

Flora understood this all right, but she was not to be defeated.

"*I* believed you, Louise. I'm sure she will. And she hates Birmingham so much, I know she'll come."

I had no more protests left. I repeated the address until I was sure I could say it quickly without any mistake. Then I stood up very straight to make my wish. My heart was beating rather fast.

"Wait!" said Charlie very loudly. "Wait! I'm coming with you. Birmingham's a big place, you said so yourself. And I've heard that parts of it are pretty rough even now."

I was touched by his concern, but still doubtful.

"That would mean three of us to come back," I pointed out, "and I'm not sure that Bast meant more than one companion to come with me. She said it in the singular—'what companion you will.' "

"Then I'll just have to wait behind in Birmingham until you can come back for me. Anyway you promised me you'd take me with you on your next trip and then went without me."

"That wasn't my fault. I never meant to go at all."

"I'm glad you did," Flora soothed me. "Charlie's right, Louise. Even the police won't go into some of the slums. Perhaps you ought to take Bertram too."

"A fat lot of use he'd be. He'd fraternize with a burglar if we had one. But all right, thanks, Charlie."

I was more grateful than I sounded, but I didn't want to give away that I was nervous. I began to concentrate again, but this time my aunt interrupted.

"Stop! You can't go like that. You'd have a crowd around you in two minutes. We'll have to find you

124

some clothes that won't be noticed."

Organizing people have their virtues! I'd never have thought of our appearance. Other worries had made me forget my first arrival in Weymouth. Aunt Harriet took us up to the attic and heaved up the lid of an old black trunk.

"There's a lot of stuff here that we used for charades when we were children." (I was getting some surprising new lights on Aunt Harriet these days.) "There are plenty of things that would do for you, Charlie. Ah, here's something—an old pair of trousers—they must have been Grandfather's. And there's a corduroy jacket somewhere too. Louisa, you must find something warmer than what you came back in. Take this big shawl."

We carried an armload of stuff downstairs. Aunt Harriet insisted on airing it, and Charlie's trousers had to be hastily taken in at the waist. Luckily the jacket covered the worst of the moth holes. I began to feel rather sick while all the delays gnawed at my courage. More and more I was glad that Charlie was coming too.

But at last we were ready. Charlie's hand, warm and steady, closed on my cold fingers. I stood straight, shut my eyes, and gabbled very quickly.

"I wish that Charlie and I were at Seven Maytree Gardens, Birmingham, in 1862."

The purring darkness flowed up, submerged us, and dissolved. Something soft and wet was blowing into our faces, and my feet—in good stout boots rather too large for me—felt dreadfully cold.

It was snowing. A wet persistent snow that settled into black slush along dirty pavements. If there had

125

ever been may trees or gardens, they had long since gone beneath rows of mean, terraced houses. They were imprisoned by ugly iron railings, separating the street from tiny courts about four feet wide. Most of them were just strips of cobble or brick, but here and there a disconsolate laurel bush struggled for life and some optimistic weeds pushed up through the snow. The front doors had panels of crudely colored glass, above which were the numbers of the houses. There was a seven on the nearest door. I heaved a great sigh of relief.

"It's the right place anyway. But it was spring last week—or whenever it was. I wonder what year this is. Perhaps she's got it wrong again."

"We could ask someone."

"We couldn't. Whatever would they think?"

"I suppose you're right."

There were one or two people about, but all intent on going their way as quickly as possible through the cold, driving flakes. They were neatly but shabbily dressed, and our own clothes, so obviously handed down and ill fitting, would have caused no surprise in this district if anyone had noticed us. Then a boy came around the far corner of the road with a bundle of papers under his arm.

"Paper! Paper! Moseley man tried for murder. Read all about it. Paper! Paper!"

"That'll tell us," I said.

I ran to meet the paper boy, thankful that I had my purse in my pocket.

"Here, I'll take one. How much?"

"Penny, miss."

I took the newspaper and was holding out my coin

before I stopped to think. Then, red with embarrassment, I tried to take it back. But it was too late.

"What's this then? I said a penny, not a farthing. Gimme back my paper, you little brat, or—"

"I'm sorry." I tried to speak with dignity. "I've got the wrong purse with me."

"Oh, all la-di-da now, are we? I'll say you've got the wrong purse, you have."

There were quick steps behind me and Charlie pushed me aside.

"Lay off. You heard what she said. It was a mistake. Leave her alone."

The boy took a step back and raised his fist. Then he took in Charlie's height and weight and changed his mind.

"Aw, I don't want no trouble. Loony, is she? You ought to keep an eye on her, you ought."

He went on down the street, shouting his headlines again. Charlie turned angrily to me.

"You idiot, Scrap. You could have had us in trouble right at the start."

"I know. I didn't think. I won't forget again, I promise. Anyway it's 1862 all right. December third. I saw the date on the paper."

He grinned. "Trust you to have the last bark! Come on, let's tackle Number Seven before we freeze."

I felt pretty nervous as we climbed the steps and knocked. It made a cavernous echo as if the house was empty. But we tried again and I put my ear to the mail slot.

"It's all right. Someone's coming."

Slapping, slithering sounds came toward us. They suggested a performing seal rather than a person. I shifted, putting my eye to the mail slot and pushing the flap. But the door opened more quickly than I expected. Scarlet and ashamed, I groped around my feet.

"Sorry!" I mumbled. "I dropped something."

Over my head Charlie's voice covered up for me.

"Miss Higgs? Miss Daisy Higgs?"

Oh no! It couldn't be! This carpet-slippered mountain of a woman surely couldn't be Flora's Aunt Daisy. My heart was in my mouth till she answered, in a wheezy little squeak.

"Oh no, dearie. Miss Higgs is out. I can give a message to her if you like."

I giggled inwardly as possible messages flashed into my mind. "Your niece Flora would like to meet you in another century." Or "Would you mind dropping in at Deep End in a hundred years' time." Luckily Charlie was never distracted by flights of fancy.

"I'm afraid it wouldn't help. We need to speak to her, you see. I suppose we couldn't wait?"

"It would be a long wait. She doesn't get back from work until seven o'clock. Nothing wrong, I hope?"

"Oh no." It was time I took my part. "We've just come a very long way to see her, that's all."

"You'd better come in for a minute. No use us all getting frozen, is it?" The mountain heaved and squeezed to one side, leaving a narrow space. We edged through into the little hall.

"I didn't know she lived with anyone," I said in some surprise.

"Oh, she doesn't live with me, dearie. This is my house, but it was too big when I was widowed and all the children gone. So I let rooms, you see. Miss

128

Higgs is my second floor back. Would you be relatives?"

"I am," I said truthfully. "Charlie's a friend of the family."

"Funny thing, I never heard her mention any but the one niece."

"Well, I haven't seen her for years," I said hurriedly.

Her eyes grew bright with curiosity. "You wouldn't have news of the other niece, would you? The one who ran away?"

"We think we might have," said Charlie. "That's why we're so anxious to see her."

"Poor thing," said the fat woman darkly. I wasn't sure whether she meant Flora or her aunt. "I'll always say it was the fault of that Wittering woman." She had a moment of caution. "You aren't relatives of *hers*, are you?"

"Certainly not."

"Ah, I thought you looked too good for her. I couldn't abide that woman when she came here badgering poor Miss Higgs to give her the child. She'd give her a home, indeed! Cheap labor, that's what *she* was after. Broke both their poor hearts, it did. Then that Mrs. Wittering pushing her way in here in a tantrum, about Flora having run away and some cock-and-bull story about a stolen pin. Wicked nonsense! 'Don't you worry, dearie,' I said to Miss Higgs. 'If a pin was stolen she did it herself to cover up how she'd driven that poor child to run away.' I gave that old battle-axe a piece of my mind, I did, and she was out of here double quick, I can tell you." Righteous anger glowed in her face at the memory, and I had a happy vision of the routing of Aunt Gladys.

129

"But now," she went on sadly, "now there's Miss Higgs crying in her room every night. Fading away she is, poor soul. Fading away! She worries me so I could do the same myself."

I wondered how long it would take the fat woman to fade. But Charlie was single-minded.

"Can you tell us where to find her, please?"

"Of course, dearie. And me just rattling on! But you'll have a glass of something hot before you go, just to keep out the cold?"

It would have been a lovely idea. I was shivering. But Charlie's fingers pressed my arms for silence. He was right, of course. More gossip meant more danger of discovery.

"It's awfully kind of you, but I think we'd better get on. If you could just give us directions."

Reluctantly she gave them. She was obviously yearning for a nice long chat.

"You can't miss it," she assured us. "It'll take you about twenty minutes."

We did miss it—twice—and it took us nearly an hour. We were chilled through and wet and miserable. But if Charlie regretted our adventure, he wasn't going to let me know.

We left the shabby respectability of Maytree Gardens for mean dark streets where gaunt figures loitered in alleys and doorways, pitiful and menacing. There were whining beggars' voices and insulting catcalls and whistles. I would have been terrified on my own, but Charlie kept a firm grip of my arm and walked on boldly. His face was grim and his eyes watchful, and no one actually attacked us. Then the dim alleys gave onto main streets and shops, and we felt safer. But the shop where Aunt Daisy worked was small and tucked away between two bigger ones. We'd passed it more than once before I noticed, in a window half obscured by snow, a monstrous hat. It was a huge thing with a whole garden of cherries and daisies and goodness knows what around the brim. I pulled Charlie's arm.

"Look! That must be it."

"What now?" said Charlie.

I dithered. The thought of whisking Aunt Daisy out of her place of work had not occurred to me before.

"I suppose we just go in and ask for her."

"Not me," said Charlie firmly. "I'm not going to go into a ladies' hat shop, not even for a hundred aunts."

"There's only one," I snapped crossly. But I saw his point. In fact, dressed as we were and bedraggled with wet snow, I wasn't likely to get much favorable attention myself. But a few yards away another little alley led to the street behind.

"Let's scout around," I suggested. "That must lead to the back of the shop."

From the back it was difficult to tell which house was which, but we worked out what was the most likely one.

"I know," I said. "You wait here—you'll be less noticed than you would on the main street—and I'll try to bring her out by the back way. Or we'll come from the front and join you. I'll go in and ask for her. I'll just say it's an urgent message."

"Be careful, Scrap. And yell your head off if you need me."

"Don't be silly. I can't get into any trouble in a hat shop."

I forgot that I have this knack of being able to get into trouble anywhere. I shook the snow off my clothes as well as I could, took a deep breath, and marched boldly into the shop.

A woman rose at once and rustled forward, placing herself neatly and unobtrusively between me and the door. A shy customer would find it hard to escape.

"Can I help—?" she began. Then she took in my appearance and her smile of welcome curdled like sour cream.

"No children here," she said sharply.

"I'm not a customer," I reassured her. "I've got a message for Miss Higgs."

"Miss *Higgs*?" She was outraged. "Miss Higgs does not receive messages while she is paid to be at work."

"But it's urgent."

"I daresay it can wait till she leaves work. Go away, little girl."

The back of the shop was closed by curtains, and I had darted through them before she could stop me. Beyond them a narrow passage lined with shelves and boxes led to a door at the farther end. The door opened, as I had hoped, into the workroom. Four women were bent over the tables around the walls, cutting and stitching with a kind of nervous hurry among piles of hat shapes, velvet flowers, waxed fruits, tulle, feathers, and ribbon. The remaining space was almost entirely filled by a heavily built, blue jawed man, who was bullying the youngest assistant.

". . . take it all out in your own time tonight and do it again. . . ."

At that moment he caught sight of me, with the sour-faced woman in angry pursuit.

"Miss Mistledene! What is the meaning of this?"
Miss Mistledene almost cringed.

"I'm sorry, Mr. Jarman, I couldn't help it. This
young person pushed her way in before I could stop
her."

I'd had time to take in the ladies in front of me.
Besides the frightened girl who was being scolded
there was another not much older. Next to her was
an elderly acid-faced woman (as she well might be
if she'd worked very long for the awful Mr. Jarman).
The other gave me a timidly sympathetic smile, which
was brave of her in the circumstances. Nature had
designed her with comfortable curves, though poverty
had sharpened them. Everything about her was
faded—her eyes, her hair like dusty straw that must
once have been red-gold, her soft cheeks that should
have been pink and white. She gave a general impression of falling hairpins and clothes buttoned in the
wrong places. I looked straight at her as I spoke.

"She shouldn't have tried to stop me. I told her I
had an urgent message for Miss Higgs—from her
niece, Flora."

It was Aunt Daisy all right. She'd been holding a
heavily beribboned hat in one hand and a pair of
scissors in the other. She gasped as I spoke and the
scissors closed sharply on the ribbons. A shower of
colored ruins fell around her feet. It was clearly the
last straw for her employer. He stood over her, glar-
ing. His words began as a shaking whisper and rose
almost to a shriek.

"Miss Higgs, this is enough! More than enough!
You are a stupid, woolgathering, incompetent woman.
It's been a charity to keep you on. But no longer! I

133

am finished with you, Miss Higgs. Finished! This morning you put the wrong flowers on the model for the window. And now you have ruined, *ruined*, Miss Gadsby's hat that I promised to deliver to her tonight. Ruined it! Go! This minute! Out!"

He put his great hairy hand on her shoulder and I dragged it off.

"Don't touch her, you great bully. She's going anyway. She doesn't need your beastly job."

"Oh, but my dear, I do!" Aunt Daisy was on her feet, trembling and crying. "I'm too old to get another. Please, Mr. Jarman, if you'd only—"

"Out!" roared Mr. Jarman. "And take this brat with you."

This time he grabbed both of us, and he had the strength of a bull. With a triumphant grin Miss Mistledene had flung open another door and he literally threw us out of it. We could have broken our necks. A yard beyond it a steep staircase led down to the back door, and I grabbed Aunt Daisy just in time to stop her from falling headlong. Then I ran down ahead of her and opened the door, yelling for Charlie.

Six more stone steps led down to the sidewalk, and we were just at the bottom when Mr. Jarman appeared again behind us, shouting.

"And take your rubbish with you!"

He hurled after us a crook-handled umbrella and a lumpy string bag. The bag caught Miss Higgs in the chest so that she staggered and nearly fell in the soft snow.

Out of the whirling flakes Charlie erupted like a cannon ball, charged the steps with a roar of anger, and punched Mr. Jarman as high as he could reach. Taken by surprise, the big man lost his balance, and they flailed down the steps together. But he outmatched Charlie in sheer weight and strength. He raised a great red fist like a sledgehammer that would have finished anyone.

It was lucky that I'd caught the umbrella as it fell. I lunged joyfully, catching him around the ankle with the crooked handle. He hit the pavement with a most satisfactory crash and I heard all the air come gasping out of his lungs.

"Run!" I shouted to an unwilling Charlie. "He's too big for us. Run before he gets up."

We grabbed Aunt Daisy, one on each side, and raced her down the street, into a side turning, and then another. There we had to stop, all of us gasping for breath and poor Miss Higgs looking ready to collapse.

"He won't follow so far," I said. "He'll have to go back to his beastly shop. Look, there's a church on the corner. Let's go in and shelter while we talk."

The church was graveyard cold, but better than the driving snow. Huddled in a pew, breathing more easily and her color returning to normal, Miss Higgs asserted herself.

"My dear children, this is quite dreadful! Suppose Mr. Jarman is injured!"

"Serve him right," I said viciously. "I hope he is."

She tried to look shocked, but secretly she may have felt the same. For she abandoned Mr. Jarman's troubles for something more important.

"Flora? You said you had a message from Flora. Where is she? Is she well?"

"She's quite well, thank you. And she sends you her love. And she's hoping you'll be together very soon."

"Oh my dears, if only we could! Nobody knows how I've missed her. Where have you come from? Are you friends of hers?"

"Charlie's a friend," I said. "I'm a sort of relation. And a friend too, of course."

"A relation? But we've seen nothing of any other relations for many years—not since my dear brother died."

I swallowed. This was going to be much, much more difficult than I'd realized. How do you explain to an elderly and exhausted lady, who has just been fired because of the interference of two strangers, that you'd like to take her into another century to meet her niece? She'd probably have a heart attack. The whole truth had better wait.

"I worked with Flora at the Bellevue," I told her. "And then we found we were sort of connected. But Mrs. Wittering was horrible to us and accused us of stealing. And she was going to beat us and send for the police, so we ran away."

"That wicked woman!" Aunt Daisy's worn face was quite pink with indignation. "I should never have let Flora go to her. We'd have managed somehow. You must both have been so unhappy."

"It was pretty awful," I admitted.

"We *will* manage," declared Aunt Daisy. "I'll find another position somehow. And Flora is older now. She too can get employment." There was a defiant courage in her voice that reminded me of Flora herself, but her eyes were anxious and frightened.

136

"You needn't do that. Not if you'll come with us. We ran away to *my* aunt, who lives in the country. There's plenty of room for you as well."

"But where? My dear child—what is your name, my dear?—"

"Louise."

Charlie began to say "Higgs," but I quashed him with a look. We couldn't give her too much all at once.

"Louise." She smiled at me warmly. "What a pretty name. But Louise, you still haven't told me *where*."

"It's just a little village," I said cautiously. "You won't have heard of it. But we can get there ever so quickly if you'll come."

"It may be *too* quickly," broke in Charlie uneasily.

"Oh dear, I don't know." Miss Higgs was dithering. "I ought to go home first perhaps. And I'm sure I ought to find out about Mr. Jarman. If I told him how sorry I was—"

"No," I said firmly.

"No," said Charlie.

"I expect you're right. But your aunt won't want a complete stranger. Perhaps Flora should come to me first. You see"—she blushed—"there's the matter of money. I can't really afford to take a vacation."

"You don't have to worry about that," Charlie assured her. "You'll get a pension or Social Security or something."

I wasn't at all sure that he was right. You have to fill in forms, and date of birth would be a tricky thing in this case. Miss Higgs was frankly bewildered.

"I'm sorry, I don't understand. What do you—?"

"Never mind," I said hurriedly. "He just means

that it will be all right. Please say you'll come. Flora's longing to see you. She couldn't come herself—I'll explain that later—but I promised I'd bring you."

"The country," said Aunt Daisy longingly. "I lived in the country as a girl, you know. I dream of it often. But really I'm not sure whether I ought—"

Somebody would have to make up her mind for her if we were ever to get anywhere. I took a firm line.

"That's settled then. You're coming, aren't you?"

"Well, yes. Yes, I will. How do we get there?"

"Like this," I said. I clasped her hand in mine, and took Charlie's on the other side of me. I held his very tightly, for now was the test of whether I could take more than one person with me. At the thought that I might lose Charlie in this alien century I was almost too frightened to speak. I think he knew, for his fingers pressed hard and encouragingly against mine.

"I wish we were all three back home in Deep End."

The sound rose all around us, deep and throbbing, as if the organ of the church were stirring into life. The shadows gathered and darkened. Then the heavenly warmth of the spring sunshine caressed our frozen bodies, and we opened our eyes onto the pleasant, shabby comfort of the living room at Deep End.

"My dear," said Aunt Harriet, as if our ever-so-great-aunt had just arrived in the usual way by the Birmingham train and the bus from Allington, "how delightful to see you. But you must be exhausted."

138

12
Windfall

Exhausted, bewildered, even scared Aunt Daisy may have been. But there must be something indestructible in the Higgs temperament. In a very few days she had absorbed the shock of her arrival and the strange discovery of our relationships. Modern life, however alarming, fascinated her. Her delight in the countryside filled the old house with happiness as if every day were a celebration. She and Aunt Harriet became firm friends almost at once.

Sid was told that the lawyer had indeed found another member of the family, but that she needed rest and quiet. But Sid recognized Flora and Aunt Daisy as true Higgses in a way that I was not, and that was quite enough for him. In his own crabbed grumbling way he was devoted to all three of them, and sometimes I felt left out.

"Never mind, Scrap," Charlie consoled me.

"They're fond of you too. But you're more than just another Higgs. You're a person on your own as well. You won't want to stay at Deep End all your life."

I remembered my performance as a lost lone orphan at the Bellevue.

"No," I said. "I'll live in London again. I'm going to be an actress."

He grinned. "You're pretty dramatic already. But you'd hate London."

"No, I wouldn't. Anyway I'd come back to Deep End between jobs."

"You'd better!" said Charlie.

The arrival of our relatives had one splendid result. My schooling was postponed for another term. Aunt Harriet told the headmaster that her two nieces had been unwell and needed a vacation before they joined the school. It was more or less true. Both our visitors were in great need of rest and good meals; and I had quite enough problems with them without adding to them by a start at a new school. Charlie, of course, had to go back, and I missed him. But Flora and I had a lot of fun on our own.

Within a week or two they might both have lived with us always. But it was Aunt Daisy who most astonished us. She fell in love with cars at her first sight of an elderly Ford that was ambling along the road at the end of the field path. After that she would spend hours down there, watching for any vehicle that went by. Aunt Harriet couldn't afford to have a car herself, but to gratify Aunt Daisy's longing she hired a taxi to take us for a drive. Apart from the glow of excitement in her eyes our guest tried gallantly to behave as if this form of travel were quite familiar to her,

and the driver suspected nothing odd about his passengers. Flora was interested in the experience. But
her aunt went about in a kind of dream for hours
afterward.

In the fresh country air her soft face grew pink
and white and round as it was meant to be. She was
a willing helper in the house, though inclined to mislay
things and to forget whether she had put salt into
the potatoes or not. But in the garden she came into
her own. She might work in it with her hair escaping
in wisps, her cardigan buttoned awry, and wearing
two halves of two separate pairs of boots. But the
plants knew who was boss. They did just as they were
told. Aunt Harriet, who cared much more for the hens,
was only too glad to give her full control.

"It isn't only because she loves it," Flora explained
to me one morning. "She's worried because we must
be costing Aunt Harriet so much."

"You shouldn't call her Aunt Harriet. She should
call you Aunt Flora."

She giggled. "So should you. I wonder what Sid
would say if he heard! But honestly, Louise, we do
eat an awful lot, and I don't think she can really afford
it."

"She wouldn't worry about that."

"No, but we do. We couldn't bear to go back, but
Aunt Daisy says we must both find work as soon as
possible. But we've got so much to learn first, and
this is one way she can repay your aunt a little."

"She's doing that all right. Even Sid says he's never
seen the garden look so good. They've got time now
to start building that proper hen house they've needed
for years. I heard them talking about it."

141

There was sudden uproar from the house. Bertram was greeting the postman. We always knew when we had visitors since he greeted them all with the same noisy enthusiasm, from the vicar to the gypsies. The mail didn't reach us till midmorning, as we were near the end of Mr. Larkins's round. I waved to him as he retrieved his cap from the doormat, where Bertram had accidentally knocked it, and picked up his bicycle.

"I like Mr. Larkins," I said. "His spaniel bitch had puppies last month. We could go down and look at them." I was no longer afraid of taking her to the village. Both of them had learned so much that they'd even been shopping in Allington with us, though Aunt Daisy still got flustered by decimal coinage and was inclined to call a tenpenny piece a florin.

We started to stroll toward the gate, but we didn't get far. Aunt Harriet appeared suddenly at the front door, waving something in her hand.

"Daisy," she called across the garden. "Daisy, can you come a minute?"

Her voice sounded odd.

"Something's up," I said. "Let's go in."

We followed our seniors into the kitchen, where Aunt Harriet was making an apple pie and Casca was playing gleefully with the peelings. No one told us to go away. My aunt's face was very pink, and streaked with flour where she'd rubbed her hand across it. I'd swear she was trembling as she passed an important-looking typed letter to Aunt Daisy.

"Read that."

She read it twice, and her face too got pinker and pinker.

"Oh, my dear Harriet—if it's true—can it be true—?"

"I'll have to get legal advice first. But I think it's genuine. And to think that I've kept the conveyance all these years just for sentiment's sake."

I could bear it no longer.

"What's it all about? Please, what are you talking about?"

She seemed suddenly aware of our presence as if she'd come abruptly to earth out of the clouds.

"I don't see why you shouldn't know. But don't get too excited. There may be a catch in it somewhere."

"A catch in what?" If only she'd get on with it!

"It's that wasteland in Spain that your father gave me—more or less as a joke. It seems it's now in the middle of a resort area. I've had a letter from a property development company that wants to build a hotel on it."

"Oh good! Perhaps it would pay for the new hen house."

She laughed, more excited than I'd ever seen a grown-up before.

"Oh, it would pay for that. It would pay enough to put Deep End back on its feet as it ought to be and to keep us all from any real financial worry for the rest of our days. It's a huge sum. But it may not happen at all. Don't get too excited."

But of course we all did get excited.

"Can I tell Charlie?" I asked, when we'd all talked our heads off for about ten minutes.

"Well, yes, I suppose so. He's a trustworthy boy. But you must tell him to keep it secret, Louisa.

Remember it may be a mistake or not legal. Or even a hoax."

But it was not a hoax and it was perfectly legal. There were more letters and visits to a lawyer and anxious days of waiting. And then Aunt Harriet was suddenly quite a rich woman. She insisted on dividing the money, and she was a person no one could stop when she'd made up her mind. Some she put into a fund for the restoration and maintenance of Deep End. The rest she divided equally between herself and Aunt Daisy.

"With Deep End run as it should be," she declared, "it will earn enough for us both to live on. But if either of us has to give up work we shall still be able to live with modest comfort. And there will still be enough to launch Louisa and Flora—yes, and Charlie—into whatever career they choose."

"Will there be enough for drama school?"

"I'm not sure that you need it," said Aunt Harriet drily. "But, yes, I think we can manage that too when the time comes."

Later that day I tagged along when the two grown-ups went to talk with Sid Jennings. He was busily sawing lengths of wood for the new hen house.

"You can stop that, Sid," said Aunt Harriet. "We aren't going to make it after all."

Sid's face changed slowly from disbelief to outrage.

"Women!" he exploded. "Ain't we been talking about it for months? Wasn't it only last week as you told me to get the wood? And ain't I been at work on it ever since, chopping and sawing, chopping and sawing, and me with my back so bad I couldn't hardly pull the skin off scalded milk?" He groaned, and

144

clapped his hands dramatically to the small of his back.

"Try the top of a beer can," suggested Aunt Harriet unkindly. "You'd find it easier. No, we aren't having a makeshift homemade affair like this, Sid. We're going to have two ready-made ones from Sisson and Steele's—just like Mr. Carter's at Hill Farm."

Sid jerked upright with surprising agility for a man with acute lumbago.

"Whatever be you a-thinking of, Miss Harry? Do you know what them things cost?"

"I know exactly. I ordered them this morning." She laughed. "Don't worry, Sid. We can afford them now. We've had a windfall."

She told him about the land in Spain, and his old face flushed dully as he listened, like a last autumn's apple withered by long keeping.

"Did you ever hear the like on it? He was a deep one, young Albert was. Didn't I always say he had the brains of the family if he cared to use 'em?"

He let out a sudden wheezy bellow that scared all the sparrows for half a mile. He was laughing outright for the first time in years. What he'd actually always implied about my father was that he was the family's biggest failure, best forgotten, and that I was probably his biggest mistake. But I didn't remind him.

Life was full of surprises after that. There was the next Saturday morning, when our two aunts sent us all out to the small barn as soon as Charlie arrived. There were three shining new bicycles there, exactly the right sizes for each of us. Then there was the day that we all went into Allington. The aunts gave Flora and me the money for the movie while they went shopping. When we met at the bus stop to catch the 5:30 back again, Flora was in an enchanted daze after her first experience of the big screen and Aunt Harriet was carrying two large packages and looking slightly sly. Aunt Daisy arrived at the very last minute just as we were getting worried. She was pinkly flustered and shedding even more hairpins than usual.

"No, dear, I didn't exactly buy anything," she explained as we sat down. "I was just looking around, you know. So many things to choose from." She spoke as if Allington were Regent Street and the bazaars of Baghdad all rolled into one.

Aunt Harriet carried her packages upstairs and came down some time later, rather self-conscious, in an elegant new tweed suit and a soft blue sweater. They suited her. I'd never before seen her in anything but baggy and shapeless sweaters and skirts. She was reassured by our pleased surprise, but very soon went upstairs again to change, and returned looking more familiar.

We were all fully occupied in the days that followed. Charlie and I taught Flora to ride her bicycle, and we all three spent quite a lot of time comforting the animals. They disapproved the changes in our lives, for the local builder had moved in to repaint the house and do long-needed repairs. Bertram tried to help and was hurt when he was rejected, while Casca wailed and spat and arched himself into angry hoops and glared balefully at any workman reckless enough to approach him. I hoped anxiously that he wasn't complaining to Bast about us. I remembered the strong fine hands, with catlike claws, that had rested on the rail of my bed that night. I shouldn't like to see those claws unsheathed!

146

The house looked more and more as it had in the old photograph, bright and shining in clear fresh color.

"Just like it did in your granddad's time, Miss Harry," approved Sid. "I never thought to see the day."

"Nonsense," said Aunt Harriet. "You can't remember that far back."

"Ay, I can and all. Nothing but a nipper I was then, and your Aunt Cissie—your granddad's youngest, that was—in her pinafore and her little frilly drawers."

Nobody contradicted him this time. Perhaps it was true—Sid's age might have been anything. He and Aunt Harriet were as usual immersed in plans for developing a full-scale poultry farm.

"Couldn't we do some general farming too?" suggested Aunt Daisy. "Like Deep End used to be. We could start quite simply, with perhaps half a dozen piglets and a couple of cows."

"I've always fancied pigs," said Sid thoughtfully. "Mind you, I'd need a lad to give me a hand."

"We can think about all that later on. Let's organize one thing at a time."

Aunt Daisy's face fell and she wandered away. But it was in that week that I first noticed *The Farmer and Stock Breeder* lying about in the kitchen. It was not a paper that Aunt Harriet had ever subscribed to. We were all happily busy with our own affairs at the time, and no one really noticed how often Aunt Daisy didn't seem to be around.

It was I who caught sight of her one morning, slipping quietly out of the house in time to catch the 8:30 bus to Allington. She put her fingers to her lips.

"Hush, dear. Don't tell Harriet you've seen me. I've got a little surprise for you. You'll know all about it as soon as I come back."

"All right," I said. "I won't tell a soul."

What on earth was the old dear up to, I wondered. But I soon forgot it. Flora and I had promised to cook the midday meal that day. Flora, who loved cooking, was trying out a new pudding recipe, and I didn't mind preparing the vegetables as long as we had the chance of a talk. It reminded us both of our days at the Bellevue and how different things were then.

"I wonder what Aunt Gladys is doing," said Flora dreamily. "And what she'd say if she could see us now."

"I expect—" I said. Then I stopped and listened. There was a noise in the distance, a perfectly ordinary noise but not often so close to Deep End. Somewhere along the field track someone was tooting a horn.

"Someone's coming!"

Nowadays we felt that almost any new arrival might mean something unexpected. We scampered to the open front door to have a look. Rapidly approaching us, at a speed that suggested the good news from Ghent, was a shiny bright-red car—a Mini. It bounced cheerfully along the track and drew up with a flourish at the yard gate, tooting for someone to open it.

"It can't be!" I said.

"It is!" said Flora.

And it was.

As we ran to open the gate, Aunt Daisy's face beamed like the sun from the driver's window.

"Isn't she beautiful? I passed my test this morning. The young man was perfectly delightful to me."

I doubt if anyone could have had the heart to fail

her. She got as much thrill from that car as Columbus might have from the discovery of America. She proved to be a remarkable driver too. In the house she gave a general impression of apologetic muddle. In church she looked like just what she was, a quiet, self-effacing elderly lady, as gentle as summer. But once inside that car, she changed. She combined the instincts of a London taxi driver with those of a pirate. She would shoot with airy ruthlessness, like an impertinent goldfish, into the narrowest gap in the traffic, right under the noses of uniformed chauffeurs. Her split-second timing at traffic lights brushed the very edges of the rules without actually breaking them. To go with her through Allington on a market day was an exhilarating but breathless experience. I think Aunt Harriet found it rather aging. Bertram loved the Mini too, and would spend long happy hours inside it whenever he could, distracted only by mealtimes or a call from his owner.

"If only that horrible Mr. Jarman could see her now," said Flora. "Oh Louise, I don't think you'll ever know quite how glad I am that you found us. And your aunt's been so marvelously kind to us both. I wish I had some money that she hadn't given me herself. I'd love to give her a present."

"But you have got money," I said. "Don't you remember? In Aunt Gladys's box that we brought from the Bellevue. We put it in my wardrobe until we could find a way to open it."

"So we did." Her face lit up. "So many things have been happening that I quite forgot about it. Let's try it now."

But we couldn't find a key anywhere that would fit the lock.

"We might lever it with a screwdriver," I suggested.

"But it's a pretty box. It seems a pity to spoil it. Come to think of it, the coinage is different now. It won't be worth anything, will it?"

"Yes, it will. People buy old coins for a lot of money. But we'd have to ask someone about that, so I suppose we may as well get help anyway."

Everyone was interested in the box, but there seemed no way of opening it except by force. We were still fiddling with it when Charlie dropped in on his way back from school. He took it from my hands.

"Let me have a go. Have you got a piece of wire?"

"Would a hairpin do?" offered Aunt Daisy.

"Yes. Thanks." He put one end into the lock and began to twiddle.

"Wherever did you learn things like that?" Aunt Harriet was slightly shocked.

He grinned at her. "A boy at school showed me. It might come in useful one day if I want to be a professional burglar. Wait a minute—yes—it's coming." There was a click and the lid came up in his hand. "There you are."

There were papers in the box as well as coins. Flora picked them up and flicked through them. Suddenly she paused and looked up in perplexity.

"I don't think this belonged to her. It's poor Mr. Banting's writing. I've seen it before. And look, it's addressed to someone. To Mr. Reginald Banting. That was the uncle he told me about."

13
Reappearance of a Goddess

"That's it! That's why he never had an answer. We guessed it was something like that."

"Whatever are you talking about, Scrap?"

"Don't you remember? When Mr. Banting lost all his money he wrote to an uncle for help. But he never got an answer. The letters at the Bellevue were always left in a box on the hall table until they were collected and taken to be mailed. Mrs. Wittering usually took them herself. She must have stolen his letters to keep him a sort of prisoner. Because he was useful and she didn't have to pay him."

"That dreadful, dreadful woman!" exclaimed Aunt Daisy.

"She stole more than his letters." Aunt Harriet's face was grim. She had turned the box upside down

151

so that all its contents fell on the table. Among them was a shabby leather wallet, quite empty of money.

"Why on earth did she keep it?" wondered Charlie. "You'd think she'd get rid of the evidence."

"She hated to throw anything away," said Flora. "And she'd feel perfectly safe about anything in the box. She always carried the key with her. And Bessie and I were the only people who ever went into her room."

"We'd better look at all of it," said Aunt Harriet.

There was a small canvas bag full of coins, and a little velvet one that Flora picked up with a cry of joy.

"My necklace! My mother's necklace."

She tipped it out into the palm of her hand, a slender, delicate thing of dark red stones linked with a fine gold chain. Aunt Daisy touched it gently.

"I remember her wearing it when she was married. Such a pretty thing, and she such a pretty young girl then."

"I expect the money is mostly yours too, Flora. Yes, it's still worth something. There are people who buy old coins. But we'd better look at these papers."

All three of Mr. Banting's letters were there and she read them aloud. In spite of their fear and desperation they had a pathetic dignity that brought him very vividly to mind. Flora could easily have cried.

"Oh, poor Mr. Banting! If only we could have brought him here too."

But Aunt Harriet and Aunt Daisy were still reading the other papers, Aunt Harriet looking more angry every minute and Aunt Daisy more upset. Two or three of them were letters in different hands, certainly

152

not Mrs. Wittering's. Last of all they picked up a stiff black notebook and began to turn the pages. Trying to look at it upside down, I could see it was a sort of account book with bits of writing as well. Once or twice they exclaimed at something, and Aunt Daisy's look of shock and distress increased. At last Aunt Harriet closed it and looked up. There was a set, hard anger in her face that I had never seen before. It almost frightened me, though I knew I was not the object of it. She spoke very quietly, in a voice of ice.

"A very nice profitable little business! Little thefts here and there, so that her wretched lodgers could be charged interest on the money they then had to owe her. Little bits of scandal (nosed out by your Mrs. Merry, I should guess). Nothing very terrible, but enough for the victims to pay to keep them quiet. And Mr. Merry to frighten them with his legal talk and threats. As nasty a trio as anyone could think of!"

"My dearest Flora!" exclaimed Aunt Daisy. "How very, very fortunate that you escaped! I can never be grateful enough. I blame myself that I ever let you go to her."

"But poor Mr. Banting!" said Flora again. "I just can't bear to think we left him behind. And perhaps he thinks we ran away because we really did take that horrible pin."

"Nonsense," said Aunt Harriet. "He would never think that of you. But certainly he should be rescued. And this shameful business must be stopped. Louisa!"

"Louise," I protested feebly, playing for time as I guessed what was coming. But she took the correction without a flicker and went straight on.

"Louise then, if you really prefer it. We must organize the journey very carefully this time. We can't afford any mistakes."

There was a part in another of my stories, *Vengeance of the Hawk*, where Colonel Hawk swore his two friends to help him in his revenge. He had a face of flint and eyes of steel that made men quail before him. But he had nothing on my Aunt Harriet just then. (Perhaps I really would throw all those stories away.) Certainly I quailed at her look myself.

"I'll try. Of course I will. But I don't know whether I can manage all three of them."

"You won't have to. Do you think I'd let you go alone to deal with people like that?" I shall come myself. And I think Daisy and Flora must come too, to face them with the evidence."

"I'm coming as well then," insisted Charlie. "In case Scrap gets carried away by some crazy idea in all the excitement."

I tried unsuccessfully to wither him with a look.

"That only makes five of us," I said ironically. "Why don't we take Sid too?"

"No," said my aunt, perfectly serious. "He's too old. It would worry him. And we don't want him here when we come back either, in case of any surprises. It will have to be on his next half day."

"It may not work." I was alarmed and stubborn as I remembered the gleam of Bast's strange eyes. "I think she meant the gift for me and one companion. I'm sure she never expected a crowd."

"And I'm sure that a goddess must be on the side of justice," declared Aunt Harriet. "She will want to help us."

154

I wasn't all that sure myself. None of them had looked, as I had, into that smiling face, secret and enigmatic as a cat's. But caught between her and my formidable Aunt Harriet, I didn't seem to have much choice. I felt that at least I should ask Bast's permission before presuming to take them with me. But I didn't know quite how or where to pray to a heathen goddess, and I wasn't all that sure that the vicar would like it. I could think of only one person who might help. I went off to look for Casca.

I found him sunning himself among the late daffodils. He was in his elegant upright pose, wearing his scarlet collar as if it were a Pharaoh's jeweled band. He was in so evidently royal a mood that I spoke to him very politely, kneeling on the grass beside him.

"Will you help me, Casca? I don't know what to do."

Casca got up with a sense of casual leisure. He stood and stretched his forelegs in slow luxury, shook his hind feet one after the other, and climbed purring onto my knees. I clasped him in a passion of gratitude.

"Oh Casca, I do love you. And I'm sure you know what's going on. If anyone knows how to speak to the goddess it must be you. Do you think you could ask her if she would mind terribly just for this once? I promise we won't do it again."

Perhaps he understood. He rubbed amiably under my chin, bit me sharply on my left thumb, and stalked off into the long grass, the tip of his tail waving gently above it.

This was a Monday morning, with two days to go before Sid's half day. Aunt Harriet used them to organize us like a general preparing an assault. She

155

brought down piles of clothes and pieces of material from the trunk in the attic, and she and Aunt Daisy (rather unwillingly helped by Flora and me) made suitable garments for all of us so that we could pass unnoticed in the Weymouth of a century ago. Since we couldn't be certain of what season it would be, she insisted that we each have something warm. On Tuesday afternoon she went into Allington alone, on some business that she didn't explain. Then in the evening she packed us each a small package of food and divided the coins from the box between us in case, as she said, we became separated and needed to fend for ourselves. Then she packed a shopping bag with the black notebook, extra scarves, a box of matches, candles, some string, and various other odds and ends that she thought might be useful, some of them in a big tin box that felt very heavy. I grew more and more anxious. Not only had Bast never suggested more than one companion; she had never even mentioned luggage.

"I wish we could take Albertine too," sighed Aunt Daisy wistfully. "*That* would stop Gladys Wittering from telling me what I couldn't afford!"

Albertine was her Mini. "After your dear father, Louise," she had explained to me. "Without him I would never have had it. And Albertine is my favorite rose as well." I too was sorry that it couldn't be done. She deserved a bit of one-upmanship against Aunt Gladys. But things were sufficiently cluttered and complicated already. By Tuesday night I was too worried even to sleep. I held Casca close against my chest for comfort and tried unsuccessfully not to think about the coming day.

I was just beginning to drowse at last when the scent disturbed me. A sweet, heavy scent. Like lilies? Like incense? Flowers in a hot, hot sun? With a sudden lurch of the stomach I knew where I had smelled it before. It had been on the terrace in ancient Egypt, where the heaped flowers at our feet had mingled with the strange scents drifting from the temple behind us.

The light in my bedroom was growing too, a pale greenish-yellow radiance that flowed from the tall figure at the end of my bed. I sat up abruptly. Casca was erect and quivering on the pillow beside me.

"Child!" The throaty purr thrilled through the surrounding dark.

I wondered what I should call her. The most exalted person in any of my stories had been a duchess. All the servants addressed her as "Your Grace," but everyone else just said "Duchess."

"Goddess!" I replied in the politest tone possible.

"My servant tells me that you have great doings afoot. With many aunts."

Was there a faint cat hiss on the sibilants?

"Oh dear," I quavered, "I knew you wouldn't like it. But one thing led to another—you know how it is. I'm ever so sorry."

"You have good reason for these doings?"

Perhaps she wasn't so angry after all?

"Oh yes, truly we have. Aunt Gladys and the Merrys have been so wicked and cruel and poor Mr. Banting is so unhappy. I know it's asking a lot, and you've been so kind. But please, do you think you could help us again just this once? I promise I'll never ask you to do anything anymore."

157

Casca wailed softly beside me, a long wavering sound as if he were talking to her. Faintly in the lemon-colored light I saw her face as if it were beginning to smile. A flicker of reviving courage brought back a memory.

"Mrs. Merry is horrible to cats," I said. "She's afraid of them. Flora told me one day Mrs. Merry caught her trying to feed a stray kitten and she threw the poor little thing out into the rain and got Flora into awful trouble with Aunt Gladys for wasting the milk."

"Sssoo? Wicked women who are cruel to my little ones?" The splitting crackle on each word made Casca shiver beside me, and I heard the rake of her curved nails along the end of my bed. "Those who punish such evil serve the gods. Perhaps I too will come."

"No! Oh please no! I mean," I stumbled wildly, "we couldn't possibly bother you to do a thing like that. Only I can't manage it all by myself. But if you would let the others come with me just this once—"

Slowly the baleful glow faded from her huge cat eyes.

"You say well. A goddess should leave such matters to those who serve her. Very well, child. For such a cause you shall take whom you will on this journey, and have my blessing. When your task is done, those who wish may return and those who wish may stay. Let them take care to choose wisely."

"You mean if they decide to stay they must stay there always? There won't be any way back?"

"Yes. For all but one—with the little cat and one human companion—there shall be no more journeyings. Too much time has flowed past me since the

158

days of my glory. My strength ebbs and each use of it draws upon it. The centuries waste me, hour by hour."

I remembered all that I owed to her and for the moment forgot everything else.

"Then we mustn't go. Not if it does you harm."

I know that she smiled at me then.

"You are a good child. You have used my gift with courage and kindness, and you have learned much, I think. You will not need my help much longer. For you, when this task is done, there can be one more journey if you choose to take it, and one companion to go with you. Think well and wisely before that choice is made."

A great sadness fell on me as I were losing something that I loved.

"Goddess, you speak as if you were saying good-bye."

"All meetings end in farewells, my child. But no one should grieve when the meetings have been good. Come here to me, little cat."

Casca walked toward her very softly, his tail high and quivering at the tip. She picked him up and held him in her strong fine hands.

"Be blessed, my little one. Remember your royal blood and be always of good courage."

Gently she set him down again and looked me full in the eyes. I knew at that moment that I would never see anyone more beautiful. Lithe and sleek and graceful as the loveliest of cats, loving as a woman at her best, dangerous as a tiger. She was all things at once, beauty and terror, satisfaction and desire.

"Good go with you too, always. My creatures shall

always love you, O savior of little cats. Farewell now. Farewell."

The light was dissolving, fading. Just before it flickered out into the dark I heard her voice once more, as if from very far away.

"Remember! Choose carefully, all of you! Choose wisely. Choose!"

14
Tyranny Defeated

Sid's old bicycle clanked and jolted away along the field track, growing smaller in the distance. The five of us, standing together at the living-room window, watched him go.

I think all of us were more nervous than we would admit. In one way I was less anxious than usual. Since Bast knew and approved our purpose, I thought she would be more attentive to time. But her last words still sounded in my ears like a solemn warning.

They all looked at me expectantly.

"Now, Louisa—Louise!" said Aunt Harriet.

"Wait!" I said, suddenly half frightened. "Bast warned us to be careful. And you said we might get separated. We must take the animals with us too. Just in case."

I didn't say in case of what. In case Bertram and Casca should wait and wait for an owner who didn't come back. But I think they all understood. Casca seemed to understand too, for he sprang from the windowsill to my shoulder without any invitation. Bertram had been lying in a far corner, his lion head on his paws, exuding gloom and sorrow. He was not one, he had been telling us for the last half hour, to indulge in silent reproach—well, not very often. But Something Was Going On and he had not been asked to be in on it. Aunt Harriet's call produced a joyous explosion of feeling from which it took two or three minutes for the party to recover itself. Then she took a firm grip on his collar, and I clasped Casca very closely and closed my eyes.

Standing there in the full afternoon sun, I shivered suddenly, touched by a twilight sadness. "Those who wish may return and those who wish may stay." Would Flora and Aunt Daisy feel homesick for their own world when they found it again? Had I made a friend only to lose her? It was best not to think about it.

"I wish that all of us were at the Bellevue Boarding House in Weymouth in 1862."

The darkness closed in, throbbing like a dynamo. I felt an instant's check in the power that lifted us. It was like one of the waves I had sometimes watched, that seemed almost to pause just before it broke, gathering all its strength for the final plunge. Then the darkness swept past like the broken wave itself. We opened our eyes into the level sunshine of a summer evening.

We were standing in the roadway outside the Bellevue Boarding House. It looked more drab and spiritless than ever. The day was so warm that the front door stood open. It was the hour when most visitors

161

were returning to their evening meal, and the promenade was busy with couples and families and nursemaids and perambulators; all the vacation life of Weymouth at the height of its season.

"They'll be in the living room," said Flora, "ready to go in to supper."

We all looked at Aunt Harriet, who by unspoken consent had somehow become the mastermind of the operation. She was rather pale from her first experience of a goddess-borne journey, but there was a light of excitement in her eyes that made her seem ten years younger. She was looking all around her at the houses and people and carriages, and murmuring under her breath.

"Beautiful! So elegant! Just what I thought it would be!"

Flora had to speak to her a second time before she heard. She came out of her thoughts with a little jerk, and then spoke briskly enough.

"Good! It will be as well to have witnesses. I think, Flora, we will go in by the side door, where we shall be less observed. You and Louisa go in to them first and we shall see what they say or do. Don't be nervous. We shall be close behind you. But it will be as well to see how they behave before they realize you have other protectors."

We walked around to the side door as quickly and quietly as possible. Flora knocked. There was a pause and then the scurry of feet along the hall. The door opened to show a tall thin girl, pale, untidy, and flurried. At the sight of Flora she gave a little breathless gasp and held out both her hands.

"Miss Flora! Oh Miss Flora! I never thought to see you again!"

"Dear Bessie! I did so hope you'd still be here. No, hush! Don't say anything about the others. Just let them wait in the hall. I'll explain it all later, but we've got a little surprise for Aunt Gladys. This is my friend Louise. She and I will go in first."

"But miss, she says dreadful things about you. She and them two Merrys. She'll be terrible angry—"

"I'm sure she will be," I said happily. I was looking forward to seeing her face when we walked in.

Standing just inside the living-room door she didn't notice us at first. She was near the window, saying something to Mr. Banting. Whatever it was, judging by her expression and his nervous gestures, it was very unpleasant. Mr. Merry, seated in the most comfortable armchair, was reading a book, and his wife was patronizing the half dozen boarders with her conversation. For the summer weather she was drearily expensive in a thin gray silk, with the jet pin pinned at her throat.

"Good evening, Aunt Gladys," said Flora, her quiet clear voice carrying easily across the room.

Mrs. Wittering spun around with a gasp that nearly choked her, her face flushing to an unbecoming purple. Mr. Merry's book thudded to the floor. I smiled very politely at his wife.

"You found your pin then, Mrs. Merry?"

Her hand went defensively to her throat, but nothing deprived her of speech.

"If you had dusted properly you would have found it yourself. You shameless girl! Coming back here as bold as brass . . ."

But Mr. Banting interrupted her. He ran across the room between the astounded boarders and caught our hands in his.

"Oh, my dear children! How wonderful to see you! I have been so anxious for you, so very anxious."

"Mr. Banting!"

Mrs. Wittering had recovered her breath. Responding to sad years of habit, Mr. Banting stopped speaking at once, but he faced her bravely, still holding our hands.

"Ladies and gentlemen, I am sorry for this rude interruption." Aunt Gladys addressed her boarders like a public meeting. "You see before you two girls who repaid kindness by shocking conduct and dishonesty."

"Mrs. Wittering, this is unjust!" Mr. Banting's broken spirit was restored as I had never seen it. "The children were innocent. The pin was found."

"If the beastly thing was ever lost," I said.

"You hear her!" squawked Mrs. Merry. "Insolent as well as ungrateful. I am astonished at your interference, Mr. Banting."

"Perhaps someone would explain," suggested an elderly gentleman. "This is a very extraordinary happening."

He must have arrived quite recently, I thought. His landlady had not yet cowed him as she did most of her visitors. Mr. Merry rose, gaunt and menacing.

"It is easy to explain, sir. These young persons have sadly proved themselves to be monsters of ingratitude. Mrs. Wittering took them in out of the kindness of her heart, employed them, protected them. Nay, I will say she even mothered them. For all her goodness they returned insult and thoughtless desertion, and finally ran away to escape proper inquiry into their conduct."

164

"To escape cruelty and injustice," said Aunt Daisy's voice, coldly angry, just behind us.

My late employer's face, already flushed, grew so dark that I wondered with interest if she was going to have a fit. She gulped for words like a stranded fish.

"Daisy Higgs! You—I might have known—you put them up to this—this monstrous intrusion."

"Pull yourself together, Gladys." Aunt Daisy gathered the attention of the assembled company with considerable dignity. "I have come here for justice. This woman enticed these young girls here with false promises and then used them as free labor. Overworked and half starved! You cannot know how much these poor innocent children have suffered."

I must admit that I had felt neither poor nor innocent during my time at the Bellevue, but I was greatly enjoying Aunt Daisy's version of it. But now she moved farther into the room, revealing Aunt Harriet, Charlie, and Bertram just behind her.

"How dare you?" stormed Mrs. Wittering. "How dare you come here with your wicked accusations? And who are these people with you?"

It was my aunt who answered her.

"I am Harriet Higgs, Mrs. Wittering. Flora had more relations to protect her than you realized when you took advantage of her poverty. I am sorry that your visitors should be inconvenienced and embarrassed by our visit, but it is necessary that we should have witnesses. I am sure that Mr. Merry, as a lawyer, will agree that it is a wise precaution."

"Witnesses?" Aunt Glady's voice shook lightly. "The woman must be mad!"

Aunt Harriet went on as if she hadn't spoken.

"I'm sure everyone here will be interested to know how you have run your business. By overcharging, theft, fraud, and petty blackmail—helped by your two precious friends here."

"Dear lady, you are right as always. She must be mad." Mr. Merry boomed into the fray with the expectation of immediate victory. "My good woman, unfounded accusations in the presence of witnesses are grounds for an action for slander. I shall see to it that you are prosecuted with the utmost rigor."

"Pray do so!" retorted my aunt. (She seemed oddly to be picking up Victorian turns of speech.) "I am sure the court will be most interested in this." She fished in her bag and held up the fat black notebook. "A record of your combined transactions for the past seven years. Shall I read you some examples?"

Mrs. Merry whirled on Aunt Gladys, looking ready to stab her with her sharp beak of a nose.

"Where did she get that?"

The dark flush had faded from her friend's face, leaving it a pasty white that shone with little flecks of perspiration.

"I didn't want to worry you by telling you. The girls stole my box when they left."

"They didn't steal it," said Charlie furiously. They all stared at him, but by now were too bewildered even to ask who he was. "They had a right to take it. It had all the money that *you* stole from them."

Mrs. Merry's feelings exploded beyond all control. With a scream of rage she picked up her husband's book and hurled it at Aunt Gladys. It missed its mark, but crashed against a small table loaded with miniatures and china ornaments, all swept in ruins to the ground.

The racket assaulted the nerves of the one person we'd all forgotten. I was still clasping Casca closely to me under my cape, as I had when we left Deep End. But now with a violent kick he shot out of my grasp and landed in the middle of the room, his tail lashing like a demented pendulum and his voice raised to its full pitch of protest. With another scream, this time of terror, Mrs. Merry leaped back.

"A cat! It's a cat! Take the brute away."

It was too much. Used to respect and affection, and faced suddenly with an apparently lunatic woman who shrieked at him, Casca lost his head entirely and went for her. For a heart-stopping moment, watching the sinuous grace and fire of that flashing spring, I thought Bast herself had come for her revenge. But Casca could manage very nicely without divine assistance. He sank all his sharp teeth into her wrist and his claws left a red weal down her hand as she beat him off. One bite was enough. (Probably her blood tasted of acid.) He leaped superbly for the mantelpiece, knocking down a hideous toby jug as he landed, and crouched there wailing quite unrepeatable things. It was lucky that he spoke Abyssinian, but everyone caught the gist of his remarks.

Mrs. Merry, sobbing with fright and clutching her hand, made a dash for the hall and the stairs, falling over Bertram on her way. Bertram too was upset. People often fell over him, but only with apologies. They never rudely trampled and rushed on. He lumbered to his feet with something surprisingly like a growl.

167

"Go after her, please," said Aunt Harriet to Bessie, who was watching goggle-eyed and openmouthed beside the wilting aspidistra. "I expect there are smelling salts or sal volatile in the house. When she is calmer you can help her with her packing. I don't think she will be staying here anymore."

Mr. Merry bore down upon her.

"Miss Higgs—if that is your name—this is enough. You have burst in here with this rabble of strangers. You have slandered us and upset our visitors. You have allowed a fierce animal to attack and injure my wife. I shall make charges of trespass and assault. Give me that book."

My aunt dropped the notebook neatly back into her bag.

"Mr. Merry, you may be accustomed to getting your own way by bullying defenseless people. But you will not bully me."

Mr. Merry said something that even Casca listened to with respectful admiration, and made a grab for the bag. Perhaps Bertram thought his beloved mistress was in danger. Or perhaps he just distrusted Mr. Merry's smell. At any rate, for the first and probably the last time in his life, he was consumed with a violent dislike for a human being.

It was lucky for his enemy that he was standing by the living-room door and that the front door was still open. He made it just in time, though with a great rip in his sleeve. He was down the front steps and along the promenade, with Bertram pounding at his heels. Flora, Charlie, and I dashed out after them. Neither of them was used to such a speed, but this was Bertram's finest hour and he knew it. Yard by thundering yard he gained upon his quarry. I'm not sure whether in the end he sprang or simply collided with him. There was the sound of ripping cloth and a yell from Mr. Merry. Fear must have sharpened his wits, for at that moment an empty carriage was driving past him, one of those that were for hire by sight-seeing visitors. With surprising agility he dragged at the door and leaped inside. Catching up breathlessly ourselves, we heard him call to the driver.

"Drive on! Quickly!"

The man turned his head, looked at his passenger, and deliberately pulled up his horse.

"Here! Remember me?"

"Of course I don't. I don't know you. Drive on, I tell you."

"No, you wouldn't remember, would you? I'm only the chap you tried to get into trouble last month. Poking your long nose into none of your business! Get out, and look sharp about it."

"Your carriage is for hire. You have no legal right to refuse a customer."

"Ho, ain't I? I'll have who I please in my own carriage, and that ain't you, mister. Now get out!"

Leaning backward he opened the far door, gave Mr. Merry a sharp push, and at the same time flicked his horse forward. The lawyer saved himself from falling only by an ungainly jump which left him standing in the roadway, clutching his coat as tightly as he could around his torn trousers.

By now we had caught up with Bertram and were all three holding on to his collar. But the temporary disappearance of his quarry had baffled him. His unaccustomed rage had already spent itself in the chase and he was wondering what all the fuss was about.

169

He allowed us quite peacefully to turn him around and ambled back panting between us. The promenade was still full of people. One or two ladies were making sympathetic sounds, but there was no mistaking the titters of laughter all around.

"Isn't that Merry, the lawyer?" I heard one man say. "Slimy rogue, if ever there was one."

"A good dog, that," said his companion, equally delighted. "I wish mine had as much sense."

We left Mr. Merry alone with his troubles and walked back to the Bellevue as quickly as we could. I suppose he took refuge somewhere in the end.

As we reentered the house, Aunt Harriet, followed by Aunt Daisy, was gently but firmly propelling Mrs. Wittering into the hall. Our late employer's solid figure seemed to have sagged in the last few minutes so that, instead of her filling her clothes to bursting, her clothes now supported her. Her round bumpy face looked like a badly cooked doughnut.

"Ah, children," said my aunt briskly, "I trust you were able to preserve Mr. Merry from serious injury?"

"His clothes were torn," I admitted, "but I don't think he was really hurt. But I don't know if he's coming back."

"He will have gone to his office premises, no doubt. His wife will probably wish to join him there. We and Mrs. Wittering have matters to discuss together. But I am sure that you will all help Bessie as much as possible, and see to it that supper is now served. There will be time for explanations afterward."

Aunt Gladys stared at us with eyes of cold hatred, but went unprotesting into the small living room, and Aunt Harriet shut the door firmly behind them.

170

15
Destinations

Aunt Harriet's flair for generalship was never more useful than that evening. Before the five of us had sat down in the kitchen to our own very late supper, she had everything under control. She had told the boarders an interesting and convincing story of how Flora and I, unjustly accused, had fled from the Bellevue and by most providential chance had found the protection of our relatives. The notebook had been accidentally taken, but its revelation of wrongdoing and petty tyranny had made our interference necessary. It would soon be destroyed. Meanwhile Mrs. Wittering herself was in need of a vacation, and our two aunts would run the boardinghouse in her absence. She apologized for their disturbed evening but assured them that the rest of their stay would be happy and comfortable. (Most of them, I think, had enjoyed the disturbance. But I'm sure that some went to bed with lighter hearts after hearing that the notebook would be destroyed.) Bessie and Mr. Banting received exactly the same explanation. Bessie was a good, kind, willing girl, but not very bright. She needed a life that took only its familiar course. As for Mr. Banting, we all felt that his nerves had suffered strain enough. He was looking even more ill and tired than when we had last seen him.

The aunts themselves carried up supper trays to Aunt Gladys and Mrs. Merry. And between them they found sleeping places for us all. Flora and I and Casca were to share one room, the aunts another, and Charlie and Bertram were to have makeshift beds in the basement.

Just as we were coping with these arrangements a sudden rumpus brought us all into the hall. Aunt Gladys and Mrs. Merry, each carrying a small valise, were jockeying for position on the staircase. Aunt Gladys had the advantage of sheer size and weight, but Mrs. Merry's small vicious elbows were having their effect. As we arrived she swung her valise against her friend's, rather as if she were playing conkers. But both ladies lost their grip at the same time and their luggage rolled down the staircase to our feet.

"I will not stay another moment under this roof," declaimed Mrs. Merry. "After all that my husband and I have done for you, all his advice and help. To be spoken to like this! The monstrous ingratitude of it!" She caught sight of Charlie. "Boy, call a cab for me at once."

Aunt Gladys drew so deep a breath that it nearly burst the upper seams of her dress.

"Ingratitude? When you've lived here all these years on terms that made it a charity to keep you?

A charity! And look what your precious husband's advice has led to! You have been snakes within my bosom."

Aunt Gladys's bosom had little room for anything but itself, but this splendid counterattack for once deprived her opponent of speech. Aunt Harriet took advantage of it.

"Ladies! Ladies! Compose yourselves, I beg you. Charlie, you had better summon two cabs. It seems that Mrs. Wittering also intends to leave us."

"Indeed I am leaving." Aunt Gladys came slowly and heavily down the staircase, effectively blocking all the space so that Mrs. Merry had to follow. "I am ill, Miss Higgs. Your accusations—your cruel, unfounded accusations—have shattered my nerves. I shall spend the night with my friend, Arabella Hinton. I shall tell her that I am ill and need immediate rest. I will send for my possessions when I have made further arrangements.

"I am sure that is wise," said Aunt Daisy quite kindly. "Flora, Louise, will you fetch two chairs for the ladies while they wait."

Obediently we fetched them. But Mrs. Merry at once seized hers and removed it to the far side of the hall table so that the aspidistra acted as a barrier between them. They waited there in dragon-eyed silence, each slightly averted from the other. There were several embarrassing minutes, and furtive sounds from the landing above us showed that some of the boarders too were interested in all these goings-on. Then there was a rumbling of wheels outside, and the clop of hooves, and Charlie came in slightly breathless.

"I'm awfully sorry. I tried everywhere, but it's so

late. I could only find one cab."

"Then that is mine," said Mrs. Merry. "I was the first to order it."

"Nonsense. I was the first downstairs. Take my valise, boy."

"I think," said Aunt Daisy with quite unexpected firmness, "that you had better share it. We will see that all your things are ready for you when you send for them."

Aunt Gladys rose and stalked heavily to the door, where she turned and faced us with a kind of ruined majesty.

"I hope you are satisfied. You have stolen the living of a poor defenseless widow. The thought of it will haunt you on your deathbeds."

It was a magnificent exit. For the first and last time I could have applauded her. But Mrs. Merry stopped beside Flora and me, nearly piercing us with her nose.

"Wicked, ungrateful, and deceitful girls! As for you, Louise, your character is written in your face. You will come to a bad end."

She followed Aunt Gladys into the cab, but sat down in it as if no one else was there. Each at the same moment gave a different address to the driver. Aunt Harriet closed the front door. There was a pause and then the cab rattled away, bearing them into the summer night and out of our lives forever.

I wondered what would become of the Bellevue without its owner. But when I asked Aunt Harriet about it next morning she told me not to worry.

"We are considering arrangements and will tell you when something is settled. Meanwhile we owe it to the present guests to make the rest of their stay as pleasant as possible. And I've no doubt a few days of sea air will do all of us good."

Probably they did. And certainly the change of management did the boarding house good. It even seemed to look better, despite its dull and peeling paint. We were all pressed into service, until everything indoors looked clean and cared for. We even washed the horrible curtains, which were still horrible afterward, but at least a brighter color, and the windows were polished and open to the sun.

All of us sat on the promenade one afternoon, looking at the house from the outside. (All of us, that is, except Casca, who had taken a fancy to that awful kitchen stove.) It was that brief blessed hour for those who keep lodgings, when the midday meal is over and cleared away and it's not yet time to begin the evening tasks.

"It looks better," said Aunt Daisy with satisfaction. "A pity it can't be repainted this season."

"Wouldn't it be lovely if it looked like the others," said Flora. "What color would you choose, Aunt Daisy?"

"Pale green would be very attractive, don't you think?"

"Turquoise," said Aunt Harriet. "It has more definition."

"We could have flowered curtains too," suggested Flora.

"Come on," I said quietly to Charlie. "They'll go on like this for ages. Let's throw stones for Bertram."

We left them to it and went down onto the beach. Bertram lumbered gratefully after every stone we threw for him, but usually trotted back to apologize

175

after a worried search. The trouble was, he explained, that there were such a lot of stones and they all looked alike. He couldn't be sure which was ours. He didn't really mind when we tired of the game and sat down. He plumped down heavily between us, showering us with damp sand and shingle.

Charlie looked at me sideways after a longish silence.

"What is it, Scrap? Something's bothering you."

"Oh, I dunno. I suppose I'm just bored. It's all this house talk. Who cares about the rotten old boardinghouse?"

"I think your aunts quite like it. But it can't be for long. They're only sort of caretaking until things are straightened out, aren't they? They must have come to some sort of an arrangement with Mrs. Wittering."

"I suppose so. But they haven't said. Flora seems quite pleased to be back."

That was the real rub and I knew it. Flora and Aunt Daisy were back in their own world, the place where they belonged and I didn't. But, next to Charlie himself, Flora was the best friend I had. The words of the goddess ran to and fro in my mind like the endless stir of the waves. "All meetings end in farewells." End in farewells. Farewells.

Charlie leaned comfortably toward me.

"There'll be lots to do at Deep End when we get back home. And there's all the summer to come. We'll have had two summers in one year!"

He was trying to cheer me up, and I smiled back at him. But Deep End just then was a whole century away and its concerns were as small to me as if I

176

saw them through the wrong end of a telescope.

It was after breakfast next morning that the aunts called us to a meeting in the small living room. I took Casca with me. He was unusually affectionate, as if he sensed that I felt depressed. As Bertram came too, the place seemed full.

"I think, my dears," said Aunt Harriet, "that it's time for us to consider our plans. You have told us of Bast's warning, Louise, that this time there can be only one more journey, and with no return."

I nodded, suddenly finding it difficult to speak.

"We must be very careful then as to what we do. But I must tell you first that the Bellevue belongs now to me."

"*Belongs* to you?" Charlie gaped at her.

"Harriet has so much more forethought than I have," said Aunt Daisy. "She felt that Aunt Gladys should be prevented if possible from continuing this business. So she arranged for her bank to buy her sufficient sovereigns to purchase this house if the owner would consent to sell—which we very easily persuaded her to do after the revelation of her dishonesty."

"So *that* was what you brought in the tin box!" I said. "Whatever will you do with the place now?"

"That's what we're here to discuss. If it's properly run, there's an excellent living to be made from it. Daisy, this is the world you know, and you like Weymouth. How would you like to take it on?"

Watching her, I was puzzled by her expression, as if she were half afraid of the answer. Aunt Daisy was suddenly flustered.

"Oh my dear! So wonderfully kind to give me the

chance! But I'm not sure . . ." She ran a distracted hand over her hair, dislodging several hairpins. "Deep End is so beautiful. And then there's Albertine. But of course there's Flora to consider. If you feel you would be happier here, Flora . . ."

"Aunt Daisy! Do you really mean it? You mean you wouldn't mind going back to Deep End? I'd love it more than anything. But I thought you'd want to stay here."

"Oh no, dear. Of course it's been very interesting to come back. But there's so much to do on the farm now that we can afford it. And so many exciting new things. And I do so love my Mini."

A surge of happiness swept through me, and I saw Charlie grinning from ear to ear.

"Then everything's all right," I said. "I would have hated you to stay behind. Let's go soon. We can all go back now, can't we?"

Aunt Harriet looked down, tapping her fingers nervously on the desk. If it had not been impossible to believe, I would have sworn she was shy.

"Well, perhaps not all. Daisy, if you are quite, quite sure that you don't want the Bellevue—"

"I'm quite sure, Harriet."

"Then I really think I'd like to stay here and manage it myself."

She could hardly have caused more surprise if she'd let off a bomb on the carpet. Aunt Daisy got her breath back first.

"But, my dear! Have you really thought? What about Deep End and all your plans for the farm?"

"All *your* plans really, Daisy. The poultry are my real interest, you know. It's you and Sid who want to expand the farm. I don't honestly like cows and pigs all that much."

"But the hens? You'd miss them dreadfully."

"I can keep hens here. The garden has been shamefully neglected but there's plenty of space. Just think, there would be fresh eggs every day for the boarders."

"Aunt Harriet," I said. And my voice sounded small in my own ears.

"Come here, Louisa." She held out both her hands to me and took mine when I stood beside her, looking very straight into my eyes. "Yes, we shall miss each other. Quite a lot at first. You didn't want to come to me, did you, and heaven knows I didn't want to have you. I'm not used to children and I'm not much good with them. But we've grown fond of each other, haven't we?"

My throat ached and I couldn't speak, but after a moment she went on.

"Yes, we'll miss each other at first. But less and less, until we are each only a happy memory to the other. But Aunt Daisy will look after you as she does Flora."

"Of course I will," said Aunt Daisy warmly. And Flora moved across to me and slipped her arm through mine.

"There are Mr. Banting and Bessie to think of too," said Aunt Harriet. "They are neither of them very fitted to care for themselves. They need both employment and protection. But you, Louisa, I think you are one of those who will shape your world much as you want it. You may even make a mark in it someday. Just before we left home I saw my lawyer and set up a trust for you, to make sure that you can go

179

to that drama school of yours—or whatever other training you may want by then."

"What about Sid Jennings?" asked Charlie.

Aunt Harriet smiled. "Sid's quite fond of me in his own way. But he sees much more eye to eye with Daisy. And as long as there's a Higgs who really cares about Deep End, Sid will be happy. I shall write a letter for you to take with you, explaining that I've been called away on urgent business. And another that you can give him later, with a reason I can't come back."

She'd thought it all out in every detail. The more she talked about it, the more we realized that she had really found what she most needed. There was so much to plan and do, the whole house to be painted and repaired, the garden to be salvaged, the poultry installed, the catering and cooking, and ways to make the Bellevue the most comfortable and delightful boardinghouse in Weymouth. She looked younger and happier and more handsome than I had ever known her. Aunt Harriet was about to engage on the organizing spree of a lifetime.

No one could grudge her so much enthusiasm. And I knew in my heart that she was right about me. I couldn't stay at Deep End all my life. When I grew up I would in any case have left her and the years would have drawn us apart.

All the same, tears were running unashamedly down my cheeks when the time came for us to say good-bye to her. All but Bertram, who was amiably disposed to us but passionately loved Aunt Harriet alone. Wherever she was he would be content.

We had already told Mr. Banting and Bessie that

180

the rest of us would have to go home. Bessie, almost pretty in a smart new dress and cap and apron, was sorry to see Flora go. But Aunt Harriet had chosen two young girls from a charity school to help her in the house and, beaming like the morning sun in the splendor of her new role as head housemaid, Bessie could not be dismayed by anything for long. Mr. Banting too looked different, in a neatly respectable dark suit and walking still a little crooked but entirely without his nervous scurry.

"Your aunt is a wonderful woman," he told me warmly. "She's keeping me on, you know, as her accountant and financial adviser, and at a most generous salary."

I thought secretly that any financial advice was likely to be my aunt's, but we told him how delighted we were and how glad that she could have his help. As he took our hands to say good-bye, he pressed a sovereign upon each of us. I began to protest.

"No, no, my dear child. Of course I can afford it. And I should be happy if you would buy some small keepsake to remember me by."

I doubted if he really could afford it, even on his new salary. But still less could he afford to be refused. We took his gifts and thanked him affectionately. I still have that sovereign to this day and will never part with it.

But now it was time to leave. We had thought it wiser not to risk observation in the house, so were gathered very early at the farthest end of the promenade. The sea had the pale silver quietness of a warm still day to come. The sand stretched smooth, unmarked, and shining toward the outgoing tide, reflect-

181

ing the paddling sea gulls and pools of blue light from the morning sky. Aunt Harriet kissed each of the others in turn, then caught me in her arms in a loving though slightly awkward embrace. I think perhaps she was crying a little too. Then I stood away from her, holding Casca tightly with both hands, and spoke aloud into the waiting silence of the untouched morning.

"I wish that all of us except Aunt Harriet and Bertram were safely home again at Deep End."

For one uneasy moment I thought the magic had failed to work. Then the darkness filtered in, slowly, very slowly, coiling like fine mist between us and the pale-blue brightness of the day. Aunt Harriet's face grew dimmer, smaller, withdrawing into infinite distance. Casca was purring under my chin, with a deep throbbing hum that filled the whole darkening world.

And there we stood again, Aunt Daisy, Flora, Charlie, Casca, and I, looking through the living-room window of Deep End at the promise of the spring afternoon.

Of course we missed her, quite a lot at first. But we knew she was fulfilled and happy in the life that she had chosen. And time moved forward, always forward, and there were so many things to do and think about. "All meetings end in farewells. But no one should grieve when the meetings have been good."

There is still that one journey that I can take if I choose—and Charlie with me too, if he will come. So many places in the world, so many possible adventures! But I think Charlie might only be really happy in England, and I don't suppose anywhere else would be much fun without him.

182

Sometimes Casca sits and watches me, with a long inscrutable stare. Is he willing me to think about Abyssinia, I wonder? That might be pretty exciting. But I don't suppose they have a drama school there.

Bishop Hilliard's poignant message to the Church—us—to hear Christ's call to minister to a dying generation, is must reading. He reminds us that the power of God's love among people willing to minister is greater than all the forces of evil. Death and despair will only lose their sting on this generation if the Church responds prayerfully and actively to the challenges articulated in this timely book. We must do more—now. Don Hilliard teaches us how.

—David Black, President
Eastern College, Saint Davids, Pennsylvania

Few men address present-day situations more clearly than Bishop Donald Hilliard. He has an insight that is the basis for challenging all of us to our greatest potential in finding solutions for our day.

In this book he deals with a generation "that is determined to kill itself," and I share with him the notion that it is the Church's responsibility to stop our young people and families that are set on self-destruction. As Jesus stopped the funeral and restored the son back to his widowed mother, even so, we must use the anointing and the authority that God has given us to stop the onslaught of the enemy to destroy us today.

Bishop Hilliard is not only a great preacher and author, but he lives out in his community service a model that we need for the Church of the new millennium. I can, without reservation, recommend anything that this man of God takes the time to pen. I pray this book will challenge anyone who reads it.

—Earl P. Paulk, Bishop
Chapel Hill Harvester Church, Decatur, Georgia

Stop the Funeral!

Reaching a Generation Determined to Kill Itself

by

Donald Hilliard Jr., D.Min.

ALBURY PUBLISHING
Tulsa, Oklahoma

Stop the Funeral!
Reaching A Generation Determined to Kill Itself
ISBN 1-57778-116-3
Copyright © 2000 by Donald Hilliard Jr., D.Min.
277 Madison Avenue
Perth Amboy, NJ 08861

Published by ALBURY PUBLISHING
P. O. Box 470406
Tulsa, Oklahoma 74147-0406
Printed in the United States of America.

Dedication

This book is dedicated to the greater glory of God
and to my beloved parents,
Alease (Crawford) Hilliard-Chapman
and the late Donald Hilliard Sr. (1930-1983).
Their consistent love and active presence stopped the
funeral in my life before it had a chance to begin.

It is also dedicated to my family: my dear wife and
partner, Phyllis, and our beloved children,
Leah, Charisma, and Destiny.

Contents

Acknowledgments

This first effort has been long-coming. Someone has said, "Procrastination is my sin, it brings me nothing but sorrow-I know I should do something about it, I will . . . tomorrow!" Hopefully this publication will release the "writer within"—or so I am told. I am grateful to the many patient souls who have labored with me and encouraged me in these endeavors. Special thanks to the ever-supportive membership of the Cathedral Second Baptist Church—Perth Amboy and Asbury Park, New Jersey—truly a great people; and our gifted pastoral staff, Dr. B. Glover-Williams, the Rev. Patricio Wilson, and the Rev. Denice Reid—thanks for your love, support, and raw honesty. Special thanks to our secretarial and support staff personnel—Sylvia A. Haire, Carol Dortch-Wright, Phyllis Moore, and Monee McGuire. Thank you, Pastor Vaughn Foster Sr. and Minister Harry Williams II for your editorial assistance and encouragement. I appreciate the preachers and prophets of God who consistently declared, "Write! Write! Write!" Chief among them were the late Rev. Dr. Samuel D. Proctor and the late Rev. Tom Skinner, beloved ministers of God, mentors, and friends. Finally, my greatest love and appreciation to my beloved wife of eighteen years, Phyllis Denise Thompson-Hilliard—a writer, teacher, and exemplary journalist in her own right—who has always breathed quiet, consistent support and encouragement into my every dream and vision; and our beloved children— Leah Joy Alease, Charisma Joy Denise, and Destiny Joy

The'ma, our joys! I am especially proud to feature some of my daughter Leah's writings in this publication.

Foreword

We, the Church, have failed to carry out our God-given assignment. Our risen Savior has given us the duty to be catalysts for change, transformation, and restoration, not only in our personal lives, but in our society as a whole. We have miserably failed our country, our society, and our communities at this task, and now our young people and our families are dying a slow and agonizing death.

The message of deliverance and restoration that God has placed in Bishop Donald Hilliard is a timely message to this generation, particularly as we embark upon a new millennium. He sets forth a challenge to the body of Christ to stop this funeral procession and, through the anointing and ability God has given us, to raise that which was dead. Bishop Hilliard reminds us that we have a "charge to keep" and a "God to glorify" while here on this earth.

I pray that as you read these pages, the conviction and call of the Holy Spirit will reach out and grab you and challenge you to act. I am convinced that Bishop Hilliard is a gift to the body of Christ and the kind of prophetic voice that the Church has needed to shock us into action. I guarantee that this man of God and integrity will speak the truth to you throughout the pages of this book.

Bishop Eddie L. Long, D.D., D.H.L.
Senior Pastor
New Birth Missionary Baptist Church
Decatur, Georgia

Introduction

Bang! Bang! Bang! That is the familiar refrain heard throughout urban neighborhoods and increasingly in the rural and suburban communities in America. Where I grew up in Houston, Texas, these would have been the sounds coming from the guns of hunters in search of game. Now, the hunted are young men and women on street corners and in school buildings. This carnage has unnecessarily destroyed many families and has created an atmosphere where children are experiencing funerals early and often during their juvenile and adolescent years. The mortuaries have become the preeminent businesses operating within many communities.

Donald Hilliard Jr.'s *Stop the Funeral!* offers keen insight into the kind of psychosis that has created an atmosphere where life is devalued and where a false sense of respect is earned through the killing of another individual. He has analyzed these attitudes by focusing not merely on the dead who have been embalmed, but also on the walking dead who still have the physical attributes of life but have lost their dreams, hopes, desires, and aspirations. The categorizing of the problems of Generation X, which seems determined to kill itself, is one of the most telling aspects of this thoughtful and challenging work.

Stop the Funeral! points us to deathbeds in various arenas of life where people are losing out on the joys of living by having made negative choices. Bishop Hilliard relates some of the fundamental attitude changes toward death to a paradigm shift in culture, lifestyles, and societal changes that reflect new definitions of ethics and morality. Through movies and music, entertainment has been an overwhelming factor in orienting young people to a mentality of greed, selfishness, low self-esteem, and a callous disregard for life. There is a feeling of invincibility, even in the face of certain death. Having seen youth who are "packing" weapons, driving luxury cars, and dressed in designer labels, there is among many a sense that these are the ultimate necessities for "the good life." Therefore, they are willing to sacrifice another life in order to gain those things which they believe give them meaning and definition. They are searching for life among the relics that symbolize death.

Stop the Funeral! challenges some of the socially accepted norms which emerged during the last several decades. Chapter Four is especially compelling since it addresses the fatherless generation. It is a challenge to fathers who do not assume responsibility for their families or the children that they sire. It also calls upon fathers to understand the necessity for providing child support, both financial and emotional, when the relationship with the mother ceases to exist. We have been made aware, by various statistical indexes, that many of our children who live in poverty are the products of families where the father has absented himself from total responsibility to and for the children.

Dr. Hilliard is not one-dimensional by merely challenging men, but also draws attention to the plight of so many young girls who believe themselves to have gained a sense of fulfillment and satisfaction by giving birth to a child. He shares some of the well-known "sayings" of parents and others from days gone by when discussion about sex was taboo on one level, but addressed in language that became memory verses which kept many young women from making poor choices.

In my twenty-three years as Pastor of Allen A.M.E. Church, I have seen enough caskets roll into the church with the bodies of individuals who could have lived had they chosen different lifestyles. So, Dr. Hilliard's poignant discussion about AIDS and other sexually-transmitted diseases is appropriate for dissemination in church groups who are interested in getting to the root of the problem. Too many others are dying from cancer because they refuse to have necessary check-ups or change their diets. Most of these deaths could be averted if we take seriously the admonitions and directives contained in this book. We should not be satisfied with "death by choice," where people have made improper decisions.

Chapters Seven and Eight must be read by every pastor who is sincere about utilizing God's resurrecting power to rebuild people's lives, relationships, communities, families, and churches. There is no excuse for dying churches to exist in the midst of a dying people when the Church of our Lord and Savior Jesus Christ has been called to be the instrument for the giving of life.

The Honorable Rev. Floyd H. Flake, D.Min.
Pastor and U.S. Congressman, Retired

A Young Man's Testimony

"Yo, I got dat man!" he whispered. "This stuff will get you high . . . straight to the brain, yo!"

He approached me this morning just two blocks away from the church building. His gangly, six-foot frame was swallowed up in the thick, insular padding of his dark green, down overcoat. A black woolen cap shielded his face from instant recognition. He ducked his head between his shoulder blades in an attempt to ward off the harsh winter winds.

He might have been seventeen, but he was not young. Two tightly clenched fists plunged themselves deep into his green pockets. A fistful of crack vials may well have filled one pocket; a nine-millimeter handgun quite possibly lodged itself in the other. He was dealing hell in a capsule to the last survivors of the urban wasteland. Employment and prosperity left these streets for the safety of the suburbs long ago. In his mind, crack dealing may have been the only economic opportunity left to him.

His clientele are the emaciated, living cadavers who haunt the dark gin mills and crack houses of the inner city. Their toothless grins reveal more heartbreak than joy, more frustration than contentment. For the most part, they are completely unaware that death has come to call, but it has. Just look at the angry tears that stream from the faces of their loved ones, the mourners.

"I'm a born-again Christian," I said to the young drug dealer. "Jesus Christ will set you free."

He lowered his head, embarrassed, ashamed. His stride quickened. His fists seem to plunge deeper into his coat pockets. He marched off into the cold winds of forever. It was the terrifying loneliness of his gaze that I recall so vividly. His deep-set, brown eyes burned themselves into my soul like twin laser beams. They seemed to say, "Somebody stop the funeral."

Spiritual death has become the number one growth industry in America. It cuts across all gender, race, and class lines. It affects all ages and ethnicities. Spiritual death is a worldwide franchise with unlimited growth potential. It can be found in both the public housing project and the corporate boardroom. The sweet scent of formaldehyde wafts through the sacred corridors of many of our churches. The anointing, the men, and the young people have all faded away, leaving questions perplexing both the pulpit and the pew.

Tearful last words are being said over many marriages. Many saints have lost their moral compass while wandering in the dry heat of a spiritual desert. Disenchanted, rebellious youth have left their heartbroken parents to wring their hands at the gravesite. All over America people are shouting, "Somebody stop the funeral!"

Jesus of Nazareth was heralded for His uncanny ability to stop a funeral. Two thousand years after his resurrection, we sit in awe over the biblical accounts of those He raised from the dead. Sometimes, Jesus would not even appear on the scene until after the corpse was cold and the situation deemed absolutely hopeless.

When Jesus ascended to the right hand of the Father, He left His work to be completed by His followers. Bishop Dr. Donald Hilliard Jr. is a Christian who has sought to walk in the footsteps of the Messiah. God has used this consecrated vessel to redeem many lives for His glory and eternal purposes. My life was among them.

The "unforgettable experience" is the descriptive term sometimes used to explain the incredible move of God at the Second Baptist Church Cathedral in Perth Amboy, New Jersey. The praise and worship component of the service lifted me to heaven's gate during my first visit in 1992. However, it was the preached Word that I shall never forget. I recall thinking that Bishop Hilliard was perhaps the greatest preacher I had ever heard in my life. The church responded with foot stomping and affirmations of "Preach!" as time and time again, the man of God reached for oratorical heights. Scores of people responded to the altar call.

I joined the Cathedral not long after that first visit. Soon, I too was part of the resurrection. Life began to take place in the wastelands of my lost dreams. Bishop Hilliard would challenge his congregation to make the promises of God real in their lives. He was not preaching a "pie in the sky" religion, but holiness and biblical precepts relevant to everyday life. The two-edged sword of the Gospel found a ready sheath in his mouth. His sermons cut away the apathy, complacency, and the "I-can't-do-it" spirit ruthlessly and relentlessly. In 1993, I enrolled at Kean University in Union, New Jersey. I graduated three years later with honors. The funeral dirge had ceased.

In 1997, I was licensed as an associate minister of the Second Baptist Church Cathedral. Soon, I will graduate with a Master of Divinity degree from Eastern Baptist Theological Seminary. Last week, I sat in the studios of WLIB radio in New York City. I racked my brain as the talk show host stormed me with questions. I was there to talk about my recently released first book, *No Easy Walk*. Today, I find myself both grateful and amazed as interview requests come in each week from all around the country. The funeral has stopped in my life. It is Easter Sunday morning.

Has death taken root in some area of your life? Have your dreams fallen into the casket? Is your ministry on the rocks? Is your family life in chaos? Have you lost your song? Do not despair. God is still in the resurrection business.

I challenge you to turn off the television. Lock the bedroom door. Unplug the phone. Now, prayerfully and carefully read each page of this heavily anointed book. You haven't picked up this book by accident. There is power in each of its pages. Truth rushes through every line of Bishop Donald Hilliard Jr.'s pen, like water overflowing a dam. What he has to say may very well stop the funeral in your life situation. I know, because it happened to me.

Harry Williams
Author, *No Easy Walk: The Dramatic Journey of African-Americans* (InterVarsity Press)

one

Jesus, Stop the Funeral!

Now it happened, the day after, that He went into a city called Nain; and many of His disciples went with Him, and a large crowd.

And when He came near the gate of the city, behold, a dead man was being carried out, the only son of his mother; and she was a widow. And a large crowd from the city was with her.

LUKE 7:11-12

While traveling the paths of His ministry, Jesus encountered a funeral procession on the outskirts of the city of Nain. A young boy, the only son of his widowed mother, was being carried to his grave.

When I read Luke's text, I can envision this bereaved mother staggering beneath the supportive grip of relatives and friends, numb from grief. Do you know what it's like to have someone hug you and talk to you and to be unable to hear a word they're saying? Heavy grief can make you so numb that you are blind to your surroundings. You can't remember who was at the funeral. You are at a loss to remember who sent the flowers or who brought the food. And this woman had become so overwhelmed with grief that it really didn't matter. Today she was burying her only son. She was burying her last hope. She had previously lost a husband and now a son. She was numb, empty, and broken.

But the Scripture goes on to say there was a crowd gathered around this woman. Some in the crowd were family members, and some were friends. Others may have been drawn by the enormity of her tragedy. Bereavement often tends to draw crowds. People are attracted by things that appear to be gruesome. Some come because of the grisly circumstances surrounding the death; others come out of curiosity. Then there are those who celebrate the pain and suffering others experience. I've seen this at the funerals of murder victims.

So here we go again, outside the city gates to another funeral. Here we go again to another gravesite, to another situation of failure, to another situation of bondage. *Here we go again.* Have you ever felt like your life was an endless procession of brokenness, pain, death?

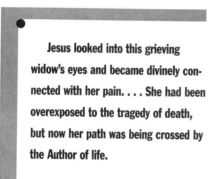

Jesus looked into this grieving widow's eyes and became divinely connected with her pain. . . . She had been overexposed to the tragedy of death, but now her path was being crossed by the Author of life.

Suddenly, the crowd encountered a band of travelers with a unique, compassionate leader. When this tragedy crossed His path, this caring captain said, "No! Not this time, Death," and He had compassion on this grieving mother.

> *When the Lord saw her, He had compassion on her and said to her, "Do not weep."*
>
> LUKE 7:13

The *New International Version* of the Bible says, "And when the Lord saw her, His heart went out to her." Jesus looked into this grieving widow's eyes and became divinely connected with her pain. He was concerned about her plight. She had been overexposed to the tragedy of death, but now her path was being crossed by the Author of life. Jesus is a life-giver in the midst of dying situations.

Culture of Death

Today in America, we are subjected to the culture of death. We have become far too familiar with drive-by shootings, teenage pregnancy, and abandoned children. A spirit of murder has been loosed upon the nation. We have become so used to the funeral processions that surround the burying of our children that they have become normative to us. We watch children go to their graves on a daily basis, figuratively and realistically, and it means nothing to us because we are overexposed and have become too intimate with the culture of death.

Here is this woman, previously crushed by the death of her husband, and now her son is dead. But Jesus said, "ENOUGH!" and stopped the funeral. Then He looked into this widow's puffy, tear-glazed eyes and said, "Do not weep." Jesus ministered to the grieving widow first, because you cannot stop the funeral in your family until God stops the funeral in you. You can't stop the bondage and brokenness in your children until you let God stop the bondage and brokenness in you. So Jesus stopped the funeral in the widow first by looking into her eyes and telling her to stop weeping. Let's deal with your issues first. Let's deal with your personal pain. Let's deal with you so that you can deal with your son!

Then Jesus did something that every orthodox Jew under the Law was forbidden to do: He touched the deceased. Why? Before we can bring life to a corpse we have to take a long hard look at it, get close to it, and touch it. We must be willing to touch what is broken, bound, and scheduled for burial. Jesus cared enough to touch the dead.

This isn't going to be business as usual, Jesus demonstrated, as He moved in compassionately and stopped the death march.

No, we've been shuffling in procession to the cemetery long enough.

No, this won't become another statistic. This won't reach the morning newspaper.

This won't be on Nightline *or* Larry King.

Sorry. No. Not here, not now! Stop this funeral!

Jesus reached over and touched the dead boy. None of the mourners had a clue as to what was going on. All they knew was that He had broken the Law, and the boy was now sitting up and talking. The crowd, including the boy's mother, stood stunned by the miracle they'd all just witnessed.

> *Then He came and touched the open coffin, and*
> *those who carried him stood still. And He said,*
> *"Young man, I say to you, arise."*

So he who was dead sat up and began to speak.
And He presented him to his mother.

Then fear came upon all, and they glorified God,
saying, "A great prophet has risen up among us";
and, "God has visited His people."

LUKE 7:14-16

Just One Touch

Just one touch of Jesus has the power to make all things new. Just one touch from Him can bring life out of death. Today, Jesus desires for us to experience the same miraculous touch this young man did. He wants to cross our paths and raise us up.

Jesus stopped the widow's funeral by touching and speaking. This is the much-needed remedy for our culture today. We must touch our children. However, some of us live in homes where our children know nothing about parental affection and T.L.C. (Tender Loving Care). Few memories are greater in the minds of children than the ones where Mommy or Daddy holds them and says, "Everything is going to be all right" or "Great job!"

> Few memories are greater in the minds of children than the ones where Mommy or Daddy holds them and says, "Everything is going to be all right" or "Great job!"

Yet, it's not enough to just touch them. Children need more than hugs and kisses. We must be there as an influence in their lives and speak God's Word over them. That's why we invite the children of our congregation up to the altar for prayer several Sundays a year. We call it "The Children's Moment." We don't do this to be cute. Our aim is not to hear the people say, "Oh, isn't that just wonderful. They have a children's moment. I think it's so nice to include the children in the service."

No! We do it because we're determined to save the lives of our children! We touch them and speak to them because we know hell has marked them for death. Hell desires to ruin our young people's beauty and their intelligence. For this reason, our church is determined to be in the funeral-stopping business.

We invite young people up to the altar, touch them, and declare that they will not become pregnant before they're married. We declare that they won't end up on drugs. We say they won't end up in jail. We say it regardless of the negative messages they often receive from Easy E, Master P, DMX, Motley Crew, and others through video and radio on a regular basis. Many voices in our death-ridden culture want our children in the grave. But God gives us the authority to say, "NO!" And through us, Jesus tells them, "Arise!"

Today Jesus is saying, "Young man, young woman, I say to you, arise! Arise from dead religion! Arise from dead relationships! Arise from the culture of death! Arise from self-hatred! Arise from poor self-esteem! ARISE!" Old folks used to say, "Honey, if you lay down with dogs, you'll get up with fleas!" When you don't love yourself you will lie with anything. Arise! You are better than that. This generation has something significant to say. Get up, young people! Arise! Take your place in the nation and speak.

But you can't arise when you're dead. When you're dead, all you can do is lie there. When you're dead, you can't say, "Stop." When you're dead, you can't keep your zipper closed or your panties up. When you're dead, you can't stop smoking drugs. When you're dead, you can't stop pickling your brain with liquor. Far too many of our children are on dead-end streets morally, spiritually, and academically.

So every Sunday at the Cathedral we declare, ARISE!

Jesus wants to deal with our national epidemic of dying children. He wants to deal with the young men and women with dreary hollowed-out eyes we see daily on street corners and in vacant lots. He wants to deal with this culture that continues to say it's all right to act like dogs in heat, because in reality, they are playing a deadly game of Russian roulette.

Culture of Sleaze

I'll never forget the young woman who told me she contracted the AIDS virus after having sex on her prom night. This was a good girl who got caught up with the wrong young man. He seemed right; but like a chameleon, he changed behavior as the night went on. She was naive to the perils of petting; and in a moment of heated passion, she let her guard down.

We must speak openly and honestly with our children about sexuality and holiness. They must have as much information as possible to make a God-informed choice. The pull to do what "feels right" is so strong in our culture. If we are to stop the funeral, we must develop strategies that teach this generation to resist the pull of the enemy of their soul.

In today's culture of sleaze, the pull involves every imaginable perversion. At first, they feel convicted because they know deep inside that their lifestyles displease the heart of God. But after awhile, they become hooked. Before you know it, they're bringing perversion in the church. It's unclean, it's unholy, and it's *happening in the Church*. Romans 1 says those who choose to live like that will be turned over to a reprobate mind:

> *And even as they did not like to retain God in their knowledge, God gave them over to a reprobate mind, to do those things which are not convenient.*
>
> ROMANS 1:28 KJV

A reprobate mind is incapable of distinguishing right from wrong. In other words, those who allow themselves to be fully seduced into perversion will not feel convicted or condemned. This may seem like a pretty low-grade reality, but it is, nonetheless, a reality. Immorality and perversion are in the Church.

Within America's children today, there is a tug of war going on. This is why we don't have time to play church. We're out of time for foolishness. Jesus is raising a funeral-stopping church because the funerals are occurring daily, and we're fighting for our lives. If pastors aren't going to serve, we need to find a nice pew. If we don't have a prayer life and no sincere desire for relevant ministry, then it may be time to step away from leadership for a season and get refocused.

Misplaced Trust

The widow of Nain's boy wasn't raised back to life through philosophy or education, the things so many put their trust in today. Don't get me wrong. We need education and we need good jobs, but knowledge and money can't stop the funerals taking place in our culture of death today. Education will inform you, but it takes Jesus Christ to transform you. It takes Jesus to show our children the difference between good and evil, life and death, and right and wrong. As Proverbs 14:12 and 16:25 say, **There is a way that seems right to a man [or woman], but its end is the way of death.**

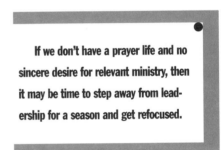

If we don't have a prayer life and no sincere desire for relevant ministry, then it may be time to step away from leadership for a season and get refocused.

When that young boy's hand is sliding all over that young girl's behind, she doesn't feel it. When a young girl is unbuttoning that young boy's shirt, guilt goes out the window. It's not until they wake up in the morning and all of a sudden he's gone, she's gone . . . then they feel it. She misses and craves him. He wants her again. You just don't give anybody that much power over your life! When a teenager's presence or lack of it controls a young girl's emotions, that's just too much power. But many are the teenage girls who can sing along with Mary J. Blige, "I'm going down 'cause you're not around." What a foolish song!

These young brothers on the make say, "Well, if you don't, Baby, you know I can always go to somebody else. You know, there's always Claudette, Shanice, Sally, Sue, or So-and-so. Young sisters will say, "I can always get Bobby or Darnell. But you know, Baby, if you want to make it, it'll just be me and you. You know what I'm saying. But if you don't . . . " Sadly, too many of our children are buying the hype and end up pregnant or dying with AIDS. The pressure against handling sexuality in a biblical, responsible way is very challenging for this generation.

At the Cathedral we embrace and speak over our children to give them the power to say, "No Brother, you can leave because I'm with God, and one with God is a majority. You're offering me death, and I choose life. So keep stepping! See ya!"

This is the message we must preach and teach today to reach a generation determined to kill itself.

■ Daddy Hunger

Sometimes we don't like what we see in our children because we see in them what we couldn't control in ourselves. Something's driving them into perversion because it drove us into perversion. But if we will start looking at the funeral in us and let God deal with the promiscuity in us, He will deliver our children too. Too many of our young girls are hungry for Daddy love. The absence of Daddy has given birth to an angry generation. In some homes, children are introduced to a different father every three months. It's Sam in September, Danny in December, and Maurice in March! The cycle continues with the next generation, because we tend to imitate what we've grown up with.

It's important for us who are biological and spiritual fathers to bridge the gap. We need to make wholesome covenants with our children. However, some men have too much dog residue to touch or compliment a young girl in a wholesome manner. There is too much nasty lust in their lives. They can't even compliment their daughters correctly. They try, but it comes out like, "You look so nice. Girl, you sure got some big legs for a young girl." This is inappropriate communication. Deliverance is needed, along with learning new and healthy ways of communication. They need to come back to the altar and let God stop their own funerals so they can start touching their children in godly love and speaking life over them.

God has called every man to be a man of integrity. He wants to deliver all of us from the darkness and death of the soul. When Adam fell, humanity fell. So don't say what you will or won't do. Don't point your finger at what others are doing. **All have sinned** (Romans 3:23). That's why Jesus died. Nothing can wash away our sin but the precious blood of Jesus! What can make us whole again? *Nothing but the blood.* It takes more than twelve steps. It takes more than psychotherapy. We need the blood.

I'm not against the twelve steps or psychotherapy, but we need more than these things. We need the blood of Jesus because the blood says once and for all, "This line is drawn, Sin, and you can't cross over it." The blood doesn't dance around on the fact that you've messed up. There is no claiming victimization with Jesus. The blood won't allow you to just lie there and get comfortable in excuses.

The blood says, "The funeral stops here!" Sin killed your grandfather and your father, but it won't kill you. So what if your grandmother never married your grandfather? So what if your mother never married that man? The blood says you can get married and *stay* married for a lifetime—with or without the so-called "monogamy gene." *The blood says the funeral stops here.* Everybody has a past, and your past is not as important as your future. Jesus Christ gives us a future and a hope!

Parents First

The dead boy Jesus raised needed deliverance, but so did his mother. So Jesus stopped the funeral in the mother first—just as He needs to stop the funeral in American parents today. Jesus is raising up parents. Of course, friendship with our children is important, but we are called to be parents first. And that means we have to take a hard stand sometimes.

I am, first, the father of my children, then I am their friend. The same is true in my public ministry. I am, first, the pastor of my congregation, then I am their friend. As a pastor I've got to tell the truth, the whole truth, and nothing but the truth, so help me God. And it is the same for parents.

Parents have to make tough choices. First of all, you've got to choose to *be there.* You've got to be there, Daddy! And I mean you've got to be there for *all* of your children. Maybe you've sown some wild oats and they're growing up somewhere outside of your home now. If that's so, you've still got to be there for every one of them. If you married a woman who didn't know you had five or six kids out of wedlock, you'll have to humble yourself

A generation determined to kill itself with unbridled sex needs the resurrection touch of Jesus.

and say, "Honey, I know you're upset. You're the first thing in my life, but I still have an obligation to these children. I may not be able to afford the mink coat because I have an obligation to put food on the table for these children."

"Yes, I know I'm saved today, Honey, but I was a dog yesterday. And I've got to reap what I've sown. I've got to be involved in the lives of these children so they don't die. I want them to progress toward life, not toward death. I've got to make the decision. Can you see what I mean, Honey?"

A generation determined to kill itself with unbridled sex needs the resurrection touch of Jesus.

Some of the influences on our children are national figures, professional athletes, and entertainers whose lifestyles are contrary to everything we teach. I recently heard one talk show host say that the morals of many professional athletes have proven them to be nothing more than "dogs with sneakers on." Our children plaster their walls with their superstar's posters and wear them on their shirts. Many of these men move from town to town, sleeping around, leaving fatherless children behind. We allow them to become our children's role models!

Listen! When your child is three years old and is wearing an earring because What's-his-name on his poster is wearing an earring, you need to take that thing out of his ear. He's three years old, for God's sake! I don't care how good a game this star plays. If you know he's a bad example, take those posters down and throw that T-shirt out! I'm talking about being an example as a parent first.

Get To Work!

Parenting is hard work that involves sacrifice and time. We're trying to stop the funerals by playing genie and fulfilling our children's every wish—VCRs, expensive sneakers, coats, TVs, and CDs. But when we get to heaven, God is not going to ask us for a Christmas list inventory. He's going to ask how much of Him we put into our children.

"Did you teach her how to pray?" He will ask. "Did you teach him the Bible?"

Are your children saved? Are they grasping life with Jesus in their view or are they lying symbolically in an open coffin on its way to the outskirts of Nain?

Parenting also means there are some things you shouldn't do in front of your children. Fathers, how do your children see you handling their mother? Do they see you slap her? Do they hear you cuss her and see you throwing chairs across the room? If they have, there's a funeral taking place in you.

Mothers, do you belittle your husband and tell him that he is less than worthless as a man? If you do, there's a funeral taking place in you. You will reap what you sow in the eyes of your children. If you sow disrespect, you will reap disrespect in them. If you sow love and respect, you will reap love and respect in them.

> *So he who was dead sat up and began to speak.*
> *And He presented him to his mother.*
>
> LUKE 7:15

God is raising funeral-stopping churches!

To the young Christian people of America today I say, "Arise. It's time for you to arise and walk into your destiny and the blessings of God. It doesn't matter who your parents are, you can live! Your daddy may be in jail, your momma may be a street walker, but that doesn't make a bit of difference. Arise!"

So what if your father or mother is an alcoholic? Jesus was born in the ghetto to a teenage mother. Jesus can take what others have condemned and bring you out. He loves proving wrong those who say, "You ain't gonna be nothing. Your daddy wasn't nothing. Your mamma wasn't nothing." God delights in taking those who were looked at as nothing and making them into something. Arise!

The widow of Nain's dead son sat up and began to speak because there was something in him to say. And there will be something in America's youth to say when Jesus touches them. Resurrection power and the Word of the Lord will be in them.

Speak Up, Samuel

The young boy Samuel was aroused from his sleep in the temple by a voice calling his name in the middle of the night. Samuel thought that Eli the priest was calling, so he went to him. But Eli responded, "I didn't call you. Go back to bed."

The voice came again: "Samuel, Samuel." So Samuel went to Eli again, but this time Eli told him it was probably the Lord. "The next time you hear the voice," Eli told him, "say 'Speak, Lord, Thy servant is listening.'" So Samuel went back to bed, and the third time the voice spoke, he asked the Lord to speak. (See 1 Samuel 3.)

If we'll quiet ourselves before Him, He will speak. He will speak to the dark, dry places in our lives, our homes, and our families, and give purpose and promise. The rest of Samuel's story is world and Bible history. God used Samuel to stop the spiritual funerals of His people.

"Speak, Lord, I'm listening," will be the response that stops our children's funerals. "Speak, Lord, I'm listening.

I may be young, but I'm listening! I may not have it all together, but I'm listening! Speak to me, Jesus, because I'm listening."

Angry, Hungry Youth

We live in an age of angry children. In our search for the source of this anger, many have concluded that the access to guns and violence on television, in music, and in video games plays a major part. Surely, we must be concerned about firearms' accessibility to our children, and no sane person can deny that many of them are living out the promiscuity and lawlessness they hear in music and see on television. However, access to guns alone does not make a person kill, nor do negative media examples alone produce promiscuous teenagers. I submit to you, we have to take a closer look at the family. Those who have an understanding of the times know that the destabilization of the family plays a major part in the plight of this generation, perhaps the greatest part.

In May 1998, a fifteen-year-old Springfield, Oregon, boy killed one classmate and wounded twenty-three others. One immediately wonders how he was raised, a question that cannot be answered by his parents—he killed them before going to school. Reports say the boy wanted revenge for being tossed out of school for bringing a gun to school. However, evidence also showed that his problems started long before the murders. His friends reported that he told them that it would be fun to kill someone. He also did an oral report in school on how to build a bomb. Perhaps the saddest thing of all is that although his classmates had opportunity to see the dark side of his mind, no one recognized how dark it was until it was too late.

In 1996, 93,000 juveniles were charged with violent crimes. Two thousand of them were charged with murder.

We're going to have to lobby harder for handgun control to stop the funerals literally. According to Angela Daidone, a freelance writer and communications specialist with St. Joseph's Hospital and Medical Center, Paterson, New Jersey, "Every day, 10 children in the United States are killed by handguns. That's 3,650 precious young lives lost senselessly each year. That startling number does not reflect the many more children that are shot and seriously injured. For every child killed by gunfire, hospital emergency departments treat four children for gunshot wounds."[1] According to the Children's Defense Fund "seventy-nine percent of the victims of juvenile homicide offenders were killed with a firearm." In addition, sixty-four percent of these victims were relatives or acquaintances.[2] It's all a part of the pathology and pain that confronts this generation. We need to help our angry, hungry youth. They're angry with absentee parents and hungry for the unconditional love of a mother and father.

We have to stop the funerals of America's dying, fractured, families. A fracture is a break, and we must deal

[1] Angela Daidone. "Stopping the Gunfire." The Parent Paper Community. Website. Update date: none. Access date: 16 September 1999. http://www.parentpaper.com/household/story.cfm?id=8

[2] "Issue Basics: Youth Violence—Children and Guns." Children's Defense Fund. Webpage. Update date: none. Access date: 16 September, 1999. http://www.childrensdefense.org/youthviolence/childandguns.html

with the break. Ethically and morally, we are on a downward spiral. Our youth are morally bankrupt and mentally disturbed. Therefore, we must deal with these fractures. Fathers must take their proper places. Mothers must learn to trust the Lord. Powerless religion must be recognized and rejected. We must learn to lean on Jesus, who alone gives us power to stop the funerals of this generation.

> We need to help our angry, hungry youth. They're angry with absentee parents and hungry for the unconditional love of a mother and father.

Throughout biblical history, God has been stopping funerals and healing fractures in the family. Through Elijah, God raised the widow of Zarephath's son and gave him back to her. (See 1 Kings 17.) Elijah's protégé, Elisha, brought the Shunammite's son back to life and gave him back to his mother. (See 2 Kings 4.) Then Jesus raised the widow of Nain's son and Jairus' daughter before giving them back to their parents. (See Luke 7:11-15 and Luke 8:41-42, 49-56.) In the same manner, Jesus wants to raise the children of this generation and give them back to their parents. This He wants to do and will do through us. After all, Jesus said in John 14:12, **Most assuredly, I say to you, he who believes in Me, the works that I do he will do also; and greater works than these he will do, because I go to My Father.**

We can ally ourselves with God to stop the nation's funeral of a generation determined to kill itself. Fathers, mothers, sisters, and brothers all have a responsibility in this desperate fight. If we are to wage war on death, every member of the family must proclaim to the other and the surrounding world, "Arise, and choose life!"

"I say to you, arise."

LUKE 7:14

Why'd He Have to Leave So Soon?

A friend of mine lost his chance;
He didn't get another.
He died while at some stupid dance,
Unexpected, just like his mother.

He was someone that you didn't have to know,
Just his smile could brighten your day,
He could pick you up when you were feeling low,
In his own very special way.

His life ended because of a knife,
A utensil that I now hate.
He was torn by that sword with strife—
Now I'll never see our fate.

Now we are all left to mourn.
There's nothing else we can do.
Our hearts are filled with remorse and scorn
'Cause he was so young, only twenty-two.

He was supposed to go far in life,
But drugs took him off track.
He knew the difference between wrong and right,
But he chose to go out and sell crack.

And I'm sad
'Cause I miss my brother.
I'm sad
'Cause I miss my friend.

I'm mad because of the way he died.
Why'd his life have to end so soon?

Leah Joy Alease Hilliard

■ Helpful Hints

Our central scripture offers us helpful hints to stopping funerals:

> And when the Lord saw her, he had compassion on her, and said unto her, Weep not.
>
> And he came and touched the bier: and they that bare him stood still. And he said, Young man, I say unto thee, Arise.
>
> And he that was dead sat up, and began to speak. And he delivered him to his mother.
>
> LUKE 7:13-15 KJV

We need to see. We must not continue to look over, around, through, or past those hurting around us. Our actions should mirror the actions of Jesus as found here with this widow. We need to look directly at them and acknowledge their humanity, their hurting, and their need for help.

We need to feel. When we look at the wounded, we should not be filled with arrogance, disgust, or fear. We should feel and be filled with compassion. Considering this woman's present predicament and the future that awaited her, Jesus could only feel compassion for her. We should groan in our innermost beings when we consider the present situation and the future that awaits those who are outside of the ark of safety.

We need to touch. We need to touch the unclean without concern of being made unclean. When we touch the unclean, the dying, and the dead in the name of the Lord, we do not become unclean or begin to die. Rather, the touch of Jesus Christ cleanses and imparts life.

We need to speak. Often we are faced with forces that are stronger than we are. We must never forget the power that is in the name of Jesus. The name of Jesus has power over the living and the dead. No matter how strange or foolish it may seem, sometimes we need to shelve our pride and speak out loud to those things that have died and command them to rise in the name of Jesus.

We need to reunite. Once we have been the agents through which the dead are brought to life, we need to reunite that which was previously dead with that which awaited its resurrection. While living among the tombs of this life, many have caused intense pain and heartbreak to family members. Now that they have been delivered, we need to reunite them with the behind-the-scenes intercessors they thought would never speak to them again. When Jesus raises the children from the dead or calls the prodigal sons and daughters to their senses, we must return them to the families and communities who need to see what the power of Jesus Christ can do.

two

Life After Death

I am He that liveth, and was dead, and behold, I am alive forevermore, Amen; and have the keys of hell and of death.

REVELATION 1:18 KJV

We have become so used to the processions that accompany the burying of our children in America's cities today that we have grown numb to them. They have become the norm to us. However, today we aren't only dealing with the physical death of our children, we're also dealing with the death of hope. The death of possibility and promise is a disturbing reality. We hear this sound in much of today's music. The theme is seen in today's movies. Gone are the lofty themes where they lived happily ever after.

Enough Is Enough

For many people the concept of life is so foreign that a miraculous touch from Jesus is all that will wake them up. The widow of Nain in Luke 7 found herself in this condition. She was devastated by the deaths of her husband and son. So when the Lord saw her, He said "ENOUGH!" This is what this book is all about— ENOUGH!

The mourners in the funeral procession were holding hands and rubbing one another on the head as they offered condolences. Then Jesus crossed their path and said, "You don't need another sympathizer right now.

You have enough mourners, dear woman. There are enough folks falling out. No, what you need is compassion." And suddenly there was life after death.

Jesus is the only one who can give life after death. The foundation of our Christian faith rests upon this truth. Paul writes

> that Christ died for our sins according to the Scriptures,
> and that He was buried, and that He rose again the third day according to the Scriptures.
>
> 1 CORINTHIANS 15:3-4

Jesus announced Himself to His good friend Martha as **the resurrection and the life** before He raised Martha's brother out of four days of death. (See John 11:25.) The daughter of the synagogue ruler Jairus lay dead on her bed until Jesus said, **"Talitha, cumi," which is translated, "Little girl, I say to you, arise"** (Mark 5:41). Tabitha was a corpse until Peter knelt in prayer and said, **"Tabitha arise."** (See Acts 9:40.) The mothers in Shunam and Zarepath received their dead sons back to life by the hands of two different men of God. (See 1 Kings 17; 2 Kings 4.) And Paul called on the power of God to raise a young man who fell out of a window during an all-night meeting. (See Acts 20:9-10.) Jesus can bring life out of death.

Not long ago, *Time* magazine's featured article was, "Does Heaven Exist?"[3] and *U.S. News and World Report* published, "Is There Life After Death?"[4] These articles covered the lives of various people who had died temporarily and found themselves floating away into a tunnel that was filled with light. When these people died, most of them discovered another experience awaiting them in an afterlife.

However, you don't need a near-death experience to know there is life after death. The Bible teaches the spiritual realities of eternal life. It teaches that all men are dead in sin until salvation gives them life and that Jesus was raised from the dead to give those who receive Him new life. It also teaches about a coming resurrection to a higher plane of life. As Jesus is today, someday the Church will be—resurrected and immortal.

■ Death Is Only a Comma

As we discovered in the last chapter, Jesus wants to stop the funerals of our children's physical and spiritual destiny. He who lives and was dead and behold is alive forevermore wants to visit their desperate lives. (See Revelation 1:18.) Jesus described Himself in that way to the apostle John when he was imprisoned on the isle of Patmos.

At this time in his life, John certainly needed the Lord's touch. He had been condemned by the Roman authorities to live out his life in seclusion. His crime was

[3]Richard N. Ostling, Elisabeth Kauffman, Victoria Rainert, Greg Burke, and S. C. Gwynne. "Does Heaven Exist?" *Time.* Online. 149:12 (24 March 1997), (n.p.).
http://pathfinder.com/time/magazine/1997/int/970331/religion_but_american.html

[4]Joshua Rich. "Is There Life After Death?" *U. S. News & World Report.* Online. 31 March 1997.
http://www.usnews.com/usnews/issue/970331/31near.htm

spreading the Gospel. So the Roman government meant to keep John desperate and alone on this prison island. They meant to keep John spiritually and emotionally dead. But Jesus had other plans. Jesus visited Patmos to keep John's ministry alive and useful to the end. It was on Patmos that John received his Revelation of humankind's victorious Christian end! And it all began with Jesus' touch:

> *And when I saw Him, I fell at His feet as dead. But He laid His right hand on me, saying to me, "Do not be afraid; I am the First and the Last.*
> *"I am He who lives, and was dead, and behold, I am alive forevermore. Amen. And I have the keys of Hades and of Death."*
>
> REVELATION 1:17-18

When John saw Jesus, he fell at His feet as though dead. Then he looked around to see a fiery figure standing in front of him. I believe he recognized the voice and face of the one he saw die on Golgatha. But now Jesus was glorified. He had gone through the temporary prison of death and was now telling John, **"I am He who lives, and was dead."**

As far as Rome was concerned, their government had carried out the funeral for John's ministry. But Jesus moved into John's life and said, "John, I died and stayed dead for three days. But now I'm on the other side of death. I rose on the third day, and I am alive forevermore." Having experienced a type of death through exile, John needed to see that Jesus was **alive forevermore**.

When John saw the resurrected Jesus, He had a golden sash across His chest. This revealed He was the high priest who goes into the presence of God to atone for your sins and mine. (See Revelation 1:13.) His white hair represented wisdom and divine nature, and His flaming eyes symbolized the judgment of all evil. (See v. 14.)

> Jesus has conquered the power of death, but there are many Christians who fear it. . . . When you have Jesus in your life, you don't have to fear death.

After Jesus touched John, He spoke:

"Do not be afraid; I am the First and the Last. I am He who lives, and was dead, and behold, I am alive forevermore. Amen. And I have the keys of Hades and of Death."

REVELATION 1:17-18 (emphasis mine)

Jesus has conquered the power of death, but there are many Christians who fear it. They're afraid to go to cemeteries and funeral parlors. When you have Jesus in your life, you don't have to fear death. Right now, He is standing in eternity on the other side of death and saying, "Been there, done that, Child. There is no reason to fear death. I beat it for you."

Death is not a period. Death is a comma. It is only a transition between this life and the life to come.

■ John Gets a Life

Jesus moved into John's life on Patmos, touched his ministry's coffin, and gave him the New Testament's only prophetic book. Have you ever been so isolated that you wondered if you would ever come out? Jesus stepped into John's isolation on this remote island, and He can step into your isolation.

Jesus can resurrect you from your sadness. He can resurrect you from your pain. He can resurrect you from your hang-ups because He is God. Jesus is the omnipotent, God Almighty, who spoke into existence everything we can see. The resurrection power of Jesus established the Church. Remember? The disciples thought it was over until Jesus walked into the room where they were hiding, hopeless, and in fear. (See John 20:19.) Today we need a resurrection just like theirs.

Jesus wants to resurrect America's inner cities today the same way He resurrected John's situation. There is life for America's cities, who are filling their morgues with the dead. There is life for America's families, who are fractured and dead on the vine. There is life after the death of a dream, which Satan's cruel work has tried to bury. There is life. There is life after death—and only Jesus can bring it.

The crack and the heroin epidemics that plague America are signs that we have become an isolated, materialistic, and self-centered people. We are high tech but low touch. America needs a resurrection in Jesus' name! Love needs to be resurrected in Jesus' name! Caring needs to be resurrected in Jesus' name! Good manners need to be res-urrected in Jesus' name! Hope needs to be resurrected in Jesus' name!

We are currently raising the first generation in our nation that has no hope for tomorrow. In many cities and towns across America, instead of our children preparing for lifetime careers, they're preparing for their funerals. They're talking about the day on which they will die. They want to die young so they can die pretty. They aren't expecting to live; for them hope and promise are dead.

Jesus, Resurrect Our Communities!

Girl X, as they called her, was a resident of the Cabrini Green projects in Chicago where she was beaten, molested, and left for dead. Where was the community when this young girl was being beaten? Where was the community during those days that she lay dying in the stall of the projects? They were somewhere, but not there. The African proverb that states, "It takes a village to raise a child," is a relevant message. Jesus desires to resurrect community concern.

Jesus wants to step into our American situation, per-sonally, through the community of His people. The late Rev. Dr. Martin Luther King Jr. said, "We must all learn to live together as brothers, or we will all perish together as fools," and we've been perishing as fools. We need sit-uational, societal, and cultural resurrection. I'm talking now to the Hassans, the W.C.s, the Theresas, and the Darnels of our church congregations. I'm also talking to you, Mother; to you Father; to you, Son; and to you, Daughter.

We need a cultural resurrection! We need to be lifted on every level, in Jesus' name, because as a people we're losing ground. As a people, we are sinking when we should be rising. Don't be fooled by the few of us who are doing relatively well. Don't even be fooled by the few of us who hold membership in the Church. If the truth be told, we've been teaching one message in the Church and living another in the home.

We need cultural resurrection! The death of popular rappers Tupac Shakur and Biggie Smalls points to a larger problem. The hip-hop artist Little Kim, with songs like "Queen B," points to a larger problem. These messengers of violence and loose morals add to the degradation of our culture and set negative examples for our children with their lifestyles and words, and we need to be resurrected. The Bible says that if you live by the sword—if you preach and talk about the sword—you shall perish by the sword. (See Matthew 26:52.) Far too many of us are the walking dead. We're breathing and talking, but dead in the mind and soul! We need to be resurrected!

Parents need to be resurrected to an understanding of what it means to be a parent. We need a resurrection of God's wisdom in training up our children so that when they grow older, they won't depart from God. Saying grace over meals, training young ones to stand up when old folk walk into the room, men tipping their hats when a lady is present—these simple honors need to be resurrected. An old saint once told me, "Honey, good manners can take you where money can't." It's still true today. Parents need a resurrection of what it means to train up their children!

There are a whole lot of folk in our communities today who are raising terrorists in their homes. That's right, terrorists, children who have lost respect for authority; and, in many cases, they are calling the shots. Sadly, the teachers at school are afraid to discipline the children. I hear their parents say, "Can't nobody touch my child. The teacher better not say nothing to Benji." But what they are really saying is that they're scared of that little terrorist they're raising in their home.

Any time a child raises a hand to his mother or has enough nerve to cuss or speak disrespectfully in any way, that child is a fool. A fool is someone who has no regard for authority and no reverence for God. A fool is his or her own little terrorist god. And the Bible says that the only way to deal with a foolish little terrorist is with the rod:

> *Foolishness is bound up in the heart of a child;*
> *The rod of correction will drive it far from him.*
> PROVERBS 22:15

If you don't sting their backsides a few times with the rod, the police will—and worse. And the police won't do it because they love your children. The police will do it just to get them off the streets.

After you use the rod, when you see their heart has become soft again, then you need to give them chapter and verse and tell them you love them. Tell them how they were acting the fool and that you won't let them grow up to be a fool. The Bible says that the fool walks in darkness (Ecclesiastes 2:14). Those who walk in darkness have no clue. They are constantly falling down, hurting others, and disgracing—even killing—themselves.

> We need Jesus to show up on the prison islands of our poverty and show us how and where to work. God wants us to stand up in Jesus' name and stop begging for everybody to bail us out of our problems.

Not only does Jesus want to resurrect the way we train our children, He wants us to grow up in how we treat our neighbors. Do we treat each other with justice and mercy? Are we honoring God? God is calling for a consistent Christian lifestyle of honesty and integrity.

Jesus wants to raise our economic situation. We need Jesus to show up on the prison islands of our poverty and show us how and where to work. God wants us to stand up in Jesus' name and stop begging for everybody to bail us out of our problems. We need to stop blaming others for what we don't have. Aren't you tired of hanging around shortsighted folk who have no vision? I am. The God I serve is more than able! He is risen and wants to touch our economic lives!

The Jesus Touch

John wasn't sure why Jesus visited him on Patmos that Sunday. He recognized and heard Jesus, but he needed to be assured that Jesus was still his loving Savior. So Jesus put His hand on John to assure him of His care. (See Revelation 1:17.) Indeed, that's what Jesus wants to do for every mother and father today. The Lord wants to put His hand on you, Mother. He wants to put His hand on you, Father. Jesus puts His hand on the shoulder of everyone who seeks Him. He will put His hand on you; and when you feel like you're falling, He will help you stand.

The touch of Jesus elevates our way of living. When we have been touched by Jesus, our focus, our aim, and our desires change so that they reflect life and not death. Paul instructed the church at Colosse:

> *If then you were raised with Christ, seek those things which are above, where Christ is, sitting at the right hand of God.*
>
> COLOSSIANS 3:1

In other words, if we are truly raised with Jesus Christ, we ought to walk like it. If we are raised with Him, we ought to talk like it. Our hearts should have no desire to stay where doubts arise and fears dismay. Our aim should be higher ground! Our goal should be Jesus Christ above.

There is a higher plane I have found for my feet. There is a higher plane for America. There is a plane where God reveals what He has done for us through the cross and His plan for our lives. There is another level! There is more than what we can naturally see. But it is there to be seen all the same, through faith in Jesus' name.

There is life after death, Jesus proved it! And He wants to prove it in America today. Jesus has more to offer! Indeed, He has come that we might have abundant life. You can rise up from welfare. You can rise up from ghetto living. There's more to life than that sad excuse for what you call a job. God has more for you! But you have to start believing it.

> So then faith comes by hearing, and hearing by the word of God.
>
> ROMANS 10:17

As an African-American, it pains me to see the disproportionate amount of death and devastation in our communities. The African-American community needs a resurrected understanding of our current culture and ourselves. This is why we don't support each other's businesses. This is why we don't love anything that looks like us. God knows I don't want to get into this; but, the truth is, many African-Americans don't love anything that looks like them.

Several hundred years of slavery have destroyed our sense of self-esteem. Our families were purposely ripped apart and opportunities denied us. It has been said that "when White America gets a cold, the African-American community gets pneumonia." Resurrection of self-reliance, focus, and empowerment are desperately needed for a community in crisis. Coming out of slavery, this community of disenfranchised people built schools and established societies and businesses. While we in contemporary society have much more economically and educationally than our forebears, we have done much less than they in stabilizing our communities. The Church played a critical role in our sanity, solace, and structure. I have very little hope for our communities without direct intervention, guidance, and direction from our churches. Only through the touch of Jesus Christ is there hope for torn-down communities.

Remember, those who carried the coffin of the widow's son in Luke stood still as Jesus touched the dead. In the same way, our communities will stand still when we choose to touch the hopeless and the dead. Parents and churches are going to have to be willing to touch the dead if former dope dealers, gang bangers, murderers, and adulterers are ever going to fill our church pews. We must be willing to say, "What the devil said was going to die is going to live. You're going to live and come out of the graveyard into the abundant life that Jesus gives."

I often invite my church members to honor the goodness of God by remembering

> I have very little hope for our communities without direct intervention, guidance, and direction from our churches. Only through the touch of Jesus Christ is there hope for torn-down communities.

who they used to hang out with. Then I ask them to think of how many of their former friends are either in cemeteries, insane asylums, or on death row. There are many who know people who still have hypodermic needles in their arms and carry bottles of liquor wrapped in brown paper bags. They can give thanks to God that Jesus touched them and raised them from the dead. Someone was willing to cross the path of their funeral in prayer and action in Jesus' name. If we're going to raise a fearless generation, we must first touch that which is dead, that which stinks, that which is ugly.

Death is not only found among the poor. Death is everywhere. There are a whole lot of folk making six-figure salaries living in custom-made homes up in the hills, but they're lost. They may look like they've made it. They're rich, educated, and well-meaning. But they're lost. They're just lost in nice suburban homes with brand-new cars and nice jobs. They just live in finer graveyards.

Rich folks may *look* real good, but when you get in with them behind that shiny face, car, and home, they're just as depressed as the poor man down the alley with a needle in his arm. They wear fancy wigs on their head, but they're dead. They have $500 shoes on their feet, but they're dead. Their fingers are covered with $10,000 rings, but they're dead. They hold honorable positions in all the right fraternities and sororities, but they're dead. Some of them are even standing up in church and are preaching the Gospel, but *they are dead*. The rich, the poor, the black, the white, the red, and the yellow—all need the touch of Jesus.

Dead is dead, no matter who you are or where you live, and Jesus wants to stop the funeral! He wants to get into our graveyards to save us, fill us with His Holy Spirit, and continually lead us along His path.

We the People

Jesus wants to resurrect our concept of who we are as a people! The psalmist says we are fearfully and wonderfully made, but we've lost sight of our marvelous value and are seeing ourselves as some movie aberration. (See Psalm 139:14.) We can't find time or money to go to fine historical or positive movies like *Rosewood*, *Get on the Bus*, or *The Preacher's Wife*. However, if Hollywood slaps together a movie like *Booty Call*, where the brothers are running after "some tail" and the black folk are made to look like fools in every negative and nasty stereotype that has ever depicted us, we'll line up around the block to see it. We need to be resurrected!

Do we always have to be laughed at? Do we always have to live up to every negative stereotype about us? Jesus says, NO! He wants to step into our situation. Jesus wants to stop the funeral procession we have been trudging in as a people since America's moral values took a nosedive in the 1960s. Jesus wants to step into our culture and resurrect us from where we are to where we ought to be! And He will—when we ask Him! He will do it because He died to do it! He will do it because He is the Savior of the world. Regardless of the darkness and decay around us, Jesus is still the light of the world.

Jesus Christ is the Savior of those living in godless confusion and reaping its rotten fruit of death. He experienced death to give us abundant life, and today He is alive!

"I am He who lives, and was dead, and behold, I am alive forevermore. Amen. And I have the keys of Hades and of Death."

REVELATION 1:18

Today Jesus is saying, "I am alive enough to step into your circumstances. I'm alive enough to step into your pain. I'm alive and I want to step into your victimization. As I did for the widow in Nain, I want to do for you. I want to stop your weeping and speak to your heartbreak. I want to resurrect your shattered dreams. I want to restore your messed up marriage. There is life after death because I am alive!"

Admit It, Quit It, and Forget It

It's time that we started living like Jesus is alive. It's time to stop our own funerals. Have you made a mess of your life? Jesus came to give you abundant life, and part of that abundance is abundant forgiveness. There is life after your mistakes! Far too many of us are walking around today in guilt and shame. If this is you, you must understand what Jesus is saying: "There is life after your sin!" There is life after your rage and anger! There is life after your extra-marital sexual rendezvous! There is life after your mess-up!

> It's time to rise out of your coffins and leave the funeral march. Resurrection comes to those who are touched by Jesus.

It's time to rise out of your coffins and leave the funeral march. Resurrection comes to those who are touched by Jesus. To start the process, admit it. You aren't the first, and you won't be the last to do whatever you may have done. While the devil would have you believe that your sin has caused God to forsake you, God says through Isaiah,

> *"But on this one will I look: on him who is poor and of a contrite spirit, and who trembles at My word."*
>
> ISAIAH 66:2

The Lord is near to those who have a broken spirit, so there is life after the death of your broken home. There is life after your victimization. There is life after a dead-end job. There is life after your dead relationship, and there is life after your dead dream. There is fresh new life for all willing to receive it. There is life for the drug addicted. There is life for the drug dealer, for the hit man, for the gangster, for the prostitute, for the sugar daddy, for the educated, for the fool, for the financially well off, and for the spiritually bankrupt. There is life after death for you and for me.

So wherever you are reading this now, my brother or my sister, please understand, there is life after death. As I work within the African-American community, I can look around and see positive proof through the lives of so many that Jesus is alive in American cities. So many of us present positive proof that no one has to stay in the grave. Jesus touched and spoke to our lives, and we are here to be counted. But our nation as a whole must hear, and it is up to us to make them listen!

Today in many of our communities, it may look like Good Friday, when Jesus hung dead on the cross. Good Friday, with all of its pain; Good Friday, with all of its shame; Good Friday, with all of its ugliness, isolation, gloom, and darkness. But Sunday is on the way! One of my college professors, Dr. Anthony Campolo, Eastern College of St. Davids, Pennsylvania, would often make reference to a sermon he heard his pastor preach. His pastor was an elderly African-American Baptist, unlettered, but not unlearned. He would mount the pulpit, gaze into the eyes of his waiting congregation and say, "I know life has not been easy for you. I know you're hurting. It's Good Friday now, but Sunday's coming!" This I truly believe! Hope always carries us through the pain of Good Friday to the glory, peace, and joy of Easter Sunday.

I am he that liveth, and was dead; and, behold, I am alive for evermore, Amen; and have the keys of hell and of death.

REVELATIONS 1:18 KJV

Helpful Hints

Time and eternity are in God's hand; nothing is lost forever.

The Holy Spirit inspired John to include in his gospel the resurrection of Lazarus to teach us that when Jesus comes late, He is still on time. Also, even when relationships, circumstances, and situations are dead and buried, Jesus is able to resurrect them. So often because of our relationship with the One who is the Resurrection and the Life, what appears to be a period in our lives is really only a comma.

Jesus resurrects communities.

While social reform and community outreach programs help to bring stability to our communities, only Jesus can bring resurrection. Until the presence and power of Jesus touch our community leaders and residents, our communities can never be what God has called them to be.

Resurrection: one by one and all together.

When God wanted to turn the world upside down, He did not simply change the world. Each disciple had to make a personal and individual decision to follow Jesus and to be used by Him. As we make individual decisions to follow Jesus, He will resurrect us. He then will resurrect our homes. It is only then that He can and will resurrect our communities and our world.

Admit it, Quit it, Forget it.

Personal resurrection begins with admitting our sinful nature and our inadequacy to do anything about it.

By trusting in the person and power of the resurrected Christ, we must strive to quit behavior that does not glorify Him. Lastly, inasmuch as the old places, people, and things hold us to a past filled with spiritual, physical, economic, and emotional death, we must forget them. It is through admitting, quitting, and forgetting that God is able to bring us into a new life that is filled with resurrection power.

The Devil's Honoree

Single Black female
Really puts up a fight,
Between doing wrong, and doing right.
Sometimes doing what's wrong can get you into lots
   of trouble,
Like it did this woman that I knew.

Thought she was all that.
Could get any guy she wanted, and let's keep it real,
   some girls wanted her too,
Often being offered "Can I buy you a CD, a pair of
   Enzo shoes?"
Tempted though she was,
She did not yield at first.

Now I'm watching her life go by quickly, like she's
   been cursed.
After getting tired of not yielding to temptation,
A sugar daddy arrived.
He could put a smile on the face of a vampire,
And whenever he came around she felt like she was
   on fire.

He got her so hot and excited
She didn't see that she was being invited
To the devil's party.
She was the honoree.
The honoree on her way to hell.

In style, so she thought.
Only because she was constantly being bought.
Bought by shoes, clothes, you name it.
Everything that her heart ever desired, she could
   claim it.

For he would do anything to keep her as his honoree,
His escort to hell.

Awhile back, she sat in the corner of her room, talk-
ing to walls,
Plates and silverware like spoons.
She talked to them as if to another person.
What she didn't realize was that he messed her up
With his ways of perversion that seemed so sweet.
She was found somewhere in the street.
In the street, possibly an alley, I don't know for sure,
I was told that she almost got arrested for trying to
steal candy from a store.
For what, you may ask? She has everything she ever
wanted.

Everything we thought,
But this sugar daddy only flaunted
His outer colors,
So no one could see what his plans to destroy her
might be.

This isn't the end of my not-real-to-my-knowledge-
but-true-to-life tale,
Because I know that she's alive and well
Somewhere,
In her right mind,
Going in the right direction.

Jesus is our only hope. Young people, please use
much discretion.
Carefully choose who you affiliate yourself with.
Don't end up like this woman did, getting whipped.
Thank God she got better;
Many of them don't.

With God there is hope;
Just don't test Him.
Know your limits;
Make boundaries.
Don't cross them; for when you go through,
You don't go through with ease.

And your possibilities for coming out without Him
are slim.

—Leah Joy Alease Hilliard

three

Looking for Love in All the Wrong Places

*Now on the first day of the week, very early in the
morning, they, and certain other women with them,
came to the tomb bringing the spices which they had
prepared.*

LUKE 24:1

We have put spiritual stumbling blocks in the way
of finding Jesus. Too many in their grief, like Mary
Magdalene, have been looking for Jesus among the dead;
but when those who seek find Him, He will resurrect whatever they bring to Him. We need to believe in the resurrection instead of dwelling among the tombstones.

Mary was one of the few followers of Jesus who was
bold enough to stand near Jesus as He hung on the cross.
Jesus' mother and aunt, John, Mary the wife of Clopas,
and the mother of James and John were at the crucifixion. The rest of Jesus' closest followers all fled in fear to
hide from the Jews. Why? Because they thought their
cause had been lost. Jesus wasn't supposed to die
between two criminals. He was supposed to conquer the
Romans. And when He died, they concluded all was lost!
None of them believed Jesus would rise from the dead.

Mary had heard Jesus' promise of rising from the
dead. At the foot of the cross she witnessed the pitch
darkness that visited the earth between the hours of 9 A.M.
and noon. She felt the earthquake that the gospel of

Matthew says split rocks when Jesus gave up His Spirit. And she also saw the soldiers take Jesus' broken, bleeding body down once He was dead.

Jesus' body was buried in a borrowed tomb; and, after His execution, the sisterhood came to the graveyard hoping to recapture His love.

> Now on the first day of the week, very early in the morning, they [the women who followed Jesus closely] and certain other women with them, came to the tomb bringing the spices which they had prepared.
> But they found the stone rolled away from the tomb.
> Then they went in and did not find the body of the Lord Jesus.
>
> LUKE 24:1-3

I can see these women as they enter the gates of the graveyard with the spices they had prepared. Their eyes are still welled with tears. They are full of despair, and they are depressed. God wants to take us from graveyard experiences into a new and resurrected life in Him. He wants to resurrect joy from sorrow, peace from confusion, and life from death.

> Then they went in and did not find the body of the Lord Jesus.
> And it happened, as they were greatly perplexed about this, that behold, two men stood by them in shining garments.

Then, as they were afraid and bowed their faces to the earth, they said to them, "Why do you seek the living among the dead?

"He is not here, but is risen! Remember how He spoke to you when He was still in Galilee,

"saying, 'The Son of Man must be delivered into the hands of sinful men, and be crucified, and the third day rise again.'"

And they remembered His words.

LUKE 24:3-8

Mary and her companions were looking for the love of Jesus in the wrong place. They were in the wrong place because Jesus wasn't dead. The disciples really didn't believe that Jesus was going to be raised on the third day, so why should these women? They didn't.

"Now I can show you some of his ancestors," one of the angels could have said. "Or I can show you the remains of His cousin, John the Baptist, who lost his head. They're dead and they're buried. But if you're looking for Him who is alive forevermore, you're in the wrong place. He left here early this morning."

Then the angels reminded them: "Don't you remember that Jesus said on the third day He would rise from the dead? Maybe, sisters, you don't know what time it is?"

Perhaps they were so preoccupied with their own agendas and were so perplexed by their own pain that they forgot what time it really was. The sisterhood was in the graveyard looking for Jesus' love in the wrong place. And the Church today is not unlike them. Like our early

Christian ancestors, we're also looking for love in the wrong places. Like them, we aren't expecting Jesus to do what He said He would do.

Walking the Talk

We talk a good talk in the Church today. We talk about God making a way out of no way; that is, until we ourselves need a way made. We talk about God being a healer; that is, until we need healing. We talk about heaven, while we fear and run from death. We say God can do anything; that is, until we need Him to do something for us that seems impossible. Like our spiritual ancestors, we are walking around in a graveyard of dead religion that keeps Jesus dead and in the tomb—especially when we need Him.

When we don't allow Jesus to be our All-in-All, we find ourselves looking for love in different graveyards. And we always come up short. I've seen women and men in dead-end love affairs and common-law marriages, connected, but not in covenant.

The church of our culture of death fills buildings with religious people who never really come to know God. We're full of religion but we don't know the difference between Jesus and Mohammed. We're in a building, but we're not in Christ. Oh, we know the church protocol: what to wear and when to sit, stand, and shout. But we don't know the GOD of the Church. Some who were raised by godly parents can only hold to what their saintly mothers and fathers told them about God. In all honesty, they never pressed in to really know God and church is only a graveyard to visit week after week.

Looking for Love in Godless Marriages

Some men and women are looking for Prince or Princess Charming when they get married. They look for a fairy godmother match in a flawless man or woman. And the moment their perfect match fails the test, it's over. Within each person is a void that only God can fill; and until you allow yourself to experience and thus begin to understand the irreplaceable love of God, the person you claim to love will never be enough. As soon as they come up to a certain set standard, you'll raise the bar because you don't love yourself. While singing, "I'm not your super woman," you are looking for superman. Yes! You are only human, and any man expecting to emotionally dog you and expect for you to just take it needs serious counseling. If you're not married to him, it's time for him to rise to responsibility or

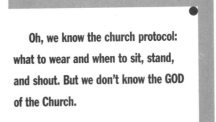

Oh, we know the church protocol: what to wear and when to sit, stand, and shout. But we don't know the GOD of the Church.

to receive his walking papers. If you're married, you shouldn't expect a superman—roses on Monday, dinner on Tuesday, a poem on Wednesday, candy on Thursday, a movie on Friday, bowling on Saturday, and church on Sunday. Some women want the world. Yet, while their husbands are out trying to earn enough money to buy it, they complain about the lack of time he spends with the family or the lack of energy he has at night. Then some men expect their wives to work full-time jobs, take care of the children, and do all of the housework. It's no wonder the passion has left the marriage. It's no wonder she barely has enough energy to turn off the light. You will never find a truly satisfying, perfected love in a husband or a wife because we are all flawed. It takes God's unconditional love and strength to make that marriage live and work.

Looking for Love in Sex

There are many graveyard folk who have been enslaved to the culture's quest for fulfillment in sex. They go from bar to bar, but they make sure they're in some religious graveyard on Sunday morning. They go from bedroom to bedroom because of an insatiable sexual appetite that is tied to a poor sense of somebodiness. There is only heartache and temporary gratification to be found in the graveyard of casual sex. Many of the diseases confronting us are the result of lifestyles of casual sex. This is no place to look for love. Still, many do it.

Those who prowl around to satisfy sexual appetite suffer from a lack of true identity. Knowledge of self begins with the knowledge of God. You cannot love anyone else fully until you first love yourself. And you can't truly love yourself until you find the love of God. Some ladies settle for trash because they feel like trash. When you feel like trash, you'll let a brother treat you like trash. I'm very disturbed to hear some of our hip-hop songs demean young women. They refer to women in highly unflattering and insulting ways. Sister, you will never be treated any better than you demand to be treated.

At the same time, every so often, good brothers who love God will ask, "What's up with these women today? I was dating this woman, and I treated her right. I opened doors, bought her gifts, took her out, and she left me for a drug dealer who disrespects her and cheats on her." As crazy as it seems, many of these women don't feel they deserve a good man. Years later some of them will tell you, "I left because you were too good for me." They never really come to know God and His love for them, so they don't love themselves.

When a decent brother sees in a woman what God sees but what they don't see in themselves, they are frightened and confused and they run. There are many well-intentioned, God fearing, hard working, clean men out there. However, there are also those men who will treat you like a dog if you let them. And sister, if you allow it, they'll take advantage of you every time. Some uncaring men make their wives work so hard that they wear them out. Then, after fifteen or twenty years of marriage, they start sniffing around for something young and fresh because their wives allow themselves to be treated like mules. Woman, you are better than that! We all desire love and affection. Love, however, is patient, kind, and gentle.

Sometimes love must be tough, do you hear me? Sometimes love has got to say, "Because I love God and because I love myself, I can't stay in this kind of abuse." Because Jesus is risen, He provides ways out of abusive relationships. Sadly, the abused and abuser are often carbon copies of models they have seen as children. Without divine intervention, the model continues from one generation to the next.

Two Kinds of Suffering

Dr. Becker, a professor I had at Princeton Theological Seminary, talked about two kinds of suffering: needless suffering and meaningful suffering. When we insist on doing things our way without involving the will and the way of God, we often end up in a mess. That is needless suffering! Meaningful suffering, on the other hand, ultimately lifts you to another level of self-awareness and resurrection.

> **Sometimes love has got to say, "Because I love God and because I love myself, I can't stay in this kind of abuse."**

Meaningful suffering will work for your good. If telling the wrong man or woman who doesn't have a clue who Jesus is to scamper off brings a little persecution your way, that's all right. Suffer a bit for right, and God will take care of you. God will lead you in paths of righteousness for His name's sake, and He will comfort you with goodness and mercy when you're right!

Sometimes goodness and mercy will follow you into the club and tell you to get out. Sometimes goodness and mercy will follow you into the tavern and tell you to put down the drink and walk out. Sometimes goodness and mercy will follow you into a bed of adultery and tell you to get out before you hit the sheets. Truly, it is better late than never. And if meaningful suffering takes place because of it, you will have life.

Too many of us have become satisfied with mediocrity, jumping into bed with every dog on the block. Far too many of us allow loneliness to decide our partners. We settle for mediocrity. We settle for short-term and often dead-end relationships. You were not created to be a one-night stand! So I ask, Girl, if he's your baby, and you're his baby tonight, what about tomorrow morning? In this troubled culture, so many have become satisfied with short-term solutions for long-term problems. So they spend their lives in "a tale told by an idiot, full of sound and fury, signifying nothing" (William Shakespeare, *MacBeth*, Act V, Scene 5). When they come to the end of their journey, very few of them can say their lives amounted to anything, because they spent their lives seeking love and acceptance in all the wrong places.

We seek acceptance on the job and in the lives of our friends. We want to be accepted in the church without really understanding that God loves us right now, where we are and who we are. We need to be looking for real love. Jesus is no longer in the graveyard, so quit looking there.

You can see right through those who are living in a graveyard. I've pastored for a number of years, and I can spot the pew-sitting dead. You can see the funeral in their eyes. You can see the pain in the eyes of women who at one time were beautiful and men who were hopeful. You can see the pain of heartbreak in those who gave their Prince Charming and Cinderella the best years of their lives. Some lived with their first prince for five years before they got involved with another for seven, and on and on it went. Before they knew it, they were forty years old, and nobody wanted them because they were considered used merchandise.

Stop the Funeral in the Church!

I'll never forget the testimony of one preacher who passed on some time ago. He had been delivered from a lifestyle of sin early in life; but, before being delivered, he had already contracted the AIDS virus. Where did he catch it? He got it in the choir, in the church. We should not be moved by titles or position. Because a man's or woman's name is Preacher this, Reverend that, Deacon this, or Elder whatever does not mean that they have character and integrity. How does he live outside of the spotlight? What is she like when the crowds aren't around? Don Basham, in his book *Lead Us Not Into Temptation*, addresses how easily the people of God can become so intoxicated by the signs and wonders that they never look beneath the surface. There always have been and always will be leaders with big names and powerful gifts who become involved in all types of sin. Some are weak, and others are wicked. An unchecked, unbridled weakness can lead to wickedness. They need our prayers, but they do not need our worship.

Jesus stops the funeral in leaders too. He touches that which is dead and says, "Get up and quit dragging my name through the mud." When you're living in a graveyard, the stench of sin will follow you. But many of us still choose to live there. Some can't make it to church on Sunday mornings because they were clubbing at the Tombstone Inn on Saturday night. The Maybelline and Fashion Fair we try to wrap ourselves in can't hide our pain; neither can our daily workouts at the health club. When we take off our designer clothes and stand before a mirror, there we are,

> When you're living in a graveyard, the stench of sin will follow you. But many of us still choose to live there.

naked and dead! If we were to ask ourselves, "What have I done today that will help somebody?" we would have to answer: "Nothing, because I can't even help myself. I'm living in the graveyard."

Graveyard Kids

Of course, because so many are living in the graveyard, our kids are forced to live there too. Kids today think they're grown when they reach the age of ten. It's difficult trying to tell them everybody isn't going to be their friend when they desire to be accepted by the cool. Too often they have to make a decision to be popular or to be smart. Wrong decisions, bad relationships, and poor upbringing have far too many in the grave. Many are in jail. You can see others on some corner with no teeth and bloodshot eyes. Dead folk continue to worship at the altars of liquor, violence, and drugs built on a foundation of childhood aimlessness.

These children needed a relationship with the King of Kings, but they've got a bedroom in the graveyard; and

death produces death. They needed a life-giving relationship with the Lord of Lords, but what they got was
dead religion. Sadly, some of their parents drag them
weekly to churches where there is no relevant ministry
that speaks to the loneliness of their lives.

Jesus Doesn't Live in Tombs

You can't find love in dead-end religion either. You
need a living faith and relationship with the risen Christ
who was raised and moved on from the graveyard.
Matthew 27:51-53 tells us the power of His resurrection
was so great that many of the dead saints entombed
around Jerusalem were also raised when Jesus was raised
from the dead.

> *Then, behold, the veil of the temple was torn in*
> *two from top to bottom; and the earth quaked, and*
> *the rocks were split,*
> *and the graves were opened; and many bodies of*
> *the saints who had fallen asleep were raised;*
> *and coming out of the graves after His resurrection,*
> *they went into the holy city and appeared to many.*
>
> MATTHEW 27:51-53

We need a living relationship like Mary discovered
when Jesus appeared to her in the garden:

> *But Mary stood outside by the tomb weeping, and*
> *as she wept she stooped down and looked into the tomb.*

And she saw two angels in white sitting, one at the head and the other at the feet, where the body of Jesus had lain.

Then they said to her, "Woman, why are you weeping?" She said to them, "Because they have taken away my Lord, and I do not know where they have laid Him."

Now when she had said this, she turned around and saw Jesus standing there, and did not know that it was Jesus.

Jesus said to her, "Woman, why are you weeping? Whom are you seeking?" She, supposing Him to be the gardener, said to Him, "Sir, if You have carried Him away, tell me where You have laid Him, and I will take Him away."

Jesus said to her, "Mary!" She turned and said to Him, "Rabboni!" (which is to say, Teacher).

Jesus said to her, "Do not cling to Me, for I have not yet ascended to My Father; but go to My brethren and say to them, 'I am ascending to My Father and your Father, and to My God and your God.'"

Mary Magdalene came and told the disciples that she had seen the Lord, and that He had spoken these things to her.

JOHN 20:11-18

When Mary Magdalene encountered her risen Master, she was thrilled and filled with new hope. She was looking to honor her dead Lord, but she found Him risen. Mary was looking in the wrong place for life, so the angels pointed her in the right direction. She found the living Lord—and so can we!

But we want to come to the tomb of our buildings and worship a concept.

We want Reverend Doe's religion without relationship.

We want to be in Christ, but we don't want Christ in our business.

We want to be in Christ, but we don't want Christ to tell us who we can or cannot marry.

We want to be in Christ, but we don't want to stop playing the numbers.

We want to be in Christ, but we don't want to stop running around on the side.

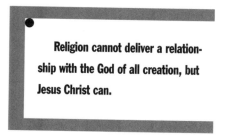

Religion cannot deliver a relationship with the God of all creation, but Jesus Christ can.

We want to be in Christ, but we don't want to leave our part-time lover and go back home to the person we're married to.

We want a religion without absolutes that requires nothing of us.

We want religion without relationship and religion without restraints!

We want to be in the church, but we don't want the church to have any rule over our lives.

Religion cannot deliver a relationship with the God of all creation, but Jesus Christ can. We must be careful not to worship our family roots. To do so is to return to ancestral graveyards and become entangled with foolishness that has bound up our families for generations. If we check our family lineage and this country's history, there's a lot of religion there. Many slave owners were religious. Many wife beaters, drunks, and child abusers were religious.

When people say, "Oh, you know he's so religious," they're not saying he's born again or renewed—because you can be religious and a devil worshipper. You can be religious and worship cultural identity. You can be religious and worship your job. You can be religious and worship yourself. No one can get into the bathroom when a self-worshipper gets in ahead of them. Every morning they're primping and combing and stuck on themselves. But they're looking for love in the wrong place. There are a lot of evil folk out there searching for good-looking people to use up and throw away like trash. You can't find love in the outward appearance.

A living faith in Jesus Christ will show that you can't have everything you see. We can't have every woman, no matter what she looks like. We can't have every brother. We can't have every car. We can't have everything that everybody else has. Living in Christ involves restraints. We are called to a disciplined lifestyle.

◼ Religious Folk and Relationship Folk

May I suggest to you that there are even sanctified church folk who are graveyard religious? I believe in the prophetic gift and the prophetic office, but some of our churches have abused the prophetic office to the point of losing balance. And people eat it up. Many just wait around when they hear a so-called prophet is coming to town, hoping for a word. You see them walk up and say, "You have a word for me? You got a word? Did the Lord tell you something about me the other night?" And they miss out on the fact that God always has a Word for them—between Genesis and Revelation. They are sanctified and religious, but don't read God's Word. So they look everywhere else to hear from Him. Ignorance and religion are dangerous companions!

Religious folk and relationship folk are like night and day. Religious folk will give an offering, but they won't tithe regularly. Religious folk always have a problem when church gets too long. They breathe God's air twenty-four hours a day, drink God's water, eat the food He provides, wear the clothes He gives, drive the cars, and live in the houses He gave them, but as soon as church runs past their schedule, they throw a fit. You see them looking at their watches and scowling at you behind the pulpit if the Spirit moves you to go into overtime. Religious folk preach against abortion and adultery, but they will walk around the poor and homeless and leave a suffering brother on the corner. We are called to self-sacrifice, to live the whole cross. We are called to justice and righteousness.

Listen, God hasn't called us to be religious in the way most people think about religion! That kind of religion is a graveyard. But because we are so dead and religious, watching the funerals that march by us every day is easy, even expected. True religion involves relationship—

relationship with God and one another. James Martineau defines religion as "the belief in an ever-living God, that is, in a Divine Mind and Will ruling the Universe and holding moral relations with mankind."[5] The apostle James wrote,

> *Pure and undefiled religion before God and the Father is this: to visit orphans and widows in their trouble, and to keep oneself unspotted from the world.*
>
> JAMES 1:27

Any religion that divorces people from a relationship with God and isolates them from one another is useless. In fact, in the preceding verse (verse 26) James goes so far as to say, if a person cannot control what they say, then their religion is empty.

Looking for Love in Education and Success

Some of us have made a religion out of going back to school. We have made a religion out of success. When someone asks us how we're doing, we tell them, "Well, I'm really doing fine. You know I got another promotion." Or, "AT&T wants me to do so-and-so." Or, "I'm going to get another degree." Now don't get me wrong, if you were to tell me that, I would be very happy for you. We ought to share in one another's successes. What I am saying is, worldly success without Jesus is still a graveyard full of dead men's bones.

---

[5] James Martinean, possibly from *A Study of Religion* (1888).

Jesus wants to address the void in each of us that comes from destiny and purpose longing to be fulfilled in our lives. However, He can only do so if we enter into relationship with Him and allow Him to direct our paths and prioritize our lives. Relationship people have their life priorities in order. Relationship people say, "Nature formed me, sin deformed me, education informed me, but it took Jesus Christ to transform me." Relationship people know Jesus isn't buried in the world's finest graveyards. He is risen! That fact changes our reality.

> Relationship people have their life priorities in order. Relationship people say, "Nature formed me, sin deformed me, education informed me, but it took Jesus Christ to transform me."

If we're ever going to stop the funeral in the church of our culture, we're going to have to start getting honest. Now, realistically speaking, sometimes life can be the pits. If we are honest, we will have to recognize that not only do we sometimes go through tough times; but, like Paul, we are often troubled on every side.

> *For indeed, when we came to Macedonia, our bodies had no rest, but we were troubled on every side. Outside were conflicts, inside were fears.*
>
> 2 CORINTHIANS 7:5

The Sunday following Jesus' crucifixion, those who were willing came to the graveyard expecting to see a dead Jesus, but He wasn't there. Instead, they found that Jesus had risen. The resurrection gave these seekers new hope, and it should give us great hope. Unfortunately, some of us don't want hope; we want pity parties.

Years ago in our churches, we would sing "Sweet Hour of Prayer" regularly during Sunday prayer time. The minister would say, "It's prayer time," and the deacons would come up to stand before the people. There they would stand, all sorrowful. Then the pastor would say, "Now I know you all have problems. All God's children have their problems. Some of you can't pay your mortgage; some of your children are in jail. But I want you to know this morning that God can work it out! The altar's open for prayer." After they came to the front, they would start crying and tell a deacon about their alcoholic son or pregnant unwed daughter. "We have no job. Not enough money!" Problems everywhere.

Now please don't misunderstand me. There's nothing wrong with *coming* to the altar like that, but there is something wrong when you *leave* the altar like that. The altar is no place to just moan and groan. The alter is the place where we touch God and allow Him to touch us. We can return to our seats full of victory and joy, confident that He heard us and answered our prayer. The altar is the place where God wants us to "get a grip." When we're troubled on all sides, we don't need a pity party; we need deliverance, hope, and peace.

■ Get Out!

If you truly want out of the graveyard, you will never get out of it by feeling sorry for yourself. You've got to see Jesus and then follow Him. When you do, the same power that resurrected Him will give you the ability to kick away whatever's binding you. When you follow Jesus, you'll get out of the graveyard.

You will never become a funeral-stopper if you're continually mourning at your own wake. See the angels announce to the women Jesus' resurrection from the dead. If you have been looking for love in all the wrong places, look at His Word today. See Jesus raise Lazarus from the dead. See Jesus raise the widow's son in that funeral march at Nain. See Him raise Jairus' daughter. Take Him at His Word. Make a decision to commit your whole life to Him. Change your address from Tombstone to Living Stone. Then see Him deliver you and raise you from the dead!

When you start looking for love in the living, risen Christ, your doctor will begin to decrease your *Xanex*, *Valium*, and *Prozac* prescriptions. When you start believing in the resurrection, you'll put that nervous breakdown, heart attack, and stroke on hold, and begin to say, "I choose to live."

"Why seek the living among the dead?"

We don't have to walk around feeling like failures. Because of the resurrection, our lives are full of possibility. Jesus got up on the third day with ALL POWER in His hand as the conquering hero of dead humanity. He is America's changeless champion. He's your champion over death. He's your champion over sickness, hell, and the grave.

But if you want victory, you've got to go where Jesus is. I did, and Jesus gave me victory over my ABCs: Anger,

Bitterness, and Complexes. Jesus has given us victory over Evil, Fear, and the Grave. He gave us victory over Hopelessness, an Inferiority complex, Jealousy, and the desire to Kill ourselves. Jesus gave us victory over Lawlessness, Mediocrity, Lack of identity, Oppression, the Poverty spirit, Rebellion, Sexual addiction, and Unforgiveness. And He will give you the Victory too.

Jesus will give you victory over the unforgiveness that has you walking around mad at everyone. Your ex-husband is deceased, and you're still sitting around angry. Your old girlfriend is married with children, and you're still sitting around trying to get back at her. *Get over it!* Don't you know God will give you victory over unforgiveness? Unforgiveness is a tombstone in the graveyard.

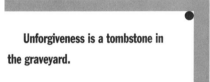

Unforgiveness is a tombstone in the graveyard.

The funeral will continue until folks quit looking for love in all the wrong places. If you know somebody who is living there, help them get out. If you've been living there and you want out, say this prayer:

Father God, I repent of my graveyard living. I want to get up and get out. So I ask You to forgive me of my sin, and I choose to move forward in faith and holiness as of today. You said if any of us sins, we have Jesus as our representative to forgive us of our sins and to cleanse us from all unrighteousness. I receive Your cleansing now, Father, in Jesus' name.

Now walk out of that graveyard! Jesus has some funeral-stopping plans for you. Jesus is alive, and He is the enemy of death!

> *O Death, where is thy sting?*
> *O grave, where is thy victory?*
>
> 1 CORINTHIANS 15:55 KJV

God raised Him so you can get up—so get up and get out!

Helpful Hints

Love yourself. Like David, realize you are a reason to praise God. He says in Psalm 139:14 KJV:

> *I will praise thee; for I am fearfully and wonderfully made: marvelous are thy works; and that my soul knoweth right well.*

Avoid destructive tendencies that lead to unhealthy relationships in search of something that can be found only within you or within God.

Don't be driven by loneliness. Learn healthy ways to enjoy yourself. Enjoy the gifts God has placed in your life, such as friends. View time alone as an opportunity to get to know God and self. Every now and then buy yourself something nice or treat yourself to dinner. Remember that no matter your status in life, you will always have to live with you; so make sure you are a person you can live with!

Be with Him. Let go of what's in your hand long enough to let God fill your heart. You can have your hands full and your heart empty. There is no deliverance in dead religion. It is possible to put on a pulpit vestment, choir robe, usher's pin, and sit in the Deacon's pew—and never be touched by God. While it is expected that we will preach the Gospel and have authority to heal sicknesses and cast out devils, it is far more important to the heart of God that we be with Him. (See Mark 3:14.)

four

Daddy, Stop the Funeral

*Now it happened on the next day, when they had
come down from the mountain, that a great multitude met Him.*

*Suddenly a man from the multitude cried out, say-
ing, "Teacher, I implore You, look on my son, for he
is my only child."*

LUKE 9:37-38

Stopping the funerals in America's homes and churches will require a resurrection of fatherhood among the men of God's community. God wants to stop the funerals of dishonorable, unaccountable men to make them honorable, accountable leaders. God wants to expand the borders of every father's mind to help him understand the importance of his role. The absence of fathers is a national crisis. There are so few fathers today in comparison to yesterday that none of us can afford to be selfish and care only for "our own". We really need to extend our love and care to our nieces, nephews, neighbors, and to the children in Sunday School.

God wants to stop the funeral in the home today and restore the hearts of children to their fathers. This is seen in Malachi's prophesy, which was fulfilled in John the Baptist's ministry of repentance:

*"Behold, I will send you Elijah the prophet before
the coming of the great and dreadful day of the Lord.*

> And he will turn the hearts of the fathers to the
> children, and the hearts of the children to their
> fathers, lest I come and smite the earth with a curse."
>
> MALACHI 4:5-6

In chapter 1 we looked at the funeral procession of a mother and saw Jesus destroy the power of death. In this chapter, I want to look at the importance of Jesus' response to a concerned, accountable father. Luke 9:37 shows us one of the few heart-turned, accountable fathers Malachi spoke about, the man brought his son to Jesus for a miracle.

> Now it happened on the next day, when they had come down from the mountain, that a great multitude met Him.
>
> Suddenly a man from the multitude cried out, saying, "Teacher, I implore You, look on my son, for he is my only child.
>
> "And behold, a spirit seizes him, and he suddenly cries out; it convulses him so that he foams at the mouth; and it departs from him with great difficulty, bruising him.
>
> "So I implored Your disciples to cast it out, but they could not."
>
> Then Jesus answered and said, "O faithless and perverse generation, how long shall I be with you and bear with you? Bring your son here."
>
> And as he was still coming, the demon threw him down and convulsed him. Then Jesus rebuked the

*unclean spirit, healed the child, and gave him back to
his father.*

LUKE 9:37-42

The father has a tremendous family responsibility,
which for the most part has been neglected during
America's current culture wars. A truly responsible father
will be concerned about what's going on in his sons' and
daughters' lives. This father in Luke 9:42 had come to his
wit's end. He had probably gone to various doctors and
others to share his concern for his son. Finally, he
brought his boy to see Jesus.

Multitudes always came to be ministered to by Jesus,
but the Scripture says this man suddenly cried out from
the multitude, **"Teacher, I implore You, look on my
son, for he is my only child."**

"Look on my son," implored this father, "for he is my
only hope."

"Teacher, please look on my son, for he is my future."

"Look on my son, for he is my seed."

"Look on my son, for he is the one who is going to
carry on my name."

"Look on my son," he shouted, "because as I look on
my son, I don't see much to be hopeful for."

And as this father looked upon his son, he probably
didn't see much that he could be proud of. He probably
didn't see the strength and the character he wanted to
see. Instead, he saw death. He saw a strange spirit that

made the boy convulse at the most inopportune times. He was strange.

How this boy became possessed by this devil, God only knows. One thing we do know is, **Evil company corrupts good habits** (1 Corinthians 15:33). Today there are many fathers who may be thinking, *Lord, look on my son. He is bound up with a bad crowd.* Today many fathers are confronted with the fact that their son's best friend is drug addicted or in a gang. "Lord, look on my son. He's not a bad boy, but his influences are concerning me here. He's hanging out late, he's become sexually active, and I don't know what I can do with him. LOOK ON MY SON."

> **Fathers, bring your sons to Jesus. Bring your daughters to Jesus. Protect them from harm and danger. Bring them to the Lord.**

Father's Day?

Father's Day in many homes today doesn't garner the same kind of celebration that Mother's Day fosters. There's a *reason* for this. We don't see the kind of concern this father in Luke showed by bringing his son to the Lord. This was a concerned father. He didn't wait for Momma or any other woman in the community to do it. No, this father took it upon himself to take care of his son's spiritual needs. This was also *his* child, so the father took *his* boy and said, "Jesus, I implore You, *look on my son.*" He teaches us a lesson today: Fathers, bring your sons to Jesus. Bring your daughters to Jesus. Protect them from harm and danger. Bring them to the Lord.

When this father broke into Jesus' ministry, *suddenly* the demon threw his boy to the ground and convulsed him. But the demon had no power. Those demons who have our children stalking around and acting like a pack of dogs have no power, but they won't go unless we also know they have no power. We've been trying to cast them out in the name of education or some fraternal order. We've been trying to deal with Satan in the name of nationalism, civil rights, and cultural pride. And there our children remain, confused and addicted, because there is no true deliverance in any of those names.

We gain insight and enlightenment as we study our history. However, regardless of how much pride you have in your culture, it won't cast out an unclean or rebellious spirit. You can only cast the devil out in that name which is above every name, the name of Jesus. God has decreed

> that at the name of Jesus every knee should bow, of those in heaven, and of those on earth, and of those under the earth,
> and that every tongue should confess that Jesus Christ is Lord, to the glory of God the Father.
>
> PHILIPPIANS 2:10-11

When Jesus was made aware of the man's child, He delivered him. **Then Jesus rebuked the unclean spirit.** And after He delivered him, the Bible says He **healed the** child (Luke 9:42). And none of it would have happened if the boy's dad hadn't pushed into that crowd.

Now let me say this about healing. I had to walk out of a loved one's room some time ago crying because my heart was breaking. I didn't like the way they looked, and I had to keep reminding myself that the Lord is still a healer. Regardless of who does or doesn't receive healing, I will continue to proclaim Jesus as healer until my dying breath. Everyone is not healed in this life, yet our God remains a healing God. He is able to heal our bodies, our minds, and our situations. *Regardless of what you see or what you read, He's still a healer.* So I continue to pray for the sick.

Fathers, lay hands on your children and pray for them in the name of Jesus. No matter what the ailment, affliction, or situation, bring them to Jesus. Pray for them, expecting them to walk. Pray, expecting them to be delivered. Pray, expecting them to come off drugs, to have changed hearts, to become all that God has destined them to be. Pray in faith, leaving the results to God.

As a minister, I don't stop praying for the sick because everybody in the line doesn't jump up with an immediate testimony. I don't stop preaching because half the crowd doesn't receive the Lord. I don't stop preaching because the shackles that bind people to their pasts don't immediately fall off. I don't stop preaching and I don't stop loving because, if you stay around the fire long enough, something's going to get on the inside of you! This is the kind of faith that moved the father to bring his son to Jesus, and Jesus set him free.

Healing the Children

Jesus wants to heal the rough and rugged children of our dangerous age. He wants to deliver our kids from the graveyard of lost dreams, sickness, and disease. He wants to heal the empty-headed. They may be walking, but they're dead. He wants to touch and speak to our kids who can play a mean game of basketball, but can't read or write.

These "precious promises" know how to make babies, but they're dead. They may have $85 worth of weave, but it covers a dead head. They may be wearing $150 shoes, but they are on dead feet. Jesus wants to touch their coffins and raise them to life. And He wants to do it through you, Daddy. You have the power to lift them to reach their potential.

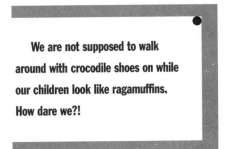

We are not supposed to walk around with crocodile shoes on while our children look like ragamuffins. How dare we?!

My three children sitting on the front row in my congregation are my responsibility. As their father, it is *my* responsibility to feed and clothe them. It is *my* responsibility to see that there are three square meals on the table every day. It's *my* job to see that they have clothes on their backs and shoes on their feet. It's *my* job to see that they have clean bed sheets and a nice place to lay their heads. This is *my* job. They are an extension of who I am.

We are not supposed to walk around with crocodile shoes on while our children look like ragamuffins. How dare we?! I'm talking to you, the father who is wearing $150 sneakers and you didn't make last month's child support payment. How dare you?! How *dare* you wear that designer sweat suit while your daughter's clothes are wrinkled and ripped?! Daddy, Jesus wants to stop the funeral in you so He can touch the lives of your children.

This father in Luke understood the importance of seeking the Lord. And when He did, Jesus handed his son back to him—because his daddy was his covering. The boy's father was responsible for him. The boy's father was his authority.

But today we're giving *everything* back to the mother. And when I say everything, I mean *everything*. So many mothers are perpetually exhausted because of too much responsibility and too little help. In many cases they are working full-time jobs outside the home; then they come home to another full-time job of cooking, cleaning, and raising. Too often the mother is the sole disciplinarian. Stop the funeral! It's your job too, Father!

Fathers, we need to get back on the job! We must make sure the rent is paid—that's our job! We must make sure the mortgage is paid on time. We must make sure the car note is paid. We must make sure the oil in the car is changed. It's time to get back on the job! There are a growing number of single-parent homes in our country. These responsibilities rest with all fathers. Even if we fathered children prior to a marriage or a divorce, our seed remains our responsibility. All of our seeds! Make sure someone takes care of what you can't do personally. When we own up to our responsibilities, Jesus will bless our homes. He will come to us and ours.

■ Thank God for Dad

Much of what is wrong with our society today is the direct result of absentee fathers. So many of our children are dying and have died from hunger for their fathers. They're hungry for Daddy's covering, care, training, and touch. But Daddy has been absent. He's not there.

Sociologists tell us that 80 percent of all men in prison today come from fragmented, fatherless homes. They also tell us that even when a father is there physically, emotionally he can be a thousand miles away. You can grow up in the same house with the man of the house, but grow up as if he wasn't even there. You can see him and even eat with him and still have no idea who your father really is. Physical and emotional presence are key factors to healthy fathering.

I thank God for a father who stayed there for me. I thank God for the late Donald Hilliard Sr., who was my concerned father. He was there for my sister and me while my mother was present at PTA meetings, Cub Scouts, and Brownies. Our father was a caring, consistent presence in the home. I didn't always like him, and God knows I didn't always understand him; but as they rolled his casket to the front of St. John's Baptist Church on October 19, 1983, all I could say was, "Thank you." As I stood over the casket and looked at and touched his loving face for the last time, I bent down and said, "Thank you." Parents, the Bible says your children will rise up and call you blessed. Together my parents taught us respect and walked side by side. My mother never had to shoulder the responsibility of rearing us alone.

I had to raise a holy fuss with my children just the other day, and I could tell I was making them angry. But they know enough not to show any disrespect. Dad taught me this. I could read on their lips the rebellious words, "I can't stand you." I could see it. You know, the Holy Spirit speaks to you. I love to turn around and catch them moving their lips and watch them just pull their lips in.

"You can feel it all you want," I told them. "You can feel it, and you can say it to each other. But I better never hear you say it." I am trying to rear them with respect. It's my job to be their father first and then their friend.

Father, your primary responsibility is not to be a friend to your children. Now, I'm not saying you're not supposed to be friendly. What I am saying is that you are the *gatekeeper* of your home. Father, it is you who must analyze what movies come into your home and what movies your children go out to see. You are the one, Father, who has to analyze who's on the phone. How old are they? Where are they from? What are they about? You're the gatekeeper of your home.

Someone may say, "Well, now, you're just too over-protective." If I don't protect my children, who do you think is going to do it? Bubba down round the corner? Jimmy? Pookie? and Big Bro? You leave it up to them and you'll be living with a terrorist house guest. No! That's *your* house, so *you* set the rules, *you* keep them, and *you* enforce them. Fathers, guard the gate to your home with love, honesty, sensitivity, and care.

It isn't God's will for us to have so many unfathered children born out of wedlock today; but because they are born, they also need to be loved and nurtured. They did not ask to come here. They are to be given the same privileges as all children, without making them feel as though something is wrong with them. If you are responsible for them being in this world, then you are responsible to father them in every way you can.

Perhaps the biggest problem with these unwed fathers and mothers is that they are a part of today's system and our moral code. And there is something pathetically wrong with a culture that congratulates irresponsible teenagers because they're going to be fathers. "Yo man, I hear you're having a baby. Congratulations," you hear so many young men say. They're acting irresponsibly and celebrating it. They don't mention marriage to the mother or commitment to the baby, so I'm not celebrating it. Irresponsibility should not be celebrated.

It wasn't too many years ago that if a young man made a young lady pregnant it didn't matter what she looked like or where she was from. If she was fine enough to be with for the night, she was fine enough to marry. For the most part, we made our sons live up to their responsibilities. While marriage is not always the best response to an unplanned pregnancy, we need to raise our sons and daughters with full knowledge of the consequences of irresponsible behavior.

Fathers, it's time to start making our young men responsible.

Daddy Pride

I'm PROUD to be a father. I couldn't wait for my wife, Phyllis, to become pregnant because I wanted to have children. We were only married three months when she conceived, and it was a very exciting season. New life, possibilities, and promise.

It's an honor to be a father. You may lose your hair because of it, but it's an honor. What hair you keep may turn gray, but it's an honor. You'll have very few quiet, tranquil moments, but it's still an honor to be a father. We don't realize that today.

Fathers, we are called to restore the sanctity of the family. We are called to train our boys to understand that one of the greatest things in life any man can do is choose the right wife and be a good father. God is calling fathers to stop the funeral in today's society by nurturing, covering, and protecting their children. Fathers, you are called to stop the funeral by taking responsibility. You are called to be the priest, protector, and provider for the home. Stability and structure are restored as fathers renew their commitment to fatherhood.

> We are called to train our boys to understand that one of the greatest things in life any man can do is choose the right wife and be a good father.

Remember, the earthly father of Jesus, Joseph, had a dream that Herod was trying to destroy his son. God informed *Joseph*, not Mary, to take his family into Egypt to protect them from Herod's plans to murder their baby. (See Matthew 2:13.) It is Dad who is called to protect and to keep the family safe. Where there is no father in the home, grandfathers, uncles, teachers, coaches, and the church must step in as surrogates.

Stop the Wrath

In most inner cities across America, we don't have many fathers. We have given birth to a generation of angry, fatherless children. Our society teems with fatherless, resentful children who have been provoked to wrath, and they're filling our jails. Some become thieves, rapists, and murderers because of what they didn't receive from their dad. Others end up like caged animals because of the rage they saw in their fathers. They hit their girlfriends because they watched their fathers hit their precious mothers.

Many of our children go astray because the home was left unguarded. Young boys have been molested and young girls have been taken advantage of because there wasn't a father figure present to protect them in life. They were left unprotected and uncared for. Those who end up having a problem with taking authority in their own lives probably didn't have a father. Others are bitter toward men because of what they did or didn't see in their fathers.

We need to stop the fatherless funeral by providing strength, structure, and order. Fathers, we need to train our young boys to know their good looks alone aren't going to get them very far. We need to train our young girls to know they are nobody's doormat. Listen to me, your teenage daughter isn't supposed to be washing some young boy's clothes. She is not supposed to become so emotionally attached to that young boy down the street that she doesn't have any other friends. It's dangerous. Don't let her be seduced by style or words. It's your job, Daddy, to protect her. It's your job to make sure she doesn't become so attached that he is the first one she talks to in the morning and the last one she talks to at night. That is *too* much emotional attachment. If we see this, it often points to a larger issue—the need for more love and attention in the home.

We Can Stop It!

Father, a trend of death haunts our homes and communities. *You* get a grip and break it up. Bind it, kill it, and stomp it in the name of Jesus. Get involved in the lives of your children! We can stop the funeral of this culture of fatherlessness. Jesus wants you to bring your girl to Him, Daddy. He wants to hear you cry out in the crowd, "Lord I implore you, look on my daughter. Set her free!"

When Father's Day arrives, we should prove worthy of celebrating. In the same sense, as a society, we need to lift up the wonderful examples of good fathers all around us. Inasmuch as we have bad pastors and good pastors, bad mothers and good mothers, bad teachers and good teachers, we also have bad fathers and good fathers. However, in today's fatherless culture, we've come to the point where the father isn't even recognized as being important. Fatherhood is a non-issue, so many sociologists are saying the family needs to be restructured. They are trying to develop a completely new standard for what a family is supposed to be. We need to stop this funeral because fathers play an important, irreplaceable role.

For a man to marry and make a covenant commitment is right in the sight of God, even though our current culture makes it out to be a joke. "I ain't gettin' married, man, no," you hear today's young people say. Why? Because they often want to live a loose life without commitments. Too often they have not seen commitments worthy of imitation in their homes.

Genuine, committed, godly fathers don't live like dogs. I encourage you men to get married! Don't run around like some unleashed animal, forever in mating season. A frightening number of

> **For a man to marry and make a covenant commitment is right in the sight of God, even though our current culture makes it out to be a joke. . . . Why? Because they often want to live a loose life without commitments.**

young people have tested positive for HIV as the direct result of loose, irresponsible living. Today we need to rebuild the whole moral structure to recapture the beauty and sanctity that marriage and commitment bring.

Godly sorrow, Paul tells us, leads to repentance, which leads to salvation. We will stop the funeral as fathers when we do the following three things:

Number one, we must be **SORRY**.

In 2 Corinthians 7:8-10, Paul corrected a moral mess that occurred in the Corinthian church. After he addressed it, he wrote: **For even if I made you sorry with my letter, I do not regret it; though I did regret it.**

When the Lord is free to minister to the deep places in our lives, He will make us sorry. True ministry uncovers and heals. He will produce godly sorrow in us because He loves us. What Paul was trying to say in this verse was, "When I corrected you, I wasn't trying to hurt you, so I did experience regret because it upset you."

One answer to our social problems today is godly sorrow for whatever role we have played in allowing such a downward slide. We need to be sorry for our sins—not sorry because we got caught. We need to be sorry enough to say, "Lord, I yield; I recognize that I should have been there. I should have shown up for Thanksgiving, but I was too busy hanging out and building my career, I'm SORRY." To say "I'm sorry" is to confess that you were wrong. The Bible says,

> If we confess our sins, He is faithful and just to forgive us our sins and to cleanse us from all unrighteousness.
>
> 1 JOHN 1:9

Then in verses 9 and 10 of 2 Corinthians, chapter 7, Paul continued,

> *Now I rejoice, not that you were made sorry, but that your sorrow led to repentance. For you were made sorry in a godly manner, that you might suffer loss from us in nothing.*
>
> *For godly sorrow produces repentance leading to salvation, not to be regretted; but the sorrow of the world produces death.*

We need godly sorrow that leads to repentance. That brings us to number two; we need to **REPENT**.

Repentance means change. When you truly repent of your sin, you will change your life. "I should have given Christmas gifts, but I didn't, and *now I repent.* I should have been more kind, but I wasn't, so I repent. I'm not just sorry; I repent, Lord. I choose to change, Lord. I choose to make every effort to right the wrong and not to repeat it." However, this cannot be accomplished without going through the next step.

Number three, we need to make a new **COMMIT-MENT**.

After true repentance, we will have a renewed commitment to God, family, and the Church because when we repent, the Holy Spirit will convict us to do something about it. Most folk who repent will try to make restitution. "I know, Son," a repentant father will say. "I know you're grown now, and I know Daddy did a whole lot wrong. Daddy wasn't there. Daddy never took you to church or read the Bible to you. Daddy never took you fishing. Daddy never took you to the ball game. But Daddy's sorry, Son.

"I'm not what I ought to be yet, but let me try to do something. I don't have any money, but can I come over every Sunday after church and sit at your table? Can I have the privilege of knowing who your children are? Can I see if perhaps God, in His mercy, will allow me to do for your children what I didn't do for you?"

Show Up

Absentee fathers need to repent, find their sons and

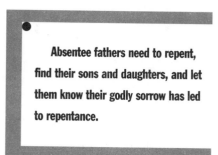

Absentee fathers need to repent, find their sons and daughters, and let them know their godly sorrow has led to repentance.

daughters, and let them know their godly sorrow has led to repentance. Fathers who are married but have other children scattered around town from a past life, need to find all of their children.

Just because children weren't born in wedlock doesn't mean they're not worthy of their father's attention. God will hold us accountable for our neglect, Father. If this is you or someone you know, the Word of the Lord is, "Repent of your past!" There is nothing you can do about yesterday except repent and turn from its evil. There is nothing any of us can do about the messes we've made. The only thing we can do is get saved from them. God is looking to see you make up that lost time by finding all of your children and showing up!

When we say, "I've made some mistakes, but God, I'm sorry," that's how we get saved. God will receive the absentee fathers of our communities just the way they are. He wants them to show up and say, "I've made some mistakes, Lord, but here I am." If you are one of these fathers, God loves you very much. However, He wants you to turn from where you are to where you ought to be—with your children—raising and providing for them.

Following the example of the accountable father in Luke, we are required to bring our sons and daughters to the Lord. God wants us to repent and stop the funeral in us so we can start doing everything possible to stop the funeral in them.

God then wants us to get this message out to our brothers in the street. It needs to grab our brothers on the corner, in the gymnasium, on the basketball court, and in the barber shop. We can stop this funeral in Jesus' name when we repent and turn to Him. But it won't happen by just turning over a new leaf. Repentance is a lifestyle of faith and accountability.

■ The Violent Take It by Force

Jesus announced the violent reality of repentance when He said:

> "And from the days of John the Baptist until now the kingdom of heaven suffers violence, and the violent take it by force."
>
> MATTHEW 11:12

In this combative statement, Jesus said the kingdom of heaven, His powerful established reign among humanity, is suffering violence. Persecution, death, and destruction threaten the kingdom of God. So the *violent* who *take it by force* are a people of keen spiritual enthusiasm and commitment. They are true spiritual radicals who are willing to propagate with complete abandonment the dynamic message of God's reign in their lives through impassioned witness and prayer.

The violent confront the demonic forces that have set up strongholds in America and around the world. The violent take the kingdom by force because they take the Bible and Christianity seriously. They believe Jesus still does heal, deliver, and save.

The violent believe Jesus is still in the funeral-stopping business. When they deal with the forces of darkness, their prayers sound like this: "I BIND EVERY DEMON SPIRIT. I COME AGAINST EVERY GENERATIONAL SPIRIT. YOU THAT ARE TRYING TO KILL MY CHILDREN AND ARE TRYING TO DESTROY MY SEED, I CURSE YOU IN THE NAME OF JESUS!"

This fight isn't against flesh and blood. I am amazed how our kids are being invaded by the body snatchers. They're being poisoned and possessed by the stuff that comes out of the TV. Demonic aliens have been coming out of the airwaves and electronically scooping them up because fathers in the home haven't been gatekeepers, and mothers have been too preoccupied to pay attention to their kids. Either they've been completely derelict and are nowhere to be found, or they've been too busy working and developing their careers. They have been too busy building their "ministries" and saving everyone else's child while their kids look at their absence and blame God for it.

> *For if a man does not know how to rule his own*
> *house, how will he take care of the church of God?*
> 1 TIMOTHY 3:5

If you don't get violent, Parent, Satan will plow you under. Just look at our communities. Many of them are war zones. Places you could walk to get a soda forty years ago look like armed camps today. We must confront the demon powers that seize our children in today's father-less communities. And we must begin with those demons that have possessed the fathers with the reck-lessness that makes them think nothing of walking away from their responsibilities. Reckless, demonic thinking breeds irresponsible activity. Demons can make a man think like that. When you can walk away from your wife and three children with no conviction, that's demonic. The violent will call upon Jesus to arrest

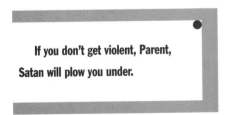

If you don't get violent, Parent, Satan will plow you under.

and cancel that spirit of abandonment. Then Jesus will scatter that wandering spirit and draw the demonized man back to responsible living.

Fathers, your children need your tenderness, time, and training. They need the training only you can give. Jesus will give your children back to you once you stop the funeral in yourself and give everything you own back to Him. Let's do it, Daddy! Bring yourself to God, bring yourself to your children, and then bring your children to Jesus. God will bless you when you choose to do it. He will stop the funeral in your home and make you a mighty man.

> *Then Jesus rebuked the unclean spirit, healed the child, and gave him back to his father.*
>
> LUKE 9:42

Helpful Hints

Love your children. Every child needs love, attention, and care. Love your children unconditionally—all of your children. Be sure your touch, your words, and your actions send the same message to each of your children—that they are loved.

Listen to their hearts. Stand still long enough to listen. While we are doing all we can, our children may need to be loved in ways that are not apparent to us. Pause from the daily routine of giving directives and offering advice to listen to your children's questions, fears, joys, and sorrows.

Lift your children. Lift them up to God daily. Pray for them and pray with them. Lift their self-esteem by your love, care, and commitment. By teaching them the Word of God and by spending quality time with them, lift them emotionally and spiritually from low places.

five

Raising Up a Fearless Generation

*Train up a child in the way he should go, and
when he is old he will not depart from it.*

PROVERBS 22:6

t's time to get out of the graveyard, America! It's time
for daddies to walk out of their tombs. It's time for
mothers to walk hand in hand with them as the shepherd-
ing team God always intended married couples to be. The
late Dr. Samuel Proctor, my dear friend and mentor, often
spoke of the home being the incubator of its young, the
place of warmth, care, and concern. Nothing can replace
the power and influence of a solid home.

Jesus wants to step into our American situation personally and culturally. He wants to touch the coffin of
our dead culture. We need a resurrection! I'm talking to
you, Parents, and to you, Children. We need a cultural
resurrection. It will start at the top of the family structure, with the father and mother loving God and training the children up in the truth.

We need to be lifted on every level in Jesus' name
because as a people, we're losing ground. As a people
we're sinking because we've been teaching one message
in the church and living in a graveyard at home. But
once we make the decision to live, Jesus will show up,
interrupt the processional, stop the funeral in us, and
raise our children back to life.

So he who was dead sat up and began to speak.
And He presented him to his mother.

LUKE 7:15

Committed Christian mothers who have been carrying the entire spiritual load: Jesus wants to stop the mourning in you. You, Mother, who have been expecting the worst because of what you have seen: Jesus wants to stop the funeral in you. He wants you to learn to take Him at His Word.

Graveyard mothers, Jesus wants to stop the funeral in you that has had you in church on Sunday mornings and rolling around in bed with somebody new every other week. This type of lifestyle sends a dying message to children in the other room. So often we attract negativity to ourselves because we give off signals that say "I don't care about myself or my future. I'm available to anyone who will show me some attention."

> You, Mother, who have been expecting the worst because of what you have seen: Jesus wants to stop the funeral in you. He wants you to learn to take Him at His Word.

My dear sister, are you in love with that brother who beat you last night? Jesus wants to stop your funeral. Are you blinded by big muscles, a smooth rap, and good sex? Wake up now! Sex is not love. When a man loves a woman—really loves a woman—he will lift her above himself and honor her.

Sister, does that young man really love you? If he did he wouldn't want you to live in fear. Stand up and respect yourself! If he loved you, he wouldn't put his hands on you. But he won't stop doing it until you start loving yourself and say, "If you put your hand on me again, I'm calling the cops. In fact, I'm outta here. It's too late. You blew it. You don't care anything about me anyway. You won't beat me again. I want your life changed. I want you saved, but from a distance."

Graveyard Fathers, Jesus wants to stop the funeral in you that has kept you out of the house—and out of Church—because when you die and face the Lord, you're going to have to give an account for what you did and didn't do. Some of your sons and daughters are on their way to the cemetery because they're starving from a lack of you. They're dying of "daddy hunger" because you didn't claim them. These precious jewels were left unprotected. They were claimed by monsters. In some cases the monsters had sneakers and sweatshirts on. Others had on suits and ties. Some monsters were wearing dresses. The message of the monsters is death and destruction. When we stand in the gap and take our rightful places as gatekeeper and caregiver, provider and protector, we are being used by God to stop the funeral. What the enemy has marked for death, the Lord Jesus can mark for life! He has done it before, and He desires to do it again!

Jesus Can Do It

Jesus didn't become God when He was baptized in the Jordan. He was born God. And death is such an enemy to Him, the Author of life, that He is compelled to stop any funeral that has the audacity to cross His path. To the woman in Luke 7, He said, "Do not weep, Woman. Sit up, Child. Here's your son, Woman." (See Luke 7:13-15.) Jesus met her where she was and handled her depression. And Jesus will meet us where we are today to deal with our depression. Jesus wants to meet our country in its national sexual obsession. He wants to meet our nation in its epidemic of violence. He wants to do it, but it is completely up to us.

> *If My people who are called by My name will humble themselves, and pray and seek My face, and turn from their wicked ways, then I will hear from heaven, and will forgive their sin and heal their land.*
>
> 2 CHRONICLES 7:14

After we make the decision to walk out of our tombs in godly sorrow, we are going to have to take up an earnest lifestyle of prayer. The Church must seek the Lord if He is ever to be found. The truth of 2 Chronicles 7:14 will invite Jesus' resurrection power into our lives. Yes, Jesus can do it, but we have got to ask for it.

Jesus is saying to the nations, "If my people who are called by my name will humble themselves and seek my face, I'll hear and forgive. I will forgive the sin of the mothers and the fathers who are so busy trying to be friends with their children that they have allowed them to become terrorists in their homes. Then I will move through them outside of their homes to touch entire communities."

Everything in This House is Going to Serve God

Once we allow God to stop the funeral in ourselves, we must learn how to say, "Baby, I'm not your friend first. I'm your father first, Baby. I'm your mother first. You may not like me right now, but you *better* do what I say, because I want you to live. When you get older, you will understand. My responsibility is to raise you right before God. You don't have to like me. That's not my job or worry. You will respect me, though, and you will understand that the Word of God is the Law in this house; and as for me and my house, we're going to serve the Lord.

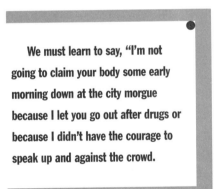

We must learn to say, "I'm not going to claim your body some early morning down at the city morgue because I let you go out after drugs or because I didn't have the courage to speak up and against the crowd.

"I'm not going to claim your body some early morning down at the city morgue because I let you go out after drugs or because I didn't have the courage to speak up and against the crowd. My love for you makes me stand up to you and sometimes against those that you have chosen as friends. You're not going to bring that filthy music that cusses me out in here. You're not going to have stuff on TV that teaches you to live like trash."

Why we pay good money to be cursed in our own homes through our music systems is beyond me. And I recently read an article where the author suggested that she needed to view any television program made after the mid 1960s before it could be seen by her children. While this may seem extreme, the truth is, there was indeed an increasingly relaxed approach in television programming that began in the 1960s. Slowly, but ever so methodically, we are accepting more profanity and nudity on primetime television. Wake up, America!

In their report, "Children, Violence and the Media," the Senate Committee on the Judiciary concluded that in 1997 123,500 juveniles were arrested for committing violent crimes, 2,500 of which were murder. The Committee is confident that the violence performed by juveniles is directly related to the fact that by age 18 an "American child will have seen 1,000 simulated murders and 200,000 acts of violence." The report attributes 10 percent of youth violence to television. If this conclusion is accurate, in 1997 alone television was responsible for 12,350 acts of violence performed by youth. Perhaps the most concise and sobering statement made within the report is, "More than 1,000 studies on the effects of television and film violence have been done over the past 40 years. The majority of these studies reach the same conclusion: television and film violence leads to real-world violence."

After you repent and allow Jesus to stop the funeral in you, Parents, you will have the moral authority to stop the mess that has been coming into your house. You will need to rattle your children's coffins and get into their lives. Who are their friends? Who are they going with? Is that young man who is coming over to take out your fifteen-year-old daughter twenty-five years old? If so, tell her, "You can't go." Is that movie her date wants her to see R-rated? If so, tell her, "You can't go."

"I don't see why I can't," she may say, "Shatty's going."

"I don't have to give an account for Shatty," we need to learn to say. "I don't have to give an account for Leroy, BoBo, Jim Bob, or Willie. I've got to give an account for my seed, and you're not going." And, Parents, our seed is the prize. The enemy of your soul and mine seeks the destination of the seed.

Parents, take charge in your houses. Rattle those coffins you have allowed to get stacked up in your homes. The Scripture says, **Train up a child in the way they should go** (Proverbs 22:6). Nobody said it was supposed to be easy. They may not like you for a season, but that's all right. You just show them you're going to love them anyway.

I know this from personal experience, because I disliked my father for a season. Yes, it's true. My dad used to make me so mad I could cry tears of fire. My father was a no-nonsense man. He left very little room for reckless, disobedient behavior. He established rules, regulations, order—and there was love. When I turned sixteen and finally found the nerve to stand up to him, Dad said,

"You say another word and I'll knock you down." But I had enough nerve to take him on. "Well, if you feel you need to knock me down, then you just ought to knock me down."

I didn't have good sense. I was young and naïve, so my mother ran in from the other room screaming, "Oh

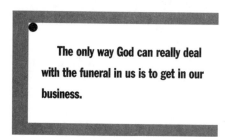

please, just get along!" My father's neck veins began to bulge, and I could feel the fire bellowing out of his nostrils. As I look back, if it wasn't for my father's stand, I wonder where I would be today. The order and stability my parents provided proved to be a strong springboard from which my future values were launched. Today I am eternally grateful for my father. Thank you, Dad, for being concerned enough to knock the devil out of me so no policeman ever would!

The Holy Spirit Will Teach Us

The Holy Spirit isn't here just to make us feel good. The Holy Spirit is here to convict us of sin. When we give our lives to God and earn the respect of our children as living examples, then the Holy Spirit will convict them of their sin. He will teach and sanctify our households. He will stand up in us when our behavior is inconsistent with His will and way. And once He does His work on the inside, He will move us on the outside.

The only way God can really deal with the funeral in us is to get in our business. Sometimes we're dead in certain areas because our daddies were dead in those areas. It is then that the Holy Spirit must set us free from the negativity of our bloodline. Why doesn't anyone stay married in your family? Why doesn't anyone in your family have the same daddy? It may be an old wound—an old demonic stronghold.

The Holy Spirit will convict you of the sin that has traveled your natural bloodline and give you the power to say, "No, you familiar spirit! You may have messed over my mother, you may have messed over my grandmother, you may have destroyed my father and my grandfather, but I've got the power in the name of Jesus to cast you out! My God is a strong tower. He is the Rock of Ages, the Lily of the Valley, the Bright and Morning Star, the Scepter, the Sanctifier, and I plead His blood over this area! In Jesus' name, get out!" We must fight for our lives and refuse to blindly give in to areas that may be painful to face.

Parents who know the power of Jesus' blood in their new family lineage have the victory over everything that happened before they met Jesus Christ. When you feel that spirit of divorce coming up in your family, there is a high probability that the spirit of divorce came down from previous generations. When everyone in the previous generation became pregnant at eighteen, and that same spirit tries to show up in your sixteen-year-old, Jesus will stop that funeral through your parental stand.

■ Take the Time

There are times parenting seems to take more than you've got to give. Sometimes, to stop a funeral you have to stop working for awhile or you have to change your working hours. Sometimes you've got to be home between the hours of three and six in the afternoon if you're going to stop the funeral in your child's life. Last year I had to cancel or postpone five preaching engagements—I mean big-time engagements. In some cases my name was already on the billboard and in the folder all over the nation. But I had to call and say, "I'm so sorry. I can't come."

They will say, "Don't you know you're booked? You sent the letter of confirmation. What's the problem? Did somebody die?" Then you have to say, "No, nobody died. I'm sorry, but I just found out my daughter's school is having a program in which she's getting promoted from the third grade. I'm terribly sorry, but I've got to be there. I promised God that my children would never grow up pointing a finger at the Church as a cause of their hurt or mistreatment. My first obligation is to be their father. I have to be Daddy first. I pray you understand and, hopefully, we can reschedule. I wish I had known about this grade promotion program before agreeing to the engagement, but I didn't. Please forgive me."

Before I'm a pastor, a bishop, or a national speaker, I'm a daddy. I am my children's father, and I won't allow my children to grow up hating God because I missed their ballet programs. I won't let them view my calling as self-ish and uncaring because I missed their dance recitals or their class promotions. It's the favor of God that we should seek in all areas. Quite frankly, our children are with us for such a brief season. We should value them, spend time with them, and love them! When we've done the very best we can in these areas, we will hear the Lord say, "Well done."

Some parents are in the midst of a family funeral now because they're simply working at the wrong time. Daddy, your daughters need you. They need you to comb their hair. My children enjoyed me combing their hair when they were younger. Little girls go through stages where they only want their daddy to do it. My daughters went through it. I remember when my wife started combing their hair and one of our girls said, "I want my daddy to do my hair." So Phyllis woke me up and said; "Get your girl, sit down here, and do her hair." I was half asleep and said, "All right, let me...come here, girl, come here."

Single mothers and fathers who manage to keep it all together are worthy of the highest respect—indeed a standing ovation. Parenting is not for cowards!

Team!

Our children are our responsibility. God is calling for team parenting. God didn't call any freelance fathers who come in on one day to help out, then watch Mom do it all the rest of the week. And sometimes you have to leave, reschedule, or even quit a job to be there, to stop a funeral when your children come home from school. You may need to be there to find out who's on the telephone with your children when you're normally at work.

Are they on the phone with an old man who is trying to seduce them?

Are they on the phone being sexually or emotionally abused through illicit conversation?

Are they on the phone with a woman who's trying to expose or convert them to a life of perversion?

Is your son on the phone with another brother who's trying to expose or convert him to a perversion?

Parents need to get involved in the lives of their kids at home and in the church because the devil is stalking about. He's marked their children for death.

> Be sober, be vigilant; because your adversary the
> devil walks about like a roaring lion, seeking whom
> he may devour.
>
> 1 PETER 5:8

Our children are being surrounded by dangerous problems and situations. Kids are coming to school with guns and shooting other children and teachers out of revenge. It's happening all around our homes. The generation that is determined to kill itself today doesn't care who or what it takes with it. The young terrorists prowling our streets and schools are often mentally disturbed and hungry for love. A spirit of murder has been released into their lives. Parents need to take the time to watch because the thief is out there trying to steal, kill, and destroy their children.

God wants to raise up Holy-Spirit-filled parents and ministries of liberating love who can bind the spirit of death that has been running rampant through their city's schools, public housing projects, and gangs for years. God wants to raise up a people who will speak to gang members in search of identity, school children without hope, and housing project tenants with no vision: "In the name of Jesus Christ, GET UP!"

But it all must start in the home. Today the Lord is saying, "Young Man, get up! Mother, get up! Father, get up! Daughter, get up! Get over your low self-esteem. Get over your low self-tolerance. Get over your spirit of violence. Arise over Smirnoff and Hennessy. Arise over chronic weed. Arise over Seagrams. Arise over music messages that sound good but lead astray. Get that villain out of your home, Parents. Arise, Parents! Get that poison off your son's or daughter's CD player. ARISE!"

> God wants to raise up a people who will speak to gang members in search of identity, school children without hope and housing project tenants with no vision: "In the name of Jesus Christ, GET UP!"

Jesus is telling us to rise over everything that is killing this generation. And when we let Him touch and talk through us, we will see results. "But oh, Pastor," you say, "I just don't know what I'm going to do. I don't know what's wrong. Jimmy just won't listen. I've tried, Pastor

Hilliard. God knows I've tried. And I know there are youth meetings at our church tomorrow, but I can't get Jimmy to do nothing. He just . . ."

"Well, how old is Jimmy?"

If you say, "He's about eight, but I just can't get him to do anything," I have bad news for you. If you can't get eight-year-old Jimmy to do anything and he's telling you what he will and won't do, listen—something's wrong with *you!* It's not Jimmy, it's you. Wake up, my friend, and bring your home into order!

You, Mother! You, Father! You have to take authority over that seed of rebellion in Jimmy. Discipline is not a bad thing. Unfortunately we have put our trust in philosophies that have been soft on order and discipline. Children need rules. Forget trying to do it in the name of your saintly grandmother. You need to get the funeral stopped in you and take authority in your home in the name of Jesus!

Jesus will break that spirit of terrorism in your home. Do you remember those little terrorists I talked about earlier? Have you ever seen them in the supermarket? "No, no, Mommy!" they scream and fuss while the mom does nothing. I have seen these children hit their parents, fall out in the floor, and run away. If I would have shown that kind of disrespect and rebellion in public when I was growing up, my parents wouldn't have cared who was looking. They wouldn't have cared less about being embarrassed. It would have been dealt with quickly and severely. All my father had to do was *look*.

He would shoot me one of those looks that could cause the walls of Jericho to come tumbling down.

I needed a strong father because my mother, God bless her, is just sweet—strong, but sweet. She is the sweetest woman I know. But as I grew older, I didn't need just *sweet*. My mother would get ready to smack me and then apologize. One time she actually did pop me. She smacked me across the cheek. Not a hard smack. The kind of smack that says, "You are a teenager and are out of line."

It shocked me. "Mother," I complained, "you . . . you smacked me." Then she quickly apologized and said, "Oh, now you know what Mommy meant. I didn't mean to . . . ." But Dad was also at the kitchen table to pick up where my mother left off. "You say another word, and I'll knock the hell out you, boy!" he commanded. Then he got up from the table, and I knew right then that the Holy Spirit had come in signs and wonders. When Dad stood up, the glory of God fell! I tell you the veil of the temple was rent, and those walls came tumbling down. Yes, sir, it got holy!

Too many homes without a good father figure have children who lack discipline. In more than half of our homes, there is no father at all. I encourage you single mothers to take your role seriously. Jesus will stand up in you in the authority of mother and father. He will lead you to a *positive* male role model in the church or the community who can provide the male support your child may be missing. Listen, Mother, you aren't helping your twenty-eight-year-old unemployed son when you let him live at home with his crusty-big-size-twelve-ashy-heels on your sofa while you're in church. You need to rise up in the power of the Holy Spirit, tell him to get his tail off that couch, and say, "If you're going to live here, you're going to church tomorrow. And get that beer out of my refrigerator. We're also gonna get rid of some of those cable channels. You will go to school and get a job! In this house, Jesus is Lord!" This is the tough love our generation needs.

Jesus is saying to the parents of America's drug and gangster-ridden cities, "Get up!" Get up from all that is killing us. Get up from all that is hindering us in Jesus' name! You won't get a response by speaking any other name. There's no power there! Power rests only in the One who created the heavens and the earth.

No Other Name

There is no other way to bring real deliverance into your children's lives but by touching and speaking to them in Jesus' name. There is no truly lasting way to touch your community other than in Jesus' name. You can only bind a demon in the name of Jesus. You can only bring biblical sense and order into your home in the name of Jesus. You can only bring life to that which is dead in the name of Jesus.

The name of Jesus will bring joy into the midst of sorrow. The name of Jesus will bring hope into the midst of despair. There is no other name given among men, women, boys, and girls through which we can be saved. Jesus Christ is the final sacrifice. There is no other name like the name of Jesus.

So Parents, ARISE! Then raise others. Start with your children. Show them how to spend time in the presence of God. Teach them how to wait on the Lord. When they learn to wait on God they will rise above dead relationships, dead culture, anger, anxiety, looseness, laziness, and self-hatred. Isaiah says that it is in waiting that they are able to rise, run, and walk without growing weary or fainting.

> *But those who wait on the Lord shall renew their strength; they shall mount up with wings like eagles, they shall run and not be weary, they shall walk and not faint.*
>
> ISAIAH 40:31

We all get weary. Some of what you see going on in your streets will get you weary and make you faint. But the strength of the Lord will raise this generation and the next.

There is no resurrection strength in our heritage alone. Our strength is in the Lord. As an African-American, I am extremely proud of the obstacles my people have overcome.

Our strength is not in being Black or White, Jewish or Asian. Our strength and deliverance is in the God who still intervenes in the affairs of humanity.

Brought to these shores as slaves, treated like animals, and living through every imaginable degradation, looked over and left out, yet we survived! The hand of God Almighty brought us out. Our strength is not in being Black or White, Jewish or Asian. Our strength and deliverance is in the God who still intervenes in the affairs of humanity. If it had not been for the Lord, where would we be?

Today we are confronted with a pervasive cultural influence that undermines all that our heritage calls us to achieve. We see this socially:

* Black children die earlier and more violently than at any other time in our history.

* An overwhelming number of children continue to fall through the cracks of society.

* We continue to swell the rolls of "out of wedlock" births.

Spiritually, we've abandoned our moral compass and our common sense—common sense that will tell us what is right:

* "If you lay down with the dogs, you're going to get up with fleas."

* "Good manners will take you where money can't."

* "Don't make your bed so hard today that you can't sleep on it tomorrow!"

* "The future belongs to those who prepare for it today."

We all need to get concretely involved in this struggle. The saying, "If you see a turtle on a fence, you know somebody helped it get there," informs us that we need to let these children ride on our coattails to a better life. The work is hard, and we need inspiration and power to do what is right. God is our refuge and our strength— and He's still able. (See Psalm 46:1.)

There is strength in Jesus to lead your family near to God and away from the ridiculous deceptions of our God—rejecting culture. Jesus is raising up a fearless generation with a hunger to preach and say yes to the Lord. He is pushing into the funeral of America's lost hopes and raising up Christian attorneys, teachers, actors, actresses, singers, athletes, playwrights, poets, businessmen and businesswomen, congressmen and congresswomen, governors, presidents, corporate executives, and entrepreneurs. These mighty ministers of the Gospel are bringing the Christian lifestyle into the world and making a difference!

Our God is seeking parents who will say yes to His will. The very child we are raising has the power to turn this world right-side up!

Is He doing it through you?

> *Train up a child in the way he should go, and when he is old he will not depart from it.*
> PROVERBS 22:6

Helpful Hints

It starts at home. Raising children is not the responsibility of the school system, government, or society as a whole. It starts at home. As previously discussed in this chapter, parents must work together as a team to set forth a standard of righteousness for the home. Children need our love, time, and consistent discipline.

Seeing is believing. We must speak and live in the same manner that we expect our children to speak and live. While there may be areas of our lives in which we would prefer that our children would do as we say and not as we do, our children cannot help but say what they hear and do what they see.

There's strength in numbers. Beyond the training that must be a part of a child's life from birth and the godly example that must be lived before them, children need to know they are not alone. While Daniel and Joseph portray great examples of individual conviction and strength, the three Hebrew boys—Shadrach, Meshach, and Abed-Nego—show us the strength and boldness found in unity. It is always easier to stand when one does not have to stand alone. Assist your children in developing healthy friendships with those of like faith and conviction. In addition to church events, pizza parties, sports outings, and movies are great ways to break the ice and help youth develop these relationships.

six

He Makes Me Lie Down

The Lord is my shepherd; I shall not want.
He maketh me to lie down.

PSALM 23:1-2 KJV

hen I discuss the need and Christian responsibility to stop funerals in our culture, I know I am speaking to some very busy ears. I know it's one thing to explain the importance of being there for the Lord and for our children and that it's another to actually make it happen. We rush so much during the course of our daily affairs that we as parents, business people, and church leaders are often poor examples of a balanced life.

Once you commit to the resurrection power of Jesus in your life, it will do little good if you're constantly tired and pulled between too many situations at one time. If you don't learn to rest in the Lord and allow Jesus to be your Good Shepherd, one day you'll look up and your children will be grown and gone. Bitterness is often bred toward God, you, and the Church because in their eyes God stole all of their daddy's and their mommy's time.

God doesn't get any glory when you burn out in His name. Once you decide to stop the funeral in your house and in your community, you're going to have to learn to lie down. If the enemy can get us too busy, he can run us into a wall. God in His infinite wisdom and mercy actually makes us to lie down so that we can discern the reality of spiritual situations which push and drive us.

You need to take certain days off when you do nothing except relax. For some that may mean playing ball, golfing, or just smelling the roses while carrying your babies and enjoying your wife or husband. God has provided the roses!

I tell you I'm living this thing as I write it. I recently had to send a letter to my church leadership to request a three-month leave of absence from all my administrative responsibilities. I needed to make an immediate adjustment due to overload. I had to personally make a decision to do what the apostles did in Acts, chapter 6—give myself completely to the ministry of the Word and prayer. While I continued preaching and teaching, greater emphasis was put on spending time with God and family. Sometimes we can be so driven that our lives get out of balance.

Yes, our responsibilities involve administration and being faithful in business affairs. You'd better be at that office if you're going to build something. Early in my ministry my office time was extremely long. The counseling and administrative responsibilities were sometimes overwhelming. I would arrive early and leave late daily. It was foundation-building time, and I needed to know every little thing that was going on. I have at this stage of my ministry learned the art of delegation. However, in every believer's life there should be times when we shut everything else out to really focus on what God is saying to us individually. We need retreats so we can revive.

Moreover, we need to go back to one of our most popular childhood activities—napping. So often children become clumsy, irritable, or silly when they do not get enough rest. Adults are no different, and the consequences of sleep deprivation for adults are far more severe. You would be amazed to know the difference a catnap can make in a person's day and ministry. In his CNN article, "Fighting Off Sleep at the Office," Mel Mandell asserts that "to lessen lethargy," corporations should provide "conveniently located, lowly lit rooms equipped with reclining chairs or easy chairs . . . in which tired employees can grab 15 to 20 minute naps during their breaks." Mandell, as well as other researchers in this area, believes that "Short naps are better than longer ones because employees are less likely to awaken feeling sluggish."[6] If those working in corporate America need and benefit from a twenty-minute nap, how much more should those who are called to stop funerals make sure they take time to rest—even if it's only for twenty minutes?

At the risk of being repetitious, let me again stress that in addition to brief moments of rest, every now and then we need to pull back from everything. In ministry, you've got to know when to turn it over and say, "Look, I'm out of here. God bless and love you, but I'll see you later!" And the same is true for lay ministers in the home. If you're *always* at work or at the church, take heed and learn to lie down and graze in the field of our Good Shepherd. If you don't, married or single, your family may suffer, not

[6]Mel Mandell. "Fighting Off Sleep at the Office." 9 April 1999. Update date: 9 April 1999. Accessed: 17 September 1999. *http://cnn.com/TECH/computing/9904/09/sleep.ent.idg/index.html*

to mention the threat of mental, emotional, and physical burnout!

Jesus makes me lie down. When I don't want to, He makes me lie down. Sometimes He will make you lie down by allowing your blood pressure to be elevated. I'm not saying that He will send sickness, but we make choices and then must bear the consequences of our decisions. If you've been trusting God for healing of a consistent migraine headache and you aren't healed yet, it could be that you're causing the migraine. We don't need to blame the devil for what we do to ourselves. If we're stressed, drained, and operating without joy, we need to spend more time in God's presence. The Scriptures tell us, **In His presence is fullness of joy** (Psalm 1:11) and **The joy of the Lord is our strength** (Nehemiah 8:10). So the question is: Are we taking time to be in His presence and enjoy His rest?

> If you're *always* at work or at the church, take heed and learn to lie down and graze in the field of our good Shepherd. If you don't, married or single, your family may suffer, not to mention the threat of mental, emotional, and physical burnout!

What's Wrong With This Picture?

No matter what our calling or profession, each of us must ask ourselves, "Is the Lord my shepherd? Is the Lord my fuel? Or am I being fueled by competition?" More often than not, when we get into the competition game everything else falls by the wayside. We find ourselves saying things like: "I'm gonna build this business or church *if it kills me.* I'm gonna get that promotion *if it kills me,* because no one ever thought I was going to be anything."

Beating out the other guy in greedy competition should never be a motivation for building a business or a church. "They never thought I would amount to anything; but, I tell you, I'm gonna make this church famous and prove them wrong." That's the wrong motive. All that is planned and pursued may, in fact, materialize. Yet, because greed and not God is what motivates you, whatever is produced will be filled with chaos. The entire process will wreak havoc on your mind and emotions. James puts it this way,

> *What causes wars, and what causes fighting among you? Is it not your passions that are at war in your members?*
> *You desire and do not have; so you kill. And you covet and cannot obtain; so you fight and wage war. You do not have, because you do not ask.*
> *You ask and do not receive, because you ask wrongly, to spend it on your passions.*
>
> JAMES 4:1-3 RSV

Settle down and ask yourself, "Who's leading me? What's fueling me?"

The Power of the Glory

We would all do well to pause for station identification. Is God truly receiving all of the glory? Often, what drives us receives the glory. But as we glorify God and serve in His name, He indeed gives us sufficient grace and strength to stop funerals and become an agent of true resurrection.

Fathers, if we are watching our families being tossed to and fro, we need to pause for station identification. If we are serious about funeral-stopping, we need to tune out distractions and tune into the Holy Spirit. If mothers are serious about stopping some funerals, they had better tune into the God channel while their children are still at home. Parents, the Holy Spirit will stand with us and visit our situations with His presence in our homes. When we make the choice to stand

> Pastors, if we are to be used as funeral-stoppers, we must reassess our priorities, turn off the home shopping channel, and tune into the servant station, J-E-S-U-S.

for righteousness, peace, and joy in the Holy Spirit, God will stand for us!

Pastors, if we are to be used as funeral-stoppers, we must reassess our priorities, turn off the Home Shopping Channel, and tune into the servant station, J-E-S-U-S. Let's get it together! Pause and think about it: Why are we in ministry?

The Spirit of the Lord God is upon Me,
Because the Lord has anointed Me
To preach good tidings to the poor;
He has sent Me to heal the brokenhearted,
To proclaim liberty to the captives.
And the opening of the prison to those who are
bound.

ISAIAH 61:1

Pastors with a heart for ministry, you need to ask yourself whether or not you are in competition with the preacher across town because they built a new sanctuary. Is this where all your efforts are directed? Are you constructing programs because your neighbor did it in her church? Everything that works in ministry in one region may not necessarily work in yours. Beware of the competition trap. Do what God has called you to do, and then work that thing!

Think about it: Are you working to build a new house because your brother down the street built a new house? Are you looking to start a new business because your friends started one? Are you going back to school because your neighbor went back to school? While people may inspire you to do more, your focus should never be competition. What is the source of your thinking? Let God get all the glory and close the door on envy, jealousy, and one-upmanship! Paul wrote,

For it is God who works in you both to will and to
do for His good pleasure.

PHILIPPIANS 2:13

We all need to pause for station identification and allow God to reveal our motives. Building churches and businesses are wonderful things when the Lord leads us to do it. Where He leads He feeds. God is not required to bless anything that is birthed out of the wrong motive.

Some dear Christian brothers and sisters are still trying to prove something to a dead parent. Overcompensating is often the result of poor self esteem and complexes. Mama or Daddy told them twenty years ago that they would never amount to anything, so they've been overachieving ever since and it's destroying them. *"Hmmmm, she said I was marrying a bum . . . I'll show her."* They work themselves to a crisp tanking up on the wrong fuel. We forfeit God's promise of blessing in our lives when our motives are not God-centered.

When you read Psalm 23, it is a time for pausing and station identification. So pause with me here for a moment:

> *The Lord is my shepherd;*
> *I shall not want.*
> *He makes me to lie down in green pastures;*
> *He leads me beside the still waters.*
> *He restores my soul;*
> *He leads me in the paths of righteousness for His name's sake.*

PSALM 23:1-3

When I read these words of David, I pause to ask myself, "Who is leading me? What is driving me? What am I building for? How is my family doing? How is my community doing? How am I affecting my church and neighborhood as a father in my community and as a bishop in His Church?"

I want to serve the purposes of God in my generation. When the Lord says, "Enough! Let someone else build," I go on and do whatever the Lord has for me to do at that time. Every now and then He'll say, "Pause and rest." I lie down to pause for station identification.

> *The Lord is my shepherd; I shall not want.*
> PSALM 23:1

When the Lord is our Shepherd, He also becomes our Source. Because He leads us, we don't have to want. When we choose to follow His plan, we don't have to worry because He supplies all of our need. (See Philippians 4:13.) The old saints would say, "He'll make a way outta no way. He may not come when you want Him, but He'll be right on time."

Oh, how we need to allow the Lord to shepherd our lives, our families, and our churches. So often churches split or die because they were started with the wrong motives. I've come across this dilemma through the years. A ministry begins because someone left another ministry angry and bruised. If the spirit of bitterness is not dealt with, it will be carried into the new work and bring disease. When the leaders are fueled by competition, the real work struggles to exist. Impacting souls for the kingdom of God gets pushed by the wayside; the focus is inward only, and the funeral procession marches on—unchallenged outside the church doors.

When the Lord is truly our Source, our times are in His hand. We have too little time to waste time. What we do with our time determines what God does in our lives and in our communities. There are two kinds of time. There is *kairos* time, that appointed, predestined time of destiny yet to come; and there is *chronos* time, the clock-ticking time which, when given to God, allows Him to work in our destiny. A preacher I know calls the connection with God's will in our life on earth the kairotic moment. The kairotic moment is that time in which we allow our time to hook up with God's time, thereby allowing every moment

> If I am on a sabbatical, God uses the sabbatical to put something in me. I retreat to refuel for the work and the struggle.

of our lives to be pregnant with possibility. When we follow the Good Shepherd, there are no wasted seasons. Every season counts for something. Even if I am resting, that time strengthens and enables me to accomplish the ensuing assignments given by God. If I am on a sabbatical, God uses the sabbatical to put something in me. I retreat to refuel for the work and the struggle.

When David says, **He makes me lie down**, he doesn't mean God is putting him out to pasture! He is saying that God makes him lie down so he can stand up and fight later. When I'm rested, **I can run through a troop and by my God I can leap over a wall** (Psalm 18:29),

because my times are in His hands. I can stand for god-
liness and truth in my home when I'm resting in God's
pasture.

Knowing His Voice

Parents, you have no time to waste. There is no time
to play with the toys of this world. Our lives are full of
potential and possibility, so we need to be restored while
we follow Him. Jesus will lead you in victory every day
when you take the time to hear His voice. Jesus describes
His relationship with the Church in terms of sheep and
shepherd in John:

> "And when he brings out his own sheep, he goes
> before them; and the sheep follow him, for they know
> his voice.
> "Yet they will by no means follow a stranger, but
> will flee from him, for they do not know the voice of
> strangers."
>
> JOHN 10:4-5

The Lord will give us the adequate rest we so desperately need in our fractured culture! I recently asked
everyone in my congregation who had high blood pressure to raise their hand and half the congregation
responded. But we aren't exclusive. If you invite Black
folk up to a prayer line in church on any given Sunday,
half of them will ask you to pray for high blood pressure
or diabetes. One out of every seven Black people today is
diabetic or suffers from high blood pressure. In many

cases, however, we cause it by running ourselves into the ground, not exercising, and eating unhealthy foods.

On occasion I want to tell some people in my healing lines, "Hear the Word of the Lord. Stop eating white bread and red meat. Stop eating pork. Give up salt. Don't waste God's time. You don't need a miracle. You need discipline! Now please get out of the prayer line. Next!"

Sometimes I hear folks complaining, "Oh child, how you feelin'?"

"Girl I'm so tired. I could just—whoo, child I'm just . . . " Then if you interrupt and ask them what time they went to bed they tell you, "Child, I didn't get to bed until four this mornin' and turned right around and got up at seven—whoo." Down at four o'clock and up at seven o'clock—she ought to be tired! It isn't the devil; it's her! So Jesus wants to make us lie down and give us His direction, including when to rest.

Most leaders are driven people by nature. When success is the goal, we run hard and rest little. Most pastors I know would be pushing to be corporate executives if they weren't pastoring. We push and often think, *I'm not doing bad. But you know, I could be doing a little bit better, considering what I give out.* Many times that's true.

What pastors give out is not always compensatory with what is put back into them, considering the enormity of their work. This is also true for the missionary on the field and for the parents in the home. Obeying the Lord promises eternal value. We are assured that payday is coming. While tangible blessings in the here and now are biblical, we must keep all things in perspective. No amount of money can ever resurrect a life out of a graveyard. During our lifetime, we may wear silk clothing and alligator shoes. We may even live in a mansion and be able to afford an ornate headstone for our burial. Still, death can reign on the inside.

Money is good, but it can't buy the Good Shepherd's rest. It may buy you a vacation, but have you ever had one of those vacations you had to take a vacation from? Money can't buy God's peace or a place in heaven. Thank God if we're living well here! Nevertheless, we mustn't forget that our real payday will come when we see Him face to face.

We don't hear much preaching about heaven anymore. Rarely do we even talk about heaven because everything is so earth-centered. When we do preach about it, we are criticized for having a "pie-in-the-sky" theology. To these critics I say, "We've been talking about seeing Him face-to-face and wearing a crown for years, so when did heaven become bad theology?" Knowing where we are headed when this life is over gives us God's perspective on the temporary nature of earthly things.

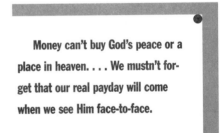

Money can't buy God's peace or a place in heaven. . . . We mustn't forget that our real payday will come when we see Him face-to-face.

Parents, if we are going to give ourselves to raising a fearless generation that is not ashamed to take a stand for God, we are going to have to find God's rest. We cannot ask God to "Bless our plans" without asking His will for our plans. The old saints often say, "If the Lord wills" or "Lord willing," or "I will serve next Sunday, if the Lord wills." Hearing this as a child helped me learn a God perspective in life. Our lives are in His hands. When the Lord wills doors to be open, they will be open. Then, and only then, should we walk through.

When God sees that we are faithful with that one door, He will open up another and another, as long as we remain focused. We will also learn to recognize that every open door hasn't been opened by God. Some are put there by Satan himself. Also, the doors meant for us to walk through do not open on demand but in their season. Consequently, the Lord makes us lie down, but not just anywhere. He makes us lie down in green pastures, to feed us with His Word.

Sheep that have good shepherds aren't allowed to graze just anywhere. They are led to fresh, green grass. Earthly shepherds are always leading and feeding, so He makes us lie down. Those of us in the ministry need someone to tell us to lie down, because we're so busy dealing with the problems of others we often just burn out. We are indeed blessed if we have someone who will come and say, "Pastor, as I look at you, I sense that for the long haul it would be good for you to take some time off right now. You need to be a hundred percent for the days that lie ahead. So take some time off. You look and sound tired!"

Our lives are not necessarily in order because we have a title and a measure of good success. God is still working on all of us. All of us are in need of the shepherd's staff to lead us, guide us, and make us lie down. To be made, we often have to be unmade. The Good Shepherd wants to unmake those areas of our lives that think, dress, and act like the "dog-eat-dog" populace of the world. He wants us to lie down.

The Holy Spirit may say to you, "Now listen, Pastor, I've called you to minister in this neighborhood. Stay faithful even though growth is slow. You are running all over the place with good intentions, but your home is fractured, and your children are lost. You've laid the complete burden of raising them on their mother, and she's too nice to say no, even when she should." We're not effective in God's kingdom if we are too tired to hear God's voice. When was the last time you took time to lie down and rest? I mean, really rest. Football coach Vince Lombardi once said, "Weariness makes cowards out of all of us." In *Christ, beloved*, there *is* rest for the weary soul.

Jesus says, "Come into a season with me, Child. Take that Bishop, Pastor, Manager, Professor, President, Vice President, or other title off of your nameplate for a season. Come and spend some time with Me because I want to remake you. I want you to see that nothing compares to what you shall see. Come and see that what you have is nothing compared to what you shall have. Come and see that where you are is nothing compared to where you shall be. Eyes have not seen and ears have not heard all that I will do for them who allow themselves to lie down and rest in me."

The funeral-stopping, world-turning Church that God wants to use to shake America will know who they are in times of trouble because they spend time with God. I know it's not easy to relax when murder, drug abuse, prostitution, and confusion are ruling the streets around our homes, but that's just my point. The Lord wants His Church to rest in the middle of the chaos. There, He can use us to touch and speak to the funeral that surrounds us.

Those who rest get blessed!

We are living in an increasingly fragmented, fast-paced society. One wonders if we can ever go back to a quieter, less hectic time. While I don't believe we can ever go back, we can, however, live as Christians within this nation, in this time. We will need a discipline strong enough to resist the pull of bowing down and bowing out. We will indeed need to stand!

> **Those who rest get blessed with the knowledge of their strength in God; so when the shooting starts, they stand strong while others run.**

During one of Dr. Martin Luther King Jr.'s civil rights marches in the sixties, a gunshot rang out that scattered his bodyguards like scared cats. These men were supposed to be guarding him, but at the first sign of danger, they ducked and ran. Evidently, no one knew what these men were really made of until the test came. Often, by then it is too late.

The same can be true for God's guardians entrusted with His work today. Those who rest get blessed with the knowledge of their strength in God; so when the shooting starts, they stand strong while others run. Stand on, Child of God, stand on! Feast regularly on Bible study, church prayer meetings, praying in the home, and Scripture memorization. These disciplines are of utmost importance for those who seriously stand! We must allow the Holy Spirit to speak to us so that we can transform our homes into missions for the war refugees in our neighborhoods.

Where the Rubber Meets the Road

The desire to stop the funeral and the power to actually do it are two different things. Right motives must be backed up with God's presence. I would burn myself out on a monthly basis doing the work of ministry if I didn't take time out to be with God. I am yet learning not to make a god out of ministry—rather to honor the God of the ministry.

> *Not by might nor by power, but by My Spirit, says the Lord of hosts.*
>
> ZECHARIAH 4:6

One day the Holy Spirit spoke to me and said, "If you don't slow down, you're just going to be walking and building, and suddenly you're going to hit a wall." So I slowed down. I didn't quit. I simply slowed down to spend time with the Good Shepherd.

Life in the fast lane can kill you if you don't watch where you're going. I could tell you story after story of leaders who wouldn't slow down and lost their ministries. Some hit that wall and started drinking. Others smashed into it and went back to the crack cocaine from which God had delivered them. Some crashed into the wall and started hitting their wives. Others crashed into it and abused their children.

Can we get real? I'm talking about business, community, and church leaders. None of us are immune. None of us should throw stones at the other, rather we all would do well from time to time to "go somewhere and sit down." Some started out to establish balanced ministries; but when problems surrounded them, they let the pressures of ministry smother God's voice and they forgot to lie down. When we truly follow the Good Shepherd, He calls us to lie down.

It is so important to support our pastors, and they need willing and obedient servants to help them in God's work. But our pastors can't use burnt-out religious folks to get the job done! It will take every one of us— rested, refueled, revived, and on top of things—to restore the inner and outer cities of America.

When the Lord cautioned me to slow down or hit the wall, I resisted for awhile because I'm a "Type A" personality to the third degree. I'm a mover and a shaker. I start the morning thinking and moving. I'm always thinking, dreaming, and wondering, *What new ministry can we bless the community with? Where do we go from here? When do we move to what the Lord is showing us?* My mind is always clicking because that's my nature. So when God cautioned me to slow down, I did it, but not without having to downshift fifteen gears in my mind.

I know that my time here on earth is temporary. I know to some extent everything I do while here on earth will change in some way or another after I leave.

Therefore, before I die I'm going to make every day count.

I must work the works of him that sent me, while it is day: the night cometh, when no man can work.
JOHN 9:4 KJV

When I stand before the Lord, I will give an account of my stewardship, not only as a pastor but as a husband, father, son, and citizen. I want to stand before Him as a faithful servant and a committed funeral-stopper.

When we follow the Good Shepherd, He will always warn us before we hit the wall. He will say, "STOP! Duck! Slow down! Lie down. Where are you going, sheep?" Jesus makes us lie down. He makes us rest. He causes us to be still. Why? He does it so He can use us effectively in our communities, lay our hands on the coffins of the dead who surround us, and raise them up! When the Church of Jesus Christ takes time to graze in His pasture, it will be a strong, relevant Church. Relevant churches are called to stop the funerals we see around us. They are the ones who will turn the world upside down.

And our world needs some upside turning!

When we slow down, we can pause and reflect. In several books in the Old Testament, especially the Psalms, we find the word *selah*. *Selah* means "pause."[7] It means to stop and think about it. *Selah* and think about God's many promises for our families and communities. *Selah* and think about the truth in God's words. When we read a psalm or another passage of Scripture publicly and come across the word *selah*, we aren't supposed to read it aloud. We are to stop right there and let everyone think

> When we feel rested, we will have the physical strength to move in, touch the coffin, raise the dead, and give the resurrected back to their family. Spending time with Jesus will help us stay refreshed and give us sweet sleep.

about what was just read. We need to think on God's Word to be world-turners for Jesus Christ.

For so He gives His beloved sleep.

PSALM 127:2

When I slow down to spend time with the Good Shepherd, I also get my sleep. Did you know there are thousands of angry, confused, sleep-deprived people today? It's true. When you sleep, your body is replenished. Most important, sleep prepares you for your day. It will give you peace to handle trouble, anxiety, and stress.

"Therefore do not worry about tomorrow, for tomorrow will worry about its own things. Sufficient for the day is its own trouble."

MATTHEW 6:34

---

[7]James Strong, LL.D., S.T.D. #5542. "Hebrew and Chaldee Dictionary" *Strong's Exhaustive Concordance of the Bible* (Atlanta: Nelson, 1990).

When we feel rested, we will have the physical strength to move in, touch the coffin, raise the dead, and give the resurrected back to their family. Spending time with Jesus will help us stay refreshed and give us sweet sleep. We then rise the next day, confident of God's new mercies and faithfulness. As a young adult our choirs would sing,

This morning when I rose,
I didn't have no doubt—
I knew the Lord would take care of me,
I knew the Lord would provide for me,
I knew the Lord would lead and guide me
All the way . . . all the way.

When the Cup Runs Over

You anoint my head with oil; my cup runs over.

PSALM 23:5

Throughout Scripture, there are various reasons for anointing a person with oil. The reason that seems to best apply to David in this particular psalm is anointing for the purpose of "refreshing or invigorating" as found in Deuteronomy 28:40; Ruth 3:3; 2 Samuel 14:2; and Psalm 104:15.[8] In Hebrew culture, when someone died the family and friends mourned for a prescribed period of time. When that time had ended, the mourners would bathe and anoint themselves with oil. Upon hearing that

---

[8]M. G. Easton. "Anoint." *Easton's Bible Dictionary*. Oklahoma City: Ellis Enterprises. QuickVerse 5.0. Hiawatha, IA: Parsons Technology, 1992-1998.

his son had died, David responded as one would upon the completion of the mourning period. The scripture reads,

> *Then David arose from the earth, and washed, and anointed himself, and changed his clothes; and he went into the house of the Lord, and worshiped; he then went to his own house; and when he asked, they set food before him, and he ate.*
>
> *Then David comforted his wife, Bathsheba, and went in to her, and lay with her; and she bore a son, and he called his name Solomon. And the Lord loved him.*
>
> 2 SAMUEL 12:20,24 RSV

In Psalm 23, David says, "God anoints my head with oil." When the Lord anoints, refreshes, and invigorates us, we will be able to comfort others and stop the funerals around us. God's anointing is not like a soda or a cup of coffee, which gives us a temporary jolt. God's anointing causes our cups to overflow. The anointing is not only for us personally, but it is for those dying and thirsty souls around us. It was not until David anointed *himself* that he could then comfort his wife. Acts 10:38 RSV states,

> *God anointed Jesus of Nazareth with the Holy Spirit and with power . . . he went about doing good and healing all that were oppressed by the devil, for God was with him.*

The anointing in Jesus' life overflowed to those He touched and those who reached out to touch Him in faith. The anointing in Paul's life overflowed **so that handkerchiefs or aprons were carried away from his body to the sick, and diseases left them and the evil spirits came out of them** (Acts 19:12 RSV). God wants to anoint us until we are refreshed and invigorated and our cups overflow. Then we can stop the funerals of those all around us. We are blessed to bless others.

> *He restores my soul.*
>
> PSALM 23:3

Jesus will give rest to His people! He will renew and restore our souls!

God is looking for a fearless generation that will live, prosper, and succeed above the tinsel-cheap image of success that the enemy of our souls has sold our culture. Every day we watch the funeral marches of a hopeless generation, and we do it without blinking because so often we see no way out. We sit and watch because we're inadequate without the Good Shepherd's rest. And without His rest, we miss His answer. Healing our national depression begins by spending time with Him, receiving His word, and following His lead.

Jesus wants us to raise a fearless generation that knows the power of His name! He wants to lead us along still waters and into green pastures to show us His will for our lives.

Take some time right now to pause. Read Psalm 23. Then get quiet before God. If you need to repent of greed and lust, do it now. If you need to repent of fear, do it. Then ask

God to bless your home and to give you—married or single—His anointing to properly shepherd your family.

Pray for your pastor and the families in your church. Ask God for the grace to shepherd your business or serve your employer in His anointing. Repent of keeping up with a certain standard that keeps you at the church or at your business all day. Ask for proper boundaries. Then read Psalm 23 and pray again tomorrow. Set a time aside every day to lie down. Stop the funeral in yourself first. Then you will be ready to help others out of their graves, and your cup will run over with blessings beyond your imagination.

> Stop the funeral in yourself first. Then you will be ready to help others out of their graves, and your cup will run over with blessings beyond your imagination.

When the Lord is our Shepherd and is living powerfully within us, we can walk up to the coffin of the widow's child, touch the situation, and bring that which has died back to life.

The Lord is my shepherd;
I shall not want.
He makes me to lie down in green pastures;
He leads me beside the still waters.
He restores my soul;
He leads me in the paths of righteousness for His name's sake.
Yea, though I walk through the valley of the shadow of death, I will fear no evil;

For You are with me;
Your rod and Your staff, they comfort me.
You prepare a table before me in the presence of
my enemies;
You anoint my head with oil;
My cup runs over.
Surely goodness and mercy shall follow me
All the days of my life;
And I will dwell in the house of the Lord forever.

Psalm 23:1-6

There is more power than we ever may have thought in this *goldie-oldie* Bible verse. We may have thought we had outgrown it, but we need a fresh revelation of this text to be funeral stoppers. When Jesus is our Shepherd, we cease to want. He makes us lie down in green pastures and feeds us His truth beside the still waters of His calming presence. It is there in His presence that He restores our soul.

Once the raging funeral is stopped in our hearts, we fear no evil because we know the Lord is with us. His rod and staff comfort us as He prepares a table before us in the presence of our enemies. In His presence, we can stand bold as a lion. He gives us His anointing beyond natural measure to proclaim His freedom to our confused, self-centered culture.

When the Lord is our Shepherd, goodness and mercy follow us all the days of our lives, now and in heaven to come.

I am the Good Shepherd; and I know my sheep,
and am known by My own.

John 10:14

Helpful Hints

Set aside family time. Sanctify at least two days of every week where the family is having a meal together. Turn the television off and focus on each other.

Take a nap. We are never too old for naps. By resting in the middle of a large task or long day, we gain the strength and focus needed to complete it.

Remember the Sabbath. God created the Sabbath out of love for His people. Jesus said "the Sabbath was made for man." Every week take a day off and rest. Worship God, praise God, and rest in God.

Delegate. Far too often it is the lack of delegation that sends hard workers to the hospital or an early grave. Have faith in God that whatever is delegated will be accomplished in a satisfactory manner. Train, prepare, organize, then delegate.

seven

The Responsible Church

We know that we have passed from death to life, because we love the brethren. He who does not love his brother abides in death.

1 JOHN 3:14

Christ is still the answer for our nation. Only Jesus can stop the funeral of our lost generation and the death that imprisons our neighborhoods. And because He is head of the body, it is His body, the Church, which is responsible to clean up this mess. If we proclaim we are the Church, the "Called Out" of God, the buck stops here!

The Church can stop the funeral. The Church can make a lasting impact. The relevant, responsible Church can win the lost and resurrect the dead. As we grow in holy boldness, we will move in to touch the coffin and raise the dead. Dead youth, families, and systems can all be resurrected in His name. We are called to be world-turners and funeral-stoppers. As it was said of the early church, so it should be said of today's church:

These who have turned the world upside down have come here too.

ACTS 17:6

But the funeral must stop in our own lives first.

■ Don't Pawn Your Crown

Satan will try to buy us off. That's where all of this competition nonsense comes in to play. Don't compromise. Remember the call of God on your life and your early zeal and commitment. Follow the Shepherd of our souls—focusing on Him will strengthen us so we won't sell out for worldly fame. When it's all over, we shall wear a crown. While here, however, we are called to a relevant, responsible Christianity. The apostle Peter put this all into eternal perspective:

> *The elders who are among you I exhort, I who am a fellow elder and a witness of the sufferings of Christ, and also a partaker of the glory that will be revealed:*
>
> *Shepherd the flock of God which is among you, serving as overseers, not by compulsion but willingly, not for dishonest gain but eagerly;*
>
> *nor as being lords over those entrusted to you, but being examples to the flock;*
>
> *and when the Chief Shepherd appears, you will receive the crown of glory that does not fade away.*
>
> 1 PETER 5:1-4

When the crown of unfading glory is the purpose and goal of Christian living, God's people can't be bought off. Although Peter is talking about the pastoral ministry in this Scripture passage, it applies just as well to men and women on the job and parents in the home. When we stay the course with the Chief Shepherd, we can't be bought off by the whimpering of our children or the seductions of our age. And when the temporal expires we will receive the crown of glory that does not fade away.

The "Chief Shepherd" Peter is referring to is Jesus. Jesus said in John 10:9-10:

> *I am the door. If anyone enters by Me, he will be saved, and will go in and out and find pasture.*
> *The thief does not come except to steal, and to kill, and to destroy. I have come that they may have life, and that they may have it more abundantly.*

The thief prowls about and kills his prey outside of God's protected pasture. So again, Psalm 23 stands as God's commentary for today's funeral-stopping Church. When the Chief Shepherd leads us, we shall not want of power, authority, finances, or faith. We won't be bought off by strategies and schemes of the devil. We will keep our crown.

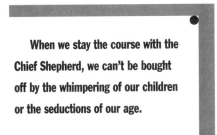

When we stay the course with the Chief Shepherd, we can't be bought off by the whimpering of our children or the seductions of our age.

The Chief Shepherd Gives Strength

So much of what we see going on today is upsetting. Although we may cry, the Lord is still our Shepherd. Responsible Christians can handle trouble. Some of us have gone through so much that we wonder why we haven't lost our minds . . . but God! Some people have gone through what many of us have gone through; they are in "rubber rooms" and unable to remember their own names. How the church is needed to share our hope with the hurting of the world . . . even Jesus, the Christ of God!

Trouble often comes to us in clusters, like bunches of grapes. In other words, you lose your job and, at the same time, you get a notice that your kids are acting up at school. Your investments go under, and your car breaks down. Trouble comes in bunches. However, the apostle Paul reminds us that,

> We are troubled on every side, yet not distressed;
> we are perplexed, but not in despair;
> persecuted, but not forsaken; cast down, but not destroyed.
>
> 2 CORINTHIANS 4:8-9 KJV

Surely God has been and is our refuge and strength, a very present help in trouble (Psalm 46:1). Listen! When we make it to the house of God, after all we have been through as a people, no one should have to tell us to throw our hands up! We should raise our hands night and day in praise to God. Our strength is in our praise. Every day is another opportunity to praise the Lord—not only with hands raised up, but hands that are "stretched out" in service to humankind.

Many think church leaders are made of stone and are invulnerable to trouble. We all bleed. We all feel pain. As leaders we learn how to press beyond the pain of consistent evaluations, gossip, and accusation. We can't lose focus—and we can't stop the work and "come down." We are on a mission. God is our present help.

One of the great challenges of pastoring for me is to visit people who are dying and then later having to bury them. I find this particularly stressful when it involves children or young mothers. I haven't been able to get to the place where I'm not challenged when a child dies. It takes two or three weeks after a little boy or girl's funeral before I really start feeling like myself again, especially if murder was involved. But I minister in this area with all my might because God has called me to do it. I recently tried to go into the pediatric ward to pray for a very sick baby with my eyes almost closed. I just wanted to walk in and say, "Point me to the baby that I'm coming to see." Then I just wanted

> Although I wasn't very fearless when I entered that hospital, once I allowed the Good Shepherd to put me *in* the funeral march, I became very bold.

to lay hands on the child, turn, and go. But I couldn't. As I prayed for the baby, I turned around and saw another baby, tubes and all. Then I made the mistake of walking into the pediatric cancer ward. Suddenly, I found myself intersecting a number of tragic funerals.

I took my authority as a man of God. I prayed for this one, turning and saying, "Lord, touch this one," and "God bless that one. Lord, help that mother. God touch that father, in Jesus' name. Lord, remember this one. Lord, remember that one." Although I wasn't very fearless when I entered that hospital, once I allowed the

Good Shepherd to put me *in* the funeral march, I became very bold.

As the Church we are called to a ministry of caring, consoling, and correcting—with the mercy and love of Jesus. All too often those of us who have been in Christian service for "some time" lose our compassion. We stop caring. Jesus calls the Church into bold action. He calls us to *do* something. Stop the funeral, reach out and touch somebody, lift the downtrodden, care for the dying, and rescue the perishing.

The Chief Shepherd Teaches

I am often surprised by the mental recall of dying Christians. It might surprise you how the old sayings and old hymns are remembered. Rarely do they recall deep, cerebral sermons from Revelation 8. Rarely do they think about those exciting prophetic words they once heard the Lord was going to do. No, the "old stuff" comes back. The old classics of long-gone years. The dying remember the Bible verses we thought were just so elementary, *milk* scriptures we supposedly matured and graduated from years ago—like Psalm 23.

Many of us learned Psalm 23 on a flannel graph in Sunday School when we were six or seven—and most of us grew out of the powerful truth of this text by the time we were twelve! Then, when the Lord is no longer our Shepherd, we wonder why our lives are rarely touched by Him. So many of us miss what we need to know because of what we already think we know. Most of the things we think we already know, we really don't know at all! We must remain teachable. As I grow older, I am moved by the foundation truths taught and embraced years ago.

When you stop to think about it, there is no better analogy that could have been used by God to show our relationship with Him than a shepherd and a sheep. We are sheep, and He is our Shepherd. If we really believed this in the Church today, and we allowed Him to teach us and give us revelation in His Word every day, there would be fewer mean, stressed out, faithless, frustrated Christians.

■ The Chief Shepherd Cares

In Psalm 23, the shepherd David describes God as a caring, dependable guide. Peter calls Him the Chief Shepherd and tells us to "cast all our cares upon Him." (See 1 Peter 5:7.) Created by God, we are marked with purpose, possibility, and promise. There isn't one sheep under heaven who was designed by God to be a failure. There may have been a generational curse that overcame us for a season, but no one was designed by God to be a lost sheep. So God sent His lost sheep a Shepherd to lead us through the valley of the shadow of death.

> *Yea, though I walk through the valley of the shadow of death, I will fear no evil; for You are with me; your rod and Your staff, they comfort me.*
>
> PSALM 23:4

As you follow the Good Shepherd through life, you walk as a blessing in the earth. If you walked into some of the neighborhoods I preach in, you would feel like you're walking into the Psalmist's valley of the shadow death. These valleys are filled with teeming tenements, homeless people lining the streets, young children with bulging eyes out all hours of the night, emaciated teenagers waiting for their next fix. It's dark and discouraging. But His rod and staff comfort me, and I touch with comfort those I am sent to bless. The relevant Church understands her call to comfort, heal, and bless. We are not to run and hide; rather, we are compelled by God's love to get into the trenches of life and make a difference. We are called to be salt and light.

> We learn victorious faith by fighting, winning, and standing our ground. We learn it by fasting and praying. Sometimes we learn it by failing, falling, and getting up again.

So often we miss it because we don't know how to follow the Shepherd of our souls. We prefer gimmicks, not God. We want formulas, not faith. Only by *living* by faith can we learn the kind of God-pleasing faith that it takes to invite His resurrection power into our lives and thereby into the lives of others. We learn victorious faith by fighting, winning, and standing our ground. We learn it by fasting and praying. Sometimes we learn it by failing, falling, and getting up again.

Anybody can fall, but a *great* man or woman gets back up. We get back up by the power of the Holy Spirit.

When we hook into and obediently follow the Shepherd of our souls, He will comfort us with His rod and staff and raise us to stand again. Jesus will guide and direct us as our light and salvation.

When we get up in the morning we need to say,

When I'm lonely, You, Lord, are my friend.
You're my water when I'm thirsty.
When I'm hungry, You're my fuel.
The Lord is my shepherd and salvation.
The Lord is my strength and my song.
The Lord is my anchor and my rock.
The Lord is my buckler.
The Lord is my director.
The Lord is my bridge over troubled water.

I'm determined to walk with Jesus, yes, I am.
I'm determined to walk with Jesus, yes, I am.
Through hard trials, tribulations, persecutions, I'll be
    faithful.
I'm determined to walk with Jesus, yes, I am!

The Lord IS and He cares for ME!

The Chief Shepherd Is Our Source

When we know the Good Shepherd as the source of all we ever need, we will cross the funeral paths of those surrounding us with love, power, care, and compassion in our hearts. We will have the answer to our community's thirst for crack cocaine, Olde English 800, chronic weed, and heroin. The Good Shepherd also will speak to us about creative solutions for teenage pregnancy and joblessness.

Folk in the tavern are there because they want someone to care for them. It wasn't too long ago that some of you were on the barstool. You just sat there paying $20 for a few thimblefuls of liquor. You could have bought a whole bottle of liquor for what you paid for those thimbles. But you were there to get some comfort and companionship. Remember?

Hear me today: If you're not a careful, blood-washed, Bible-reading, hand-waving, shouting, offering-giving child of God—if you don't get the Word of God deep down in your soul—if you don't believe and stay responsible—there are traps set ahead that will cause you to run back to that same familiar place. The enemy of your soul is always at work. Spend time with the Shepherd. Rely on Him as your source. There are some things in life that will shake you to the core of your being and have the capacity to rock your world. Be still, and know that He is God; you are not alone.

The responsible Church doesn't play church. The time for playing church is over. We must do more than get all dressed up and look the part. If we are to be the Church that turns the world upside down, then we need more than form and fashion. We need a vibrant, living faith that is relevant and responsible. We are called to a *real* relationship with a resurrected Lord.

Words of a Follower

We must hide the Word of God deep within our hearts, as the Psalmist writes in 119:

> *Your word I have hidden in my heart, that I might not sin against You.*
> *Blessed are You, O Lord! Teach me Your statutes!*
> *With my lips I have declared all the judgments of Your mouth.*
> *I have rejoiced in the way of Your testimonies, as much as in all riches.*
> *I will meditate on Your precepts, and contemplate Your ways.*
> *I will delight myself in Your statutes; I will not forget Your word.*
>
> PSALM 119:11-16

These words are the creed of a faithful follower of the Good Shepherd who seeks God every day. Nevertheless, I'm *shocked* at the numbers of people who don't feel they need Bible class and midweek prayer meeting. I'm *shocked* and amazed at the numbers of us who put *everything* in front of extracurricular Bible study as if we knew all we will ever need to know. This is why Paul says, **Let him who thinks he stands take heed lest he fall** (1 Corinthians 10:12).

Jesus died to birth a responsible Church that understands the importance of following Him as Shepherd. We are to obey the Lord's commands and prompting. Those who hope and follow Him find fulfillment, eternal life, and security. When we follow the Lord only when it's convenient, we experience discontentment, and ultimately failure and loss. Then that loss of care and compassion causes apathy.

Apathetic Christians don't care about the state of the world. They just sit idly by and say "Whatever." Someone says, "I hear that they're phasing out another thousand folk at the firm. They will lose their jobs next month."

And you say, "Whatever . . . "

"A child was molested by her father." And you say, "Whatever."

"Whatever . . . Whatever the devil wants to do in my life is all right by me. Whatever happens in the community is all right with me. Whatever happens is what happens, that's all. What will be will be. Whatever . . . "

> **When we follow the Lord only when it's convenient, we experience discontentment, and ultimately failure and loss. Then that loss of care and compassion causes apathy.**

This is the kind of thinking that watches funerals pass by everyday. You say, "Kids on drugs, forced into prostitution, shot down by a drive-by, can't do anything about it. Whatever . . . " Now what kind of responsibility is that? Quite frankly, I am tiring of the Church saying, "Whatever." We should be concerned about the state of things. Wherever there is pain, the Church needs to not only "show up" but find creative ways to deal with societal ills.

When we learn to rest in God and trust Him, He will lead us to minister. He will move through us to confront the funeral processions in our homes, down the street, and in our churches. We must get to the place where we don't just *say*, "The Lord is my shepherd." We must get to the place where He is our Shepherd and we are the sheep of His pasture, feeding on His Word, resting in His presence. Jesus is our Good Shepherd because He cares for us and meets all our needs. He is our source for everything in life.

I heard a story at a ministerial convention that helps to illustrate this point. A story was told about an Arab shepherd in the Middle East. One day, as a Christian group was touring Israel, a shepherd told some ministers, "Your Jesus spoke of sheep and shepherd. I, Shepherd Abdul know every sheep by name. When I call, they come."

So the preachers walked over and said, "Please, Abdul, call that sheep right there."

So Abdul said, "Give me two dollars."

"What do you mean, give you two dollars? Is this some sort of game?" the ministers asked.

"I need two dollars so I can go buy some oats," Abdul replied. "Because when I put the oats in my hand and call their names, the sheep come to eat the oats. No oats, no sheep."

The point of this story is that the sheep come to where the food is. It is the shepherd's responsibility to make sure sheep are fed with food that is nourishing. In these days of compromise, it is refreshing to know that there are pastors and churches who take seriously feeding the sheep. Sheep will go to where the food and nourishment are.

John 10:11 refers to Jesus as the Good Shepherd who gives His life for the sheep. No poison there. The writer of Hebrews refers to Jesus as the Great Shepherd of the sheep, who equips us to do God's will:

> *Now may the God of peace who brought up our Lord Jesus from the dead, that great Shepherd of the sheep, through the blood of the everlasting covenant,*
> *make you complete in every good work to do His will, working in you what is well pleasing in His sight, through Jesus Christ, to whom be glory forever and ever. Amen.*
>
> HEBREWS 13:20-21

Peter refers to Jesus as the Chief Shepherd:

> *And when the Chief Shepherd appears, you will receive the crown of glory that does not fade away.*
>
> 1 PETER 5:4

So we see Jesus as the Good Shepherd, the Great Shepherd, and the Chief Shepherd. In Psalm 23 David simply refers to Him as "the shepherd," the faithful guide and leader. Those who follow Him have a life that is marked with purpose. The Lord is our source and our strength. It is sad to witness the compromised standards of Christians in need. When the need is great, the faith needs to be strongest. The Lord will supply. Periodically I caution young women not to get caught up in the "sugar daddy" syndrome. A sugar daddy is often a man who is older and well-heeled financially—certainly in a better financial situation than the woman at the time. A sugar daddy rarely comes into a covenant relationship with the young woman. Rather, he helps her out with her bills and responsibilities. She, single and needy, pays him back by being available for varied and sundry "fleshly" favors.

> You don't need a sugar daddy when you have a heavenly Father who cared enough to send His only Son to save our souls.

Now, young lady, your sugar daddy is not your source! I know that around the thirtieth of the month the bills need to be paid. I know that your light bill is late, and you need cereal for the children. But hold on! You're better than that. You are nobody's toy. God will provide wholesome and healthy ways to meet your need. I've pastored fifteen years, and I've seen it.

You don't need a sugar daddy when you have a heavenly Father who cared enough to send His only Son to save your soul. He prepares a table before you and asks nothing in return. I'm telling you right now, you won't get anything from that sugar daddy but a *quid pro quo*— Sugar Daddy isn't giving you anything for free. He expects a lot in return. By the time he writes you that check, you have given everything to him.

But he is not the real problem. The problem is that you don't know who you are and who your true Source is. You are God's child. God is your source! And Mother, you need to teach this to your daughter. I wish more women would take time with young girls today. Your testimony, your story, and your strength could prevent young women from falling into the sugar daddy trap and others.

> *There is a way that seemeth right unto a man* (or a woman), *but the end thereof are the ways of death.*
>
> PROVERBS 14:12 KJV

Because so many of our sisters are living in the graveyard and have no idea who they are, some brothers think they can walk in and out of their lives night or day. And they do. "Johnny" watches as this sweet young thing has one foot in church on Sunday and is in his pocket the other six days. Then one morning, Sugar Daddy's baby wakes up, singing in the choir with a forced, holy smile on her face because she found out Johnny gave her AIDS. Because when Johnny was walking in and out of her life, he was also walking in and out of Diane's life and Laquita's life and on and on. Young woman, whoever you are—understand this—you are a queen, regardless of the hard knocks and the disappointments you've experienced. You are a beautiful princess. You matter to God, and there are those who genuinely care for you.

I've seen it, believe me. I've seen it.

I believe our churches could do more to help meet the needs of women in hard times. Sadly, some of us are just so phony and graveyard spiritual that we won't write anyone a check when we know they're hurting. We have become a very self-centered, self-obsessed people. We forget too quickly when we were going through hard times. Somebody helped us. Somebody cared enough to give us a spare car, a refrigerator . . . a job! This is true, relevant, Christianity. Some folk have five cars but won't volunteer to pick up a single parent with three children and bring them to church. That's stingy and cold. They see the cab pull up to the church, and they see it go. They see her walking to the bus stop in the rain week after week. If the Lord were truly their shepherd, He would be telling them to minister to that need. Are the days gone completely when you could depend on the saints in the church to help you in hard times?

Most of us would be surprised how much we have accumulated around the house that could prove to be a real blessing to people. I know folk who plan garage sales that couldn't earn them more than $15. They could spare themselves the trouble and give that "for sale" cabinet to some struggling parent in the church. Some church lady says, "Child, this is a Rothchild's coat, girl. And I know I can get $50 because I paid $125 for it." But there is another saint in the church that has a child the same age as hers who could be blessed by that coat. While she can't afford to buy it, it would be worth much more to her and her daughter than $50!

I'm talking about being the Responsible Church! I'm talking about being responsible Christians. When you know your neighbor's husband had a stroke and is incapacitated, who do you think God is going to use to help that wife through? When you know a blizzard's coming, who do you think is going to shovel Mother Brown's driveway and walk—if you don't do it? Responsible Christianity sees the need and moves in Jesus' name to meet it.

"Mother Brown, has anyone been to your house to shovel?

"No, Baby."

"Mother, I'll be right there."

"Baby, I ain't got nothin' to pay you, but I made some fried chicken yesterday. You take your wife Ernestine a piece of this cake."

"If you say so, Mother."

Now that is real Christianity!

"Mother Perry, I know your sons have moved to California, so has anybody changed the oil in your car? Anybody rotated the tires?"

"No, darlin', nobody rotated those tires."

"I'll be right over, Mother."

"I can't pay you, darlin'."

"Mother, I *wouldn't* take it if you could."

This is responsible Christianity! It is up to us as responsible Christians to show everyone we know that Jesus is their source, and He uses people—ordinary, everyday people who love God enough to want to make a difference. The Scripture states, **We know that we have passed from death to life, because we love the brethren** (1 John 3:14).

Sometimes people are in a position where they can't pay you. "I raked your leaves, Mother," that young man says, waiting for a payoff.

If all Mother says is "Thank you. God bless you," that should be payment enough!

You who have teenage sons and daughters can start putting this kind of Christian responsibility into their lives today. You can point out Mother's need and put the rake in their hand. You can start showing them how to respect and honor their own grandparents.

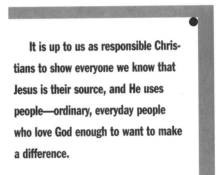

It is up to us as responsible Christians to show everyone we know that Jesus is their source, and He uses people—ordinary, everyday people who love God enough to want to make a difference.

"Did you see your grandmother? Get over there and speak to your grandmother." Make your children get up.

Let's be the responsible Church that knows the Lord is our source, and then He will move through us to meet one another's needs. I'm talking about looking for needs in your church and community. **Let your light so shine before** [humanity,] **that they may see your good works and glorify your Father who is in heaven** (Matthew 5:16, insert mine).

The responsible Church says, "The Lord is my shepherd, guide, and director. The Lord leads me, not the past. The Lord leads me, not anger. The Lord leads me, not revenge. The Lord leads me, not competition. The Lord is my fuel." The responsible Church reaches out and looks "Chavelle" in the eye and says, "How you doing this morning, Sister? You know, that child looks just like you. I want to buy him some milk."

"How are you this morning, young man? Daddy still out? Ask your mother if you can spend the afternoon with my two sons and me today. We're going to a ballgame. Let me see if your mother will have supper with us. If she's busy, maybe you can come by yourself. All right?"

"How are you this morning, Brother? You need any help around your place this week? Oh, you're painting? Need any help? I whip a mean brush."

This is how saints in the responsible Church are supposed to live. Let's do it!

> *Then the righteous will answer Him, saying, 'Lord, when did we see You hungry and feed You, or thirsty and give You drink?*
>
> *'When did we see You a stranger and take You in, or naked and clothe You?'*
>
> MATTHEW 25:37-38

Helpful Hints

Remember the Basics. Always go back to the basics. Growing in God does not mean that we forsake the basics. Reading and reciting the 23rd Psalm, praying "the Lord's Prayer," and singing "Yes, Jesus Loves Me" can often minister in ways that "deep" things cannot.

Remember the least. Jesus' parable regarding ministry to the least is timeless. God has always held a special place in His heart for the widow, the orphan, and the stranger. We must always seek to minister to the overlooked, the outcast, the diseased, depressed, distraught, and disenfranchised.

Remember your Source. God and God alone is our Source. If we are going to be the Church He is calling for today, we must allow God to use us as the "source" of blessings for others. *What we make happen for others God will make happen for us!* God will provide all we need as we put our trust in Him and not in the temporary schemes this world offers.

(Your local directory lists spouse abuse hotline phone numbers. Call today!)

The Funeral-Stopping Church

These who have turned the world upside down have come here too.

ACTS 17:6

Then Jesus went about all the cities and villages, teaching in their synagogues, preaching the gospel of the kingdom, and healing every sickness and every disease among the people.

But when he saw the multitudes, He was moved with compassion for them, because they were weary and scattered, like sheep having no shepherd.

And then He said to His disciples, "The harvest is plentiful, but the laborers are few.

"Therefore, pray the Lord of the harvest to send out laborers into His harvest."

MATTHEW 9:35-38

How to Reach the Masses

The widow of Nain was a beneficiary of the everyday ministry of Jesus. The Gospel of Luke describes Jesus' ministry in a nutshell. The ministry of Jesus is not necessarily about "bless me" programs, rather it is a holistic ministry of compassion, healing, and deliverance:

> *"The Spirit of the Lord is upon me,*
> *Because He has anointed me*

> *To preach the gospel to the poor;*
> *He has sent Me to heal the brokenhearted,*
> *To preach deliverance to the captives,*
> *And recovering of sight to the blind;*
> *To set at liberty them that are bruised,*
> *To preach the acceptable year of the Lord."*
>
> LUKE 4:18-19 KJV

I believe this is the acceptable year of the Lord and, should the Lord tarry and I live, I will declare next year is the acceptable year of the Lord and the following year is the acceptable year of the Lord.[9] As we live and grow in God, each year, each time, each season ought to get better; and we ought to become more effectively engaged in the ministry of Jesus until He comes. For example, Matthew 9 shows Jesus forgiving sins and healing paralytics. In this chapter we see Jesus ministering life to a girl

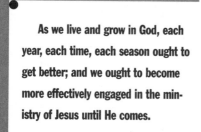

As we live and grow in God, each year, each time, each season ought to get better; and we ought to become more effectively engaged in the ministry of Jesus until He comes.

who was thought to have been dead and also healing two men. Then in verse 32 we see a man who once was a deaf mute but is now able to speak and hear. Jesus is moved by human need, and He desires to intervene in the affairs of humanity. What appears to be human extremity is God's opportunity.

---

[9]*Matthew Henry's Commentary* (6 vols.). Book. *PC Study Bible,* Version 2.1J. CD-ROM. (Seattle: Biblesoft, 1993-1998), n.p.

In one sense or another, Jesus is seen stopping funeral after funeral. He stops literal funerals, but He also stops the funerals of dead hopes, dead dreams, and destinies cut short. **"When He saw the multitudes . . ."** He touched and healed the empty, lonely, broken, and misguided—indeed, huddled masses yearning to be free. Matthew describes the people: **they fainted, and were scattered abroad, like sheep without a shepherd** (Matthew 9:36 KJV). The *Revised Standard Version* of the Bible says they were **harassed and helpless, like sheep without a shepherd**. As he had done for so many individuals on prior occasions, Jesus ministers to the masses and stops what would inevitably be a great funeral culminating with a mass burial.

In many of our churches, we know how to stop one or two funerals. We know how to prepare food baskets. We know how to pray for the sick. Many of our churches even cast out demons. But how shall we reach the masses? In this hour of cynicism and suspicion, where so many see the Church as increasingly irrelevant, we must reach the masses with *effective* and *engaging* ministry. I believe the answer to reaching the masses and stopping the funerals among them is found here in this 9th chapter of Matthew. The Bible says that Jesus went about all the cities and villages in their synagogues teaching and preaching the Gospel of the kingdom. Effective ministry begins with the Gospel of the kingdom; and wherever there is the Gospel of the kingdom, God is king! We are called to live our lives under God as authority and ruler. We are *under*; God is *over*. For Christians, King Jesus is ruling and the King is reigning. The

King rules in our homes, and the King rules in our families. The King rules in our relationships and in our behavior. We cannot have the authority of the King without yielding to the King. And we cannot be effective without the power of the King.

Jesus went about doing effective ministry, and that included teaching in their synagogues and preaching the Gospel of the kingdom. Jesus did not teach or preach the gospel of religion. We will never reach the masses if we preach the gospel of religion. We must preach the Gospel of the kingdom. We will never reach the masses by preaching the gospel of denominationalism. We must preach the Gospel of the kingdom. Preaching anything else is ineffective against the funerals in their lives.

The church of Christ is called to a ministry that is effective and engaging. Sadly, some of our churches are more museum than ministry. These are buildings that *look* like church. On the inside there is beauty, but no light. It is so easy to become a church that is more fluff than substance—music with no ministry, programs with no power. When I was a child, a product called *Fluffernutter* was very popular. It was a sweet, marshmallow spread. It had no nutritional value whatsoever; just a lot of fat calories that tasted good and gave you a good warm feeling. Effective ministry moves beyond fluff. In order for our ministries to be effective, we must be engaged in those areas that Jesus was engaged in.

Jesus is concerned about the poor, the broken, the blind, and the lost. He is concerned about the sick, and He is concerned about the dying. Yet, some of us have been operating in ineffective, non-nutritional ministry for so long, we are not sure what effective ministry looks like. To be effective means to meet the need. To be effective means to be life changing, to serve a purpose. That's effective. And to be effective you have to be present. A church that is not present in the presence of God or in the community cannot be effective. If we want effective churches, we need to

> **In some of our communities, the people don't even know our churches are open for ministry. Twice a week we crack the doors of the church to let members in and out, but we are never present among the people.**

spend time seeking the face of God. As the Church we must ask, "Lord, what is Your agenda for the city? What are Your concerns?" When clergy and laity gather together in one accord, something will happen that will be the first step in reaching the masses. God will show up and begin to speak to leadership regarding effective ministry.

> *When the Day of Pentecost had fully come, they were all with one accord in one place.*
> *And suddenly. . . .*
> ACTS 2:1-2

Jesus was functioning in effective ministry when He saw the multitudes. He was present with the Father and among the people. In some of our communities, the people don't even know our churches are open for ministry. Twice a week we crack the doors of the church to let members in and out, but we are never present among the people.

Perhaps the only thing worse than an absent church is a complacent church. A complacent church stands by and watches the funeral procession and sometimes even joins in the procession but never does anything to stop the funeral. But Jesus was far from complacent! Jesus did not ignore what was going on around Him. His presence put Him in touch with the grief, the weariness, and the despair of the masses, and He was moved with compassion. To reach the masses we must be moved with compassion and not judgement. To reach the masses we must have empathy. Someone once said, "People do not care how much you know until they know how much you care." We should be genuinely concerned for the weary, scattered, and dying masses around us.

The masses are people like you and me—people who look like us but so often are misdirected and overlooked by us. The masses are the hurting. The masses include the broken. They include those with five babies and no husband. They include those who have had three abortions by the time they are fourteen. They include the unemployed. They include the uneducated. Some have not been properly parented. Some don't love themselves; and, therefore, they feel like trash. Because they feel like trash, they lay with trash, and they get up with trash. They have bitterness for breakfast, loneliness for lunch, and disaster for dinner. These are the masses. These are the multitudes. We often overlook the multitude of professional, educated, well-heeled, and connected people.

These are folk who have power and position in life but are void of peace and joy in their souls. We often overlook this crowd because at first glance they look like they have it all together. If we look closely, however, we will find that they too are broken, shallow, and hurting. They too need the healing touch of the Savior's hand.

> *For what will it profit a man if he gains the whole world, and loses his soul?*
>
> MARK 8:36

The multitudes are scattered, needy, and in need of someone who can identify with where they are and where they've been.

I once heard a story about a young boy who was scared to go to bed and scared to turn his light off at night. His father said, "Boy, go to bed. Turn the light off. Don't be afraid of the dark. Jesus is with you." The boy responded, "I know He's with me, but I want somebody with skin on them." This young boy wanted to identify with something he could touch and something he could feel. The multitudes on the outside of the Church are no different. We are called to present to the multitudes a Jesus who can be touched.

Our ministries would grow in effectiveness if we would just take some time and tell our story. We all have a story: what we were, what we're struggling through, or what the Lord delivered us out of. Therefore, when they look at us, they see a *real* person they can identify with. We are real people with real stories, delivered and set free by a real God! We'd like people to believe we've been sanctified our whole lives. We'd like people to believe we've been elders our whole lives. We'd like people to believe that we have a right to wear our liturgical robes, play the piano, or sing the songs of Zion. But the truth is, the blood has covered us. None of us are worthy of the blessings we enjoy. It is the grace and mercy of God. If any man, boy, woman, or girl be in Christ, he or she is a new creature, old things have passed away. (See 2 Corinthians 5:17.) Every now and then we need to talk about those old things because those old things continue to bind the masses.

The Pharisees didn't want to have anything to do with the multitudes. They thought the multitudes were like chaff to be burned by the fire. I read a book years ago concerning a church in the South. The pastor in the book was trying to draw people to Jesus by encouraging his members to get out and minister, to hit the neighborhoods and knock on doors. Then one of the good deacons wearing shined black shoes, a black mohair suit, a white starched shirt, a black silk tie, and a white pocket square with the watch going across the side of the vest stood and said, "Brother preacher, I'm not sure if our church was meant to be a *mass* church. I believe that our ministry is not to be for the masses, but our ministry is meant to be for our class." Because he had been blessed to make it to the top, get an education, and be a part of a national fraternity, he wanted a church that reflected his standing in society. Although he was a grandchild of a slave, he wanted to be a part of an upwardly mobile church filled with an influential membership. The emphasis here is not people but position. This kind of elitism does not represent the heart of Jesus. When we come to Jesus, we are all on the same playing field—sinners saved by grace.

Effective churches are empathetic with where people are and how they got there. They are compassionate enough to help get them through to where they ought to be without always asking questions. How a person contracted AIDS, why a person is in prison, or why a marriage broke up should not determine the degree of our compassion. While each situation may need a different type of ministry, all need the empathy and compassion of Jesus Christ.

I believe we can turn this mess around. Our local church stands on a four-pillar mission that involves a call to EVANGELIZE, EDUCATE, EMANCIPATE, AND EMPOWER. Our *first* calling is to save those who are lost. *We must be enthusiastic about souls.* We must be enthusiastic about raising the sights of humanity. We are more than flesh and blood. We are also spirit. Their spirits are down. Their spirits are worn out. Many of them don't know where to go or what to do to rise from their present state of death. While sharing with a church that I have the privilege of covering in the belly of the hood in southeast Washington, D.C., I met with the young pastor and the leaders of the church. I asked each

> **How a person contracted AIDS, why a person is in prison, or why a marriage broke up should not determine the degree of our compassion. While each situation may need a different type of ministry, all need the empathy and compassion of Jesus Christ.**

of them to tell me why they were a part of that church. One woman's response incorporated a concern for the community. She said, "We need to be real careful because they don't trust the Church. They don't trust the saints. They don't trust the people of God because they see that we are irrelevant. They see that we are not in touch with what's really going on in society." I laid out what I believed to be a blueprint for reaching and resurrecting the masses in that area, and it begins with souls. It begins with raising the spirits of people, saving their souls, and giving them hope. In our church, this would come under the first pillar of our mission statement—EVANGELIZE.

Secondly, the church needs to be serious about education. Article after article tells the sad story of how poor so many of our inner city public education institutions are. While many of our teachers, principles, and administrators are concerned and still have a heart for what they're doing, an equal number seem to have lost their passion. If the truth be told, many of them are in education because it is all they know. Many are still teaching because they are contracted to do so. It is not as though they love teaching or the students, but that they've got a job. Some don't care about our children, and we must begin to point our children toward the right direction, even if we have to educate them ourselves.

The public school system as we know it is in need of a major overhaul. I am glad to see states across the nation grapple with this weighty issue. The Church should build its own schools as a viable alternative in the community. Multitudes are seeking private Christian schools to educate their children because of the questionable ethical and moral integrity and lack of safety in public schools. We cannot run—and we surely can't hide—but we can make a difference. Education should include sound Bible teaching, Christian lifestyle and behavior, marriage, family, and economics. These are not exhaustive subjects, but they are a good starting point.

Third, funeral-stopping churches are called to the ministry of emancipation. In our church sanctuary, there is a larger than life stained glass window depicting the resurrected Christ. At the bottom of the window, at His feet, are broken chains. The message here is that Jesus can break away binding chains. Emancipation is the act of setting free. The Church's message of love, forgiveness, grace, and mercy can indeed set humanity free.

> He breaks the power of cancelled sin.
> He sets the prisoner free.
> His blood can make the foulest clean,
> His blood availed for me.[10]

Countless numbers of God's children are bound up by alcohol, drugs, sex, perversion, fear, and violence. Every fifteen seconds a woman is victimized by domestic violence and struck by the hand she loves. The number of children sexually molested by their fathers is staggering. These silent, often undetected killers can be

[10] Charles Wesley, "O For a Thousand Tongues to Sing", *Progressive Baptist Hymnal*, (Progressive National Baptist Convention, Inc. Headquarters, Washington D. C., 1976).

found not only in the streets, but on the pews of our churches. If we are to be relevant, we must face relevant issues and help emancipate people from the chains that bind them. Soul salvation is the first step; then people need to be educated and fully emancipated in Jesus' name.

Fourth, funeral-stopping churches empower people. Empowerment on several fronts need attention; however, economic empowerment is at the helm. Economic empowerment is the result of kingdom financial management—pay the tithe (10 percent), pay yourself (save 10 percent) and live on the 80 percent.

> If we are to be relevant, we must face relevant issues and help emancipate people from the chains that bind them. Soul salvation is the first step; then people need to be educated and fully emancipated in Jesus Name.

God wants to bless inner-city communities with prosperous businesses that serve as mission outposts and give glory to His name. When we give glory and honor to His name in our communities, the funeral will come to us for resurrection life. When the Lord is leading His people, the downcast and hopeless will come to our business doors for joy and peace. When God's Church has the answers, people will come to us for answers.

Our congregations are filled with people who have dreams and ideas just waiting to be tapped. As the Church moves into the twenty-first century, she will need to teach economics. Across the nation churches are putting far more emphasis on economics than ever before. Indeed, the "wealth of the wicked is laid up for the righteous" (see Proverbs 13:22)—but we need to learn how to handle this wealth.

If we're going to be a Church that reaches the masses and resurrects the multitudes we must be effectively engaged, we must be empathic with those where we are, and then, by God, we need to get enthusiastic about what we are doing. If we are going to half-step, we need to sit down. If we are not going to be enthusiastic about ministry, about singing in the choir, about playing an instrument, about serving God and His people, then perhaps we should make way for those who are. We need to go back and lie down with the Good Shepherd until He rekindles our fire and restores our excitement about what He has called us to do. We cannot expect the masses to want something that we are not excited about. Jesus said,

> *Every branch of mine that bears no fruit, he takes away, and every branch that does bear fruit he prunes, that it may bear more fruit.*
>
> JOHN 15:2 RSV

A branch that bears fruit is effective. God wants every church to be an effective church and every Christian to be an effective Christian. It helps me to think back on why I came into ministry in the first place—to make a difference.

Funeral Stoppers Are Full of Joy

Have you ever been to a funeral and seen someone falling apart walk over to someone else who was falling apart and try to console them? Compounded grief is not a pretty sight. Yet, in the same way that we expect people to get excited about a Gospel that doesn't excite us, we expect them to embrace a God who does nothing for our character. Funeral-stoppers ought to possess something on the inside that outshines the darkness around them. Funeral-stoppers ought to have joy.

> *The joy of the Lord is our strength.*
>
> NEHEMIAH 8:10 RSV

I visited a church some time ago when I was on vacation, and I was wearing my loafers with no socks. I was on vacation and just wanted to enjoy the Lord. I entered the service with my little Bible and tried to tip-toe in without disturbing anyone.

"Excuse me, uh, excuse me, is this seat taken?" I asked a brother.

"NO!" he replied sternly.

"Excuse me," I asked again. "Where are the hymnals?"

"This is the hymnal. It says *Hymnal* on it," the brother said again.

So I just tried to sit, but I was extremely uncomfortable. I didn't feel embraced. I didn't want to stay. This church was certainly a poor reflection of hospitality and warmth.

Most of our churches would be larger if our members were warmer. So often, when someone comes in that doesn't look the way we think they should look, we act cold and unfriendly. We're supposed to be the Church!

Always remember that we were strangers at one time too, but somebody cared for us and embraced us in His name.

Have you ever seen a person who is blessed but rigid? They're the kind of folk Jesus ran into in the temple at Jerusalem. They were the overly pious, self-righteous who were busy with their religious services and schedules. You had to wash your hands "just right," bow down "just right," and keep every law. You couldn't walk more than a certain number of steps on the Sabbath day. You couldn't heal on the Sabbath day, and on and on. Jesus came with power and deliverance with boldness. The traditions of men could not hinder His ministry.

You don't know when a church visitor just may be an angel unaware. And most folk who come in are looking to have a funeral stopped. So those of us who claim to know the Lord need to learn how to rejoice. I'm speaking of a rejoicing that is beyond hand-clapping and dancing. We do that well. *However, we can dance with reckless abandon and leave the service the same as we came in!*

Demonstrating our joy in the Lord through worship and praise is important, but the rejoicing I'm talking about has to do with having a strong sense of peace and well-being at all times on the *inside* of us. "This joy that I have, the world didn't give it to me, and the world can't take it away." This peace passes all understanding. And this kind of joy is deeper than merely being happy. Happiness is often relative to what we have going on at the time.

"I'm happy because I just bought a car."

"I'm happy because I just got a raise."

Real joy has little to do with what's in your hand, rather what's in your heart and soul. People can tell the difference between temporary happiness and genuine joy. Genuine joy is a fruit of the Spirit, and like life itself, a gift from God. I came across this quotation from an anonymous author recently: "Yesterday was history, tomorrow is a mystery, and all we have is the gift of today; and that is why they call it the present." This is why life is a gift: God, the Blesser, promises us a full, abundant life. Jesus said this when He introduced himself as our Good Shepherd:

> Real joy has little to do with what's in your hand, rather what's in your heart and soul. People can tell the difference between temporary happiness and genuine joy.

> The thief does not come except to steal, and to kill, and to destroy. I have come that they may have life, and that they may have it more abundantly.
> I am the good shepherd. The good shepherd gives His life for the sheep.
>
> JOHN 10:10-11

The abundant life God gives overpowers death and establishes His kingdom of peace. Life in Jesus gives us reason to rejoice! We need to learn how to rejoice and lighten up. That's right—lighten up! Life is too short to be petty and in a perpetually bad mood. I truly believe more people would be drawn to Jesus Christ through us if we were more joyful. We would have more believers and visitors coming to our meetings if our churches were happier.

> But the fruit of the Spirit is love, joy, peace, long-suffering, gentleness, goodness, faith,
> Meekness, temperance: against such there is no law.
>
> GALATIANS 5:22-23 KJV

ARISE!

The abundant life of God is blessed with His peace. Today's funeral-stopping Church is destined to raise America from its death. It will touch the coffins of our cities. Today's funeral-stopping Church is destined to raise our culture from the graveyard to a place of spiritual abundance in Jesus Christ.

God desires to expand our horizons so He can move through us in His resurrection power. He desires the communities living in the valley of the shadow of death to rise above their hopeless circumstances. However, communities will not and cannot, except we come to their aid. The Church is to show the world that death is only a shadow to those who are free from fear.

It is time to arise, Church!

> Arise, shine; for thy light is come, and the glory of the Lord is risen upon thee.
>
> ISAIAH 60:1 KJV

Jesus wants to look into our eyes, touch us, and speak His life into our lives. He wants us to sing that old hymn,

This Is My Father's World, like we really *know* it and believe it. There are families to raise, churches to build, neighborhoods to win, and many funerals to stop.

Every moment counts. The clock is always ticking as the pallbearers of this generation march daily in our streets. Jesus appears to the Marys who are looking in the graveyard for love and hope. He raises the sons of widows and gives new life to the dead. And Jesus desires to raise many others. He can and He will—through us. The late Dr. Benjamin Elijah Mays of Morehouse College, Atlanta, would often recite this quotation:

> We only have one minute, only sixty seconds in it. We didn't seek it; we didn't choose it. Thrust upon us, we can't refuse it. But we will suffer if we lose it, give account if we abuse it. Just one tiny little minute, but eternity is in it.
>
> Anonymous

Let Him use you, and say, YES! I WILL ARISE!

> *Now it happened, the day after, that He went into a city called Nain; and many of His disciples went with Him, and a large crowd.*
>
> *And when He came near the gate of the city, behold, a dead man was being carried out, the only son of his mother; and she was a widow. And a large crowd from the city was with her.*
>
> *When the Lord saw her, He had compassion on her and said to her, "Do not weep."*
>
> *Then He came and touched the open coffin, and those who carried him stood still. And He said, "Young man, I say to you, arise."*
>
> *So he who was dead sat up and began to speak. And He presented him to his mother.*

Then fear came upon all, and they glorified God, saying, "A great prophet has risen up among us"; and, "God has visited His people."

And this report about Him went throughout all Judea and all the surrounding region.

LUKE 7:11-17

Selah.

Appendix

More Funeral-Stopping Testimonies

And you shall be witnesses to Me in Jerusalem, and in all Judea and Samaria, and to the end of the earth.

ACTS 1:8

When the Lord delivered me from a life of drugs and perversion and allowed me to return to the "land of the living," He blessed me to sit under the instruction of Dr. Donald Hilliard Jr., my bishop and spiritual father. I have learned much about living a Christ-centered life as an African-American man in today's society. Traits such as responsibility, compassion, confronting emotions, true manhood, and mentoring—amongst a myriad of other important topics—have been taught openly and effectively by Bishop Hilliard.

If it had not been for this ministry and his leadership, I don't believe I would have had the fortitude or determination to stand in the face of adversity, fight for my faith, my family, or my future, or to endure the struggles of daily living that drive many converts back to the worldly tombs from whence they came. I thank God for Jesus and for allowing Bishop Hilliard to become such an important part of my life.

—Dwayne Trawick

In March of 1991, I was crying on my way to get drugs one night because I didn't want to go, but the enemy had a grip on me. While I was doing the drugs, I fell on my knees and asked the Lord to please help me. I couldn't take it anymore. That morning I checked myself into the hospital detox. By this time everyone had given up on me except my mother. They said I would never be anything. Well, by the grace of God I have been free from drug addiction since that time!

I came out of the hospital clean of drugs, but not knowing how to live this life, not knowing how to be a lady, and the Lord led me to Second Baptist Church. There, I watched you, Sister Hilliard, and learned how to be not just a lady, but a lady of God, and I am still learning. My third week there, the Lord came into my home and filled me with the Holy Ghost, and my life has never been the same.

Pastor, my life has been changed through your preaching, teaching, love, and honesty. You are the father I never had, and I thank the Lord for you and your wife. Words will never express how I love you and your family. But most of all, I thank the Lord for saving a nothing like me and for loving me enough to call me into His grace. He keeps me and He blesses me with joy. I love Him!

—Eleathia Gunther

As usual, I was paid on Friday and smoked crack until noon Saturday. Then the money was gone, so I went home to sleep. When I awoke on Sunday afternoon, a real surprise awaited me. My mother, grandparents, and mother- and father-in-law were waiting for me. They didn't yell or scream. They very calmly announced that the party was over. I was either going to rehab or Susan and my children were leaving.

When I refused to go to a rehab hospital because I had seen so many people go in and come out twice as bad, they suggested I go to Second Baptist Church, where there was a ministry to struggling addicts. I went on Monday night, and I met men who had been delivered from twenty-year heroine addictions and had their families restored. I accepted Jesus Christ into my life that night and cried just like a baby. I had found brotherhood and hope where there was none. I've never used drugs since that night back in July of 1991. I love the Lord!

I received my bachelor's degree in May of 1999 and own my own home and business, which employs men who have been down and need to be inspired and introduced to a lifestyle that is Christ-centered. I want to thank God for putting people like Bishop Hilliard and Mother Jessie Smallwood in my life. When I was down and had lost all hope, they told me about a God who loved me and wanted to use me for His honor and glory. I love the Lord and will serve Him forever.

—Kevin R. Smallwood

As I stood before the judge, he began to read off the charges. A total of 25 years plus. As I faced a life of incarceration, my life seemed over, but I was released after serving only a little more than two years. A free man again, I was looking forward to a very successful venture with my drug supplier, but one day an old acquaintance stopped by to talk with me. She told me about Second Baptist Church, but my mind was not ready for church! Thankfully, the sister didn't give up on me and finally convinced me to come to a Sunday service.

The service was wonderful, and my soul was touched. All the longing for material things that came with the drug dealing life left as I sat there. For the first time, I struggled with my desire to return to drug dealing. Suddenly, I wanted to learn about God and the place He wanted to have in my life. I returned home feeling strangely different and canceled the meeting with my supplier.

I continued to go to church even though I was afraid to make a commitment. I knew it would mean a drastic change in my lifestyle, but more than that was my unbelief that I was worthy of God's love. After all, how could God forgive or love someone who sold drugs, fought in bars and clubs, carried guns, and shot at people. But I thank God for His steadfast love shown to me through the man of God leading Second Baptist Church. Through Bishop Hilliard's continuous teaching and preaching, it wasn't long before I was loosed from the devil's hold and released to live out the true purpose and plan God had for my life.

More than two decades later, I stand delivered from a life of drugs and crime that all started with a simple dare as a teenager. I now serve God as an aide to Bishop Hilliard and ministry head of a support group for men and women who struggle with addictions of all kinds. Thank God for stopping the funeral!

—Gary L. Elliott

About the Author

Dr. Hilliard and his wife, Phyllis Thompson-Hilliard, have three daughters, Leah, Charisma, and Destiny. Reverend Hilliard was called to the pastorate of the Second Baptist Church in Perth Amboy in 1983. He was 26 years old. Since those early days, attendance at the Cathedral Second Baptist Church has skyrocketed. Church membership has grown from 125 members in 1983 to over 4,000 at the time of this publication. The church worships in Perth Amboy and also in Asbury Park, New Jersey, where the Cathedral Assembly by the Shore is a satellite congregation.

Dr. Hilliard is widely known for his church's part in the economic rebirth and revitalization of Perth Amboy's commercial area. The church and its Community Development Corporation where he serves as CEO, own numerous properties in the city through which they provide encouragement and outreach ministry to many. He is also President of Millennium Ministries, Inc. The ministry of Cathedral Second Baptist Church can be experienced weekly on television and radio.

Dr. Hilliard has earned degrees from Eastern College of St. Davids, Pennsylvania; Princeton Theological Seminary, Princeton, New Jersey; and in 1990, a Doctor of Ministry degree from United Theological Seminary in Dayton, Ohio, as a Samuel D. Proctor Fellow. He has been a visiting professor at Drew University, the School of Theology (Parish Administration) in Madison, New Jersey; Boston University, School of Theology (Black Preaching and Religion); New Brunswick Theological

Seminary (Evangelism and Church Growth); and Princeton Theological Seminary, Princeton, New Jersey. Dr. Hilliard is the recipient of the Distinguished Alumnus Award from both Princeton Theological Seminary (1995) and Eastern College (1997), and Entrepreneur of the Year from the Perth Amboy Chamber of Commerce.

Dr. Hilliard's ministry has been the agent by which countless lives have been resurrected for the sake of our Lord. A preacher who refuses to pull any punches, his poignant, oratorical genius brings the Gospel alive in a dynamic, life-altering way for his listeners. His understanding of the holistic Gospel places emphasis on themes as diverse as holiness and home ownership, deep faith and debt reduction, and the Holy Spirit and higher education.

Dr. Hilliard can be contacted at the following:

The Cathedral Second Baptist Church
277 Madison Ave.
P. O. 1608
Perth Amboy, New Jersey 08861

———

Millennium Ministries, Inc.
P. O. Box 1216
Jackson, New Jersey 08526

Other Books by Albury Publishing

Free to Dream
Bishop Charles Blake

The Princess Within
Serita Jakes

Woman, Thou Art Loosed!
Bishop T. D. Jakes

Loose That Man and Let Him Go!
Bishop T. D. Jakes

Six Pillars From Ephesians Series
Loved by God
Experiencing Jesus
Intimacy With God
Life Overflowing
Celebrating Marriage
Overcoming the Enemy
Bishop T. D. Jakes

I Don't Want Delilah, I Need You!
Bishop Eddie L. Long

Why Kingdoms Fall
Bishop Paul Morton

Additional copies of this book and other book titles
from **ALBURY PUBLISHING** are
available at your local bookstore.

ALBURY PUBLISHING
Tulsa, Oklahoma

For a complete list of our titles,
visit us at our website:

www.alburypublishing.com

For international and Canadian orders,
please contact:

Access Sales International
2448 East 81st Street
Suite 4900
Tulsa, Oklahoma 74137
Phone 918-523-5590   Fax 918-496-2822